OZ

THE COMPLETE COLLECTION

VOLUME 1

L. FRANK BAUM

The Wonderful Wizard of Oz
The Marvelous Land of Oz
Ozma of Oz

Classic Editions

OZ, THE COMPLETE COLLECTION
VOLUME 1
Complete and Unabridged
By L. Frank Baum

ISBN NO. 978-1-80445-086-4

Classic Editions

This edition published by
Fox Eye Publishing Ltd.
Vulcan House Business Centre
Vulcan Road, Leicester, LE5 3EF
United Kingdom

This edition is published in 2022

Cover Design by Haitenlo Semy
Cover Illustration by Ishan Trivedi

In association with
Wilco Publishing House
Mumbai, India

© *Wilco* Publishing House 2022

Printed in India

This book is dedicated to my good friend & comrade
My Wife
L.F.B.

Publisher's Note

An iconic classic, *The Wizard of Oz* by Frank L. Baum is a must-read for adults and children alike. This collection follows the adventurous journey of Dorothy, Scarecrow, the Cowardly Lion and Tin Woodman through the Four Countries of the Land of Oz and the glorious Emerald City. Come and let your imaginations run wild with the strange and magical creatures of Oz.

Wilco has been bringing out the finest Classic titles since 1958. Now the thrust of our endeavour is to extend the list and present more of these treasures to our readers, at the most affordable prices.

About the Author

LYMAN FRANK BAUM

(1856-1919)

L. F. Baum was born in New York in May 1856. Young Lyman surprised his peers by first becoming a reporter for *New York World* in his teens, and then, within two years, by bringing out his own newspaper in Pennsylvania.

Baum wrote and acted in a musical play '*Arran*' (1880), which was well received. Two years later he married Maud Gage. The couple was devoted to their four sons. Baum edited a trade journal to sustain the family while writing fiction. His first commercial break came with his maiden work *Father Goose* (1899). The enchanting fable *The Wizard of Oz* was published a year later. It became such a roaring success that Baum wrote as many as thirteen sequels to 'Oz', which were translated in many languages and filmed extensively.

Using a feminine pseudonym 'Edith Van Dyke', Baum also brought out lucid books for girls. Baum died in 1919 in his home in Hollywood, California. His last words to his wife, Maud, were "Now we can cross the shifting sands," referring to the sands that separate our world with that of the 'Oz'.

AUTHOR'S NOTE

After the publication of *The Wonderful Wizard of OZ* I began to receive letters from children, telling me of their pleasure in reading the story and asking me to "write something more" about the Scarecrow and the Tin Woodman. At first I considered these little letters, frank and earnest though they were, in the light of pretty compliments; but the letters continued to come during succeeding months, and even years.

Finally I promised one little girl, who made a long journey to see me and prefer her request,—and she is a "Dorothy," by the way—that when a thousand little girls had written me a thousand little letters asking for the Scarecrow and the Tin Woodman I would write the book.

Either little Dorothy was a fairy in disguise, and waved her magic wand, or the success of the stage production of "The Wizard of OZ" made new friends for the story, For the thousand letters reached their destination long since—and many more followed them.

And now, although pleading guilty to long delay, I have kept my promise in this book.

L. FRANK BAUM.

Chicago, June, 1904

CONTENTS

INTRODUCTION

FOLKLORE, legends, myths and fairy tales have followed childhood through the ages, for every healthy youngster has a wholesome and instinctive love for stories fantastic, marvelous and manifestly unreal. The winged fairies of Grimm and Andersen have brought more happiness to childish hearts than all other human creations.

Yet the old time fairy tale, having served for generations, may now be classed as "historical" in the children's library; for the time has come for a series of newer "wonder tales" in which the stereotyped genie, dwarf and fairy are eliminated, together with all the horrible and blood-curdling incidents devised by their authors to point a fearsome moral to each tale. Modern education includes morality; therefore the modern child seeks only entertainment in its wonder tales and gladly dispenses with all disagreeable incident.

Having this thought in mind, the story of "The Wonderful Wizard of Oz" was written solely to please children of today. It aspires to being a modernized fairy tale, in which the wonderment and joy are retained and the heartaches and nightmares are left out.

L. Frank Baum

Chicago, April, 1900.

THE WONDERFUL WIZARD OF OZ

CONTENTS

Chapter 1

THE CYCLONE

DOROTHY lived in the midst of the great Kansas prairies, with Uncle Henry, who was a farmer, and Aunt Em, who was the farmer's wife. Their house was small, for the lumber to build it had to be carried by wagon many miles. There were four walls, a floor and a roof, which made one room; and this room contained a rusty looking cookstove, a cupboard for the dishes, a table, three or four chairs, and the beds. Uncle Henry and Aunt Em had a big bed in one corner, and Dorothy a little bed in another corner. There was no garret at all, and no cellar—except a small hole dug in the ground, called a cyclone cellar, where the family could go in case one of those great whirlwinds arose, mighty enough to crush any building in its path. It was reached by a trap door in the middle of the floor, from which a ladder led down into the small, dark hole.

When Dorothy stood in the doorway and looked around, she could see nothing but the great gray prairie on every side. Not a tree nor a house broke the broad sweep of flat country that reached to the edge of the sky in all directions. The sun had baked the plowed land into a gray mass, with little cracks running through it. Even the grass was not green, for the sun had burned the tops of the long blades until they were the same gray color to be seen everywhere. Once the house had been painted, but the sun blistered the paint and the rains washed it away, and now the house was as dull and gray as everything else.

When Aunt Em came there to live she was a young, pretty wife. The sun and wind had changed her, too. They had taken the sparkle from her eyes and left them a sober gray; they had taken the red from her cheeks and lips, and they were gray also. She was thin and gaunt, and never smiled now. When Dorothy, who was an orphan, first came to her, Aunt Em had been so startled by the child's laughter that she would scream and press her hand upon her heart whenever Dorothy's merry voice reached her ears; and she still looked at the little girl with wonder that she could find anything to laugh at.

Uncle Henry never laughed. He worked hard from morning till night and did not know what joy was. He was gray also, from his long beard to his rough boots, and he looked stern and solemn, and rarely spoke.

It was Toto that made Dorothy laugh, and saved her from growing as gray as her other surroundings. Toto was not gray; he was a little black dog, with long silky hair and small black eyes that twinkled merrily on either side of his funny, wee nose. Toto played all day long, and Dorothy played with him, and loved him dearly.

Today, however, they were not playing. Uncle Henry sat upon the doorstep and looked anxiously at the sky, which was even grayer than usual. Dorothy stood in the door with Toto in her arms, and looked at the sky too. Aunt Em was washing the dishes.

From the far north they heard a low wail of the wind, and Uncle Henry and Dorothy could see where the long grass bowed in waves before the coming storm. There now came a sharp whistling in the air from the south, and as they turned their eyes that way they saw ripples in the grass coming from that direction also.

Suddenly Uncle Henry stood up.

"There's a cyclone coming, Em," he called to his wife. "I'll go look after the stock." Then he ran toward the sheds where the cows and horses were kept.

Aunt Em dropped her work and came to the door. One glance told her of the danger close at hand.

"Quick, Dorothy!" she screamed. "Run for the cellar!"

Toto jumped out of Dorothy's arms and hid under the bed, and the girl started to get him. Aunt Em, badly frightened, threw open the trap door in the floor and climbed down the ladder into the small, dark hole. Dorothy caught Toto at last and started to follow her aunt. When she was halfway across the room there came a great shriek from the wind, and the house shook so hard that she lost her footing and sat down suddenly upon the floor.

Then a strange thing happened.

The house whirled around two or three times and rose slowly through the air. Dorothy felt as if she were going up in a balloon.

The north and south winds met where the house stood, and made it the exact center of the cyclone. In the middle of a cyclone the air is generally still, but the great pressure of the wind on every side of the house raised it up higher and higher, until it was at the very top of the cyclone; and there it remained and was carried miles and miles away as easily as you could carry a feather.

It was very dark, and the wind howled horribly around her, but Dorothy found she was riding quite easily. After the first few whirls around, and one other time when the house tipped badly, she felt as if she were being rocked gently, like a baby in a cradle.

Toto did not like it. He ran about the room, now here, now there, barking loudly; but Dorothy sat quite still on the floor and waited to see what would happen.

Once Toto got too near the open trap door, and fell in; and at first the little girl thought she had lost him. But soon she saw one of his ears sticking up through the hole, for the strong pressure of the air was keeping him up so that he could not fall. She crept to the hole, caught Toto by the ear, and dragged him into the room again, afterward closing the trap door so that no more accidents could happen.

Hour after hour passed away, and slowly Dorothy got over her fright; but she felt quite lonely, and the wind shrieked so loudly all about her that she nearly became deaf. At first she had wondered if she would be dashed to pieces when the house fell again; but as the hours passed and nothing terrible happened, she stopped worrying and resolved to wait calmly and see what the future would bring. At last she crawled over the swaying floor to her bed, and lay down upon it; and Toto followed and lay down beside her.

In spite of the swaying of the house and the wailing of the wind, Dorothy soon closed her eyes and fell fast asleep.

Chapter 2

THE COUNCIL WITH THE MUNCHKINS

SHE was awakened by a shock, so sudden and severe that if Dorothy had not been lying on the soft bed she might have been hurt. As it was, the jar made her catch her breath and wonder what had happened; and Toto put his cold little nose into her face and whined dismally. Dorothy sat up and noticed that the house was not moving; nor was it dark, for the bright sunshine came in at the window, flooding the little room. She sprang from her bed and with Toto at her heels ran and opened the door.

The little girl gave a cry of amazement and looked about her, her eyes growing bigger and bigger at the wonderful sights she saw.

The cyclone had set the house down very gently—for a cyclone—in the midst of a country of marvelous beauty. There were lovely patches of greensward all about, with stately trees bearing rich and luscious fruits. Banks of gorgeous flowers were on every hand, and birds with rare and brilliant plumage sang and fluttered in the trees and bushes. A little way off was a small brook, rushing and sparkling along between green banks, and murmuring in a voice very grateful to a little girl who had lived so long on the dry, gray prairies.

While she stood looking eagerly at the strange and beautiful sights, she noticed coming toward her a group of the queerest people she had ever seen. They were not as big as the grown folk she had always been used to; but neither were they very small. In fact, they seemed about as tall as Dorothy, who was a well-grown child for her age, although they were, so far as looks go, many years older.

Three were men and one a woman, and all were oddly dressed. They wore round hats that rose to a small point a foot above their heads, with little bells around the brims that tinkled sweetly as they moved. The hats of the men were blue; the little woman's hat was white, and she wore a white gown that hung in pleats from her shoulders. Over it were sprinkled little stars that glistened in the sun like diamonds. The men were dressed in blue, of the same shade as their hats, and wore well-polished boots with a deep roll of blue at the tops. The men, Dorothy thought, were about as old as Uncle Henry, for two of them had beards. But the little woman was doubtless much older. Her face was covered with wrinkles, her hair was nearly white, and she walked rather stiffly.

When these people drew near the house where Dorothy was standing in the doorway, they paused and whispered among themselves, as if afraid to come farther. But the little old woman walked up to Dorothy, made a low bow and said, in a sweet voice:

"You are welcome, most noble Sorceress, to the land of the Munchkins. We are so grateful to you for having killed the Wicked Witch of the East, and for setting our people free from bondage."

Dorothy listened to this speech with wonder. What could the little woman possibly mean by calling her a sorceress, and saying she had killed the Wicked Witch of the East? Dorothy was an innocent, harmless little girl, who had been carried by a cyclone many miles from home; and she had never killed anything in all her life.

But the little woman evidently expected her to answer; so Dorothy said, with hesitation, "You are very kind, but there must be some mistake. I have not killed anything."

"Your house did, anyway," replied the little old woman, with a laugh, "and that is the same thing. See!" she continued, pointing to the corner of the house. "There are her two feet, still sticking out from under a block of wood."

Dorothy looked, and gave a little cry of fright. There, indeed, just under the corner of the great beam the house rested on, two feet were sticking out, shod in silver shoes with pointed toes.

"Oh, dear! Oh, dear!" cried Dorothy, clasping her hands together in dismay. "The house must have fallen on her. Whatever shall we do?"

"There is nothing to be done," said the little woman calmly.

"But who was she?" asked Dorothy.

"She was the Wicked Witch of the East, as I said," answered the little woman. "She has held all the Munchkins in bondage for many years, making them slave for her night and day. Now they are all set free, and are grateful to you for the favor."

"Who are the Munchkins?" inquired Dorothy.

"They are the people who live in this land of the East where the Wicked Witch ruled."

"Are you a Munchkin?" asked Dorothy.

"No, but I am their friend, although I live in the land of the North. When they saw the Witch of the East was dead the Munchkins sent a swift messenger to me, and I came at once. I am the Witch of the North."

"Oh, gracious!" cried Dorothy. "Are you a real witch?"

"Yes, indeed," answered the little woman. "But I am a good witch, and the people love me. I am not as powerful as the Wicked Witch was who ruled here, or I should have set the people free myself."

"But I thought all witches were wicked," said the girl, who was half frightened at facing a real witch. "Oh, no, that is a great mistake. There were only four witches in all the Land of Oz, and two of them, those who live in the North and the South, are good witches. I know this is true, for I am one of them myself, and cannot be mistaken. Those who dwelt in the East and the West were, indeed, wicked witches; but now that you have killed one of them, there is but one Wicked Witch in all the Land of Oz—the one who lives in the West."

"But," said Dorothy, after a moment's thought, "Aunt Em has told me that the witches were all dead—years and years ago."

"Who is Aunt Em?" inquired the little old woman.

"She is my aunt who lives in Kansas, where I came from."

The Witch of the North seemed to think for a time, with her head bowed and her eyes upon the ground. Then she looked up and said, "I do not know where Kansas is, for I have never heard that country mentioned before. But tell me, is it a civilized country?"

"Oh, yes," replied Dorothy.

"Then that accounts for it. In the civilized countries I believe there are no witches left, nor wizards, nor sorceresses, nor magicians. But, you see, the Land of Oz has never been civilized, for we are cut off from all the rest of the world. Therefore we still have witches and wizards amongst us."

"Who are the wizards?" asked Dorothy.

"Oz himself is the Great Wizard," answered the Witch, sinking her voice to a whisper. "He is more powerful than all the rest of us together. He lives in the City of Emeralds."

Dorothy was going to ask another question, but just then the Munchkins, who had been standing silently by, gave a loud shout and pointed to the corner of the house where the Wicked Witch had been lying.

"What is it?" asked the little old woman, and looked, and began to laugh. The feet of the dead Witch had disappeared entirely, and nothing was left but the silver shoes.

"She was so old," explained the Witch of the North, "that she dried up quickly in the sun. That is the end of her. But the silver shoes are yours, and you shall have them to wear." She reached down and picked up the shoes, and after shaking the dust out of them handed them to Dorothy.

"The Witch of the East was proud of those silver shoes," said one of the Munchkins, "and there is some charm connected with them; but what it is we never knew."

Dorothy carried the shoes into the house and placed them on the table. Then she came out again to the Munchkins and said:

"I am anxious to get back to my aunt and uncle, for I am sure they will worry about me. Can you help me find my way?"

The Munchkins and the Witch first looked at one another, and then at Dorothy, and then shook their heads.

"At the East, not far from here," said one, "there is a great desert, and none could live to cross it."

"It is the same at the South," said another, "for I have been there and seen it. The South is the country of the Quadlings."

"I am told," said the third man, "that it is the same at the West. And that country, where the Winkies live, is ruled by the Wicked Witch of the West, who would make you her slave if you passed her way."

"The North is my home," said the old lady, "and at its edge is the same great desert that surrounds this Land of Oz. I'm afraid, my dear, you will have to live with us."

Dorothy began to sob at this, for she felt lonely among all these strange people. Her tears seemed to grieve the kind-hearted

Munchkins, for they immediately took out their handkerchiefs and began to weep also. As for the little old woman, she took off her cap and balanced the point on the end of her nose, while she counted "One, two, three" in a solemn voice. At once the cap changed to a slate, on which was written in big, white chalk marks:

"LET DOROTHY GO TO THE CITY OF EMERALDS"

The little old woman took the slate from her nose, and having read the words on it, asked, "Is your name Dorothy, my dear?"

"Yes," answered the child, looking up and drying her tears.

"Then you must go to the City of Emeralds. Perhaps Oz will help you."

"Where is this city?" asked Dorothy.

"It is exactly in the center of the country, and is ruled by Oz, the Great Wizard I told you of."

"Is he a good man?" inquired the girl anxiously.

"He is a good Wizard. Whether he is a man or not I cannot tell, for I have never seen him."

"How can I get there?" asked Dorothy.

"You must walk. It is a long journey, through a country that is sometimes pleasant and sometimes dark and terrible. However, I will use all the magic arts I know of to keep you from harm."

"Won't you go with me?" pleaded the girl, who had begun to look upon the little old woman as her only friend.

"No, I cannot do that," she replied, "but I will give you my kiss, and no one will dare injure a person who has been kissed by the Witch of the North."

She came close to Dorothy and kissed her gently on the forehead. Where her lips touched the girl they left a round, shining mark, as Dorothy found out soon after.

"The road to the City of Emeralds is paved with yellow brick," said the Witch, "so you cannot miss it. When you get to Oz do not be afraid of him, but tell your story and ask him to help you. Good-bye, my dear."

The three Munchkins bowed low to her and wished her a pleasant journey, after which they walked away through the trees. The Witch gave Dorothy a friendly little nod, whirled around on her left heel three times, and straightway disappeared, much to the surprise of little Toto, who barked after her loudly enough when she had gone, because he had been afraid even to growl while she stood by.

But Dorothy, knowing her to be a witch, had expected her to disappear in just that way, and was not surprised in the least.

Chapter 3

HOW DOROTHY SAVED THE SCARECROW

When Dorothy was left alone she began to feel hungry. So she went to the cupboard and cut herself some bread, which she spread with butter. She gave some to Toto, and taking a pail from the shelf she carried it down to the little brook and filled it with clear, sparkling water. Toto ran over to the trees and began to bark at the birds sitting there. Dorothy went to get him, and saw such delicious fruit hanging from the branches that she gathered some of it, finding it just what she wanted to help out her breakfast.

Then she went back to the house, and having helped herself and Toto to a good drink of the cool, clear water, she set about making ready for the journey to the City of Emeralds.

Dorothy had only one other dress, but that happened to be clean and was hanging on a peg beside her bed. It was gingham, with checks of white and blue; and although the blue was somewhat faded with many washings, it was still a pretty frock. The girl washed herself carefully, dressed herself in the clean gingham, and tied her pink sunbonnet on her head. She took a little basket and filled it with bread from the cupboard, laying a white cloth over the top. Then she looked down at her feet and noticed how old and worn her shoes were.

"They surely will never do for a long journey, Toto," she said. And Toto looked up into her face with his little black eyes and wagged his tail to show he knew what she meant.

At that moment Dorothy saw lying on the table the silver shoes that had belonged to the Witch of the East.

"I wonder if they will fit me," she said to Toto. "They would be just the thing to take a long walk in, for they could not wear out."

She took off her old leather shoes and tried on the silver ones, which fitted her as well as if they had been made for her.

Finally she picked up her basket.

"Come along, Toto," she said. "We will go to the Emerald City and ask the Great Oz how to get back to Kansas again."

She closed the door, locked it, and put the key carefully in the pocket of her dress. And so, with Toto trotting along soberly behind her, she started on her journey.

There were several roads nearby, but it did not take her long to find the one paved with yellow bricks. Within a short time she was walking briskly toward the Emerald City, her silver shoes tinkling merrily on the hard, yellow road-bed. The sun shone bright and the birds sang sweetly, and Dorothy did not feel nearly so bad as you might think a little girl would who had been suddenly whisked away from her own country and set down in the midst of a strange land.

She was surprised, as she walked along, to see how pretty the country was about her. There were neat fences at the sides of the road, painted a dainty blue color, and beyond them were fields of grain and vegetables in abundance. Evidently the Munchkins were good farmers and able to raise large crops. Once in a while she would pass a house, and the people came out to look at her and bow low as she went by; for everyone knew she had been the means of destroying the Wicked Witch and setting them free from bondage. The houses of the Munchkins were odd-looking dwellings, for each was round, with a big dome for a roof. All were painted blue, for in this country of the East blue was the favorite color.

Toward evening, when Dorothy was tired with her long walk and began to wonder where she should pass the night, she came to a house rather larger than the rest. On the green lawn before it many men and women were dancing. Five little fiddlers played as loudly as possible, and the people were laughing and singing, while a big table nearby was loaded with delicious fruits and nuts, pies and cakes, and many other good things to eat.

The people greeted Dorothy kindly, and invited her to supper and to pass the night with them; for this was the home of one of the richest Munchkins in the land, and his friends were gathered with him to celebrate their freedom from the bondage of the Wicked Witch.

Dorothy ate a hearty supper and was waited upon by the rich Munchkin himself, whose name was Boq. Then she sat upon a settee and watched the people dance.

When Boq saw her silver shoes he said, "You must be a great sorceress."

"Why?" asked the girl.

"Because you wear silver shoes and have killed the Wicked Witch. Besides, you have white in your frock, and only witches and sorceresses wear white."

"My dress is blue and white checked," said Dorothy, smoothing out the wrinkles in it.

"It is kind of you to wear that," said Boq. "Blue is the color of the Munchkins, and white is the witch color. So we know you are a friendly witch."

Dorothy did not know what to say to this, for all the people seemed to think her a witch, and she knew very well she was only an ordinary little girl who had come by the chance of a cyclone into a strange land.

When she had tired watching the dancing, Boq led her into the house, where he gave her a room with a pretty bed in it. The sheets were made of blue cloth, and Dorothy slept soundly in them till morning, with Toto curled up on the blue rug beside her.

She ate a hearty breakfast, and watched a wee Munchkin baby, who played with Toto and pulled his tail and crowed and laughed in a way that greatly amused Dorothy. Toto was a fine curiosity to all the people, for they had never seen a dog before.

"How far is it to the Emerald City?" the girl asked.

"I do not know," answered Boq gravely, "for I have never been there. It is better for people to keep away from Oz, unless they have business with him. But it is a long way to the Emerald City, and it will take you many days. The country here is rich and pleasant, but you must pass through rough and dangerous places before you reach the end of your journey."

This worried Dorothy a little, but she knew that only the Great Oz could help her get to Kansas again, so she bravely resolved not to turn back.

She bade her friends good-bye, and again started along the road of yellow brick. When she had gone several miles she thought she would stop to rest, and so climbed to the top of the fence beside the road and sat down. There was a great cornfield beyond the fence, and not far away she saw a Scarecrow, placed high on a pole to keep the birds from the ripe corn.

Dorothy leaned her chin upon her hand and gazed thoughtfully at the Scarecrow. Its head was a small sack stuffed with straw, with eyes, nose, and mouth painted on it to represent a face. An old, pointed blue hat, that had belonged to some Munchkin, was perched on his head, and the rest of the figure was a blue suit of clothes, worn and faded, which had also been stuffed with straw.

On the feet were some old boots with blue tops, such as every man wore in this country, and the figure was raised above the stalks of corn by means of the pole stuck up its back.

While Dorothy was looking earnestly into the queer, painted face of the Scarecrow, she was surprised to see one of the eyes slowly wink at her. She thought she must have been mistaken at first, for none of the scarecrows in Kansas ever wink; but presently the figure nodded its head to her in a friendly way. Then she climbed down from the fence and walked up to it, while Toto ran around the pole and barked.

"Good day," said the Scarecrow, in a rather husky voice.

"Did you speak?" asked the girl, in wonder.

"Certainly," answered the Scarecrow. "How do you do?"

"I'm pretty well, thank you," replied Dorothy politely. "How do you do?"

"I'm not feeling well," said the Scarecrow, with a smile, "for it is very tedious being perched up here night and day to scare away crows."

"Can't you get down?" asked Dorothy.

"No, for this pole is stuck up my back. If you will please take away the pole I shall be greatly obliged to you."

Dorothy reached up both arms and lifted the figure off the pole, for, being stuffed with straw, it was quite light.

"Thank you very much," said the Scarecrow, when he had been set down on the ground. "I feel like a new man."

Dorothy was puzzled at this, for it sounded queer to hear a stuffed man speak, and to see him bow and walk along beside her.

"Who are you?" asked the Scarecrow when he had stretched himself and yawned. "And where are you going?"

"My name is Dorothy," said the girl, "and I am going to the Emerald City, to ask the Great Oz to send me back to Kansas."

"Where is the Emerald City?" he inquired. "And who is Oz?"

"Why, don't you know?" she returned, in surprise.

"No, indeed. I don't know anything. You see, I am stuffed, so I have no brains at all," he answered sadly.

"Oh," said Dorothy, "I'm awfully sorry for you."

"Do you think," he asked, "if I go to the Emerald City with you, that Oz would give me some brains?"

"I cannot tell," she returned, "but you may come with me, if you like. If Oz will not give you any brains you will be no worse off than you are now."

"That is true," said the Scarecrow. "You see," he continued confidentially, "I don't mind my legs and arms and body being stuffed, because I cannot get hurt. If anyone treads on my toes or sticks a pin into me, it doesn't matter, for I can't feel it. But I do not want people to call me a fool, and if my head stays stuffed with straw instead of with brains, as yours is, how am I ever to know anything?"

"I understand how you feel," said the little girl, who was truly sorry for him. "If you will come with me I'll ask Oz to do all he can for you."

"Thank you," he answered gratefully.

They walked back to the road. Dorothy helped him over the fence, and they started along the path of yellow brick for the Emerald City.

Toto did not like this addition to the party at first. He smelled around the stuffed man as if he suspected there might be a nest of rats in the straw, and he often growled in an unfriendly way at the Scarecrow.

"Don't mind Toto," said Dorothy to her new friend. "He never bites."

"Oh, I'm not afraid," replied the Scarecrow. "He can't hurt the straw. Do let me carry that basket for you. I shall not mind it, for I can't get tired. I'll tell you a secret," he continued, as he walked along. "There is only one thing in the world I am afraid of."

"What is that?" asked Dorothy; "the Munchkin farmer who made you?"

"No," answered the Scarecrow; "it's a lighted match."

Chapter 4

THE ROAD THROUGH THE FOREST

AFTER a few hours the road began to be rough, and the walking grew so difficult that the Scarecrow often stumbled over the yellow bricks, which were here very uneven. Sometimes, indeed, they were broken or missing altogether, leaving holes that Toto jumped across and Dorothy walked around. As for the Scarecrow, having no brains, he walked straight ahead, and so stepped into the holes and fell at full length on the hard bricks. It never hurt him, however, and Dorothy would pick him up and set him upon his feet again, while he joined her in laughing merrily at his own mishap.

The farms were not nearly so well cared for here as they were farther back. There were fewer houses and fewer fruit trees, and the farther they went the more dismal and lonesome the country became.

At noon they sat down by the roadside, near a little brook, and Dorothy opened her basket and got out some bread. She offered a piece to the Scarecrow, but he refused.

"I am never hungry," he said, "and it is a lucky thing I am not, for my mouth is only painted, and if I should cut a hole in it so I could eat, the straw I am stuffed with would come out, and that would spoil the shape of my head."

Dorothy saw at once that this was true, so she only nodded and went on eating her bread.

"Tell me something about yourself and the country you came from," said the Scarecrow, when she had finished her dinner. So she told him all about Kansas, and how gray everything was there, and how the cyclone had carried her to this queer Land of Oz.

The Scarecrow listened carefully, and said, "I cannot understand why you should wish to leave this beautiful country and go back to the dry, gray place you call Kansas."

"That is because you have no brains" answered the girl. "No matter how dreary and gray our homes are, we people of flesh and blood would rather live there than in any other country, be it ever so beautiful. There is no place like home."

The Scarecrow sighed.

"Of course I cannot understand it," he said. "If your heads were stuffed with straw, like mine, you would probably all live in the beautiful places, and then Kansas would have no people at all. It is fortunate for Kansas that you have brains."

"Won't you tell me a story, while we are resting?" asked the child.

The Scarecrow looked at her reproachfully, and answered:

"My life has been so short that I really know nothing whatever. I was only made day before yesterday. What happened in the world before that time is all unknown to me. Luckily, when the farmer made my head, one of the first things he did was to paint my ears, so that I heard what was going on. There was another Munchkin with him, and the first thing I heard was the farmer saying, 'How do you like those ears?'

"'They aren't straight,'" answered the other.

"'Never mind,'" said the farmer. "'They are ears just the same,'" which was true enough.

"'Now I'll make the eyes,'" said the farmer. So he painted my right eye, and as soon as it was finished I found myself looking at him and at everything around me with a great deal of curiosity, for this was my first glimpse of the world.

"'That's a rather pretty eye,'" remarked the Munchkin who was watching the farmer. "'Blue paint is just the color for eyes.'

"'I think I'll make the other a little bigger,'" said the farmer. And when the second eye was done I could see much better than before. Then he made my nose and my mouth. But I did not speak, because at that time I didn't know what a mouth was for. I had the fun of watching them make my body and my arms and legs; and when they fastened on my head, at last, I felt very proud, for I thought I was just as good a man as anyone.

"'This fellow will scare the crows fast enough,' said the farmer. 'He looks just like a man.'

"'Why, he is a man,' said the other, and I quite agreed with him. The farmer carried me under his arm to the cornfield, and set me up on a tall stick, where you found me. He and his friend soon after walked away and left me alone.

"I did not like to be deserted this way. So I tried to walk after them. But my feet would not touch the ground, and I was forced to stay on that pole. It was a lonely life to lead, for I had nothing to think of, having been made such a little while before. Many crows and other birds flew into the cornfield, but as soon as they saw me they flew away again, thinking I was a Munchkin; and this pleased me and made me feel that I was quite an important person. By and by an old crow flew near me, and after looking at me carefully he perched upon my shoulder and said:

"'I wonder if that farmer thought to fool me in this clumsy manner. Any crow of sense could see that you are only stuffed with straw'. Then he hopped down at my feet and ate all the corn he wanted. The other birds, seeing he was not harmed by me, came to eat the corn too, so in a short time there was a great flock of them about me.

"I felt sad at this, for it showed I was not such a good Scarecrow after all; but the old crow comforted me, saying, 'If you only had brains in your head you would be as good a man as any of them, and a better man than some of them. Brains are the only things worth having in this world, no matter whether one is a crow or a man.'

"After the crows had gone I thought this over, and decided I would try hard to get some brains. By good luck you came along and pulled me off the stake, and from what you say I am sure the Great Oz will give me brains as soon as we get to the Emerald City."

"I hope so," said Dorothy earnestly, "since you seem anxious to have them."

"Oh, yes; I am anxious," returned the Scarecrow. "It is such an uncomfortable feeling to know one is a fool."

"Well," said the girl, "let us go." And she handed the basket to the Scarecrow.

There were no fences at all by the roadside now, and the land was rough and untilled. Toward evening they came to a great forest, where the trees grew so big and close together that their branches met over the road of yellow brick. It was almost dark under the trees, for the branches shut out the daylight; but the travelers did not stop, and went on into the forest.

"If this road goes in, it must come out," said the Scarecrow, "and as the Emerald City is at the other end of the road, we must go wherever it leads us."

"Anyone would know that," said Dorothy.

"Certainly; that is why I know it," returned the Scarecrow. "If it required brains to figure it out, I never should have said it."

After an hour or so the light faded away, and they found themselves stumbling along in the darkness. Dorothy could not see at all, but Toto could, for some dogs see very well in the dark; and the Scarecrow declared he could see as well as by day. So she took hold of his arm and managed to get along fairly well.

"If you see any house, or any place where we can pass the night," she said, "you must tell me; for it is very uncomfortable walking in the dark."

Soon after the Scarecrow stopped.

"I see a little cottage at the right of us," he said, "built of logs and branches. Shall we go there?"

"Yes, indeed," answered the child. "I am all tired out."

So the Scarecrow led her through the trees until they reached the cottage, and Dorothy entered and found a bed of dried leaves in one corner. She lay down at once, and with Toto beside her soon fell into a sound sleep. The Scarecrow, who was never tired, stood up in another corner and waited patiently until morning came.

Chapter 5

THE RESCUE OF THE TIN WOODMAN

WHEN Dorothy awoke the sun was shining through the trees and Toto had long been out chasing birds around him and squirrels. She sat up and looked around her. There was the Scarecrow, still standing patiently in his corner, waiting for her.

"We must go and search for water," she said to him.

"Why do you want water?" he asked.

"To wash my face clean after the dust of the road, and to drink, so the dry bread will not stick in my throat."

"It must be inconvenient to be made of flesh," said the Scarecrow thoughtfully, "for you must sleep, and eat and drink. However, you have brains, and it is worth a lot of bother to be able to think properly."

They left the cottage and walked through the trees until they found a little spring of clear water, where Dorothy drank and bathed and ate her breakfast. She saw there was not much bread left in the basket, and the girl was thankful the Scarecrow did not have to eat anything, for there was scarcely enough for herself and Toto for the day.

When she had finished her meal, and was about to go back to the road of yellow brick, she was startled to hear a deep groan nearby.

"What was that?" she asked timidly.

"I cannot imagine," replied the Scarecrow; "but we can go and see."

Just then another groan reached their ears, and the sound seemed to come from behind them. They turned and walked through the forest a few steps, when Dorothy discovered something shining in a ray of sunshine that fell between the trees. She ran to the place and then stopped short, with a little cry of surprise.

One of the big trees had been partly chopped through, and standing beside it, with an uplifted axe in his hands, was a man made entirely of tin. His head and arms and legs were jointed upon his body, but he stood perfectly motionless, as if he could not stir at all.

Dorothy looked at him in amazement, and so did the Scarecrow, while Toto barked sharply and made a snap at the tin legs, which hurt his teeth.

"Did you groan?" asked Dorothy.

"Yes," answered the tin man, "I did. I've been groaning for more than a year, and no one has ever heard me before or come to help me."

"What can I do for you?" she inquired softly, for she was moved by the sad voice in which the man spoke.

"Get an oil-can and oil my joints," he answered. "They are rusted so badly that I cannot move them at all; if I am well oiled I shall soon be all right again. You will find an oil-can on a shelf in my cottage."

Dorothy at once ran back to the cottage and found the oil-can, and then she returned and asked anxiously, "Where are your joints?"

"Oil my neck, first," replied the Tin Woodman. So she oiled it, and as it was quite badly rusted the Scarecrow took hold of the tin head and moved it gently from side to side until it worked freely, and then the man could turn it himself.

"Now oil the joints in my arms," he said. And Dorothy oiled them and the Scarecrow bent them carefully until they were quite free from rust and as good as new.

The Tin Woodman gave a sigh of satisfaction and lowered his axe, which he leaned against the tree.

"This is a great comfort," he said. "I have been holding that axe in the air ever since I rusted, and I'm glad to be able to put it down at last. Now, if you will oil the joints of my legs, I shall be all right once more."

So they oiled his legs until he could move them freely; and he thanked them again and again for his release, for he seemed a very polite creature, and very grateful.

"I might have stood there always if you had not come along," he said; "so you have certainly saved my life. How did you happen to be here?"

"We are on our way to the Emerald City to see the Great Oz," she answered, "and we stopped at your cottage to pass the night."

"Why do you wish to see Oz?" he asked.

"I want him to send me back to Kansas, and the Scarecrow wants him to put a few brains into his head," she replied.

The Tin Woodman appeared to think deeply for a moment. Then he said:

"Do you suppose Oz could give me a heart?"

"Why, I guess so," Dorothy answered. "It would be as easy as to give the Scarecrow brains."

"True," the Tin Woodman returned. "So, if you will allow me to join your party, I will also go to the Emerald City and ask Oz to help me."

"Come along," said the Scarecrow heartily, and Dorothy added that she would be pleased to have his company. So the Tin Woodman shouldered his axe and they all passed through the forest until they came to the road that was paved with yellow brick.

The Tin Woodman had asked Dorothy to put the oil-can in her basket. "For," he said, "if I should get caught in the rain, and rust again, I would need the oil-can badly."

It was a bit of good luck to have their new comrade join the party, for soon after they had begun their journey again they came to a place where the trees and branches grew so thick over the road that the travelers could not pass. But the Tin Woodman set to work with his axe and chopped so well that soon he cleared a passage for the entire party.

Dorothy was thinking so earnestly as they walked along that she did not notice when the Scarecrow stumbled into a hole and rolled over to the side of the road. Indeed he was obliged to call to her to help him up again.

"Why didn't you walk around the hole?" asked the Tin Woodman.

"I don't know enough," replied the Scarecrow cheerfully. "My head is stuffed with straw, you know, and that is why I am going to Oz to ask him for some brains."

"Oh, I see," said the Tin Woodman. "But, after all, brains are not the best things in the world."

"Have you any?" inquired the Scarecrow.

"No, my head is quite empty," answered the Woodman. "But once I had brains, and a heart also; so, having tried them both, I should much rather have a heart."

"And why is that?" asked the Scarecrow.

"I will tell you my story, and then you will know."

So, while they were walking through the forest, the Tin Woodman told the following story:

"I was born the son of a woodman who chopped down trees in the forest and sold the wood for a living. When I grew up, I too became a woodchopper, and after my father died I took care of my old mother as long as she lived. Then I made up my mind that instead of living alone I would marry, so that I might not become lonely.

"There was one of the Munchkin girls who was so beautiful that I soon grew to love her with all my heart. She, on her part, promised to marry me as soon as I could earn enough money to build a better house for her; so I set to work harder than ever. But the girl lived with an old woman who did not want her to marry anyone, for she was so lazy she wished the girl to remain with her and do the cooking and the housework. So the old woman went to the Wicked Witch of the East, and promised her two sheep and a cow if she would prevent the marriage. Thereupon the Wicked Witch enchanted my axe, and when I was chopping away at my best one day, for I was anxious to get the new house and my wife as soon as possible, the axe slipped all at once and cut off my left leg.

"This at first seemed a great misfortune, for I knew a one-legged man could not do very well as a wood-chopper. So I went to a tinsmith and had him make me a new leg out of tin. The leg worked very well, once I was used to it. But my action angered the Wicked Witch of the East, for she had promised the old woman I should not marry the pretty Munchkin girl. When I began chopping again, my axe slipped and cut off my right leg. Again I went to the tinsmith, and again he made me a leg out of tin. After this the enchanted axe cut off my arms, one after the other; but, nothing daunted, I had them replaced with tin ones. The Wicked Witch then made the axe slip and cut off my head, and at first I thought that was the end of me. But the tinsmith happened to come along, and he made me a new head out of tin.

"I thought I had beaten the Wicked Witch then, and I worked harder than ever; but I little knew how cruel my enemy could be. She thought of a new way to kill my love for the beautiful Munchkin maiden, and made my axe slip again, so that it cut right through my body, splitting me into two halves. Once more the tinsmith came to my help and made me a body of tin, fastening my tin arms and legs and head to it, by means of joints, so that I could move around as well as ever. But, alas! I had now no heart, so that I lost all my love for the Munchkin girl, and did not care whether I married her or not. I suppose she is still living with the old woman, waiting for me to come after her.

"My body shone so brightly in the sun that I felt very proud of it and it did not matter now if my axe slipped, for it could not cut me. There was only one danger—that my joints would rust; but I kept an oil-can in my cottage and took care to oil myself whenever I needed it. However, there came a day when I forgot to do this, and, being caught in a rainstorm, before I thought of the danger my joints had rusted, and I was left to stand in the woods until you came to help me. It was a terrible thing to undergo, but during the year I stood there I had time to think that the greatest loss I had known was the loss of my heart. While I was in love I was the happiest man on earth; but no one can love who has not a heart, and so I am resolved to ask Oz to give me one. If he does, I will go back to the Munchkin maiden and marry her."

Both Dorothy and the Scarecrow had been greatly interested in the story of the Tin Woodman, and now they knew why he was so anxious to get a new heart.

"All the same," said the Scarecrow, "I shall ask for brains instead of a heart; for a fool would not know what to do with a heart if he had one."

"I shall take the heart," returned the Tin Woodman; "for brains do not make one happy, and happiness is the best thing in the world."

Dorothy did not say anything, for she was puzzled to know which of her two friends was right, and she decided if she could only get back to Kansas and Aunt Em, it did not matter so much whether the Woodman had no brains and the Scarecrow no heart, or each got what he wanted.

What worried her most was that the bread was nearly gone, and another meal for herself and Toto would empty the basket. To be sure, neither the Woodman nor the Scarecrow ever ate anything, but she was not made of tin nor straw, and could not live unless she was fed.

Chapter 6

THE COWARDLY LION

ALL this time Dorothy and her companions had been walking through the thick woods. The road was still paved with yellow brick, but these were much covered by dried branches and dead leaves from the trees, and the walking was not at all good.

There were few birds in this part of the forest, for birds love the open country where there is plenty of sunshine. But now and then there came a deep growl from some wild animal hidden among the trees. These sounds made the little girl's heart beat fast, for she did not know what made them; but Toto knew, and he walked close to Dorothy's side, and did not even bark in return.

"How long will it be," the child asked of the Tin Woodman, "before we are out of the forest?"

"I cannot tell," was the answer, "for I have never been to the Emerald City. But my father went there once, when I was a boy, and he said it was a long journey through a dangerous country, although nearer to the city where Oz dwells the country is beautiful. But I am not afraid so long as I have my oil-can, and nothing can hurt the Scarecrow, while you bear upon your forehead the mark of the Good Witch's kiss, and that will protect you from harm."

"But Toto!" said the girl anxiously. "What will protect him?"

"We must protect him ourselves if he is in danger," replied the Tin Woodman.

Just as he spoke there came from the forest a terrible roar, and the next moment a great Lion bounded into the road. With one blow of his paw he sent the Scarecrow spinning over and over to the edge of the road, and then he struck at the Tin Woodman with his sharp claws. But, to the Lion's surprise, he could make no impression on the tin, although the Woodman fell over in the road and lay still.

Little Toto, now that he had an enemy to face, ran barking toward the Lion, and the great beast had opened his mouth to bite the dog, when Dorothy, fearing Toto would be killed, and heedless of danger, rushed forward and slapped the Lion upon his nose as hard as she could, while she cried out:

"Don't you dare to bite Toto! You ought to be ashamed of yourself, a big beast like you, to bite a poor little dog!"

"I didn't bite him," said the Lion, as he rubbed his nose with his paw where Dorothy had hit it.

"No, but you tried to," she retorted. "You are nothing but a big coward."

"I know it," said the Lion, hanging his head in shame. "I've always known it. But how can I help it?"

"I don't know, I'm sure. To think of your striking a stuffed man, like the poor Scarecrow!"

"Is he stuffed?" asked the Lion in surprise, as he watched her pick up the Scarecrow and set him upon his feet, while she patted him into shape again.

"Of course he's stuffed," replied Dorothy, who was still angry.

"That's why he went over so easily," remarked the Lion. "It astonished me to see him whirl around so. Is the other one stuffed also?"

"No," said Dorothy, "he's made of tin." And she helped the Woodman up again.

"That's why he nearly blunted my claws," said the Lion. "When they scratched against the tin it made a cold shiver run down my back. What is that little animal you are so tender of?"

"He is my dog, Toto," answered Dorothy.

"Is he made of tin, or stuffed?" asked the Lion.

"Neither. He's a—a—a meat dog," said the girl.

"Oh! He's a curious animal and seems remarkably small, now that I look at him. No one would think of biting such a little thing, except a coward like me," continued the Lion sadly.

"What makes you a coward?" asked Dorothy, looking at the great beast in wonder, for he was as big as a small horse.

"It's a mystery," replied the Lion. "I suppose I was born that way. All the other animals in the forest naturally expect me to be brave, for the Lion is everywhere thought to be the King of Beasts. I learned that if I roared very loudly every living thing was frightened and got out of my way. Whenever I've met a man I've been awfully scared; but I just roared at him, and he has always run away as fast as he could go. If the elephants and the tigers and the bears had ever tried to fight me, I should have run myself—I'm such a coward; but just as soon as they hear me roar they all try to get away from me, and of course I let them go."

"But that isn't right. The King of Beasts shouldn't be a coward," said the Scarecrow.

"I know it," returned the Lion, wiping a tear from his eye with the tip of his tail. "It is my great sorrow, and makes my life very unhappy. But whenever there is danger, my heart begins to beat fast."

"Perhaps you have heart disease," said the Tin Woodman.

"It may be," said the Lion.

"If you have," continued the Tin Woodman, "you ought to be glad, for it proves you have a heart. For my part, I have no heart; so I cannot have heart disease."

"Perhaps," said the Lion thoughtfully, "if I had no heart I should not be a coward."

"Have you brains?" asked the Scarecrow.

"I suppose so. I've never looked to see," replied the Lion.

"I am going to the Great Oz to ask him to give me some," remarked the Scarecrow, "for my head is stuffed with straw."

"And I am going to ask him to give me a heart," said the Woodman.

"And I am going to ask him to send Toto and me back to Kansas," added Dorothy.

"Do you think Oz could give me courage?" asked the Cowardly Lion.

"Just as easily as he could give me brains," said the Scarecrow.

"Or give me a heart," said the Tin Woodman.

"Or send me back to Kansas," said Dorothy.

"Then, if you don't mind, I'll go with you," said the Lion, "for my life is simply unbearable without a bit of courage."

"You will be very welcome," answered Dorothy, "for you will help to keep away the other wild beasts. It seems to me they must be more cowardly than you are if they allow you to scare them so easily."

"They really are," said the Lion, "but that doesn't make me any braver, and as long as I know myself to be a coward I shall be unhappy."

So once more the little company set off upon the journey, the Lion walking with stately strides at Dorothy's side. Toto did not approve of this new comrade at first, for he could not forget how nearly he had been crushed between the Lion's great jaws. But after a time he became more at ease, and presently Toto and the Cowardly Lion had grown to be good friends.

During the rest of that day there was no other adventure to mar the peace of their journey. Once, indeed, the Tin Woodman stepped upon a beetle that was crawling along the road, and killed the poor little thing. This made the Tin Woodman very unhappy, for he was always careful not to hurt any living creature; and as he walked along he wept several tears of sorrow and regret. These tears ran slowly down his face and over the hinges of his jaw, and there they rusted. When Dorothy presently asked him a question the Tin Woodman could not open his mouth, for his jaws were tightly rusted together. He became greatly frightened at this and made many motions to Dorothy to relieve him, but she could not understand. The Lion was also puzzled to know what was wrong. But the Scarecrow seized the oil-can from Dorothy's basket and oiled the Woodman's jaws, so that after a few moments he could talk as well as before.

"This will serve me a lesson," said he, "to look where I step. For if I should kill another bug or beetle I should surely cry again, and crying rusts my jaws so that I cannot speak."

Thereafter he walked very carefully, with his eyes on the road, and when he saw a tiny ant toiling by he would step over it, so as not to harm it. The Tin Woodman knew very well he had no heart, and therefore he took great care never to be cruel or unkind to anything.

"You people with hearts," he said, "have something to guide you, and need never do wrong; but I have no heart, and so I must be very careful. When Oz gives me a heart of course I needn't mind so much."

Chapter 7

THE JOURNEY TO THE GREAT OZ

THEY were obliged to camp out that night under a large tree in the forest, for there were no houses near. The tree made a good, thick covering to protect them from the dew, and the Tin Woodman chopped a great pile of wood with his axe and Dorothy built a splendid fire that warmed her and made her feel less lonely. She and Toto ate the last of their bread, and now she did not know what they would do for breakfast.

"If you wish," said the Lion, "I will go into the forest and kill a deer for you. You can roast it by the fire, since your tastes are so peculiar that you prefer cooked food, and then you will have a very good breakfast."

"Don't! Please don't," begged the Tin Woodman. "I should certainly weep if you killed a poor deer, and then my jaws would rust again."

But the Lion went away into the forest and found his own supper, and no one ever knew what it was, for he didn't mention it. And the Scarecrow found a tree full of nuts and filled Dorothy's basket with them, so that she would not be hungry for a long time. She thought this was very kind and thoughtful of the Scarecrow, but she laughed heartily at the awkward way in which the poor creature picked up the nuts. His padded hands were so clumsy and the nuts were so small that he dropped almost as many as he put in the basket. But the Scarecrow did not mind how long it took him to fill the basket, for it enabled him to keep away from the fire, as he feared a spark might get into his straw and burn him up. So he kept a good distance away from the flames, and only came near to cover Dorothy with dry leaves when she lay down to sleep. These kept her very snug and warm, and she slept soundly until morning.

When it was daylight, the girl bathed her face in a little rippling brook, and soon after they all started toward the Emerald City.

This was to be an eventful day for the travelers. They had hardly been walking an hour when they saw before them a great ditch that crossed the road and divided the forest as far as they could see on either side. It was a very wide ditch, and when they crept up to the edge and looked into it they could see it was also very deep, and there were many big, jagged rocks at the bottom. The sides were so steep that none of them could climb down, and for a moment it seemed that their journey must end.

"What shall we do?" asked Dorothy despairingly.

"I haven't the faintest idea," said the Tin Woodman, and the Lion shook his shaggy mane and looked thoughtful.

But the Scarecrow said, "We cannot fly, that is certain. Neither can we climb down into this great ditch. Therefore, if we cannot jump over it, we must stop where we are."

"I think I could jump over it," said the Cowardly Lion, after measuring the distance carefully in his mind.

"Then we are all right," answered the Scarecrow, "for you can carry us all over on your back, one at a time."

"Well, I'll try it," said the Lion. "Who will go first?"

"I will," declared the Scarecrow, "for, if you found that you could not jump over the gulf, Dorothy would be killed, or the Tin Woodman badly dented on the rocks below. But if I am on your back it will not matter so much, for the fall would not hurt me at all."

"I am terribly afraid of falling, myself," said the Cowardly Lion, "but I suppose there is nothing to do but try it. So get on my back and we will make the attempt."

The Scarecrow sat upon the Lion's back, and the big beast walked to the edge of the gulf and crouched down.

"Why don't you run and jump?" asked the Scarecrow.

"Because that isn't the way we Lions do these things," he replied. Then giving a great spring, he shot through the air and landed safely on the other side. They were all greatly pleased to see how easily he did it, and after the Scarecrow had got down from his back the Lion sprang across the ditch again.

Dorothy thought she would go next; so she took Toto in her arms and climbed on the Lion's back, holding tightly to his mane with one hand. The next moment it seemed as if she were flying through the air; and then, before she had time to think about it, she was safe on the other side. The Lion went back a third time and got the Tin Woodman, and then they all sat down for a few moments to give the beast a chance to rest, for his great leaps had made his breath short, and he panted like a big dog that has been running too long.

They found the forest very thick on this side, and it looked dark and gloomy. After the Lion had rested they started along the road of yellow brick, silently wondering, each in his own mind, if ever they would come to the end of the woods and reach the bright sunshine again. To add to their discomfort, they soon heard strange noises in the depths of the forest, and the Lion whispered to them that it was in this part of the country that the Kalidahs lived.

"What are the Kalidahs?" asked the girl.

"They are monstrous beasts with bodies like bears and heads like tigers," replied the Lion, "and with claws so long and sharp that they could tear me in two as easily as I could kill Toto. I'm terribly afraid of the Kalidahs."

"I'm not surprised that you are," returned Dorothy. "They must be dreadful beasts."

The Lion was about to reply when suddenly they came to another gulf across the road. But this one was so broad and deep that the Lion knew at once he could not leap across it.

So they sat down to consider what they should do, and after serious thought the Scarecrow said:

"Here is a great tree, standing close to the ditch. If the Tin Woodman can chop it down, so that it will fall to the other side, we can walk across it easily."

"That is a first-rate idea," said the Lion. "One would almost suspect you had brains in your head, instead of straw."

The Woodman set to work at once, and so sharp was his axe that the tree was soon chopped nearly through. Then the Lion put his strong front legs against the tree and pushed with all his might, and slowly the big tree tipped and fell with a crash across the ditch, with its top branches on the other side.

They had just started to cross this queer bridge when a sharp growl made them all look up, and to their horror they saw running toward them two great beasts with bodies like bears and heads like tigers.

"They are the Kalidahs!" said the Cowardly Lion, beginning to tremble.

"Quick!" cried the Scarecrow. "Let us cross over."

So Dorothy went first, holding Toto in her arms, the Tin Woodman followed, and the Scarecrow came next. The Lion, although he was certainly afraid, turned to face the Kalidahs, and then he gave so loud and terrible a roar that Dorothy screamed and the Scarecrow fell over backward, while even the fierce beasts stopped short and looked at him in surprise.

But, seeing they were bigger than the Lion, and remembering that there were two of them and only one of him, the Kalidahs again rushed forward, and the Lion crossed over the tree and turned to see what they would do next. Without stopping an instant the fierce beasts also began to cross the tree. And the Lion said to Dorothy:

"We are lost, for they will surely tear us to pieces with their sharp claws. But stand close behind me, and I will fight them as long as I am alive."

"Wait a minute!" called the Scarecrow. He had been thinking what was best to be done, and now he asked the Woodman to chop away the end of the tree that rested on their side of the ditch. The Tin Woodman began to use his axe at once, and, just as the two Kalidahs were nearly across, the tree fell with a crash into the gulf, carrying the ugly, snarling brutes with it, and both were dashed to pieces on the sharp rocks at the bottom.

"Well," said the Cowardly Lion, drawing a long breath of relief, "I see we are going to live a little while longer, and I am glad of it, for it must be a very uncomfortable thing not to be alive. Those creatures frightened me so badly that my heart is beating yet."

"Ah," said the Tin Woodman sadly, "I wish I had a heart to beat."

This adventure made the travelers more anxious than ever to get out of the forest, and they walked so fast that Dorothy became tired, and had to ride on the Lion's back. To their great joy the trees became thinner the farther they advanced, and in the afternoon they suddenly came upon a broad river, flowing swiftly just before them. On the other side of the water they could see the road of yellow brick running through a beautiful country, with green meadows dotted with bright flowers and all the road bordered with trees hanging full of delicious fruits. They were greatly pleased to see this delightful country before them.

"How shall we cross the river?" asked Dorothy.

"That is easily done," replied the Scarecrow. "The Tin Woodman must build us a raft, so we can float to the other side."

So the Woodman took his axe and began to chop down small trees to make a raft, and while he was busy at this the Scarecrow found on the riverbank a tree full of fine fruit. This pleased Dorothy, who had eaten nothing but nuts all day, and she made a hearty meal of the ripe fruit.

But it takes time to make a raft, even when one is as industrious and untiring as the Tin Woodman, and when night came the work was not done. So they found a cozy place under the trees where they slept well until the morning; and Dorothy dreamed of the Emerald City, and of the good Wizard Oz, who would soon send her back to her own home again.

Chapter 8

THE DEADLY POPPY FIELD

Our little party of travelers awakened the next morning refreshed and full of hope, and Dorothy breakfasted like a princess off peaches and plums from the trees beside the river. Behind them was the dark forest they had passed safely through, although they had suffered many discouragements; but before them was a lovely, sunny country that seemed to beckon them on to the Emerald City.

To be sure, the broad river now cut them off from this beautiful land. But the raft was nearly done, and after the Tin Woodman had cut a few more logs and fastened them together with wooden pins, they were ready to start. Dorothy sat down in the middle of the raft and held Toto in her arms. When the Cowardly Lion stepped upon the raft it tipped badly, for he was big and heavy; but the Scarecrow and the Tin Woodman stood upon the other end to steady it, and they had long poles in their hands to push the raft through the water.

They got along quite well at first, but when they reached the middle of the river the swift current swept the raft downstream, farther and farther away from the road of yellow brick. And the water grew so deep that the long poles would not touch the bottom.

"This is bad," said the Tin Woodman, "for if we cannot get to the land we shall be carried into the country of the Wicked Witch of the West, and she will enchant us and make us her slaves."

"And then I should get no brains," said the Scarecrow.

"And I should get no courage," said the Cowardly Lion.

"And I should get no heart," said the Tin Woodman.

"And I should never get back to Kansas," said Dorothy.

"We must certainly get to the Emerald City if we can," the Scarecrow continued, and he pushed so hard on his long pole that it stuck fast in the mud at the bottom of the river. Then, before he could pull it out again—or let go—the raft was swept away, and the poor Scarecrow was left clinging to the pole in the middle of the river.

"Good-bye!" he called after them, and they were very sorry to leave him. Indeed, the Tin Woodman began to cry, but fortunately remembered that he might rust, and so dried his tears on Dorothy's apron.

Of course this was a bad thing for the Scarecrow.

"I am now worse off than when I first met Dorothy," he thought. "Then, I was stuck on a pole in a cornfield, where I could make-believe scare the crows, at any rate. But surely there is no use for a Scarecrow stuck on a pole in the middle of a river. I am afraid I shall never have any brains, after all!"

Down the stream the raft floated, and the poor Scarecrow was left far behind. Then the Lion said:

"Something must be done to save us. I think I can swim to the shore and pull the raft after me, if you will only hold fast to the tip of my tail."

So he sprang into the water, and the Tin Woodman caught fast hold of his tail. Then the Lion began to swim with all his might toward the shore. It was hard work, although he was so big; but by and by they were drawn out of the current, and then Dorothy took the Tin Woodman's long pole and helped push the raft to the land.

They were all tired out when they reached the shore at last and stepped off upon the pretty green grass, and they also knew that the stream had carried them a long way past the road of yellow brick that led to the Emerald City.

"What shall we do now?" asked the Tin Woodman, as the Lion lay down on the grass to let the sun dry him.

"We must get back to the road, in some way," said Dorothy.

"The best plan will be to walk along the riverbank until we come to the road again," remarked the Lion.

So, when they were rested, Dorothy picked up her basket and they started along the grassy bank, to the road from which the river had carried them. It was a lovely country, with plenty of flowers and fruit trees and sunshine to cheer them, and had they not felt so sorry for the poor Scarecrow, they could have been very happy.

They walked along as fast as they could, Dorothy only stopping once to pick a beautiful flower; and after a time the Tin Woodman cried out: "Look!"

Then they all looked at the river and saw the Scarecrow perched upon his pole in the middle of the water, looking very lonely and sad.

"What can we do to save him?" asked Dorothy.

The Lion and the Woodman both shook their heads, for they did not know. So they sat down upon the bank and gazed wistfully at the Scarecrow until a Stork flew by, who, upon seeing them, stopped to rest at the water's edge.

"Who are you and where are you going?" asked the Stork.

"I am Dorothy," answered the girl, "and these are my friends, the Tin Woodman and the Cowardly Lion; and we are going to the Emerald City."

"This isn't the road," said the Stork, as she twisted her long neck and looked sharply at the queer party.

"I know it," returned Dorothy, "but we have lost the Scarecrow, and are wondering how we shall get him again."

"Where is he?" asked the Stork.

"Over there in the river," answered the little girl.

"If he wasn't so big and heavy I would get him for you," remarked the Stork.

"He isn't heavy a bit," said Dorothy eagerly, "for he is stuffed with straw; and if you will bring him back to us, we shall thank you ever and ever so much."

"Well, I'll try," said the Stork, "but if I find he is too heavy to carry I shall have to drop him in the river again."

So the big bird flew into the air and over the water till she came to where the Scarecrow was perched upon his pole. Then the Stork with her great claws grabbed the Scarecrow by the arm and carried him up into the air and back to the bank, where Dorothy and the Lion and the Tin Woodman and Toto were sitting.

When the Scarecrow found himself among his friends again, he was so happy that he hugged them all, even the Lion and Toto; and as they walked along he sang "Tol-de-ri-de-oh!" at every step, he felt so gay.

"I was afraid I should have to stay in the river forever," he said, "but the kind Stork saved me, and if I ever get any brains I shall find the Stork again and do her some kindness in return."

"That's all right," said the Stork, who was flying along beside them. "I always like to help anyone in trouble. But I must go now, for my babies are waiting in the nest for me. I hope you will find the Emerald City and that Oz will help you."

"Thank you," replied Dorothy, and then the kind Stork flew into the air and was soon out of sight.

They walked along listening to the singing of the brightly colored birds and looking at the lovely flowers which now became so thick that the ground was carpeted with them. There were big yellow and white and blue and purple blossoms, besides great clusters of scarlet poppies, which were so brilliant in color they almost dazzled Dorothy's eyes.

"Aren't they beautiful?" the girl asked, as she breathed in the spicy scent of the bright flowers.

"I suppose so," answered the Scarecrow. "When I have brains, I shall probably like them better."

"If I only had a heart, I should love them," added the Tin Woodman.

"I always did like flowers," said the Lion. "They seem so helpless and frail. But there are none in the forest so bright as these."

They now came upon more and more of the big scarlet poppies, and fewer and fewer of the other flowers; and soon they found themselves in the midst of a great meadow of poppies. Now it is well known that when there are many of these flowers together their odor is so powerful that anyone who breathes it falls asleep, and if the sleeper is not carried away from the scent of the flowers, he sleeps on and on forever. But Dorothy did not know this, nor could she get away from the bright red flowers that were everywhere about; so presently her eyes grew heavy and she felt she must sit down to rest and to sleep.

But the Tin Woodman would not let her do this.

"We must hurry and get back to the road of yellow brick before dark," he said; and the Scarecrow agreed with him. So they kept walking until Dorothy could stand no longer. Her eyes closed in spite of herself and she forgot where she was and fell among the poppies, fast asleep.

"What shall we do?" asked the Tin Woodman.

"If we leave her here she will die," said the Lion. "The smell of the flowers is killing us all. I myself can scarcely keep my eyes open, and the dog is asleep already."

It was true; Toto had fallen down beside his little mistress. But the Scarecrow and the Tin Woodman, not being made of flesh, were not troubled by the scent of the flowers.

"Run fast," said the Scarecrow to the Lion, "and get out of this deadly flower bed as soon as you can. We will bring the little girl with us, but if you should fall asleep you are too big to be carried."

So the Lion aroused himself and bounded forward as fast as he could go. In a moment he was out of sight.

"Let us make a chair with our hands and carry her," said the Scarecrow. So they picked up Toto and put the dog in Dorothy's lap, and then they made a chair with their hands for the seat and their arms for the arms and carried the sleeping girl between them through the flowers.

On and on they walked, and it seemed that the great carpet of deadly flowers that surrounded them would never end. They followed the bend of the river, and at last came upon their friend the Lion, lying fast asleep among the poppies. The flowers had been too strong for the huge beast and he had given up at last, and fallen only a short distance from the end of the poppy bed, where the sweet grass spread in beautiful green fields before them.

"We can do nothing for him," said the Tin Woodman, sadly; "for he is much too heavy to lift. We must leave him here to sleep on forever, and perhaps he will dream that he has found courage at last."

"I'm sorry," said the Scarecrow. "The Lion was a very good comrade for one so cowardly. But let us go on."

They carried the sleeping girl to a pretty spot beside the river, far enough from the poppy field to prevent her breathing any more of the poison of the flowers, and here they laid her gently on the soft grass and waited for the fresh breeze to waken her.

Chapter 9

THE QUEEN OF THE FIELD MICE

"WE cannot be far from the road of yellow brick, now," remarked the Scarecrow, as he stood beside the girl, "for we have come nearly as far as the river carried us away."

The Tin Woodman was about to reply when he heard a low growl, and turning his head (which worked beautifully on hinges) he saw a strange beast come bounding over the grass toward them. It was, indeed, a great yellow Wildcat, and the Woodman thought it must be chasing something, for its ears were lying close to its head and its mouth was wide open, showing two rows of ugly teeth, while its red eyes glowed like balls of fire. As it came nearer the Tin Woodman saw that running before the beast was a little gray field mouse, and although he had no heart he knew it was wrong for the Wildcat to try to kill such a pretty, harmless creature.

So the Woodman raised his axe, and as the Wildcat ran by he gave it a quick blow that cut the beast's head clean off from its body, and it rolled over at his feet in two pieces.

The field mouse, now that it was freed from its enemy, stopped short; and coming slowly up to the Woodman it said, in a squeaky little voice:

"Oh, thank you! Thank you ever so much for saving my life."

"Don't speak of it, I beg of you," replied the Woodman. "I have no heart, you know, so I am careful to help all those who may need a friend, even if it happens to be only a mouse."

"Only a mouse!" cried the little animal, indignantly. "Why, I am a Queen—the Queen of all the Field Mice!"

"Oh, indeed," said the Woodman, making a bow.

"Therefore you have done a great deed, as well as a brave one, in saving my life," added the Queen.

At that moment several mice were seen running up as fast as their little legs could carry them, and when they saw their Queen they exclaimed:

"Oh, your Majesty, we thought you would be killed! How did you manage to escape the great Wildcat?" They all bowed so low to the little Queen that they almost stood upon their heads.

"This funny tin man," she answered, "killed the Wildcat and saved my life. So hereafter you must all serve him, and obey his slightest wish."

"We will!" cried all the mice, in a shrill chorus. And then they scampered in all directions, for Toto had awakened from his sleep, and seeing all these mice around him he gave one bark of delight and jumped right into the middle of the group. Toto had always loved to chase mice when he lived in Kansas, and he saw no harm in it.

But the Tin Woodman caught the dog in his arms and held him tight, while he called to the mice, "Come back! Come back! Toto shall not hurt you."

At this the Queen of the Mice stuck her head out from underneath a clump of grass and asked, in a timid voice, "Are you sure he will not bite us?"

"I will not let him," said the Woodman; "so do not be afraid."

One by one the mice came creeping back, and Toto did not bark again, although he tried to get out of the Woodman's arms, and would have bitten him had he not known very well he was made of tin. Finally one of the biggest mice spoke.

"Is there anything we can do," it asked, "to repay you for saving the life of our Queen?"

"Nothing that I know of," answered the Woodman; but the Scarecrow, who had been trying to think, but could not because his head was stuffed with straw, said, quickly, "Oh, yes; you can save our friend, the Cowardly Lion, who is asleep in the poppy bed."

"A Lion!" cried the little Queen. "Why, he would eat us all up."

"Oh, no," declared the Scarecrow; "this Lion is a coward."

"Really?" asked the Mouse.

"He says so himself," answered the Scarecrow, "and he would never hurt anyone who is our friend. If you will help us to save him I promise that he shall treat you all with kindness."

"Very well," said the Queen, "we trust you. But what shall we do?"

"Are there many of these mice which call you Queen and are willing to obey you?"

"Oh, yes; there are thousands," she replied.

"Then send for them all to come here as soon as possible, and let each one bring a long piece of string."

The Queen turned to the mice that attended her and told them to go at once and get all her people. As soon as they heard her orders they ran away in every direction as fast as possible.

"Now," said the Scarecrow to the Tin Woodman, "you must go to those trees by the riverside and make a truck that will carry the Lion."

So the Woodman went at once to the trees and began to work; and he soon made a truck out of the limbs of trees, from which he chopped away all the leaves and branches. He fastened it together with wooden pegs and made the four wheels out of short pieces of a big tree trunk. So fast and so well did he work that by the time the mice began to arrive the truck was all ready for them.

They came from all directions, and there were thousands of them: big mice and little mice and middle-sized mice; and each one brought a piece of string in his mouth. It was about this time that Dorothy woke from her long sleep and opened her eyes. She was greatly astonished to find herself lying upon the grass, with thousands of mice standing around and looking at her timidly. But the Scarecrow told her about everything, and turning to the dignified little Mouse, he said:

"Permit me to introduce to you her Majesty, the Queen."

Dorothy nodded gravely and the Queen made a curtsy, after which she became quite friendly with the little girl.

The Scarecrow and the Woodman now began to fasten the mice to the truck, using the strings they had brought. One end of a string was tied around the neck of each mouse and the other end to the truck. Of course the truck was a thousand times bigger than any of the mice who were to draw it; but when all the mice had been harnessed, they were able to pull it quite easily. Even the Scarecrow and the Tin Woodman could sit on it, and were drawn swiftly by their queer little horses to the place where the Lion lay asleep.

After a great deal of hard work, for the Lion was heavy, they managed to get him up on the truck. Then the Queen hurriedly gave her people the order to start, for she feared if the mice stayed among the poppies too long they also would fall asleep.

At first the little creatures, many though they were, could hardly stir the heavily loaded truck; but the Woodman and the Scarecrow both pushed from behind, and they got along better. Soon they rolled the Lion out of the poppy bed to the green fields, where he could breathe the sweet, fresh air again, instead of the poisonous scent of the flowers.

Dorothy came to meet them and thanked the little mice warmly for saving her companion from death. She had grown so fond of the big Lion she was glad he had been rescued.

Then the mice were unharnessed from the truck and scampered away through the grass to their homes. The Queen of the Mice was the last to leave.

"If ever you need us again," she said, "come out into the field and call, and we shall hear you and come to your assistance. Good-bye!"

"Good-bye!" they all answered, and away the Queen ran, while Dorothy held Toto tightly lest he should run after her and frighten her.

After this they sat down beside the Lion until he should awaken; and the Scarecrow brought Dorothy some fruit from a tree near by, which she ate for her dinner.

Chapter 10

THE GUARDIAN OF THE GATE

IT was some time before the Cowardly Lion awakened, for he had lain among the poppies a long while, breathing in their deadly fragrance; but when he did open his eyes and roll off the truck he was very glad to find himself still alive.

"I ran as fast as I could," he said, sitting down and yawning, "but the flowers were too strong for me. How did you get me out?"

Then they told him of the field mice, and how they had generously saved him from death; and the Cowardly Lion laughed, and said:

"I have always thought myself very big and terrible; yet such little things as flowers came near to killing me, and such small animals as mice have saved my life. How strange it all is! But, comrades, what shall we do now?"

"We must journey on until we find the road of yellow brick again," said Dorothy, "and then we can keep on to the Emerald City."

So, the Lion being fully refreshed, and feeling quite himself again, they all started upon the journey, greatly enjoying the walk through the soft, fresh grass; and it was not long before they reached the road of yellow brick and turned again toward the Emerald City where the Great Oz dwelt.

The road was smooth and well paved, now, and the country about was beautiful, so that the travelers rejoiced in leaving the forest far behind, and with it the many dangers they had met in its gloomy shades. Once more they could see fences built beside the road; but these were painted green, and when they came to a small house, in which a farmer evidently lived, that also was painted green. They passed by several of these houses during the afternoon, and sometimes people came to the doors and looked at them as if they would like to ask questions; but no one came near them nor spoke to them because of the great Lion, of which they were very much afraid. The people were all dressed in clothing of a lovely emerald-green color and wore peaked hats like those of the Munchkins.

"This must be the Land of Oz," said Dorothy, "and we are surely getting near the Emerald City."

"Yes," answered the Scarecrow. "Everything is green here, while in the country of the Munchkins blue was the favorite color. But the people do not seem to be as friendly as the Munchkins, and I'm afraid we shall be unable to find a place to pass the night."

"I should like something to eat besides fruit," said the girl, "and I'm sure Toto is nearly starved. Let us stop at the next house and talk to the people."

So, when they came to a good-sized farmhouse, Dorothy walked boldly up to the door and knocked.

A woman opened it just far enough to look out, and said, "What do you want, child, and why is that great Lion with you?"

"We wish to pass the night with you, if you will allow us," answered Dorothy; "and the Lion is my friend and comrade, and would not hurt you for the world."

"Is he tame?" asked the woman, opening the door a little wider.

"Oh, yes," said the girl, "and he is a great coward, too. He will be more afraid of you than you are of him."

"Well," said the woman, after thinking it over and taking another peep at the Lion, "if that is the case you may come in, and I will give you some supper and a place to sleep."

So they all entered the house, where there were, besides the woman, two children and a man. The man had hurt his leg, and was lying on the couch in a corner. They seemed greatly surprised to see so strange a company, and while the woman was busy laying the table the man asked:

"Where are you all going?"

"To the Emerald City," said Dorothy, "to see the Great Oz."

"Oh, indeed!" exclaimed the man. "Are you sure that Oz will see you?"

"Why not?" she replied.

"Why, it is said that he never lets anyone come into his presence. I have been to the Emerald City many times, and it is a beautiful and wonderful place; but I have never been permitted to see the Great Oz, nor do I know of any living person who has seen him."

"Does he never go out?" asked the Scarecrow.

"Never. He sits day after day in the great Throne Room of his Palace, and even those who wait upon him do not see him face to face."

"What is he like?" asked the girl.

"That is hard to tell," said the man thoughtfully. "You see, Oz is a Great Wizard, and can take on any form he wishes. So that some say he looks like a bird; and some say he looks like an elephant; and some say he looks like a cat. To others he appears as a beautiful fairy, or a brownie, or in any other form that pleases him. But who the real Oz is, when he is in his own form, no living person can tell."

"That is very strange," said Dorothy, "but we must try, in some way, to see him, or we shall have made our journey for nothing."

"Why do you wish to see the terrible Oz?" asked the man.

"I want him to give me some brains," said the Scarecrow eagerly.

"Oh, Oz could do that easily enough," declared the man. "He has more brains than he needs."

"And I want him to give me a heart," said the Tin Woodman.

"That will not trouble him," continued the man, "for Oz has a large collection of hearts, of all sizes and shapes."

"And I want him to give me courage," said the Cowardly Lion.

"Oz keeps a great pot of courage in his Throne Room," said the man, "which he has covered with a golden plate, to keep it from running over. He will be glad to give you some."

"And I want him to send me back to Kansas," said Dorothy.

"Where is Kansas?" asked the man, with surprise.

"I don't know," replied Dorothy sorrowfully, "but it is my home, and I'm sure it's somewhere."

"Very likely. Well, Oz can do anything; so I suppose he will find Kansas for you. But first you must get to see him, and that will be a hard task; for the Great Wizard does not like to see anyone, and he usually has his own way. But what do YOU want?" he continued, speaking to Toto. Toto only wagged his tail; for, strange to say, he could not speak.

The woman now called to them that supper was ready, so they gathered around the table and Dorothy ate some delicious porridge and a dish of scrambled eggs and a plate of nice white bread, and enjoyed her meal. The Lion ate some of the porridge, but did not care for it, saying it was made from oats and oats were food for horses, not for lions. The Scarecrow and the Tin Woodman ate nothing at all. Toto ate a little of everything, and was glad to get a good supper again.

The woman now gave Dorothy a bed to sleep in, and Toto lay down beside her, while the Lion guarded the door of her room so she might not be disturbed. The Scarecrow and the Tin Woodman stood up in a corner and kept quiet all night, although of course they could not sleep.

The next morning, as soon as the sun was up, they started on their way, and soon saw a beautiful green glow in the sky just before them.

"That must be the Emerald City," said Dorothy.

As they walked on, the green glow became brighter and brighter, and it seemed that at last they were nearing the end of their travels. Yet it was afternoon before they came to the great wall that surrounded the City. It was high and thick and of a bright green color.

In front of them, and at the end of the road of yellow brick, was a big gate, all studded with emeralds that glittered so in the sun that even the painted eyes of the Scarecrow were dazzled by their brilliancy.

There was a bell beside the gate, and Dorothy pushed the button and heard a silvery tinkle sound within. Then the big gate swung slowly open, and they all passed through and found themselves in a high arched room, the walls of which glistened with countless emeralds.

Before them stood a little man about the same size as the Munchkins. He was clothed all in green, from his head to his feet, and even his skin was of a greenish tint. At his side was a large green box.

When he saw Dorothy and her companions the man asked, "What do you wish in the Emerald City?"

"We came here to see the Great Oz," said Dorothy.

The man was so surprised at this answer that he sat down to think it over.

"It has been many years since anyone asked me to see Oz," he said, shaking his head in perplexity. "He is powerful and terrible, and if you come on an idle or foolish errand to bother the wise reflections of the Great Wizard, he might be angry and destroy you all in an instant."

"But it is not a foolish errand, nor an idle one," replied the Scarecrow; "it is important. And we have been told that Oz is a good Wizard."

"So he is," said the green man, "and he rules the Emerald City wisely and well. But to those who are not honest, or who approach him from curiosity, he is most terrible, and few have ever dared ask to see his face. I am the Guardian of the Gates, and since you demand to see the Great Oz I must take you to his Palace. But first you must put on the spectacles."

"Why?" asked Dorothy.

"Because if you did not wear spectacles the brightness and glory of the Emerald City would blind you. Even those who live in the City must wear spectacles night and day. They are all locked on, for Oz so ordered it when the City was first built, and I have the only key that will unlock them."

He opened the big box, and Dorothy saw that it was filled with spectacles of every size and shape. All of them had green glasses in them. The Guardian of the Gates found a pair that would just fit Dorothy and put them over her eyes. There were two golden bands fastened to them that passed around the back of her head, where they were locked together by a little key that was at the end of a chain the Guardian of the Gates wore around his neck. When they were on, Dorothy could not take them off had she wished, but of course she did not wish to be blinded by the glare of the Emerald City, so she said nothing.

Then the green man fitted spectacles for the Scarecrow and the Tin Woodman and the Lion, and even on little Toto; and all were locked fast with the key.

Then the Guardian of the Gates put on his own glasses and told them he was ready to show them to the Palace. Taking a big golden key from a peg on the wall, he opened another gate, and they all followed him through the portal into the streets of the Emerald City.

Chapter 11

THE WONDERFUL CITY OF OZ

Even with eyes protected by the green spectacles, Dorothy and her friends were at first dazzled by the brilliancy of the wonderful City. The streets were lined with beautiful houses all built of green marble and studded everywhere with sparkling emeralds. They walked over a pavement of the same green marble, and where the blocks were joined together were rows of emeralds, set closely, and glittering in the brightness of the sun. The window panes were of green glass; even the sky above the City had a green tint, and the rays of the sun were green.

There were many people—men, women, and children—walking about, and these were all dressed in green clothes and had greenish skins. They looked at Dorothy and her strangely assorted company with wondering eyes, and the children all ran away and hid behind their mothers when they saw the Lion; but no one spoke to them. Many shops stood in the street, and Dorothy saw that everything in them was green. Green candy and green pop corn were offered for sale, as well as green shoes, green hats, and green clothes of all sorts. At one place a man was selling green lemonade, and when the children bought it Dorothy could see that they paid for it with green pennies.

There seemed to be no horses nor animals of any kind; the men carried things around in little green carts, which they pushed before them. Everyone seemed happy and contented and prosperous.

The Guardian of the Gates led them through the streets until they came to a big building, exactly in the middle of the City, which was the Palace of Oz, the Great Wizard. There was a soldier before the door, dressed in a green uniform and wearing a long green beard.

"Here are strangers," said the Guardian of the Gates to him, "and they demand to see the Great Oz."

"Step inside," answered the soldier, "and I will carry your message to him."

So they passed through the Palace Gates and were led into a big room with a green carpet and lovely green furniture set with emeralds. The soldier made them all wipe their feet upon a green mat before entering this room, and when they were seated he said politely:

"Please make yourselves comfortable while I go to the door of the Throne Room and tell Oz you are here."

They had to wait a long time before the soldier returned. When, at last, he came back, Dorothy asked:

"Have you seen Oz?"

"Oh, no," returned the soldier; "I have never seen him. But I spoke to him as he sat behind his screen and gave him your message. He said he will grant you an audience, if you so desire; but each one of you must enter his presence alone, and he will admit but one each day. Therefore, as you must remain in the Palace for several days, I will have you shown to rooms where you may rest in comfort after your journey."

"Thank you," replied the girl; "that is very kind of Oz."

The soldier now blew upon a green whistle, and at once a young girl, dressed in a pretty green silk gown, entered the room. She had lovely green hair and green eyes, and she bowed low before Dorothy as she said, "Follow me and I will show you your room."

So Dorothy said good-bye to all her friends except Toto, and taking the dog in her arms followed the green girl through seven passages and up three flights of stairs until they came to a room at the front of the Palace. It was the sweetest little room in the world, with a soft comfortable bed that had sheets of green silk and a green velvet counterpane. There was a tiny fountain in the middle of the room, that shot a spray of green perfume into the air, to fall back into a beautifully carved green marble basin. Beautiful green flowers stood in the windows, and there was a shelf with a row of little green books. When Dorothy had time to open these books she found them full of queer green pictures that made her laugh, they were so funny.

In a wardrobe were many green dresses, made of silk and satin and velvet; and all of them fitted Dorothy exactly.

"Make yourself perfectly at home," said the green girl, "and if you wish for anything ring the bell. Oz will send for you tomorrow morning."

She left Dorothy alone and went back to the others. These she also led to rooms, and each one of them found himself lodged in a very pleasant part of the Palace. Of course this politeness was wasted on the Scarecrow; for when he found himself alone in his room he stood stupidly in one spot, just within the doorway, to wait till morning. It would not rest him to lie down, and he could not close his eyes; so he remained all night staring at a little spider which was weaving its web in a corner of the room, just as if it were not one of the most wonderful rooms in the world. The Tin Woodman lay down on his bed from force of habit, for he remembered when he was made of flesh; but not being able to sleep, he passed the night moving his joints up and down to make sure they kept in good working order. The Lion would have preferred a bed of dried leaves in the forest, and did not like being shut up in a room; but he had too much sense to let this worry him, so he sprang upon the bed and rolled himself up like a cat and purred himself asleep in a minute.

The next morning, after breakfast, the green maiden came to fetch Dorothy, and she dressed her in one of the prettiest gowns, made of green brocaded satin. Dorothy put on a green silk apron and tied a green ribbon around Toto's neck, and they started for the Throne Room of the Great Oz.

First they came to a great hall in which were many ladies and gentlemen of the court, all dressed in rich costumes. These people had nothing to do but talk to each other, but they always came to wait outside the Throne Room every morning, although they were never permitted to see Oz. As Dorothy entered they looked at her curiously, and one of them whispered:

"Are you really going to look upon the face of Oz the Terrible?"

"Of course," answered the girl, "if he will see me."

"Oh, he will see you," said the soldier who had taken her message to the Wizard, "although he does not like to have people ask to see him. Indeed, at first he was angry and said I should send you back where you came from. Then he asked me what you looked like, and when I mentioned your silver shoes he was very much interested. At last I told him about the mark upon your forehead, and he decided he would admit you to his presence."

Just then a bell rang, and the green girl said to Dorothy, "That is the signal. You must go into the Throne Room alone."

She opened a little door and Dorothy walked boldly through and found herself in a wonderful place. It was a big, round room with a high arched roof, and the walls and ceiling and floor were covered with large emeralds set closely together. In the center of the roof was a great light, as bright as the sun, which made the emeralds sparkle in a wonderful manner.

But what interested Dorothy most was the big throne of green marble that stood in the middle of the room. It was shaped like a chair and sparkled with gems, as did everything else. In the center of the chair was an enormous Head, without a body to support it or any arms or legs whatever. There was no hair upon this head, but it had eyes and a nose and mouth, and was much bigger than the head of the biggest giant.

As Dorothy gazed upon this in wonder and fear, the eyes turned slowly and looked at her sharply and steadily. Then the mouth moved, and Dorothy heard a voice say:

"I am Oz, the Great and Terrible. Who are you, and why do you seek me?"

It was not such an awful voice as she had expected to come from the big Head; so she took courage and answered:

"I am Dorothy, the Small and Meek. I have come to you for help."

The eyes looked at her thoughtfully for a full minute. Then said the voice:

"Where did you get the silver shoes?"

"I got them from the Wicked Witch of the East, when my house fell on her and killed her," she replied.

"Where did you get the mark upon your forehead?" continued the voice.

"That is where the Good Witch of the North kissed me when she bade me good-bye and sent me to you," said the girl.

Again the eyes looked at her sharply, and they saw she was telling the truth. Then Oz asked, "What do you wish me to do?"

"Send me back to Kansas, where my Aunt Em and Uncle Henry are," she answered earnestly. "I don't like your country, although it is so beautiful. And I am sure Aunt Em will be dreadfully worried over my being away so long."

The eyes winked three times, and then they turned up to the ceiling and down to the floor and rolled around so queerly that they seemed to see every part of the room. And at last they looked at Dorothy again.

"Why should I do this for you?" asked Oz.

"Because you are strong and I am weak; because you are a Great Wizard and I am only a little girl."

"But you were strong enough to kill the Wicked Witch of the East," said Oz.

"That just happened," returned Dorothy simply; "I could not help it."

"Well," said the Head, "I will give you my answer. You have no right to expect me to send you back to Kansas unless you do something for me in return. In this country everyone must pay for everything he gets. If you wish me to use my magic power to send you home again you must do something for me first. Help me and I will help you."

"What must I do?" asked the girl.

"Kill the Wicked Witch of the West," answered Oz.

"But I cannot!" exclaimed Dorothy, greatly surprised.

"You killed the Witch of the East and you wear the silver shoes, which bear a powerful charm. There is now but one Wicked Witch left in all this land, and when you can tell me she is dead I will send you back to Kansas—but not before."

The little girl began to weep, she was so much disappointed; and the eyes winked again and looked upon her anxiously, as if the Great Oz felt that she could help him if she would.

"I never killed anything, willingly," she sobbed. "Even if I wanted to, how could I kill the Wicked Witch? If you, who are Great and Terrible, cannot kill her yourself, how do you expect me to do it?"

"I do not know," said the Head; "but that is my answer, and until the Wicked Witch dies you will not see your uncle and aunt again. Remember that the Witch is Wicked—tremendously Wicked—and ought to be killed. Now go, and do not ask to see me again until you have done your task."

Sorrowfully Dorothy left the Throne Room and went back where the Lion and the Scarecrow and the Tin Woodman were waiting to hear what Oz had said to her. "There is no hope for me," she said sadly, "for Oz will not send me home until I have killed the Wicked Witch of the West; and that I can never do."

Her friends were sorry, but could do nothing to help her; so Dorothy went to her own room and lay down on the bed and cried herself to sleep.

The next morning the soldier with the green whiskers came to the Scarecrow and said:

"Come with me, for Oz has sent for you."

So the Scarecrow followed him and was admitted into the great Throne Room, where he saw, sitting in the emerald throne, a most lovely Lady. She was dressed in green silk gauze and wore upon her flowing green locks a crown of jewels. Growing from her shoulders were wings, gorgeous in color and so light that they fluttered if the slightest breath of air reached them.

When the Scarecrow had bowed, as prettily as his straw stuffing would let him, before this beautiful creature, she looked upon him sweetly, and said:

"I am Oz, the Great and Terrible. Who are you, and why do you seek me?"

Now the Scarecrow, who had expected to see the great Head Dorothy had told him of, was much astonished; but he answered her bravely.

"I am only a Scarecrow, stuffed with straw. Therefore I have no brains, and I come to you praying that you will put brains in my head instead of straw, so that I may become as much a man as any other in your dominions."

"Why should I do this for you?" asked the Lady.

"Because you are wise and powerful, and no one else can help me," answered the Scarecrow.

"I never grant favors without some return," said Oz; "but this much I will promise. If you will kill for me the Wicked Witch of the West, I will bestow upon you a great many brains, and such good brains that you will be the wisest man in all the Land of Oz."

"I thought you asked Dorothy to kill the Witch," said the Scarecrow, in surprise.

"So I did. I don't care who kills her. But until she is dead I will not grant your wish. Now go, and do not seek me again until you have earned the brains you so greatly desire."

The Scarecrow went sorrowfully back to his friends and told them what Oz had said; and Dorothy was surprised to find that the Great Wizard was not a Head, as she had seen him, but a lovely Lady.

"All the same," said the Scarecrow, "she needs a heart as much as the Tin Woodman."

On the next morning the soldier with the green whiskers came to the Tin Woodman and said:

"Oz has sent for you. Follow me."

So the Tin Woodman followed him and came to the great Throne Room. He did not know whether he would find Oz a lovely Lady or a Head, but he hoped it would be the lovely Lady. "For," he said to himself, "if it is the head, I am sure I shall not be given a heart, since a head has no heart of its own and therefore cannot feel for me. But if it is the lovely Lady I shall beg hard for a heart, for all ladies are themselves said to be kindly hearted."

But when the Woodman entered the great Throne Room he saw neither the Head nor the Lady, for Oz had taken the shape of a most terrible Beast. It was nearly as big as an elephant, and the green throne seemed hardly strong enough to hold its weight. The Beast had a head like that of a rhinoceros, only there were five eyes in its face. There were five long arms growing out of its body, and it also had five long, slim legs. Thick, woolly hair covered every part of it, and a more dreadful-looking monster could not be imagined. It was fortunate the Tin Woodman had no heart at that moment, for it would have beat loud and fast from terror. But being only tin, the Woodman was not at all afraid, although he was much disappointed.

"I am Oz, the Great and Terrible," spoke the Beast, in a voice that was one great roar. "Who are you, and why do you seek me?"

"I am a Woodman, and made of tin. Therefore I have no heart, and cannot love. I pray you to give me a heart that I may be as other men are."

"Why should I do this?" demanded the Beast.

"Because I ask it, and you alone can grant my request," answered the Woodman.

Oz gave a low growl at this, but said, gruffly: "If you indeed desire a heart, you must earn it."

"How?" asked the Woodman.

"Help Dorothy to kill the Wicked Witch of the West," replied the Beast. "When the Witch is dead, come to me, and I will then give you the biggest and kindest and most loving heart in all the Land of Oz."

So the Tin Woodman was forced to return sorrowfully to his friends and tell them of the terrible Beast he had seen. They all wondered greatly at the many forms the Great Wizard could take upon himself, and the Lion said:

"If he is a Beast when I go to see him, I shall roar my loudest, and so frighten him that he will grant all I ask. And if he is the lovely Lady, I shall pretend to spring upon her, and so compel her to do my bidding. And if he is the great Head, he will be at my mercy; for I will roll this head all about the room until he promises to give us what we desire. So be of good cheer, my friends, for all will yet be well."

The next morning the soldier with the green whiskers led the Lion to the great Throne Room and bade him enter the presence of Oz.

The Lion at once passed through the door, and glancing around saw, to his surprise, that before the throne was a Ball of Fire, so fierce and glowing he could scarcely bear to gaze upon it. His first thought was that Oz had by accident caught on fire and was burning up; but when he tried to go nearer, the heat was so intense that it singed his whiskers, and he crept back tremblingly to a spot nearer the door.

Then a low, quiet voice came from the Ball of Fire, and these were the words it spoke:

"I am Oz, the Great and Terrible. Who are you, and why do you seek me?"

And the Lion answered, "I am a Cowardly Lion, afraid of everything. I came to you to beg that you give me courage, so that in reality I may become the King of Beasts, as men call me."

"Why should I give you courage?" demanded Oz.

"Because of all Wizards you are the greatest, and alone have power to grant my request," answered the Lion.

The Ball of Fire burned fiercely for a time, and the voice said, "Bring me proof that the Wicked Witch is dead, and that moment I will give you courage. But as long as the Witch lives, you must remain a coward."

The Lion was angry at this speech, but could say nothing in reply, and while he stood silently gazing at the Ball of Fire it became so furiously hot that he turned tail and rushed from the room. He was glad to find his friends waiting for him, and told them of his terrible interview with the Wizard.

"What shall we do now?" asked Dorothy sadly.

"There is only one thing we can do," returned the Lion, "and that is to go to the land of the Winkies, seek out the Wicked Witch, and destroy her."

"But suppose we cannot?" said the girl.

"Then I shall never have courage," declared the Lion.

"And I shall never have brains," added the Scarecrow.

"And I shall never have a heart," spoke the Tin Woodman.

"And I shall never see Aunt Em and Uncle Henry," said Dorothy, beginning to cry.

"Be careful!" cried the green girl. "The tears will fall on your green silk gown and spot it."

So Dorothy dried her eyes and said, "I suppose we must try it; but I am sure I do not want to kill anybody, even to see Aunt Em again."

"I will go with you; but I'm too much of a coward to kill the Witch," said the Lion.

"I will go too," declared the Scarecrow; "but I shall not be of much help to you, I am such a fool."

"I haven't the heart to harm even a Witch," remarked the Tin Woodman; "but if you go I certainly shall go with you."

Therefore it was decided to start upon their journey the next morning, and the Woodman sharpened his axe on a green grindstone and had all his joints properly oiled. The Scarecrow stuffed himself with fresh straw and Dorothy put new paint on his eyes that he might see better. The green girl, who was very kind to them, filled Dorothy's basket with good things to eat, and fastened a little bell around Toto's neck with a green ribbon.

They went to bed quite early and slept soundly until daylight, when they were awakened by the crowing of a green cock that lived in the back yard of the Palace, and the cackling of a hen that had laid a green egg.

Chapter 12

THE SEARCH FOR THE WICKED WITCH

THE soldier with the green whiskers led them through the streets of the Emerald City until they reached the room where the Guardian of the Gates lived. This officer unlocked their spectacles to put them back in his great box, and then he politely opened the gate for our friends.

"Which road leads to the Wicked Witch of the West?" asked Dorothy.

"There is no road," answered the Guardian of the Gates. "No one ever wishes to go that way."

"How, then, are we to find her?" inquired the girl.

"That will be easy," replied the man, "for when she knows you are in the country of the Winkies she will find you, and make you all her slaves."

"Perhaps not," said the Scarecrow, "for we mean to destroy her."

"Oh, that is different," said the Guardian of the Gates. "No one has ever destroyed her before, so I naturally thought she would make slaves of you, as she has of the rest. But take care; for she is wicked and fierce, and may not allow you to destroy her. Keep to the West, where the sun sets, and you cannot fail to find her."

They thanked him and bade him good-bye, and turned toward the West, walking over fields of soft grass dotted here and there with daisies and buttercups. Dorothy still wore the pretty silk dress she had put on in the palace, but now, to her surprise, she found it was no longer green, but pure white. The ribbon around

Toto's neck had also lost its green color and was as white as Dorothy's dress.

The Emerald City was soon left far behind. As they advanced the ground became rougher and hillier, for there were no farms nor houses in this country of the West, and the ground was untilled.

In the afternoon the sun shone hot in their faces, for there were no trees to offer them shade; so that before night Dorothy and Toto and the Lion were tired, and lay down upon the grass and fell asleep, with the Woodman and the Scarecrow keeping watch.

Now the Wicked Witch of the West had but one eye, yet that was as powerful as a telescope, and could see everywhere. So, as she sat in the door of her castle, she happened to look around and saw Dorothy lying asleep, with her friends all about her. They were a long distance off, but the Wicked Witch was angry to find them in her country; so she blew upon a silver whistle that hung around her neck.

At once there came running to her from all directions a pack of great wolves. They had long legs and fierce eyes and sharp teeth.

"Go to those people," said the Witch, "and tear them to pieces."

"Are you not going to make them your slaves?" asked the leader of the wolves.

"No," she answered, "one is of tin, and one of straw; one is a girl and another a Lion. None of them is fit to work, so you may tear them into small pieces."

"Very well," said the wolf, and he dashed away at full speed, followed by the others.

It was lucky the Scarecrow and the Woodman were wide awake and heard the wolves coming.

"This is my fight," said the Woodman, "so get behind me and I will meet them as they come."

He seized his axe, which he had made very sharp, and as the leader of the wolves came on the Tin Woodman swung his arm and chopped the wolf's head from its body, so that it immediately died. As soon as he could raise his axe another wolf came up, and he also fell under the sharp edge of the Tin Woodman's weapon. There were forty wolves, and forty times a wolf was killed, so that at last they all lay dead in a heap before the Woodman.

Then he put down his axe and sat beside the Scarecrow, who said, "It was a good fight, friend."

They waited until Dorothy awoke the next morning. The little girl was quite frightened when she saw the great pile of shaggy wolves, but the Tin Woodman told her all. She thanked him for saving them and sat down to breakfast, after which they started again upon their journey.

Now this same morning the Wicked Witch came to the door of her castle and looked out with her one eye that could see far off. She saw all her wolves lying dead, and the strangers still traveling through her country. This made her angrier than before, and she blew her silver whistle twice.

Straightway a great flock of wild crows came flying toward her, enough to darken the sky.

And the Wicked Witch said to the King Crow, "Fly at once to the strangers; peck out their eyes and tear them to pieces."

The wild crows flew in one great flock toward Dorothy and her companions. When the little girl saw them coming she was afraid.

But the Scarecrow said, "This is my battle, so lie down beside me and you will not be harmed."

So they all lay upon the ground except the Scarecrow, and he stood up and stretched out his arms. And when the crows saw him they were frightened, as these birds always are by scarecrows, and did not dare to come any nearer. But the King Crow said:

"It is only a stuffed man. I will peck his eyes out."

The King Crow flew at the Scarecrow, who caught it by the head and twisted its neck until it died. And then another crow flew at him, and the Scarecrow twisted its neck also. There were forty crows, and forty times the Scarecrow twisted a neck, until at last all were lying dead beside him. Then he called to his companions to rise, and again they went upon their journey.

When the Wicked Witch looked out again and saw all her crows lying in a heap, she got into a terrible rage, and blew three times upon her silver whistle.

Forthwith there was heard a great buzzing in the air, and a swarm of black bees came flying toward her.

"Go to the strangers and sting them to death!" commanded the Witch, and the bees turned and flew rapidly until they came to where Dorothy and her friends were walking. But the Woodman had seen them coming, and the Scarecrow had decided what to do.

"Take out my straw and scatter it over the little girl and the dog and the Lion," he said to the Woodman, "and the bees cannot sting them." This the Woodman did, and as Dorothy lay close beside the Lion and held Toto in her arms, the straw covered them entirely.

The bees came and found no one but the Woodman to sting, so they flew at him and broke off all their stings against the tin, without hurting the Woodman at all. And as bees cannot live when their stings are broken that was the end of the black bees, and they lay scattered thick about the Woodman, like little heaps of fine coal.

Then Dorothy and the Lion got up, and the girl helped the Tin Woodman put the straw back into the Scarecrow again, until he was as good as ever. So they started upon their journey once more.

The Wicked Witch was so angry when she saw her black bees in little heaps like fine coal that she stamped her foot and tore her hair and gnashed her teeth. And then she called a dozen of her slaves, who were the Winkies, and gave them sharp spears, telling them to go to the strangers and destroy them.

The Winkies were not a brave people, but they had to do as they were told. So they marched away until they came near to Dorothy. Then the Lion gave a great roar and sprang towards them, and the poor Winkies were so frightened that they ran back as fast as they could.

When they returned to the castle the Wicked Witch beat them well with a strap, and sent them back to their work, after which she sat down to think what she should do next. She could not understand how all her plans to destroy these strangers had failed; but she was a powerful Witch, as well as a wicked one, and she soon made up her mind how to act.

There was, in her cupboard, a Golden Cap, with a circle of diamonds and rubies running round it. This Golden Cap had a charm. Whoever owned it could call three times upon the Winged Monkeys, who would obey any order they were given. But no person could command these strange creatures more than three times. Twice already the Wicked Witch had used the charm of the Cap. Once was when she had made the Winkies her slaves, and set herself to rule over their country. The Winged Monkeys had helped her do this. The second time was when she had fought against the Great Oz himself, and driven him out of the land of the West. The Winged Monkeys had also helped her in doing this. Only once more could she use this Golden Cap, for which reason she did not like to do so until all her other powers were exhausted. But now that her fierce wolves and her wild crows and her stinging bees were gone, and her slaves had been scared away by the Cowardly Lion, she saw there was only one way left to destroy Dorothy and her friends.

So the Wicked Witch took the Golden Cap from her cupboard and placed it upon her head. Then she stood upon her left foot and said slowly:

"Ep-pe, pep-pe, kak-ke!"

Next she stood upon her right foot and said:

"Hil-lo, hol-lo, hel-lo!"

After this she stood upon both feet and cried in a loud voice:

"Ziz-zy, zuz-zy, zik!"

Now the charm began to work. The sky was darkened, and a low rumbling sound was heard in the air. There was a rushing of many wings, a great chattering and laughing, and the sun came out of the dark sky to show the Wicked Witch surrounded by a crowd of monkeys, each with a pair of immense and powerful wings on his shoulders.

One, much bigger than the others, seemed to be their leader. He flew close to the Witch and said, "You have called us for the third and last time. What do you command?"

"Go to the strangers who are within my land and destroy them all except the Lion," said the Wicked Witch. "Bring that beast to me, for I have a mind to harness him like a horse, and make him work."

"Your commands shall be obeyed," said the leader. Then, with a great deal of chattering and noise, the Winged Monkeys flew away to the place where Dorothy and her friends were walking.

Some of the Monkeys seized the Tin Woodman and carried him through the air until they were over a country thickly covered with sharp rocks. Here they dropped the poor Woodman, who fell a great distance to the rocks, where he lay so battered and dented that he could neither move nor groan.

Others of the Monkeys caught the Scarecrow, and with their long fingers pulled all of the straw out of his clothes and head. They made his hat and boots and clothes into a small bundle and threw it into the top branches of a tall tree.

The remaining Monkeys threw pieces of stout rope around the Lion and wound many coils about his body and head and legs, until he was unable to bite or scratch or struggle in any way. Then they lifted him up and flew away with him to the Witch's castle, where he was placed in a small yard with a high iron fence around it, so that he could not escape.

But Dorothy they did not harm at all. She stood, with Toto in her arms, watching the sad fate of her comrades and thinking it would soon be her turn. The leader of the Winged Monkeys flew up to her, his long, hairy arms stretched out and his ugly face grinning terribly; but he saw the mark of the Good Witch's kiss upon her forehead and stopped short, motioning the others not to touch her.

"We dare not harm this little girl," he said to them, "for she is protected by the Power of Good, and that is greater than the Power of Evil. All we can do is to carry her to the castle of the Wicked Witch and leave her there."

So, carefully and gently, they lifted Dorothy in their arms and carried her swiftly through the air until they came to the castle, where they set her down upon the front doorstep. Then the leader said to the Witch:

"We have obeyed you as far as we were able. The Tin Woodman and the Scarecrow are destroyed, and the Lion is tied up in your yard. The little girl we dare not harm, nor the dog she carries in her arms. Your power over our band is now ended, and you will never see us again."

Then all the Winged Monkeys, with much laughing and chattering and noise, flew into the air and were soon out of sight.

The Wicked Witch was both surprised and worried when she saw the mark on Dorothy's forehead, for she knew well that neither the Winged Monkeys nor she, herself, dare hurt the girl in any way. She looked down at Dorothy's feet, and seeing the Silver Shoes, began to tremble with fear, for she knew what a powerful charm belonged to them. At first the Witch was tempted to run away from Dorothy; but she happened to look into the child's eyes and saw how simple the soul behind them was, and that the little girl did not know of the wonderful power the Silver Shoes gave her. So the Wicked Witch laughed to herself, and thought, "I can still make her my slave, for she does not know how to use her power." Then she said to Dorothy, harshly and severely:

"Come with me; and see that you mind everything I tell you, for if you do not I will make an end of you, as I did of the Tin Woodman and the Scarecrow."

Dorothy followed her through many of the beautiful rooms in her castle until they came to the kitchen, where the Witch bade her clean the pots and kettles and sweep the floor and keep the fire fed with wood.

Dorothy went to work meekly, with her mind made up to work as hard as she could; for she was glad the Wicked Witch had decided not to kill her.

With Dorothy hard at work, the Witch thought she would go into the courtyard and harness the Cowardly Lion like a horse;

it would amuse her, she was sure, to make him draw her chariot whenever she wished to go to drive. But as she opened the gate the Lion gave a loud roar and bounded at her so fiercely that the Witch was afraid, and ran out and shut the gate again.

"If I cannot harness you," said the Witch to the Lion, speaking through the bars of the gate, "I can starve you. You shall have nothing to eat until you do as I wish."

So after that she took no food to the imprisoned Lion; but every day she came to the gate at noon and asked, "Are you ready to be harnessed like a horse?"

And the Lion would answer, "No. If you come in this yard, I will bite you."

The reason the Lion did not have to do as the Witch wished was that every night, while the woman was asleep, Dorothy carried him food from the cupboard. After he had eaten he would lie down on his bed of straw, and Dorothy would lie beside him and put her head on his soft, shaggy mane, while they talked of their troubles and tried to plan some way to escape. But they could find no way to get out of the castle, for it was constantly guarded by the yellow Winkies, who were the slaves of the Wicked Witch and too afraid of her not to do as she told them.

The girl had to work hard during the day, and often the Witch threatened to beat her with the same old umbrella she always carried in her hand. But, in truth, she did not dare to strike Dorothy, because of the mark upon her forehead. The child did not know this, and was full of fear for herself and Toto. Once the Witch struck Toto a blow with her umbrella and the brave little dog flew at her and bit her leg in return. The Witch did not bleed where she was bitten, for she was so wicked that the blood in her had dried up many years before.

Dorothy's life became very sad as she grew to understand that it would be harder than ever to get back to Kansas and Aunt Em again. Sometimes she would cry bitterly for hours, with Toto sitting at her feet and looking into her face, whining dismally to show how sorry he was for his little mistress. Toto did not really care whether he was in Kansas or the Land of Oz so long as Dorothy was with him; but he knew the little girl was unhappy, and that made him unhappy too.

Now the Wicked Witch had a great longing to have for her own the Silver Shoes which the girl always wore. Her bees and her crows and her wolves were lying in heaps and drying up, and she had used up all the power of the Golden Cap; but if she could only get hold of the Silver Shoes, they would give her more power than all the other things she had lost. She watched Dorothy carefully, to see if she ever took off her shoes, thinking she might steal them. But the child was so proud of her pretty shoes that she never took them off except at night and when she took her bath. The Witch was too much afraid of the dark to dare go in Dorothy's room at night to take the shoes, and her dread of water was greater than her fear of the dark, so she never came near when Dorothy was bathing. Indeed, the old Witch never touched water, nor ever let water touch her in any way.

But the wicked creature was very cunning, and she finally thought of a trick that would give her what she wanted. She placed a bar of iron in the middle of the kitchen floor, and then by her magic arts made the iron invisible to human eyes. So that when Dorothy walked across the floor she stumbled over the bar, not being able to see it, and fell at full length. She was not much hurt, but in her fall one of the Silver Shoes came off; and before she could reach it, the Witch had snatched it away and put it on her own skinny foot.

The wicked woman was greatly pleased with the success of her trick, for as long as she had one of the shoes she owned half the power of their charm, and Dorothy could not use it against her, even had she known how to do so.

The little girl, seeing she had lost one of her pretty shoes, grew angry, and said to the Witch, "Give me back my shoe!"

"I will not," retorted the Witch, "for it is now my shoe, and not yours."

"You are a wicked creature!" cried Dorothy. "You have no right to take my shoe from me."

"I shall keep it, just the same," said the Witch, laughing at her, "and someday I shall get the other one from you, too."

This made Dorothy so very angry that she picked up the bucket of water that stood near and dashed it over the Witch, wetting her from head to foot.

Instantly the wicked woman gave a loud cry of fear, and then, as Dorothy looked at her in wonder, the Witch began to shrink and fall away.

"See what you have done!" she screamed. "In a minute I shall melt away."

"I'm very sorry, indeed," said Dorothy, who was truly frightened to see the Witch actually melting away like brown sugar before her very eyes.

"Didn't you know water would be the end of me?" asked the Witch, in a wailing, despairing voice.

"Of course not," answered Dorothy. "How should I?"

"Well, in a few minutes I shall be all melted, and you will have the castle to yourself. I have been wicked in my day, but I never thought a little girl like you would ever be able to melt me and end my wicked deeds. Look out—here I go!"

With these words the Witch fell down in a brown, melted, shapeless mass and began to spread over the clean boards of the kitchen floor. Seeing that she had really melted away to nothing, Dorothy drew another bucket of water and threw it over the mess. She then swept it all out the door. After picking out the silver shoe, which was all that was left of the old woman, she cleaned and dried it with a cloth, and put it on her foot again. Then, being at last free to do as she chose, she ran out to the courtyard to tell the Lion that the Wicked Witch of the West had come to an end, and that they were no longer prisoners in a strange land.

Chapter 13

THE RESCUE

THE Cowardly Lion was much pleased to hear that the Wicked Witch had been melted by a bucket of water, and Dorothy at once unlocked the gate of his prison and set him free. They went in together to the castle, where Dorothy's first act was to call all the Winkies together and tell them that they were no longer slaves.

There was great rejoicing among the yellow Winkies, for they had been made to work hard during many years for the Wicked Witch, who had always treated them with great cruelty. They kept this day as a holiday, then and ever after, and spent the time in feasting and dancing.

"If our friends, the Scarecrow and the Tin Woodman, were only with us," said the Lion, "I should be quite happy."

"Don't you suppose we could rescue them?" asked the girl anxiously.

"We can try," answered the Lion.

So they called the yellow Winkies and asked them if they would help to rescue their friends, and the Winkies said that they would be delighted to do all in their power for Dorothy, who had set them free from bondage. So she chose a number of the Winkies who looked as if they knew the most, and they all started away. They traveled that day and part of the next until they came to the rocky plain where the Tin Woodman lay, all battered and bent. His axe was near him, but the blade was rusted and the handle broken off short.

The Winkies lifted him tenderly in their arms, and carried him back to the Yellow Castle again, Dorothy shedding a few tears by the way at the sad plight of her old friend, and the Lion looking sober and sorry. When they reached the castle Dorothy said to the Winkies:

"Are any of your people tinsmiths?"

"Oh, yes. Some of us are very good tinsmiths," they told her.

"Then bring them to me," she said. And when the tinsmiths came, bringing with them all their tools in baskets, she inquired, "Can you straighten out those dents in the Tin Woodman, and bend him back into shape again, and solder him together where he is broken?"

The tinsmiths looked the Woodman over carefully and then answered that they thought they could mend him so he would be as good as ever. So they set to work in one of the big yellow rooms of the castle and worked for three days and four nights, hammering and twisting and bending and soldering and polishing and pounding at the legs and body and head of the Tin Woodman, until at last he was straightened out into his old form, and his joints worked as well as ever. To be sure, there were several patches on him, but the tinsmiths did a good job, and as the Woodman was not a vain man he did not mind the patches at all.

When, at last, he walked into Dorothy's room and thanked her for rescuing him, he was so pleased that he wept tears of joy, and Dorothy had to wipe every tear carefully from his face with her apron, so his joints would not be rusted. At the same time her own tears fell thick and fast at the joy of meeting her old friend again, and these tears did not need to be wiped away. As for the Lion, he wiped his eyes so often with the tip of his tail that it became quite wet, and he was obliged to go out into the courtyard and hold it in the sun till it dried.

"If we only had the Scarecrow with us again," said the Tin Woodman, when Dorothy had finished telling him everything that had happened, "I should be quite happy."

"We must try to find him," said the girl.

So she called the Winkies to help her, and they walked all that day and part of the next until they came to the tall tree in the branches of which the Winged Monkeys had tossed the Scarecrow's clothes.

It was a very tall tree, and the trunk was so smooth that no one could climb it; but the Woodman said at once, "I'll chop it down, and then we can get the Scarecrow's clothes."

Now while the tinsmiths had been at work mending the Woodman himself, another of the Winkies, who was a goldsmith, had made an axe-handle of solid gold and fitted it to the Woodman's axe, instead of the old broken handle. Others polished the blade until all the rust was removed and it glistened like burnished silver.

As soon as he had spoken, the Tin Woodman began to chop, and in a short time the tree fell over with a crash, whereupon the Scarecrow's clothes fell out of the branches and rolled off on the ground.

Dorothy picked them up and had the Winkies carry them back to the castle, where they were stuffed with nice, clean straw; and behold! here was the Scarecrow, as good as ever, thanking them over and over again for saving him.

Now that they were reunited, Dorothy and her friends spent a few happy days at the Yellow Castle, where they found everything they needed to make them comfortable.

But one day the girl thought of Aunt Em, and said, "We must go back to Oz, and claim his promise."

"Yes," said the Woodman, "at last I shall get my heart."

"And I shall get my brains," added the Scarecrow joyfully.

"And I shall get my courage," said the Lion thoughtfully.

"And I shall get back to Kansas," cried Dorothy, clapping her hands. "Oh, let us start for the Emerald City tomorrow!"

This they decided to do. The next day they called the Winkies together and bade them good-bye. The Winkies were sorry to have them go, and they had grown so fond of the Tin Woodman that they begged him to stay and rule over them and the Yellow Land of the West. Finding they were determined to go, the Winkies gave Toto and the Lion each a golden collar; and to Dorothy they presented a beautiful bracelet studded with diamonds; and to the Scarecrow they gave a gold-headed walking stick, to keep him from stumbling; and to the Tin Woodman they offered a silver oil-can, inlaid with gold and set with precious jewels.

Every one of the travelers made the Winkies a pretty speech in return, and all shook hands with them until their arms ached.

Dorothy went to the Witch's cupboard to fill her basket with food for the journey, and there she saw the Golden Cap. She tried it on her own head and found that it fitted her exactly. She did not know anything about the charm of the Golden Cap, but she saw that it was pretty, so she made up her mind to wear it and carry her sunbonnet in the basket.

Then, being prepared for the journey, they all started for the Emerald City; and the Winkies gave them three cheers and many good wishes to carry with them.

Chapter 14

THE WINGED MONKEYS

You will remember there was no road—not even a pathway—between the castle of the Wicked Witch and the Emerald City. When the four travelers went in search of the Witch she had seen them coming, and so sent the Winged Monkeys to bring them to her. It was much harder to find their way back through the big fields of buttercups and yellow daisies than it was being carried. They knew, of course, they must go straight east, toward the rising sun; and they started off in the right way. But at noon, when the sun was over their heads, they did not know which was east and which was west, and that was the reason they were lost in the great fields. They kept on walking, however, and at night the moon came out and shone brightly. So they lay down among the sweet smelling yellow flowers and slept soundly until morning—all but the Scarecrow and the Tin Woodman.

The next morning the sun was behind a cloud, but they started on, as if they were quite sure which way they were going.

"If we walk far enough," said Dorothy, "I am sure we shall sometime come to some place."

But day by day passed away, and they still saw nothing before them but the scarlet fields. The Scarecrow began to grumble a bit.

"We have surely lost our way," he said, "and unless we find it again in time to reach the Emerald City, I shall never get my brains."

"Nor I my heart," declared the Tin Woodman. "It seems to me I can scarcely wait till I get to Oz, and you must admit this is a very long journey."

"You see," said the Cowardly Lion, with a whimper, "I haven't the courage to keep tramping forever, without getting anywhere at all."

Then Dorothy lost heart. She sat down on the grass and looked at her companions, and they sat down and looked at her, and Toto found that for the first time in his life he was too tired to chase a butterfly that flew past his head. So he put out his tongue and panted and looked at Dorothy as if to ask what they should do next.

"Suppose we call the field mice," she suggested. "They could probably tell us the way to the Emerald City."

"To be sure they could," cried the Scarecrow. "Why didn't we think of that before?"

Dorothy blew the little whistle she had always carried about her neck since the Queen of the Mice had given it to her. In a few minutes they heard the pattering of tiny feet, and many of the small gray mice came running up to her. Among them was the Queen herself, who asked, in her squeaky little voice:

"What can I do for my friends?"

"We have lost our way," said Dorothy. "Can you tell us where the Emerald City is?"

"Certainly," answered the Queen; "but it is a great way off, for you have had it at your backs all this time." Then she noticed Dorothy's Golden Cap, and said, "Why don't you use the charm of the Cap, and call the Winged Monkeys to you? They will carry you to the City of Oz in less than an hour."

"I didn't know there was a charm," answered Dorothy, in surprise. "What is it?"

"It is written inside the Golden Cap," replied the Queen of the Mice. "But if you are going to call the Winged Monkeys we must run away, for they are full of mischief and think it great fun to plague us."

"Won't they hurt me?" asked the girl anxiously.

"Oh, no. They must obey the wearer of the Cap. Good-bye!" And she scampered out of sight, with all the mice hurrying after her.

Dorothy looked inside the Golden Cap and saw some words written upon the lining. These, she thought, must be the charm, so she read the directions carefully and put the Cap upon her head.

"Ep-pe, pep-pe, kak-ke!" she said, standing on her left foot.

"What did you say?" asked the Scarecrow, who did not know what she was doing.

"Hil-lo, hol-lo, hel-lo!" Dorothy went on, standing this time on her right foot.

"Hello!" replied the Tin Woodman calmly.

"Ziz-zy, zuz-zy, zik!" said Dorothy, who was now standing on both feet. This ended the saying of the charm, and they heard a great chattering and flapping of wings, as the band of Winged Monkeys flew up to them.

The King bowed low before Dorothy, and asked, "What is your command?"

"We wish to go to the Emerald City," said the child, "and we have lost our way."

"We will carry you," replied the King, and no sooner had he spoken than two of the Monkeys caught Dorothy in their arms and flew away with her. Others took the Scarecrow and the Woodman and the Lion, and one little Monkey seized Toto and flew after them, although the dog tried hard to bite him.

The Scarecrow and the Tin Woodman were rather frightened at first, for they remembered how badly the Winged Monkeys had treated them before; but they saw that no harm was intended, so they rode through the air quite cheerfully, and had a fine time looking at the pretty gardens and woods far below them.

Dorothy found herself riding easily between two of the biggest Monkeys, one of them the King himself. They had made a chair of their hands and were careful not to hurt her.

"Why do you have to obey the charm of the Golden Cap?" she asked.

"That is a long story," answered the King, with a winged laugh; "but as we have a long journey before us, I will pass the time by telling you about it, if you wish."

"I shall be glad to hear it," she replied.

"Once," began the leader, "we were a free people, living happily in the great forest, flying from tree to tree, eating nuts and fruit, and doing just as we pleased without calling anybody master. Perhaps some of us were rather too full of mischief at times, flying down to pull the tails of the animals that had no wings, chasing birds, and throwing nuts at the people who walked in the forest. But we were careless and happy and full of fun, and enjoyed every minute of the day. This was many years ago, long before Oz came out of the clouds to rule over this land.

"There lived here then, away at the North, a beautiful princess, who was also a powerful sorceress. All her magic was used to help the people, and she was never known to hurt anyone who was good. Her name was Gayelette, and she lived in a handsome palace built from great blocks of ruby. Everyone loved her, but her greatest sorrow was that she could find no one to love in return, since all the men were much too stupid and ugly to mate with one so beautiful and wise. At last, however, she found a boy who was handsome and manly and wise beyond his years. Gayelette made up her mind that when he grew to be a man she would make him her husband, so she took him to her ruby palace and used all her magic powers to make him as strong and good and lovely as any woman could wish. When he grew to manhood, Quelala, as he was called, was said to be the best and wisest man in all the land, while his manly beauty was so great that Gayelette loved him dearly, and hastened to make everything ready for the wedding.

"My grandfather was at that time the King of the Winged Monkeys which lived in the forest near Gayelette's palace, and the old fellow loved a joke better than a good dinner. One day, just before the wedding, my grandfather was flying out with his band when he saw Quelala walking beside the river. He was dressed in a rich costume of pink silk and purple velvet, and my grandfather thought he would see what he could do. At his word the band flew down and seized Quelala, carried him in their arms until they were over the middle of the river, and then dropped him into the water.

"'Swim out, my fine fellow,' cried my grandfather, 'and see if the water has spotted your clothes.' Quelala was much too wise not to swim, and he was not in the least spoiled by all his good fortune. He laughed, when he came to the top of the water, and swam in to shore. But when Gayelette came running out to him she found his silks and velvet all ruined by the river.

"The princess was angry, and she knew, of course, who did it. She had all the Winged Monkeys brought before her, and she said at first that their wings should be tied and they should be treated as they had treated Quelala, and dropped in the river. But my grandfather pleaded hard, for he knew the Monkeys would drown in the river with their wings tied, and Quelala said a kind word for them also; so that Gayelette finally spared them, on condition that the Winged Monkeys should ever after do three times the bidding of the owner of the Golden Cap. This Cap had been made for a wedding present to Quelala, and it is said to have cost the princess half her kingdom. Of course my grandfather and all the other Monkeys at once agreed to the condition, and that is how it happens that we are three times the slaves of the owner of the Golden Cap, whosoever he may be."

"And what became of them?" asked Dorothy, who had been greatly interested in the story.

"Quelala being the first owner of the Golden Cap," replied the Monkey, "he was the first to lay his wishes upon us. As his bride could not bear the sight of us, he called us all to him in the forest after he had married her and ordered us always to keep where she could never again set eyes on a Winged Monkey, which we were glad to do, for we were all afraid of her.

"This was all we ever had to do until the Golden Cap fell into the hands of the Wicked Witch of the West, who made us enslave the Winkies, and afterward drive Oz himself out of the Land of the West. Now the Golden Cap is yours, and three times you have the right to lay your wishes upon us."

As the Monkey King finished his story Dorothy looked down and saw the green, shining walls of the Emerald City before them. She wondered at the rapid flight of the Monkeys, but was glad the journey was over. The strange creatures set the travelers down carefully before the gate of the City, the King bowed low to Dorothy, and then flew swiftly away, followed by all his band.

"That was a good ride," said the little girl.

"Yes, and a quick way out of our troubles," replied the Lion. "How lucky it was you brought away that wonderful Cap!"

Chapter 15

THE DISCOVERY OF OZ, THE TERRIBLE

The four travelers walked up to the great gate of Emerald City and rang the bell. After ringing several times, it was opened by the same Guardian of the Gates they had met before.

"What! are you back again?" he asked, in surprise.

"Do you not see us?" answered the Scarecrow.

"But I thought you had gone to visit the Wicked Witch of the West."

"We did visit her," said the Scarecrow.

"And she let you go again?" asked the man, in wonder.

"She could not help it, for she is melted," explained the Scarecrow.

"Melted! Well, that is good news, indeed," said the man. "Who melted her?"

"It was Dorothy," said the Lion gravely.

"Good gracious!" exclaimed the man, and he bowed very low indeed before her.

Then he led them into his little room and locked the spectacles from the great box on all their eyes, just as he had done before. Afterward they passed on through the gate into the Emerald City. When the people heard from the Guardian of the Gates that Dorothy had melted the Wicked Witch of the West, they all gathered around the travelers and followed them in a great crowd to the Palace of Oz.

The soldier with the green whiskers was still on guard before the door, but he let them in at once, and they were again met by the beautiful green girl, who showed each of them to their old rooms at once, so they might rest until the Great Oz was ready to receive them.

The soldier had the news carried straight to Oz that Dorothy and the other travelers had come back again, after destroying the Wicked Witch; but Oz made no reply. They thought the Great Wizard would send for them at once, but he did not. They had no word from him the next day, nor the next, nor the next. The waiting was tiresome and wearing, and at last they grew vexed that Oz should treat them in so poor a fashion, after sending them to undergo hardships and slavery. So the Scarecrow at last asked the green girl to take another message to Oz, saying if he did not let them in to see him at once they would call the Winged Monkeys to help them, and find out whether he kept his promises or not. When the Wizard was given this message he was so frightened that he sent word for them to come to the Throne Room at four minutes after nine o'clock the next morning. He had once met the Winged Monkeys in the Land of the West, and he did not wish to meet them again.

The four travelers passed a sleepless night, each thinking of the gift Oz had promised to bestow on him. Dorothy fell asleep only once, and then she dreamed she was in Kansas, where Aunt Em was telling her how glad she was to have her little girl at home again.

Promptly at nine o'clock the next morning the green-whiskered soldier came to them, and four minutes later they all went into the Throne Room of the Great Oz.

Of course each one of them expected to see the Wizard in the shape he had taken before, and all were greatly surprised when they looked about and saw no one at all in the room. They kept close to the door and closer to one another, for the stillness of the empty room was more dreadful than any of the forms they had seen Oz take.

Presently they heard a solemn Voice, that seemed to come from somewhere near the top of the great dome, and it said:

"I am Oz, the Great and Terrible. Why do you seek me?"

They looked again in every part of the room, and then, seeing no one, Dorothy asked, "Where are you?"

"I am everywhere," answered the Voice, "but to the eyes of common mortals I am invisible. I will now seat myself upon my throne, that you may converse with me." Indeed, the Voice seemed just then to come straight from the throne itself; so they walked toward it and stood in a row while Dorothy said:

"We have come to claim our promise, O Oz."

"What promise?" asked Oz.

"You promised to send me back to Kansas when the Wicked Witch was destroyed," said the girl.

"And you promised to give me brains," said the Scarecrow.

"And you promised to give me a heart," said the Tin Woodman.

"And you promised to give me courage," said the Cowardly Lion.

"Is the Wicked Witch really destroyed?" asked the Voice, and Dorothy thought it trembled a little.

"Yes," she answered, "I melted her with a bucket of water."

"Dear me," said the Voice, "how sudden! Well, come to me tomorrow, for I must have time to think it over."

"You've had plenty of time already," said the Tin Woodman angrily.

"We shan't wait a day longer," said the Scarecrow.

"You must keep your promises to us!" exclaimed Dorothy.

The Lion thought it might be as well to frighten the Wizard, so he gave a large, loud roar, which was so fierce and dreadful that Toto jumped away from him in alarm and tipped over the screen that stood in a corner. As it fell with a crash they looked that way, and the next moment all of them were filled with wonder. For they saw, standing in just the spot the screen had hidden, a little old man, with a bald head and a wrinkled face, who seemed to be as much surprised as they were. The Tin Woodman, raising his axe, rushed toward the little man and cried out, "Who are you?"

"I am Oz, the Great and Terrible," said the little man, in a trembling voice. "But don't strike me—please don't—and I'll do anything you want me to."

Our friends looked at him in surprise and dismay.

"I thought Oz was a great Head," said Dorothy.

"And I thought Oz was a lovely Lady," said the Scarecrow.

"And I thought Oz was a terrible Beast," said the Tin Woodman.

"And I thought Oz was a Ball of Fire," exclaimed the Lion.

"No, you are all wrong," said the little man meekly. "I have been making believe."

"Making believe!" cried Dorothy. "Are you not a Great Wizard?"

"Hush, my dear," he said. "Don't speak so loud, or you will be overheard—and I should be ruined. I'm supposed to be a Great Wizard."

"And aren't you?" she asked.

"Not a bit of it, my dear; I'm just a common man."

"You're more than that," said the Scarecrow, in a grieved tone; "you're a humbug."

"Exactly so!" declared the little man, rubbing his hands together as if it pleased him. "I am a humbug."

"But this is terrible," said the Tin Woodman. "How shall I ever get my heart?"

"Or I my courage?" asked the Lion.

"Or I my brains?" wailed the Scarecrow, wiping the tears from his eyes with his coat sleeve.

"My dear friends," said Oz, "I pray you not to speak of these little things. Think of me, and the terrible trouble I'm in at being found out."

"Doesn't anyone else know you're a humbug?" asked Dorothy.

"No one knows it but you four—and myself," replied Oz. "I have fooled everyone so long that I thought I should never be found out. It was a great mistake my ever letting you into the Throne Room. Usually I will not see even my subjects, and so they believe I am something terrible."

"But, I don't understand," said Dorothy, in bewilderment. "How was it that you appeared to me as a great Head?"

"That was one of my tricks," answered Oz. "Step this way, please, and I will tell you all about it."

He led the way to a small chamber in the rear of the Throne Room, and they all followed him. He pointed to one corner, in which lay the great Head, made out of many thicknesses of paper, and with a carefully painted face.

"This I hung from the ceiling by a wire," said Oz. "I stood behind the screen and pulled a thread, to make the eyes move and the mouth open."

"But how about the voice?" she inquired.

"Oh, I am a ventriloquist," said the little man. "I can throw the sound of my voice wherever I wish, so that you thought it was coming out of the Head. Here are the other things I used to deceive you." He showed the Scarecrow the dress and the mask he had worn when he seemed to be the lovely Lady. And the Tin Woodman saw that his terrible Beast was nothing but a lot of skins, sewn together, with slats to keep their sides out. As for the Ball of Fire, the false Wizard had hung that also from the ceiling. It was really a ball of cotton, but when oil was poured upon it the ball burned fiercely.

"Really," said the Scarecrow, "you ought to be ashamed of yourself for being such a humbug."

"I am—I certainly am," answered the little man sorrowfully; "but it was the only thing I could do. Sit down, please, there are plenty of chairs; and I will tell you my story."

So they sat down and listened while he told the following tale.

"I was born in Omaha—"

"Why, that isn't very far from Kansas!" cried Dorothy.

"No, but it's farther from here," he said, shaking his head at her sadly. "When I grew up I became a ventriloquist, and at that I was very well trained by a great master. I can imitate any kind of a bird or beast." Here he mewed so like a kitten that Toto pricked up his ears and looked everywhere to see where she was. "After a time," continued Oz, "I tired of that, and became a balloonist."

"What is that?" asked Dorothy.

"A man who goes up in a balloon on circus day, so as to draw a crowd of people together and get them to pay to see the circus," he explained.

"Oh," she said, "I know."

"Well, one day I went up in a balloon and the ropes got twisted, so that I couldn't come down again. It went way up above the clouds, so far that a current of air struck it and carried it many, many miles away. For a day and a night I traveled through the air, and on the morning of the second day I awoke and found the balloon floating over a strange and beautiful country.

"It came down gradually, and I was not hurt a bit. But I found myself in the midst of a strange people, who, seeing me come from the clouds, thought I was a great Wizard. Of course I let them think so, because they were afraid of me, and promised to do anything I wished them to.

"Just to amuse myself, and keep the good people busy, I ordered them to build this City, and my Palace; and they did it all willingly and well. Then I thought, as the country was so green and beautiful, I would call it the Emerald City; and to make the name fit better I put green spectacles on all the people, so that everything they saw was green."

"But isn't everything here green?" asked Dorothy.

"No more than in any other city," replied Oz; "but when you wear green spectacles, why of course everything you see looks green to you. The Emerald City was built a great many years ago, for I was a young man when the balloon brought me here, and I am a very old man now. But my people have worn green glasses on their eyes so long that most of them think it really is an Emerald City, and it certainly is a beautiful place, abounding in jewels and precious metals, and every good thing that is needed to make one happy. I have been good to the people, and they like me; but ever since this Palace was built, I have shut myself up and would not see any of them.

"One of my greatest fears was the Witches, for while I had no magical powers at all I soon found out that the Witches were really able to do wonderful things. There were four of them in this country, and they ruled the people who live in the North and South and East and West. Fortunately, the Witches of the North and South were good, and I knew they would do me no harm; but the Witches of the East and West were terribly wicked, and had they not thought I was more powerful than they themselves, they would surely have destroyed me. As it was, I lived in deadly fear of them for many years; so you can imagine how pleased I was when I heard your house had fallen on the Wicked Witch of the East. When you came to me, I was willing to promise anything if you would only do away with the other Witch; but, now that you have melted her, I am ashamed to say that I cannot keep my promises."

"I think you are a very bad man," said Dorothy.

"Oh, no, my dear; I'm really a very good man, but I'm a very bad Wizard, I must admit."

"Can't you give me brains?" asked the Scarecrow.

"You don't need them. You are learning something every day. A baby has brains, but it doesn't know much. Experience is the only thing that brings knowledge, and the longer you are on earth the more experience you are sure to get."

"That may all be true," said the Scarecrow, "but I shall be very unhappy unless you give me brains."

The false Wizard looked at him carefully.

"Well," he said with a sigh, "I'm not much of a magician, as I said; but if you will come to me tomorrow morning, I will stuff your head with brains. I cannot tell you how to use them, however; you must find that out for yourself."

"Oh, thank you—thank you!" cried the Scarecrow. "I'll find a way to use them, never fear!"

"But how about my courage?" asked the Lion anxiously.

"You have plenty of courage, I am sure," answered Oz. "All you need is confidence in yourself. There is no living thing that is not afraid when it faces danger. The True courage is in facing danger when you are afraid, and that kind of courage you have in plenty."

"Perhaps I have, but I'm scared just the same," said the Lion. "I shall really be very unhappy unless you give me the sort of courage that makes one forget he is afraid."

"Very well, I will give you that sort of courage tomorrow," replied Oz.

"How about my heart?" asked the Tin Woodman.

"Why, as for that," answered Oz, "I think you are wrong to want a heart. It makes most people unhappy. If you only knew it, you are in luck not to have a heart."

"That must be a matter of opinion," said the Tin Woodman. "For my part, I will bear all the unhappiness without a murmur, if you will give me the heart."

"Very well," answered Oz meekly. "Come to me tomorrow and you shall have a heart. I have played Wizard for so many years that I may as well continue the part a little longer."

"And now," said Dorothy, "how am I to get back to Kansas?"

"We shall have to think about that," replied the little man. "Give me two or three days to consider the matter and I'll try to find a way to carry you over the desert. In the meantime you shall all be treated as my guests, and while you live in the Palace my people will wait upon you and obey your slightest wish. There is only one thing I ask in return for my help—such as it is. You must keep my secret and tell no one I am a humbug."

They agreed to say nothing of what they had learned, and went back to their rooms in high spirits. Even Dorothy had hope that "The Great and Terrible Humbug," as she called him, would find a way to send her back to Kansas, and if he did she was willing to forgive him everything.

Chapter 16

THE MAGIC ART OF THE GREAT HUMBUG

Next morning the Scarecrow said to his friends:

"Congratulate me. I am going to Oz to get my brains at last. When I return I shall be as other men are."

"I have always liked you as you were," said Dorothy simply.

"It is kind of you to like a Scarecrow," he replied. "But surely you will think more of me when you hear the splendid thoughts my new brain is going to turn out." Then he said good-bye to them all in a cheerful voice and went to the Throne Room, where he rapped upon the door.

"Come in," said Oz.

The Scarecrow went in and found the little man sitting down by the window, engaged in deep thought.

"I have come for my brains," remarked the Scarecrow, a little uneasily.

"Oh, yes; sit down in that chair, please," replied Oz. "You must excuse me for taking your head off, but I shall have to do it in order to put your brains in their proper place."

"That's all right," said the Scarecrow. "You are quite welcome to take my head off, as long as it will be a better one when you put it on again."

So the Wizard unfastened his head and emptied out the straw. Then he entered the back room and took up a measure of bran, which he mixed with a great many pins and needles. Having shaken them together thoroughly, he filled the top of the

Scarecrow's head with the mixture and stuffed the rest of the space with straw, to hold it in place.

When he had fastened the Scarecrow's head on his body again he said to him, "Hereafter you will be a great man, for I have given you a lot of bran-new brains."

The Scarecrow was both pleased and proud at the fulfillment of his greatest wish, and having thanked Oz warmly he went back to his friends.

Dorothy looked at him curiously. His head was quite bulged out at the top with brains.

"How do you feel?" she asked.

"I feel wise indeed," he answered earnestly. "When I get used to my brains I shall know everything."

"Why are those needles and pins sticking out of your head?" asked the Tin Woodman.

"That is proof that he is sharp," remarked the Lion.

"Well, I must go to Oz and get my heart," said the Woodman. So he walked to the Throne Room and knocked at the door.

"Come in," called Oz, and the Woodman entered and said, "I have come for my heart."

"Very well," answered the little man. "But I shall have to cut a hole in your breast, so I can put your heart in the right place. I hope it won't hurt you."

"Oh, no," answered the Woodman. "I shall not feel it at all."

So Oz brought a pair of tinsmith's shears and cut a small, square hole in the left side of the Tin Woodman's breast. Then, going to a chest of drawers, he took out a pretty heart, made entirely of silk and stuffed with sawdust.

"Isn't it a beauty?" he asked.

"It is, indeed!" replied the Woodman, who was greatly pleased. "But is it a kind heart?"

"Oh, very!" answered Oz. He put the heart in the Woodman's breast and then replaced the square of tin, soldering it neatly together where it had been cut.

"There," said he; "now you have a heart that any man might be proud of. I'm sorry I had to put a patch on your breast, but it really couldn't be helped."

"Never mind the patch," exclaimed the happy Woodman. "I am very grateful to you, and shall never forget your kindness."

"Don't speak of it," replied Oz.

Then the Tin Woodman went back to his friends, who wished him every joy on account of his good fortune.

The Lion now walked to the Throne Room and knocked at the door.

"Come in," said Oz.

"I have come for my courage," announced the Lion, entering the room.

"Very well," answered the little man; "I will get it for you."

He went to a cupboard and reaching up to a high shelf took down a square green bottle, the contents of which he poured into a green-gold dish, beautifully carved. Placing this before the Cowardly Lion, who sniffed at it as if he did not like it, the Wizard said:

"Drink."

"What is it?" asked the Lion.

"Well," answered Oz, "if it were inside of you, it would be courage. You know, of course, that courage is always inside one; so that this really cannot be called courage until you have swallowed it. Therefore I advise you to drink it as soon as possible."

The Lion hesitated no longer, but drank till the dish was empty.

"How do you feel now?" asked Oz.

"Full of courage," replied the Lion, who went joyfully back to his friends to tell them of his good fortune.

Oz, left to himself, smiled to think of his success in giving the Scarecrow and the Tin Woodman and the Lion exactly what they thought they wanted. "How can I help being a humbug," he said, "when all these people make me do things that everybody knows can't be done? It was easy to make the Scarecrow and the Lion and the Woodman happy, because they imagined I could do anything. But it will take more than imagination to carry Dorothy back to Kansas, and I'm sure I don't know how it can be done."

Chapter 17

HOW THE BALLOON WAS LAUNCHED

FOR three days Dorothy heard nothing from Oz. These were sad days for the little girl, although her friends were all quite happy and contented. The Scarecrow told them there were wonderful thoughts in his head; but he would not say what they were because he knew no one could understand them but himself. When the Tin Woodman walked about he felt his heart rattling around in his breast; and he told Dorothy he had discovered it to be a kinder and more tender heart than the one he had owned when he was made of flesh. The Lion declared he was afraid of nothing on earth, and would gladly face an army or a dozen of the fierce Kalidahs.

Thus each of the little party was satisfied except Dorothy, who longed more than ever to get back to Kansas.

On the fourth day, to her great joy, Oz sent for her, and when she entered the Throne Room he greeted her pleasantly:

"Sit down, my dear; I think I have found the way to get you out of this country."

"And back to Kansas?" she asked eagerly.

"Well, I'm not sure about Kansas," said Oz, "for I haven't the faintest notion which way it lies. But the first thing to do is to cross the desert, and then it should be easy to find your way home."

"How can I cross the desert?" she inquired.

"Well, I'll tell you what I think," said the little man. "You see, when I came to this country it was in a balloon. You also came through the air, being carried by a cyclone. So I believe the best way to get across the desert will be through the air. Now, it is quite beyond my powers to make a cyclone; but I've been thinking the matter over, and I believe I can make a balloon."

"How?" asked Dorothy.

"A balloon," said Oz, "is made of silk, which is coated with glue to keep the gas in it. I have plenty of silk in the Palace, so it will be no trouble to make the balloon. But in all this country there is no gas to fill the balloon with, to make it float."

"If it won't float," remarked Dorothy, "it will be of no use to us."

"True," answered Oz. "But there is another way to make it float, which is to fill it with hot air. Hot air isn't as good as gas, for if the air should get cold the balloon would come down in the desert, and we should be lost."

"We!" exclaimed the girl. "Are you going with me?"

"Yes, of course," replied Oz. "I am tired of being such a humbug. If I should go out of this Palace my people would soon discover I am not a Wizard, and then they would be vexed with me for having deceived them. So I have to stay shut up in these rooms all day, and it gets tiresome. I'd much rather go back to Kansas with you and be in a circus again."

"I shall be glad to have your company," said Dorothy.

"Thank you," he answered. "Now, if you will help me sew the silk together, we will begin to work on our balloon."

So Dorothy took a needle and thread, and as fast as Oz cut the strips of silk into proper shape the girl sewed them neatly together. First there was a strip of light green silk, then a strip of dark green and then a strip of emerald green; for Oz had a fancy to make the balloon in different shades of the color about them. It took three days to sew all the strips together, but when it was finished they had a big bag of green silk more than twenty feet long.

Then Oz painted it on the inside with a coat of thin glue, to make it airtight, after which he announced that the balloon was ready.

"But we must have a basket to ride in," he said. So he sent the soldier with the green whiskers for a big clothes basket, which he fastened with many ropes to the bottom of the balloon.

When it was all ready, Oz sent word to his people that he was going to make a visit to a great brother Wizard who lived in the clouds. The news spread rapidly throughout the city and everyone came to see the wonderful sight.

Oz ordered the balloon carried out in front of the Palace, and the people gazed upon it with much curiosity. The Tin Woodman had chopped a big pile of wood, and now he made a fire of it, and Oz held the bottom of the balloon over the fire so that the hot air that arose from it would be caught in the silken bag. Gradually the balloon swelled out and rose into the air, until finally the basket just touched the ground.

Then Oz got into the basket and said to all the people in a loud voice:

"I am now going away to make a visit. While I am gone the Scarecrow will rule over you. I command you to obey him as you would me."

The balloon was by this time tugging hard at the rope that held it to the ground, for the air within it was hot, and this made it so much lighter in weight than the air without that it pulled hard to rise into the sky.

"Come, Dorothy!" cried the Wizard. "Hurry up, or the balloon will fly away."

"I can't find Toto anywhere," replied Dorothy, who did not wish to leave her little dog behind. Toto had run into the crowd to bark at a kitten, and Dorothy at last found him. She picked him up and ran towards the balloon.

She was within a few steps of it, and Oz was holding out his hands to help her into the basket, when, crack! went the ropes, and the balloon rose into the air without her.

"Come back!" she screamed. "I want to go, too!"

"I can't come back, my dear," called Oz from the basket. "Good-bye!"

"Good-bye!" shouted everyone, and all eyes were turned upward to where the Wizard was riding in the basket, rising every moment farther and farther into the sky.

And that was the last any of them ever saw of Oz, the Wonderful Wizard, though he may have reached Omaha safely, and be there now, for all we know. But the people remembered him lovingly, and said to one another:

"Oz was always our friend. When he was here he built for us this beautiful Emerald City, and now he is gone he has left the Wise Scarecrow to rule over us."

Still, for many days they grieved over the loss of the Wonderful Wizard, and would not be comforted.

Chapter 18

AWAY TO THE SOUTH

DOROTHY wept bitterly at the passing of her hope to get home to Kansas again; but when she thought it all over she was glad she had not gone up in a balloon. And she also felt sorry at losing Oz, and so did her companions.

The Tin Woodman came to her and said:

"Truly I should be ungrateful if I failed to mourn for the man who gave me my lovely heart. I should like to cry a little because Oz is gone, if you will kindly wipe away my tears, so that I shall not rust."

"With pleasure," she answered, and brought a towel at once. Then the Tin Woodman wept for several minutes, and she watched the tears carefully and wiped them away with the towel. When he had finished, he thanked her kindly and oiled himself thoroughly with his jeweled oil-can, to guard against mishap.

The Scarecrow was now the ruler of the Emerald City, and although he was not a Wizard the people were proud of him. "For," they said, "there is not another city in all the world that is ruled by a stuffed man." And, so far as they knew, they were quite right.

The morning after the balloon had gone up with Oz, the four travelers met in the Throne Room and talked matters over. The Scarecrow sat in the big throne and the others stood respectfully before him.

"We are not so unlucky," said the new ruler, "for this Palace and the Emerald City belong to us, and we can do just as we please. When I remember that a short time ago I was up on a pole in a farmer's cornfield, and that now I am the ruler of this beautiful City, I am quite satisfied with my lot."

"I also," said the Tin Woodman, "am well-pleased with my new heart; and, really, that was the only thing I wished in all the world."

"For my part, I am content in knowing I am as brave as any beast that ever lived, if not braver," said the Lion modestly.

"If Dorothy would only be contented to live in the Emerald City," continued the Scarecrow, "we might all be happy together."

"But I don't want to live here," cried Dorothy. "I want to go to Kansas, and live with Aunt Em and Uncle Henry."

"Well, then, what can be done?" inquired the Woodman.

The Scarecrow decided to think, and he thought so hard that the pins and needles began to stick out of his brains. Finally he said:

"Why not call the Winged Monkeys, and ask them to carry you over the desert?"

"I never thought of that!" said Dorothy joyfully. "It's just the thing. I'll go at once for the Golden Cap."

When she brought it into the Throne Room she spoke the magic words, and soon the band of Winged Monkeys flew in through the open window and stood beside her.

"This is the second time you have called us," said the Monkey King, bowing before the little girl. "What do you wish?"

"I want you to fly with me to Kansas," said Dorothy.

But the Monkey King shook his head.

"That cannot be done," he said. "We belong to this country alone, and cannot leave it. There has never been a Winged Monkey in Kansas yet, and I suppose there never will be, for they don't belong there. We shall be glad to serve you in any way in our power, but we cannot cross the desert. Good-bye."

And with another bow, the Monkey King spread his wings and flew away through the window, followed by all his band.

Dorothy was ready to cry with disappointment. "I have wasted the charm of the Golden Cap to no purpose," she said, "for the Winged Monkeys cannot help me."

"It is certainly too bad!" said the tender-hearted Woodman.

The Scarecrow was thinking again, and his head bulged out so horribly that Dorothy feared it would burst.

"Let us call in the soldier with the green whiskers," he said, "and ask his advice."

So the soldier was summoned and entered the Throne Room timidly, for while Oz was alive he never was allowed to come farther than the door.

"This little girl," said the Scarecrow to the soldier, "wishes to cross the desert. How can she do so?"

"I cannot tell," answered the soldier, "for nobody has ever crossed the desert, unless it is Oz himself."

"Is there no one who can help me?" asked Dorothy earnestly.

"Glinda might," he suggested.

"Who is Glinda?" inquired the Scarecrow.

"The Witch of the South. She is the most powerful of all the Witches, and rules over the Quadlings. Besides, her castle stands on the edge of the desert, so she may know a way to cross it."

"Glinda is a Good Witch, isn't she?" asked the child.

"The Quadlings think she is good," said the soldier, "and she is kind to everyone. I have heard that Glinda is a beautiful woman, who knows how to keep young in spite of the many years she has lived."

"How can I get to her castle?" asked Dorothy.

"The road is straight to the South," he answered, "but it is said to be full of dangers to travelers. There are wild beasts in the woods, and a race of queer men who do not like strangers to cross their country. For this reason none of the Quadlings ever come to the Emerald City."

The soldier then left them and the Scarecrow said:

"It seems, in spite of dangers, that the best thing Dorothy can do is to travel to the Land of the South and ask Glinda to help her. For, of course, if Dorothy stays here she will never get back to Kansas."

"You must have been thinking again," remarked the Tin Woodman.

"I have," said the Scarecrow.

"I shall go with Dorothy," declared the Lion, "for I am tired of your city and long for the woods and the country again. I am really a wild beast, you know. Besides, Dorothy will need someone to protect her."

"That is true," agreed the Woodman. "My axe may be of service to her; so I also will go with her to the Land of the South."

"When shall we start?" asked the Scarecrow.

"Are you going?" they asked, in surprise.

"Certainly. If it wasn't for Dorothy I should never have had brains. She lifted me from the pole in the cornfield and brought me to the Emerald City. So my good luck is all due to her, and I shall never leave her until she starts back to Kansas for good and all."

"Thank you," said Dorothy gratefully. "You are all very kind to me. But I should like to start as soon as possible."

"We shall go tomorrow morning," returned the Scarecrow. "So now let us all get ready, for it will be a long journey."

Chapter 19

ATTACKED BY THE FIGHTING TREES

THE next morning Dorothy kissed the pretty green girl good-bye, and they all shook hands with the soldier with the green whiskers, who had walked with them as far as the gate. When the Guardian of the Gate saw them again he wondered greatly that they could leave the beautiful City to get into new trouble. But he at once unlocked their spectacles, which he put back into the green box, and gave them many good wishes to carry with them.

"You are now our ruler," he said to the Scarecrow; "so you must come back to us as soon as possible."

"I certainly shall if I am able," the Scarecrow replied; "but I must help Dorothy to get home, first."

As Dorothy bade the good-natured Guardian a last farewell she said:

"I have been very kindly treated in your lovely City, and everyone has been good to me. I cannot tell you how grateful I am."

"Don't try, my dear," he answered. "We should like to keep you with us, but if it is your wish to return to Kansas, I hope you will find a way." He then opened the gate of the outer wall, and they walked forth and started upon their journey.

The sun shone brightly as our friends turned their faces toward the Land of the South. They were all in the best of spirits, and laughed and chatted together. Dorothy was once more filled with the hope of getting home, and the Scarecrow and the Tin Woodman were glad to be of use to her. As for the Lion, he sniffed the fresh air with delight and whisked his tail from side to side in pure joy at being in the country again, while Toto ran around them and chased the moths and butterflies, barking merrily all the time.

"City life does not agree with me at all," remarked the Lion, as they walked along at a brisk pace. "I have lost much flesh since I lived there, and now I am anxious for a chance to show the other beasts how courageous I have grown."

They now turned and took a last look at the Emerald City. All they could see was a mass of towers and steeples behind the green walls, and high up above everything the spires and dome of the Palace of Oz.

"Oz was not such a bad Wizard, after all," said the Tin Woodman, as he felt his heart rattling around in his breast.

"He knew how to give me brains, and very good brains, too," said the Scarecrow.

"If Oz had taken a dose of the same courage he gave me," added the Lion, "he would have been a brave man."

Dorothy said nothing. Oz had not kept the promise he made her, but he had done his best, so she forgave him. As he said, he was a good man, even if he was a bad Wizard.

The first day's journey was through the green fields and bright flowers that stretched about the Emerald City on every side. They slept that night on the grass, with nothing but the stars over them; and they rested very well indeed.

In the morning they traveled on until they came to a thick wood. There was no way of going around it, for it seemed to extend to the right and left as far as they could see; and, besides, they did not dare change the direction of their journey for fear of getting lost. So they looked for the place where it would be easiest to get into the forest.

The Scarecrow, who was in the lead, finally discovered a big tree with such wide-spreading branches that there was room for the party to pass underneath. So he walked forward to the tree, but just as he came under the first branches they bent down and twined around him, and the next minute he was raised from the ground and flung headlong among his fellow travelers.

This did not hurt the Scarecrow, but it surprised him, and he looked rather dizzy when Dorothy picked him up.

"Here is another space between the trees," called the Lion.

"Let me try it first," said the Scarecrow, "for it doesn't hurt me to get thrown about." He walked up to another tree, as he spoke, but its branches immediately seized him and tossed him back again.

"This is strange," exclaimed Dorothy. "What shall we do?"

"The trees seem to have made up their minds to fight us, and stop our journey," remarked the Lion.

"I believe I will try it myself," said the Woodman, and shouldering his axe, he marched up to the first tree that had handled the Scarecrow so roughly. When a big branch bent down to seize him the Woodman chopped at it so fiercely that he cut it in two. At once the tree began shaking all its branches as if in pain, and the Tin Woodman passed safely under it.

"Come on!" he shouted to the others. "Be quick!" They all ran forward and passed under the tree without injury, except Toto, who was caught by a small branch and shaken until he howled. But the Woodman promptly chopped off the branch and set the little dog free.

The other trees of the forest did nothing to keep them back, so they made up their minds that only the first row of trees could bend down their branches, and that probably these were the policemen of the forest, and given this wonderful power in order to keep strangers out of it.

The four travelers walked with ease through the trees until they came to the farther edge of the wood. Then, to their surprise, they found before them a high wall which seemed to be made of white china. It was smooth, like the surface of a dish, and higher than their heads.

"What shall we do now?" asked Dorothy.

"I will make a ladder," said the Tin Woodman, "for we certainly must climb over the wall."

Chapter 20

THE DAINTY CHINA COUNTRY

WHILE the Woodman was making a ladder from wood which he found in the forest Dorothy lay down and slept, for she was tired by the long walk. The Lion also curled himself up to sleep and Toto lay beside him.

The Scarecrow watched the Woodman while he worked, and said to him:

"I cannot think why this wall is here, nor what it is made of."

"Rest your brains and do not worry about the wall," replied the Woodman. "When we have climbed over it, we shall know what is on the other side."

After a time the ladder was finished. It looked clumsy, but the Tin Woodman was sure it was strong and would answer their purpose. The Scarecrow waked Dorothy and the Lion and Toto, and told them that the ladder was ready. The Scarecrow climbed up the ladder first, but he was so awkward that Dorothy had to follow close behind and keep him from falling off. When he got his head over the top of the wall the Scarecrow said, "Oh, my!"

"Go on," exclaimed Dorothy.

So the Scarecrow climbed farther up and sat down on the top of the wall, and Dorothy put her head over and cried, "Oh, my!" just as the Scarecrow had done.

Then Toto came up, and immediately began to bark, but Dorothy made him be still.

The Lion climbed the ladder next, and the Tin Woodman came last; but both of them cried, "Oh, my!" as soon as they looked over the wall. When they were all sitting in a row on the top of the wall, they looked down and saw a strange sight.

Before them was a great stretch of country having a floor as smooth and shining and white as the bottom of a big platter. Scattered around were many houses made entirely of china and painted in the brightest colors. These houses were quite small, the biggest of them reaching only as high as Dorothy's waist. There were also pretty little barns, with china fences around them; and many cows and sheep and horses and pigs and chickens, all made of china, were standing about in groups.

But the strangest of all were the people who lived in this queer country. There were milkmaids and shepherdesses, with brightly colored bodices and golden spots all over their gowns; and princesses with most gorgeous frocks of silver and gold and purple; and shepherds dressed in knee breeches with pink and yellow and blue stripes down them, and golden buckles on their shoes; and princes with jeweled crowns upon their heads, wearing ermine robes and satin doublets; and funny clowns in ruffled gowns, with round red spots upon their cheeks and tall, pointed caps. And, strangest of all, these people were all made of china, even to their clothes, and were so small that the tallest of them was no higher than Dorothy's knee.

No one did so much as look at the travelers at first, except one little purple china dog with an extra-large head, which came to the wall and barked at them in a tiny voice, afterwards running away again.

"How shall we get down?" asked Dorothy.

They found the ladder so heavy they could not pull it up, so the Scarecrow fell off the wall and the others jumped down upon him so that the hard floor would not hurt their feet. Of course they took pains not to light on his head and get the pins in their feet. When all were safely down they picked up the Scarecrow, whose body was quite flattened out, and patted his straw into shape again.

"We must cross this strange place in order to get to the other side," said Dorothy, "for it would be unwise for us to go any other way except due South."

They began walking through the country of the china people, and the first thing they came to was a china milkmaid milking a china cow. As they drew near, the cow suddenly gave a kick and kicked over the stool, the pail, and even the milkmaid herself, and all fell on the china ground with a great clatter.

Dorothy was shocked to see that the cow had broken her leg off, and that the pail was lying in several small pieces, while the poor milkmaid had a nick in her left elbow.

"There!" cried the milkmaid angrily. "See what you have done! My cow has broken her leg, and I must take her to the mender's shop and have it glued on again. What do you mean by coming here and frightening my cow?"

"I'm very sorry," returned Dorothy. "Please forgive us."

But the pretty milkmaid was much too vexed to make any answer. She picked up the leg sulkily and led her cow away, the poor animal limping on three legs. As she left them the milkmaid cast many reproachful glances over her shoulder at the clumsy strangers, holding her nicked elbow close to her side.

Dorothy was quite grieved at this mishap.

"We must be very careful here," said the kind-hearted Woodman, "or we may hurt these pretty little people so they will never get over it."

A little farther on Dorothy met a most beautifully dressed young Princess, who stopped short as she saw the strangers and started to run away.

Dorothy wanted to see more of the Princess, so she ran after her. But the china girl cried out:

"Don't chase me! Don't chase me!"

She had such a frightened little voice that Dorothy stopped and said, "Why not?"

"Because," answered the Princess, also stopping, a safe distance away, "if I run I may fall down and break myself."

"But could you not be mended?" asked the girl.

"Oh, yes; but one is never so pretty after being mended, you know," replied the Princess.

"I suppose not," said Dorothy.

"Now there is Mr. Joker, one of our clowns," continued the china lady, "who is always trying to stand upon his head. He has broken himself so often that he is mended in a hundred places, and doesn't look at all pretty. Here he comes now, so you can see for yourself."

Indeed, a jolly little clown came walking toward them, and Dorothy could see that in spite of his pretty clothes of red and yellow and green he was completely covered with cracks, running every which way and showing plainly that he had been mended in many places.

The Clown put his hands in his pockets, and after puffing out his cheeks and nodding his head at them saucily, he said:

"My lady fair,
Why do you stare
At poor old Mr. Joker?
You're quite as stiff
And prim as if
You'd eaten up a poker!"

"Be quiet, sir!" said the Princess. "Can't you see these are strangers, and should be treated with respect?"

"Well, that's respect, I expect," declared the Clown, and immediately stood upon his head.

"Don't mind Mr. Joker," said the Princess to Dorothy. "He is considerably cracked in his head, and that makes him foolish."

"Oh, I don't mind him a bit," said Dorothy. "But you are so beautiful," she continued, "that I am sure I could love you dearly. Won't you let me carry you back to Kansas, and stand you on Aunt Em's mantel? I could carry you in my basket."

"That would make me very unhappy," answered the china Princess. "You see, here in our country we live contentedly, and can talk and move around as we please. But whenever any of us are taken away our joints at once stiffen, and we can only stand straight and look pretty. Of course that is all that is expected of us when we are on mantels and cabinets and drawing-room tables, but our lives are much pleasanter here in our own country."

"I would not make you unhappy for all the world!" exclaimed Dorothy. "So I'll just say good-bye."

"Good-bye," replied the Princess.

They walked carefully through the china country. The little animals and all the people scampered out of their way, fearing the strangers would break them, and after an hour or so the travelers reached the other side of the country and came to another china wall.

It was not so high as the first, however, and by standing upon the Lion's back they all managed to scramble to the top. Then the Lion gathered his legs under him and jumped on the wall; but just as he jumped, he upset a china church with his tail and smashed it all to pieces.

"That was too bad," said Dorothy, "but really I think we were lucky in not doing these little people more harm than breaking a cow's leg and a church. They are all so brittle!"

"They are, indeed," said the Scarecrow, "and I am thankful I am made of straw and cannot be easily damaged. There are worse things in the world than being a Scarecrow."

Chapter 21

THE LION BECOMES THE KING OF BEASTS

AFTER climbing down from the china wall the travelers found themselves in a disagreeable country, full of bogs and marshes and covered with tall, rank grass. It was difficult to walk without falling into muddy holes, for the grass was so thick that it hid them from sight. However, by carefully picking their way, they got safely along until they reached solid ground. But here the country seemed wilder than ever, and after a long and tiresome walk through the underbrush they entered another forest, where the trees were bigger and older than any they had ever seen.

"This forest is perfectly delightful," declared the Lion, looking around him with joy. "Never have I seen a more beautiful place."

"It seems gloomy," said the Scarecrow.

"Not a bit of it," answered the Lion. "I should like to live here all my life. See how soft the dried leaves are under your feet and how rich and green the moss is that clings to these old trees. Surely no wild beast could wish a pleasanter home."

"Perhaps there are wild beasts in the forest now," said Dorothy.

"I suppose there are," returned the Lion, "but I do not see any of them about."

They walked through the forest until it became too dark to go any farther. Dorothy and Toto and the Lion lay down to sleep, while the Woodman and the Scarecrow kept watch over them as usual.

When morning came, they started again. Before they had gone far they heard a low rumble, as of the growling of many wild animals. Toto whimpered a little, but none of the others was frightened, and they kept along the well-trodden path until they came to an opening in the wood, in which were gathered hundreds of beasts of every variety. There were tigers and elephants and bears and wolves and foxes and all the others in the natural history, and for a moment Dorothy was afraid. But the Lion explained that the animals were holding a meeting, and he judged by their snarling and growling that they were in great trouble.

As he spoke several of the beasts caught sight of him, and at once the great assemblage hushed as if by magic. The biggest of the tigers came up to the Lion and bowed, saying:

"Welcome, O King of Beasts! You have come in good time to fight our enemy and bring peace to all the animals of the forest once more."

"What is your trouble?" asked the Lion quietly.

"We are all threatened," answered the tiger, "by a fierce enemy which has lately come into this forest. It is a most tremendous monster, like a great spider, with a body as big as an elephant and legs as long as a tree trunk. It has eight of these long legs, and as the monster crawls through the forest he seizes an animal with a leg and drags it to his mouth, where he eats it as a spider does a fly. Not one of us is safe while this fierce creature is alive, and we had called a meeting to decide how to take care of ourselves when you came among us."

The Lion thought for a moment.

"Are there any other lions in this forest?" he asked.

"No; there were some, but the monster has eaten them all. And, besides, they were none of them nearly so large and brave as you."

"If I put an end to your enemy, will you bow down to me and obey me as King of the Forest?" inquired the Lion.

"We will do that gladly," returned the tiger; and all the other beasts roared with a mighty roar: "We will!"

"Where is this great spider of yours now?" asked the Lion.

"Yonder, among the oak trees," said the tiger, pointing with his forefoot.

"Take good care of these friends of mine," said the Lion, "and I will go at once to fight the monster."

He bade his comrades good-bye and marched proudly away to do battle with the enemy.

The great spider was lying asleep when the Lion found him, and it looked so ugly that its foe turned up his nose in disgust. Its legs were quite as long as the tiger had said, and its body covered with coarse black hair. It had a great mouth, with a row of sharp teeth a foot long; but its head was joined to the pudgy body by a neck as slender as a wasp's waist. This gave the Lion a hint of the best way to attack the creature, and as he knew it was easier to fight it asleep than awake, he gave a great spring and landed directly upon the monster's back. Then, with one blow of his heavy paw, all armed with sharp claws, he knocked the spider's head from its body. Jumping down, he watched it until the long legs stopped wiggling, when he knew it was quite dead.

The Lion went back to the opening where the beasts of the forest were waiting for him and said proudly:

"You need fear your enemy no longer."

Then the beasts bowed down to the Lion as their King, and he promised to come back and rule over them as soon as Dorothy was safely on her way to Kansas.

Chapter 22

THE COUNTRY OF THE QUADLINGS

THE four travelers passed through the rest of the forest in safety, and when they came out from its gloom saw before them a steep hill, covered from top to bottom with great pieces of rock.

"That will be a hard climb," said the Scarecrow, "but we must get over the hill, nevertheless."

So he led the way and the others followed. They had nearly reached the first rock when they heard a rough voice cry out, "Keep back!"

"Who are you?" asked the Scarecrow.

Then a head showed itself over the rock and the same voice said, "This hill belongs to us, and we don't allow anyone to cross it."

"But we must cross it," said the Scarecrow. "We're going to the country of the Quadlings."

"But you shall not!" replied the voice, and there stepped from behind the rock the strangest man the travelers had ever seen.

He was quite short and stout and had a big head, which was flat at the top and supported by a thick neck full of wrinkles. But he had no arms at all, and, seeing this, the Scarecrow did not fear that so helpless a creature could prevent them from climbing the hill. So he said, "I'm sorry not to do as you wish, but we must pass over your hill whether you like it or not," and he walked boldly forward.

As quick as lightning the man's head shot forward and his neck stretched out until the top of the head, where it was flat, struck the Scarecrow in the middle and sent him tumbling, over and over, down the hill. Almost as quickly as it came the head went back to the body, and the man laughed harshly as he said, "It isn't as easy as you think!"

A chorus of boisterous laughter came from the other rocks, and Dorothy saw hundreds of the armless Hammer-Heads upon the hillside, one behind every rock.

The Lion became quite angry at the laughter caused by the Scarecrow's mishap, and giving a loud roar that echoed like thunder, he dashed up the hill.

Again a head shot swiftly out, and the great Lion went rolling down the hill as if he had been struck by a cannon ball.

Dorothy ran down and helped the Scarecrow to his feet, and the Lion came up to her, feeling rather bruised and sore, and said, "It is useless to fight people with shooting heads; no one can withstand them."

"What can we do, then?" she asked.

"Call the Winged Monkeys," suggested the Tin Woodman. "You have still the right to command them once more."

"Very well," she answered, and putting on the Golden Cap she uttered the magic words. The Monkeys were as prompt as ever, and in a few moments the entire band stood before her.

"What are your commands?" inquired the King of the Monkeys, bowing low.

"Carry us over the hill to the country of the Quadlings," answered the girl.

"It shall be done," said the King, and at once the Winged Monkeys caught the four travelers and Toto up in their arms and flew away with them. As they passed over the hill the Hammer-Heads yelled with vexation, and shot their heads high in the air, but they could not reach the Winged Monkeys, which carried Dorothy and her comrades safely over the hill and set them down in the beautiful country of the Quadlings.

"This is the last time you can summon us," said the leader to Dorothy; "so good-bye and good luck to you."

"Good-bye, and thank you very much," returned the girl; and the Monkeys rose into the air and were out of sight in a twinkling.

The country of the Quadlings seemed rich and happy. There was field upon field of ripening grain, with well-paved roads running between, and pretty rippling brooks with strong bridges across them. The fences and houses and bridges were all painted bright red, just as they had been painted yellow in the country of the Winkies and blue in the country of the Munchkins. The Quadlings themselves, who were short and fat and looked chubby and good-natured, were dressed all in red, which showed bright against the green grass and the yellowing grain.

The Monkeys had set them down near a farmhouse, and the four travelers walked up to it and knocked at the door. It was opened by the farmer's wife, and when Dorothy asked for something to eat the woman gave them all a good dinner, with three kinds of cake and four kinds of cookies, and a bowl of milk for Toto.

"How far is it to the Castle of Glinda?" asked the child.

"It is not a great way," answered the farmer's wife. "Take the road to the South and you will soon reach it."

Thanking the good woman, they started afresh and walked by the fields and across the pretty bridges until they saw before them a very beautiful Castle. Before the gates were three young girls, dressed in handsome red uniforms trimmed with gold braid; and as Dorothy approached, one of them said to her:

"Why have you come to the South Country?"

"To see the Good Witch who rules here," she answered. "Will you take me to her?"

"Let me have your name, and I will ask Glinda if she will receive you." They told who they were, and the girl soldier went into the Castle. After a few moments she came back to say that Dorothy and the others were to be admitted at once.

Chapter 23

GLINDA THE GOOD WITCH GRANTS DOROTHY'S WISH

Before they went to see Glinda, however, they were taken to a room of the Castle, where Dorothy washed her face and combed her hair, and the Lion shook the dust out of his mane, and the Scarecrow patted himself into his best shape, and the Woodman polished his tin and oiled his joints.

When they were all quite presentable they followed the soldier girl into a big room where the Witch Glinda sat upon a throne of rubies.

She was both beautiful and young to their eyes. Her hair was a rich red in color and fell in flowing ringlets over her shoulders. Her dress was pure white but her eyes were blue, and they looked kindly upon the little girl.

"What can I do for you, my child?" she asked.

Dorothy told the Witch all her story: how the cyclone had brought her to the Land of Oz, how she had found her companions, and of the wonderful adventures they had met with.

"My greatest wish now," she added, "is to get back to Kansas, for Aunt Em will surely think something dreadful has happened to me, and that will make her put on mourning; and unless the crops are better this year than they were last, I am sure Uncle Henry cannot afford it."

Glinda leaned forward and kissed the sweet, upturned face of the loving little girl.

"Bless your dear heart," she said, "I am sure I can tell you of a way to get back to Kansas." Then she added, "But, if I do, you must give me the Golden Cap."

"Willingly!" exclaimed Dorothy; "indeed, it is of no use to me now, and when you have it you can command the Winged Monkeys three times."

"And I think I shall need their service just those three times," answered Glinda, smiling.

Dorothy then gave her the Golden Cap, and the Witch said to the Scarecrow, "What will you do when Dorothy has left us?"

"I will return to the Emerald City," he replied, "for Oz has made me its ruler and the people like me. The only thing that worries me is how to cross the hill of the Hammer-Heads."

"By means of the Golden Cap I shall command the Winged Monkeys to carry you to the gates of the Emerald City," said Glinda, "for it would be a shame to deprive the people of so wonderful a ruler."

"Am I really wonderful?" asked the Scarecrow.

"You are unusual," replied Glinda.

Turning to the Tin Woodman, she asked, "What will become of you when Dorothy leaves this country?"

He leaned on his axe and thought a moment. Then he said, "The Winkies were very kind to me, and wanted me to rule over them after the Wicked Witch died. I am fond of the Winkies, and if I could get back again to the Country of the West, I should like nothing better than to rule over them forever."

"My second command to the Winged Monkeys," said Glinda "will be that they carry you safely to the land of the Winkies. Your brain may not be so large to look at as those of the Scarecrow, but you are really brighter than he is—when you are well polished— and I am sure you will rule the Winkies wisely and well."

Then the Witch looked at the big, shaggy Lion and asked, "When Dorothy has returned to her own home, what will become of you?"

"Over the hill of the Hammer-Heads," he answered, "lies a grand old forest, and all the beasts that live there have made me their King. If I could only get back to this forest, I would pass my life very happily there."

"My third command to the Winged Monkeys," said Glinda, "shall be to carry you to your forest. Then, having used up the powers of the Golden Cap, I shall give it to the King of the Monkeys, that he and his band may thereafter be free for evermore."

The Scarecrow and the Tin Woodman and the Lion now thanked the Good Witch earnestly for her kindness; and Dorothy exclaimed:

"You are certainly as good as you are beautiful! But you have not yet told me how to get back to Kansas."

"Your Silver Shoes will carry you over the desert," replied Glinda. "If you had known their power you could have gone back to your Aunt Em the very first day you came to this country."

"But then I should not have had my wonderful brains!" cried the Scarecrow. "I might have passed my whole life in the farmer's cornfield."

"And I should not have had my lovely heart," said the Tin Woodman. "I might have stood and rusted in the forest till the end of the world."

"And I should have lived a coward forever," declared the Lion, "and no beast in all the forest would have had a good word to say to me."

"This is all true," said Dorothy, "and I am glad I was of use to these good friends. But now that each of them has had what he most desired, and each is happy in having a kingdom to rule besides, I think I should like to go back to Kansas."

"The Silver Shoes," said the Good Witch, "have wonderful powers. And one of the most curious things about them is that they can carry you to any place in the world in three steps, and each step will be made in the wink of an eye. All you have to do is to knock the heels together three times and command the shoes to carry you wherever you wish to go."

"If that is so," said the child joyfully, "I will ask them to carry me back to Kansas at once."

She threw her arms around the Lion's neck and kissed him, patting his big head tenderly. Then she kissed the Tin Woodman, who was weeping in a way most dangerous to his joints. But she hugged the soft, stuffed body of the Scarecrow in her arms instead of kissing his painted face, and found she was crying herself at this sorrowful parting from her loving comrades.

Glinda the Good stepped down from her ruby throne to give the little girl a good-bye kiss, and Dorothy thanked her for all the kindness she had shown to her friends and herself.

Dorothy now took Toto up solemnly in her arms, and having said one last good-bye she clapped the heels of her shoes together three times, saying:

"Take me home to Aunt Em!"

Instantly she was whirling through the air, so swiftly that all she could see or feel was the wind whistling past her ears.

The Silver Shoes took but three steps, and then she stopped so suddenly that she rolled over upon the grass several times before she knew where she was.

At length, however, she sat up and looked about her.

"Good gracious!" she cried.

For she was sitting on the broad Kansas prairie, and just before her was the new farmhouse Uncle Henry built after the cyclone had carried away the old one. Uncle Henry was milking the cows in the barnyard, and Toto had jumped out of her arms and was running toward the barn, barking furiously.

Dorothy stood up and found she was in her stocking-feet. For the Silver Shoes had fallen off in her flight through the air, and were lost forever in the desert.

Chapter 24

HOME AGAIN

AUNT Em had just come out of the house to water the cabbages when she looked up and saw Dorothy running toward her.

"My darling child!" she cried, folding the little girl in her arms and covering her face with kisses. "Where in the world did you come from?"

"From the Land of Oz," said Dorothy gravely. "And here is Toto, too. And oh, Aunt Em! I'm so glad to be at home again!"

THE END

THE MARVELOUS LAND OF OZ

To those excellent good fellows and comedians David C. Montgomery and Frank A. Stone whose clever personations of the Tin Woodman and the Scarecrow have delighted thousands of children throughout the land, this book is gratefully dedicated by THE AUTHOR

CONTENTS

Chapter 1

TIP MANUFACTURES A PUMPKINHEAD

In the Country of the Gillikins, which is at the North of the Land of Oz, lived a youth called Tip. There was more to his name than that, for old Mombi often declared that his whole name was Tippetarius; but no one was expected to say such a long word when "Tip" would do just as well.

This boy remembered nothing of his parents, for he had been brought when quite young to be reared by the old woman known as Mombi, whose reputation, I am sorry to say, was none of the best. For the Gillikin people had reason to suspect her of indulging in magical arts, and therefore hesitated to associate with her.

Mombi was not exactly a Witch, because the Good Witch who ruled that part of the Land of Oz had forbidden any other Witch to exist in her dominions. So Tip's guardian, however much she might aspire to working magic, realized it was unlawful to be more than a Sorceress, or at most a Wizardess.

Tip was made to carry wood from the forest, that the old woman might boil her pot. He also worked in the corn-fields, hoeing and husking; and he fed the pigs and milked the four-horned cow that was Mombi's especial pride.

But you must not suppose he worked all the time, for he felt that would be bad for him. When sent to the forest Tip often climbed trees for birds' eggs or amused himself chasing the fleet white rabbits or fishing in the brooks with bent pins. Then he would hastily gather his armful of wood and carry it home. And when he was supposed to be working in the corn-fields, and the tall stalks hid him from Mombi's view, Tip would often dig in the gopher holes, or if the mood seized him—lie upon his back between the rows of corn and take a nap. So, by taking care not to exhaust his strength, he grew as strong and rugged as a boy may be.

Mombi's curious magic often frightened her neighbors, and they treated her shyly, yet respectfully, because of her weird powers. But Tip frankly hated her, and took no pains to hide his feelings. Indeed, he sometimes showed less respect for the old woman than he should have done, considering she was his guardian.

There were pumpkins in Mombi's corn-fields, lying golden red among the rows of green stalks; and these had been planted and carefully tended that the four-horned cow might eat of them in the winter time. But one day, after the corn had all been cut and stacked, and Tip was carrying the pumpkins to the stable, he took a notion to make a "Jack Lantern" and try to give the old woman a fright with it.

So he selected a fine, big pumpkin—one with a lustrous, orange-red color—and began carving it. With the point of his knife he made two round eyes, a three-cornered nose, and a mouth shaped like a new moon. The face, when completed, could not have been considered strictly beautiful; but it wore a smile so big and broad, and was so jolly in expression, that even Tip laughed as he looked admiringly at his work.

The child had no playmates, so he did not know that boys often dig out the inside of a "pumpkin-jack," and in the space thus made put a lighted candle to render the face more startling; but he conceived an idea of his own that promised to be quite as effective. He decided to manufacture the form of a man, who would wear this pumpkin head, and to stand it in a place where old Mombi would meet it face to face.

"And then," said Tip to himself, with a laugh, "she'll squeal louder than the brown pig does when I pull her tail, and shiver with fright worse than I did last year when I had the ague!"

He had plenty of time to accomplish this task, for Mombi had gone to a village—to buy groceries, she said—and it was a journey of at least two days.

So he took his axe to the forest, and selected some stout, straight saplings, which he cut down and trimmed of all their twigs and leaves. From these he would make the arms, and legs, and feet of his man. For the body he stripped a sheet of thick bark from around a big tree, and with much labor fashioned it into a cylinder of about the right size, pinning the edges together with wooden pegs. Then, whistling happily as he worked, he carefully jointed the limbs and fastened them to the body with pegs whittled into shape with his knife.

By the time this feat had been accomplished it began to grow dark, and Tip remembered he must milk the cow and feed the pigs. So he picked up his wooden man and carried it back to the house with him.

During the evening, by the light of the fire in the kitchen, Tip carefully rounded all the edges of the joints and smoothed the rough places in a neat and workmanlike manner. Then he stood the figure up against the wall and admired it. It seemed remarkably tall, even for a full-grown man; but that was a good point in a small boy's eyes, and Tip did not object at all to the size of his creation.

Next morning, when he looked at his work again, Tip saw he had forgotten to give the dummy a neck, by means of which he might fasten the pumpkinhead to the body. So he went again to the forest, which was not far away, and chopped from a tree several pieces of wood with which to complete his work. When he returned he fastened a cross-piece to the upper end of the body, making a hole through the center to hold upright the neck. The bit of wood which formed this neck was also sharpened at the upper end, and when all was ready Tip put on the pumpkin head, pressing it well down onto the neck, and found that it fitted very well. The head could be turned to one side or the other, as he pleased, and the hinges of the arms and legs allowed him to place the dummy in any position he desired.

"Now, that," declared Tip, proudly, "is really a very fine man, and it ought to frighten several screeches out of old Mombi! But it would be much more lifelike if it were properly dressed."

To find clothing seemed no easy task; but Tip boldly ransacked the great chest in which Mombi kept all her keepsakes and treasures, and at the very bottom he discovered some purple trousers, a red shirt and a pink vest which was dotted with white spots. These he carried away to his man and succeeded, although the garments did not fit very well, in dressing the creature in a jaunty fashion. Some knit stockings belonging to Mombi and a much worn pair of his own shoes completed the man's apparel, and Tip was so delighted that he danced up and down and laughed aloud in boyish ecstacy.

"I must give him a name!" he cried. "So good a man as this must surely have a name. I believe," he added, after a moment's thought, "I will name the fellow 'Jack Pumpkinhead!'"

Chapter 2

THE MARVELOUS POWDER OF LIFE

AFTER considering the matter carefully, Tip decided that the best place to locate Jack would be at the bend in the road, a little way from the house. So he started to carry his man there, but found him heavy and rather awkward to handle. After dragging the creature a short distance Tip stood him on his feet, and by first bending the joints of one leg, and then those of the other, at the same time pushing from behind, the boy managed to induce Jack to walk to the bend in the road. It was not accomplished without a few tumbles, and Tip really worked harder than he ever had in the fields or forest; but a love of mischief urged him on, and it pleased him to test the cleverness of his workmanship.

"Jack's all right, and works fine!" he said to himself, panting with the unusual exertion. But just then he discovered the man's left arm had fallen off in the journey so he went back to find it, and afterward, by whittling a new and stouter pin for the shoulder-joint, he repaired the injury so successfully that the arm was stronger than before. Tip also noticed that Jack's pumpkin head had twisted around until it faced his back; but this was easily remedied. When, at last, the man was set up facing the turn in the path where old Mombi was to appear, he looked natural enough to be a fair imitation of a Gillikin farmer,—and unnatural enough to startle anyone that came on him unawares.

As it was yet too early in the day to expect the old woman to return home, Tip went down into the valley below the farm-house and began to gather nuts from the trees that grew there.

However, old Mombi returned earlier than usual. She had met a crooked wizard who resided in a lonely cave in the mountains, and had traded several important secrets of magic with him. Having in this way secured three new recipes, four magical powders and a selection of herbs of wonderful power and potency, she hobbled home as fast as she could, in order to test her new sorceries.

So intent was Mombi on the treasures she had gained that when she turned the bend in the road and caught a glimpse of the man, she merely nodded and said:

"Good evening, sir."

But, a moment after, noting that the person did not move or reply, she cast a shrewd glance into his face and discovered his pumpkin head elaborately carved by Tip's jack-knife.

"Heh!" ejaculated Mombi, giving a sort of grunt; "that rascally boy has been playing tricks again! Very good! ve—ry *good!* I'll beat him black-and-blue for trying to scare me in this fashion!"

Angrily she raised her stick to smash in the grinning pumpkin head of the dummy; but a sudden thought made her pause, the uplifted stick left motionless in the air.

"Why, here is a good chance to try my new powder!" said she, eagerly. "And then I can tell whether that crooked wizard has fairly traded secrets, or whether he has fooled me as wickedly as I fooled him."

So she set down her basket and began fumbling in it for one of the precious powders she had obtained.

While Mombi was thus occupied Tip strolled back, with his pockets full of nuts, and discovered the old woman standing beside his man and apparently not the least bit frightened by it.

At first he was generally disappointed; but the next moment he became curious to know what Mombi was going to do. So he hid behind a hedge, where he could see without being seen, and prepared to watch.

After some search the woman drew from her basket an old pepper-box, upon the faded label of which the wizard had written with a lead-pencil:

"Powder of Life."

"Ah—here it is!" she cried, joyfully. "And now let us see if it is potent. The stingy wizard didn't give me much of it, but I guess there's enough for two or three doses."

Tip was much surprised when he overheard this speech. Then he saw old Mombi raise her arm and sprinkle the powder from the box over the pumpkin head of his man Jack. She did this in the same way one would pepper a baked potato, and the powder sifted down from Jack's head and scattered over the red shirt and pink waistcoat and purple trousers Tip had dressed him in, and a portion even fell upon the patched and worn shoes.

Then, putting the pepper-box back into the basket, Mombi lifted her left hand, with its little finger pointed upward, and said:

"Weaugh!"

Then she lifted her right hand, with the thumb pointed upward, and said:

"Teaugh!"

Then she lifted both hands, with all the fingers and thumbs spread out, and cried:

"Peaugh!"

Jack Pumpkinhead stepped back a pace, at this, and said in a reproachful voice:

"Don't yell like that! Do you think I'm deaf?"

Old Mombi danced around him, frantic with delight.

"He lives!" she screamed: "He lives! He lives!"

Then she threw her stick into the air and caught it as it came down; and she hugged herself with both arms, and tried to do a step of a jig; and all the time she repeated, rapturously:

"He lives!—he lives!—he lives!"

Now you may well suppose that Tip observed all this with amazement.

At first he was so frightened and horrified that he wanted to run away, but his legs trembled and shook so badly that he couldn't. Then it struck him as a very funny thing for Jack to come to life, especially as the expression on his pumpkin face was so droll and comical it excited laughter on the instant. So, recovering from his first fear, Tip began to laugh; and the merry peals reached old Mombi's ears and made her hobble quickly to the hedge, where she seized Tip's collar and dragged him back to where she had left her basket and the pumpkinheaded man.

"You naughty, sneaking, wicked boy!" she exclaimed, furiously: "I'll teach you to spy out my secrets and to make fun of me!"

"I wasn't making fun of you," protested Tip. "I was laughing at old Pumpkinhead! Look at him! Isn't he a picture, though?"

"I hope you are not reflecting on my personal appearance," said Jack; and it was so funny to hear his grave voice, while his face continued to wear its jolly smile, that Tip again burst into a peal of laughter.

Even Mombi was not without a curious interest in the man her magic had brought to life; for, after staring at him intently, she presently asked:

"What do you know?"

"Well, that is hard to tell," replied Jack. "For although I feel that I know a tremendous lot, I am not yet aware how much there is in the world to find out about. It will take me a little time to discover whether I am very wise or very foolish."

"To be sure," said Mombi, thoughtfully.

"But what are you going to do with him, now he is alive?" asked Tip, wondering.

"I must think it over," answered Mombi. "But we must get home at once, for it is growing dark. Help the Pumpkinhead to walk."

"Never mind me," said Jack; "I can walk as well as you can. Haven't I got legs and feet, and aren't they jointed?"

"Are they?" asked the woman, turning to Tip.

"Of course they are; I made 'em myself," returned the boy, with pride.

So they started for the house, but when they reached the farm yard old Mombi led the pumpkin man to the cow stable and shut him up in an empty stall, fastening the door securely on the outside.

"I've got to attend to you, first," she said, nodding her head at Tip.

Hearing this, the boy became uneasy; for he knew Mombi had a bad and revengeful heart, and would not hesitate to do any evil thing.

They entered the house. It was a round, dome-shaped structure, as are nearly all the farm houses in the Land of Oz.

Mombi bade the boy light a candle, while she put her basket in a cupboard and hung her cloak on a peg. Tip obeyed quickly, for he was afraid of her.

After the candle had been lighted Mombi ordered him to build a fire in the hearth, and while Tip was thus engaged the old woman ate her supper. When the flames began to crackle the boy came to her and asked a share of the bread and cheese; but Mombi refused him.

"I'm hungry!" said Tip, in a sulky tone.

"You won't be hungry long," replied Mombi, with a grim look.

The boy didn't like this speech, for it sounded like a threat; but he happened to remember he had nuts in his pocket, so he cracked some of those and ate them while the woman rose, shook the crumbs from her apron, and hung above the fire a small black kettle.

Then she measured out equal parts of milk and vinegar and poured them into the kettle. Next she produced several packets of herbs and powders and began adding a portion of each to the contents of the kettle. Occasionally she would draw near the candle and read from a yellow paper the recipe of the mess she was concocting.

As Tip watched her his uneasiness increased.

"What is that for?" he asked.

"For you," returned Mombi, briefly.

Tip wriggled around upon his stool and stared awhile at the kettle, which was beginning to bubble. Then he would glance at the stern and wrinkled features of the witch and wish he were any place but in that dim and smoky kitchen, where even the shadows cast by the candle upon the wall were enough to give one the horrors. So an hour passed away, during which the silence was only broken by the bubbling of the pot and the hissing of the flames.

Finally, Tip spoke again.

"Have I got to drink that stuff?" he asked, nodding toward the pot.

"Yes," said Mombi.

"What'll it do to me?" asked Tip.

"If it's properly made," replied Mombi, "it will change or transform you into a marble statue."

Tip groaned, and wiped the perspiration from his forehead with his sleeve.

"I don't want to be a marble statue!" he protested.

That doesn't matter I want you to be one," said the old woman, looking at him severely.

"What use'll I be then?" asked Tip. "There won't be any one to work for you."

"I'll make the Pumpkinhead work for me," said Mombi.

Again Tip groaned.

"Why don't you change me into a goat, or a chicken?" he asked, anxiously. "You can't do anything with a marble statue."

"Oh, yes, I can," returned Mombi. "I'm going to plant a flower garden, next Spring, and I'll put you in the middle of it, for an ornament. I wonder I haven't thought of that before; you've been a bother to me for years."

At this terrible speech Tip felt the beads of perspiration starting all over his body, but he sat still and shivered and looked anxiously at the kettle.

"Perhaps it won't work," he mutttered, in a voice that sounded weak and discouraged.

"Oh, I think it will," answered Mombi, cheerfully. "I seldom make a mistake."

Again there was a period of silence a silence so long and gloomy that when Mombi finally lifted the kettle from the fire it was close to midnight.

"You cannot drink it until it has become quite cold," announced the old witch for in spite of the law she had acknowledged practising witchcraft. "We must both go to bed now, and at daybreak I will call you and at once complete your transformation into a marble statue."

With this she hobbled into her room, bearing the steaming kettle with her, and Tip heard her close and lock the door.

The boy did not go to bed, as he had been commanded to do, but still sat glaring at the embers of the dying fire.

Chapter 3

THE FLIGHT OF THE FUGITIVES

TIP reflected.

"It's a hard thing, to be a marble statue," he thought, rebelliously, "and I'm not going to stand it. For years I've been a bother to her, she says; so she's going to get rid of me. Well, there's an easier way than to become a statue. No boy could have any fun forever standing in the middle of a flower garden! I'll run away, that's what I'll do—and I may as well go before she makes me drink that nasty stuff in the kettle." He waited until the snores of the old witch announced she was fast asleep, and then he arose softly and went to the cupboard to find something to eat.

"No use starting on a journey without food," he decided, searching upon the narrow shelves.

He found some crusts of bread; but he had to look into Mombi's basket to find the cheese she had brought from the village. While turning over the contents of the basket he came upon the pepper-box which contained the "Powder of Life."

"I may as well take this with me," he thought, "or Mombi'll be using it to make more mischief with." So he put the box in his pocket, together with the bread and cheese.

Then he cautiously left the house and latched the door behind him. Outside both moon and stars shone brightly, and the night seemed peaceful and inviting after the close and ill-smelling kitchen.

"I'll be glad to get away," said Tip, softly; "for I never did like that old woman. I wonder how I ever came to live with her."

He was walking slowly toward the road when a thought made him pause.

"I don't like to leave Jack Pumpkinhead to the tender mercies of old Mombi," he muttered. "And Jack belongs to me, for I made him even if the old witch did bring him to life."

He retraced his steps to the cow-stable and opened the door of the stall where the pumpkin-headed man had been left.

Jack was standing in the middle of the stall, and by the moonlight Tip could see he was smiling just as jovially as ever.

"Come on!" said the boy, beckoning.

"Where to?" asked Jack.

"You'll know as soon as I do," answered Tip, smiling sympathetically into the pumpkin face.

"All we've got to do now is to tramp."

"Very well," returned Jack, and walked awkwardly out of the stable and into the moonlight.

Tip turned toward the road and the man followed him. Jack walked with a sort of limp, and occasionally one of the joints of his legs would turn backward, instead of frontwise, almost causing him to tumble. But the Pumpkinhead was quick to notice this, and began to take more pains to step carefully; so that he met with few accidents.

Tip led him along the path without stopping an instant. They could not go very fast, but they walked steadily; and by the time the moon sank away and the sun peeped over the hills they had travelled so great a distance that the boy had no reason to fear pursuit from the old witch. Moreover, he had turned first into one path, and then into another, so that should anyone follow them it would prove very difficult to guess which way they had gone, or where to seek them.

Fairly satisfied that he had escaped—for a time, at least—being turned into a marble statue, the boy stopped his companion and seated himself upon a rock by the roadside.

"Let's have some breakfast," he said.

Jack Pumpkinhead watched Tip curiously, but refused to join in the repast. "I don't seem to be made the same way you are," he said.

"I know you are not," returned Tip; "for I made you."

"Oh! Did you?" asked Jack.

" Certainly. And put you together. And carved your eyes and nose and ears and mouth," said Tip proudly. "And dressed you."

Jack looked at his body and limbs critically.

"It strikes me you made a very good job of it," he remarked.

"Just so-so," replied Tip, modestly; for he began to see certain defects in the construction of his man. "If I'd known we were going to travel together I might have been a little more particular."

"Why, then," said the Pumpkinhead, in a tone that expressed surprise, "you must be my creator my parent my father!"

"Or your inventor," replied the boy with a laugh. "Yes, my son; I really believe I am!"

"Then I owe you obedience," continued the man, "and you owe me—support."

"That's it, exactly", declared Tip, jumping up. "So let us be off."

"Where are we going?" asked Jack, when they had resumed their journey.

"I'm not exactly sure," said the boy; "but I believe we are headed South, and that will bring us, sooner or later, to the Emerald City."

"What city is that?" enquired the Pumpkinhead.

"Why, it's the center of the Land of Oz, and the biggest town in all the country. I've never been there, myself, but I've heard all about its history. It was built by a mighty and wonderful Wizard named Oz, and everything there is of a green color—just as everything in this Country of the Gillikins is of a purple color."

"Is everything here purple?" asked Jack.

"Of course it is. Can't you see?" returned the boy.

"I believe I must be color-blind," said the Pumpkinhead, after staring about him.

"Well, the grass is purple, and the trees are purple, and the houses and fences are purple," explained Tip. "Even the mud in the roads is purple. But in the Emerald City everything is green that is purple here. And in the Country of the Munchkins, over at the East, everything is blue; and in the South country of the Quadlings everything is red; and in the West country of the Winkies, where the Tin Woodman rules, everything is yellow."

"Oh!" said Jack. Then, after a pause, he asked: "Did you say a Tin Woodman rules the Winkies?"

"Yes; he was one of those who helped Dorothy to destroy the Wicked Witch of the West, and the Winkies were so grateful that they invited him to become their ruler,—just as the people of the Emerald City invited the Scarecrow to rule them."

"Dear me!" said Jack. "I'm getting confused with all this history. Who is the Scarecrow?"

"Another friend of Dorothy's," replied Tip.

"And who is Dorothy?"

"She was a girl that came here from Kansas, a place in the big, outside World. She got blown to the Land of Oz by a cyclone, and while she was here the Scarecrow and the Tin Woodman accompanied her on her travels."

"And where is she now?" inquired the Pumpkinhead.

"Glinda the Good, who rules the Quadlings, sent her home again," said the boy.

"Oh. And what became of the Scarecrow?"

"I told you. He rules the Emerald City," answered Tip.

"I thought you said it was ruled by a wonderful Wizard," objected Jack, seeming more and more confused.

"Well, so I did. Now, pay attention, and I'll explain it," said Tip, speaking slowly and looking the smiling Pumpkinhead squarely in the eye. "Dorothy went to the Emerald City to ask the Wizard to send her back to Kansas; and the Scarecrow and the Tin Woodman went with her. But the Wizard couldn't send her back, because he wasn't so much of a Wizard as he might have been. And then they got angry at the Wizard, and threatened to expose him; so the Wizard made a big balloon and escaped in it, and no one has ever seen him since."

"Now, that is very interesting history," said Jack, well pleased; "and I understand it perfectly all but the explanation."

"I'm glad you do," responded Tip. "After the Wizard was gone, the people of the Emerald City made His Majesty, the Scarecrow, their King; and I have heard that he became a very popular ruler."

"Are we going to see this queer King?" asked Jack, with interest.

"I think we may as well," replied the boy; "unless you have something better to do."

"Oh, no, dear father," said the Pumpkinhead. "I am quite willing to go wherever you please."

Chapter 4

TIP MAKES AN EXPERIMENT IN MAGIC

THE boy, small and rather delicate in appearance seemed somewhat embarrassed at being called "father" by the tall, awkward, pumpkinheaded man, but to deny the relationship would involve another long and tedious explanation; so he changed the subject by asking, abruptly:

"Are you tired?"

"Of course not!" replied the other. "But," he continued, after a pause, "it is quite certain I shall wear out my wooden joints if I keep on walking."

Tip reflected, as they journeyed on, that this was true. He began to regret that he had not constructed the wooden limbs more carefully and substantially. Yet how could he ever have guessed that the man he had made merely to scare old Mombi with would be brought to life by means of a magical powder contained in an old pepper-box?

So he ceased to reproach himself, and began to think how he might yet remedy the deficiencies of Jack's weak joints.

While thus engaged they came to the edge of a wood, and the boy sat down to rest upon an old sawhorse that some woodcutter had left there.

"Why don't you sit down?" he asked the Pumpkinhead.

"Won't it strain my joints?" inquired the other.

"Of course not. It'll rest them," declared the boy.

So Jack tried to sit down; but as soon as he bent his joints farther than usual they gave way altogether, and he came clattering to the ground with such a crash that Tip feared he was entirely ruined.

He rushed to the man, lifted him to his feet, straightened his arms and legs, and felt of his head to see if by chance it had become cracked. But Jack seemed to be in pretty good shape, after all, and Tip said to him:

"I guess you'd better remain standing, hereafter. It seems the safest way."

"Very well, dear father." just as you say, replied the smiling Jack, who had been in no wise confused by his tumble.

Tip sat down again. Presently the Pumpkinhead asked:

"What is that thing you are sitting on?"

"Oh, this is a horse," replied the boy, carelessly.

"What is a horse?" demanded Jack.

"A horse? Why, there are two kinds of horses," returned Tip, slightly puzzled how to explain. "One kind of horse is alive, and has four legs and a head and a tail. And people ride upon its back."

"I understand," said Jack, cheerfully "That's the kind of horse you are now sitting on."

"No, it isn't," answered Tip, promptly.

"Why not? That one has four legs, and a head, and a tail." Tip looked at the saw-horse more carefully, and found that the Pumpkinhead was right. The body had been formed from a tree-trunk, and a branch had been left sticking up at one end that looked very much like a tail. In the other end were two big knots that resembled eyes, and a place had been chopped away that might easily be mistaken for the horse's mouth. As for the legs, they were four straight limbs cut from trees and stuck fast into the body, being spread wide apart so that the saw-horse would stand firmly when a log was laid across it to be sawed.

"This thing resembles a real horse more than I imagined," said Tip, trying to explain. "But a real horse is alive, and trots and prances and eats oats, while this is nothing more than a dead horse, made of wood, and used to saw logs upon."

"If it were alive, wouldn't it trot, and prance, and eat oats?" inquired the Pumpkinhead.

"It would trot and prance, perhaps; but it wouldn't eat oats," replied the boy, laughing at the idea. "And of course it can't ever be alive, because it is made of wood."

"So am I," answered the man.

Tip looked at him in surprise.

"Why, so you are!" he exclaimed. "And the magic powder that brought you to life is here in my pocket."

He brought out the pepper box, and eyed it curiously.

"I wonder," said he, musingly, "if it would bring the saw-horse to life."

"If it would," returned Jack, calmly for nothing seemed to surprise him "I could ride on its back, and that would save my joints from wearing out."

"I'll try it!" cried the boy, jumping up. "But I wonder if I can remember the words old Mombi said, and the way she held her hands up."

He thought it over for a minute, and as he had watched carefully from the hedge every motion of the old witch, and listened to her words, he believed he could repeat exactly what she had said and done.

So he began by sprinkling some of the magic Powder of Life from the pepper-box upon the body of the saw-horse. Then he lifted his left hand, with the little finger pointing upward, and said: "Weaugh!"

"What does that mean, dear father?" asked Jack, curiously.

"I don't know," answered Tip. Then he lifted his right hand, with the thumb pointing upward and said: "Teaugh!"

"What's that, dear father?" inquired Jack.

"It means you must keep quiet!" replied the boy, provoked at being interrupted at so important a moment.

"How fast I am learning!" remarked the Pumpkinhead, with his eternal smile.

Tip now lifted both hands above his head, with all the fingers and thumbs spread out, and cried in a loud voice: "Peaugh!"

Immediately the saw-horse moved, stretched its legs, yawned with its chopped-out mouth, and shook a few grains of the powder off its back. The rest of the powder seemed to have vanished into the body of the horse.

"Good!" called Jack, while the boy looked on in astonishment. "You are a very clever sorcerer, dear father!"

Chapter 5

THE AWAKENING OF THE SAW-HORSE

THE Saw-Horse, finding himself alive, seemed even more astonished than Tip. He rolled his knotty eyes from side to side, taking a first wondering view of the world in which he had now so important an existence. Then he tried to look at himself; but he had, indeed, no neck to turn; so that in the endeavor to see his body he kept circling around and around, without catching even a glimpse of it. His legs were stiff and awkward, for there were no knee-joints in them; so that presently he bumped against Jack Pumpkinhead and sent that personage tumbling upon the moss that lined the roadside.

Tip became alarmed at this accident, as well as at the persistence of the Saw-Horse in prancing around in a circle; so he called out:

"Whoa! Whoa, there!"

The Saw-Horse paid no attention whatever to this command, and the next instant brought one of his wooden legs down upon Tip's foot so forcibly that the boy danced away in pain to a safer distance, from where he again yelled:

"Whoa! Whoa, I say!"

Jack had now managed to raise himself to a sitting position, and he looked at the Saw-Horse with much interest.

"I don't believe the animal can hear you," he remarked.

"I shout loud enough, don't I?" answered Tip, angrily.

"Yes; but the horse has no ears," said the smiling Pumpkinhead.

"Sure enough!" exclaimed Tip, noting the fact for the first time. "How, then, am I going to stop him?"

But at that instant the Saw-Horse stopped himself, having concluded it was impossible to see his own body. He saw Tip, however, and came close to the boy to observe him more fully.

It was really comical to see the creature walk; for it moved the legs on its right side together, and those on its left side together, as a pacing horse does; and that made its body rock sidewise, like a cradle.

Tip patted it upon the head, and said "Good boy! Good Boy!" in a coaxing tone; and the Saw-Horse pranced away to examine with its bulging eyes the form of Jack Pumpkinhead.

"I must find a halter for him," said Tip; and having made a search in his pocket he produced a roll of strong cord. Unwinding this, he approached the Saw-Horse and tied the cord around its neck, afterward fastening the other end to a large tree. The Saw-Horse, not understanding the action, stepped backward and snapped the string easily; but it made no attempt to run away.

"He's stronger than I thought," said the boy, "and rather obstinate, too."

"Why don't you make him some ears?" asked Jack. "Then you can tell him what to do."

"That's a splendid idea!" said Tip. "How did you happen to think of it?"

"Why, I didn't think of it," answered the Pumpkinhead; "I didn't need to, for it's the simplest and easiest thing to do."

So Tip got out his knife and fashioned some ears out of the bark of a small tree.

"I mustn't make them too big," he said, as he whittled, "or our horse would become a donkey."

"How is that?" inquired Jack, from the roadside.

"Why, a horse has bigger ears than a man; and a donkey has bigger ears than a horse," explained Tip.

"Then, if my ears were longer, would I be a horse?" asked Jack.

"My friend," said Tip, gravely, "you'll never be anything but a Pumpkinhead, no matter how big your ears are."

"Oh," returned Jack, nodding; "I think I understand."

"If you do, you're a wonder," remarked the boy "but there's no harm in *thinking* you understand. I guess these ears are ready now. Will you hold the horse while I stick them on?"

"Certainly, if you'll help me up," said Jack.

So Tip raised him to his feet, and the Pumpkinhead went to the horse and held its head while the boy bored two holes in it with his knife-blade and inserted the ears.

"They make him look very handsome," said Jack, admiringly.

But those words, spoken close to the Saw-Horse, and being the first sounds he had ever heard, so startled the animal that he made a bound forward and tumbled Tip on one side and Jack on the other. Then he continued to rush forward as if frightened by the clatter of his own foot-steps.

"Whoa!" shouted Tip, picking himself up; "whoa! you idiot whoa!" The Saw-Horse would probably have paid no attention to this, but just then it stepped a leg into a gopher-hole and stumbled head-over-heels to the ground, where it lay upon its back, frantically waving its four legs in the air.

Tip ran up to it.

"You're a nice sort of a horse, I must say!" he exclaimed. "Why didn't you stop when I yelled 'whoa?'"

"Does 'whoa' mean to stop?" asked the Saw-Horse, in a surprised voice, as it rolled its eyes upward to look at the boy.

"Of course it does," answered Tip.

"And a hole in the ground means to stop, also, doesn't it?" continued the horse.

"To be sure; unless you step over it," said Tip.

"What a strange place this is," the creature exclaimed, as if amazed. "What am I doing here, anyway?"

"Why, I've brought you to life," answered the boy "but it won't hurt you any, if you mind me and do as I tell you."

"Then I will do as you tell me," replied the Saw-Horse, humbly. "But what happened to me, a moment ago? I don't seem to be just right, someway."

"You're upside down," explained Tip. "But just keep those legs still a minute and I'll set you right side up again."

"How many sides have I?" asked the creature, wonderingly.

"Several," said Tip, briefly. "But do keep those legs still."

The Saw-Horse now became quiet, and held its legs rigid; so that Tip, after several efforts, was able to roll him over and set him upright.

"Ah, I seem all right now," said the queer animal, with a sigh.

"One of your ears is broken," Tip announced, after a careful examination. "I'll have to make a new one."

Then he led the Saw-Horse back to where Jack was vainly struggling to regain his feet, and after assisting the Pumpkinhead to stand upright Tip whittled out a new ear and fastened it to the horse's head.

"Now," said he, addressing his steed, "pay attention to what I'm going to tell you. 'Whoa!' means to stop; 'Get-Up!' means to walk forward; 'Trot!' means to go as fast as you can. Understand?"

"I believe I do," returned the horse.

"Very good. We are all going on a journey to the Emerald City, to see His Majesty, the Scarecrow; and Jack Pumpkinhead is going to ride on your back, so he won't wear out his joints."

"I don't mind," said the Saw-Horse. "Anything that suits you suits me."

Then Tip assisted Jack to get upon the horse.

"Hold on tight," he cautioned, "or you may fall off and crack your pumpkin head."

"That would be horrible!" said Jack, with a shudder. "What shall I hold on to?"

"Why, hold on to his ears," replied Tip, after a moment's hesitation.

"Don't do that!" remonstrated the Saw-Horse; "for then I can't hear."

That seemed reasonable, so Tip tried to think of something else.

"I'll fix it!" said he, at length. He went into the wood and cut a short length of limb from a young, stout tree. One end of this he sharpened to a point, and then he dug a hole in the back of the Saw-Horse, just behind its head. Next he brought a piece of rock from the road and hammered the post firmly into the animal's back.

"Stop! Stop!" shouted the horse; "you're jarring me terribly."

"Does it hurt?" asked the boy.

"Not exactly hurt," answered the animal; "but it makes me quite nervous to be jarred."

"Well, it's all over now" said Tip, encouragingly. "Now, Jack, be sure to hold fast to this post and then you can't fall off and get smashed."

So Jack held on tight, and Tip said to the horse:

"Get up."

The obedient creature at once walked forward, rocking from side to side as he raised his feet from the ground.

Tip walked beside the Saw-Horse, quite content with this addition to their party. Presently he began to whistle.

"What does that sound mean?" asked the horse.

"Don't pay any attention to it," said Tip. "I'm just whistling, and that only means I'm pretty well satisfied."

"I'd whistle myself, if I could push my lips together," remarked Jack. "I fear, dear father, that in some respects I am sadly lacking."

After journeying on for some distance the narrow path they were following turned into a broad roadway, paved with yellow brick. By the side of the road Tip noticed a sign-post that read:

"NINE MILES TO THE EMERALD CITY."

But it was now growing dark, so he decided to camp for the night by the roadside and to resume the journey next morning by daybreak. He led the Saw-Horse to a grassy mound upon which grew several bushy trees, and carefully assisted the Pumpkinhead to alight.

"I think I'll lay you upon the ground, overnight," said the boy. "You will be safer that way."

"How about me?" asked the Saw-Horse.

"It won't hurt you to stand," replied Tip; "and, as you can't sleep, you may as well watch out and see that no one comes near to disturb us."

Then the boy stretched himself upon the grass beside the Pumpkinhead, and being greatly wearied by the journey was soon fast asleep.

Chapter 6

JACK PUMPKINHEAD'S RIDE TO THE EMERALD CITY

AT daybreak Tip was awakened by the Pumpkinhead. He rubbed the sleep from his eyes, bathed in a little brook, and then ate a portion of his bread and cheese. Having thus prepared for a new day the boy said:

"Let us start at once. Nine miles is quite a distance, but we ought to reach the Emerald City by noon if no accidents happen." So the Pumpkinhead was again perched upon the back of the Saw-Horse and the journey was resumed.

Tip noticed that the purple tint of the grass and trees had now faded to a dull lavender, and before long this lavender appeared to take on a greenish tinge that gradually brightened as they drew nearer to the great City where the Scarecrow ruled.

The little party had traveled but a short two miles upon their way when the road of yellow brick was parted by a broad and swift river. Tip was puzzled how to cross over; but after a time he discovered a man in a ferry-boat approaching from the other side of the stream.

When the man reached the bank Tip asked:

"Will you row us to the other side?"

"Yes, if you have money," returned the ferryman, whose face looked cross and disagreeable.

"But I have no money," said Tip.

"None at all?" inquired the man.

"None at all," answered the boy.

"Then I'll not break my back rowing you over," said the ferryman, decidedly.

"What a nice man!" remarked the Pumpkinhead, smilingly.

The ferryman stared at him, but made no reply. Tip was trying to think, for it was a great disappointment to him to find his journey so suddenly brought to an end.

"I must certainly get to the Emerald City," he said to the boatman; "but how can I cross the river if you do not take me?"

The man laughed, and it was not a nice laugh.

"That wooden horse will float," said he; "and you can ride him across. As for the pumpkinheaded loon who accompanies you, let him sink or swim it won't matter greatly which."

"Don't worry about me," said Jack, smiling pleasantly upon the crabbed ferryman; "I'm sure I ought to float beautifully."

Tip thought the experiment was worth making, and the Saw-Horse, who did not know what danger meant, offered no objections whatever. So the boy led it down into the water and climbed upon its back. Jack also waded in up to his knees and grasped the tail of the horse so that he might keep his pumpkin head above the water.

"Now," said Tip, instructing the Saw-Horse, "if you wiggle your legs you will probably swim; and if you swim we shall probably reach the other side."

The Saw-Horse at once began to wiggle its legs, which acted as oars and moved the adventurers slowly across the river to the opposite side. So successful was the trip that presently they were climbing, wet and dripping, up the grassy bank.

Tip's trouser-legs and shoes were thoroughly soaked; but the Saw-Horse had floated so perfectly that from his knees up the boy was entirely dry. As for the Pumpkinhead, every stitch of his gorgeous clothing dripped water.

"The sun will soon dry us," said Tip "and, anyhow, we are now safely across, in spite of the ferryman, and can continue our journey."

"I didn't mind swimming, at all," remarked the horse.

"Nor did I," added Jack.

They soon regained the road of yellow brick, which proved to be a continuation of the road they had left on the other side, and then Tip once more mounted the Pumpkinhead upon the back of the Saw-Horse.

"If you ride fast," said he, "the wind will help to dry your clothing. I will hold on to the horse's tail and run after you. In this way we all will become dry in a very short time."

"Then the horse must step lively," said Jack.

"I'll do my best," returned the Saw-Horse, cheerfully.

Tip grasped the end of the branch that served as tail to the Saw-Horse, and called loudly: "Get-up!"

The horse started at a good pace, and Tip followed behind. Then he decided they could go faster, so he shouted: "Trot!"

Now, the Saw-Horse remembered that this word was the command to go as fast as he could; so he began rocking along the road at a tremendous pace, and Tip had hard work—running faster than he ever had before in his life—to keep his feet.

Soon he was out of breath, and although he wanted to call "Whoa!" to the horse, he found he could not get the word out of his throat. Then the end of the tail he was clutching, being nothing more than a dead branch, suddenly broke away, and the next minute the boy was rolling in the dust of the road, while the horse and its pumpkin-headed rider dashed on and quickly disappeared in the distance.

By the time Tip had picked himself up and cleared the dust from his throat so he could say "Whoa!" there was no further need of saying it, for the horse was long since out of sight.

So he did the only sensible thing he could do. He sat down and took a good rest, and afterward began walking along the road.

"Some time I will surely overtake them," he reflected; "for the road will end at the gates of the Emerald City, and they can go no further than that."

Meantime Jack was holding fast to the post and the Saw-Horse was tearing along the road like a racer. Neither of them knew Tip was left behind, for the Pumpkinhead did not look around and the Saw-Horse couldn't.

As he rode, Jack noticed that the grass and trees had become a bright emerald-green in color, so he guessed they were nearing the Emerald City even before the tall spires and domes came into sight.

At length a high wall of green stone, studded thick with emeralds, loomed up before them; and fearing the Saw-Horse would not know enough to stop and so might smash them both against this wall, Jack ventured to cry "Whoa!" as loud as he could.

So suddenly did the horse obey that had it not been for his post Jack would have been pitched off head foremost, and his beautiful face ruined.

"That was a fast ride, dear father!" he exclaimed; and then, hearing no reply, he turned around and discovered for the first time that Tip was not there.

This apparent desertion puzzled the Pumpkinhead, and made him uneasy. And while he was wondering what had become of the boy, and what he ought to do next under such trying circumstances, the gateway in the green wall opened and a man came out.

This man was short and round, with a fat face that seemed remarkably good-natured. He was clothed all in green and wore a high, peaked green hat upon his head and green spectacles over his eyes. Bowing before the Pumpkinhead he said:

"I am the Guardian of the Gates of the Emerald City. May I inquire who you are, and what is your business?"

"My name is Jack Pumpkinhead," returned the other, smilingly; "but as to my business, I haven't the least idea in the world what it is."

The Guardian of the Gates looked surprised, and shook his head as if dissatisfied with the reply.

"What are you, a man or a pumpkin?" he asked, politely.

"Both, if you please," answered Jack.

"And this wooden horse—is it alive?" questioned the Guardian.

The horse rolled one knotty eye upward and winked at Jack. Then it gave a prance and brought one leg down on the Guardian's toes.

"Ouch!" cried the man; "I'm sorry I asked that question. But the answer is most convincing. Have you any errand, sir, in the Emerald City?"

"It seems to me that I have," replied the Pumpkinhead, seriously; "but I cannot think what it is. My father knows all about it, but he is not here."

"This is a strange affair very strange!" declared the Guardian. "But you seem harmless. Folks do not smile so delightfully when they mean mischief."

"As for that," said Jack, "I cannot help my smile, for it is carved on my face with a jack-knife."

"Well, come with me into my room," resumed the Guardian, "and I will see what can be done for you."

So Jack rode the Saw-Horse through the gateway into a little room built into the wall. The Guardian pulled a bell-cord, and presently a very tall soldier—clothed in a green uniform—entered from the opposite door. This soldier carried a long green gun over his shoulder and had lovely green whiskers that fell quite to his knees. The Guardian at once addressed him, saying:

"Here is a strange gentleman who doesn't know why he has come to the Emerald City, or what he wants. Tell me, what shall we do with him?"

The Soldier with the Green Whiskers looked at Jack with much care and curiosity. Finally he shook his head so positively that little waves rippled down his whiskers, and then he said:

"I must take him to His Majesty, the Scarecrow."

"But what will His Majesty, the Scarecrow, do with him?" asked the Guardian of the Gates.

"That is His Majesty's business," returned the soldier. "I have troubles enough of my own. All outside troubles must be turned over to His Majesty. So put the spectacles on this fellow, and I'll take him to the royal palace."

So the Guardian opened a big box of spectacles and tried to fit a pair to Jack's great round eyes.

"I haven't a pair in stock that will really cover those eyes up," said the little man, with a sigh; "and your head is so big that I shall be obliged to tie the spectacles on."

"But why need I wear spectacles?" asked Jack.

"It's the fashion here," said the Soldier, "and they will keep you from being blinded by the glitter and glare of the gorgeous Emerald City."

"Oh!" exclaimed Jack. "Tie them on, by all means. I don't wish to be blinded."

"Nor I!" broke in the Saw-Horse; so a pair of green spectacles was quickly fastened over the bulging knots that served it for eyes.

Then the Soldier with the Green Whiskers led them through the inner gate and they at once found themselves in the main street of the magnificent Emerald City.

Sparkling green gems ornamented the fronts of the beautiful houses and the towers and turrets were all faced with emeralds. Even the green marble pavement glittered with precious stones, and it was indeed a grand and marvelous sight to one who beheld it for the first time.

However, the Pumpkinhead and the Saw-Horse, knowing nothing of wealth and beauty, paid little attention to the wonderful sights they saw through their green spectacles. They calmly followed after the green soldier and scarcely noticed the crowds of green people who stared at them in surprise. When a green dog ran out and barked at them the Saw-Horse promptly kicked at it with its wooden leg and sent the little animal howling into one of the houses; but nothing more serious than this happened to interrupt their progress to the royal palace.

The Pumpkinhead wanted to ride up the green marble steps and straight into the Scarecrow's presence; but the soldier would not permit that. So Jack dismounted, with much difficulty, and a servant led the Saw-Horse around to the rear while the Soldier with the Green Whiskers escorted the Pumpkinhead into the palace, by the front entrance.

The stranger was left in a handsomely furnished waiting room while the soldier went to announce him. It so happened that at this hour His Majesty was at leisure and greatly bored for want of something to do, so he ordered his visitor to be shown at once into his throne room.

Jack felt no fear or embarrassment at meeting the ruler of this magnificent city, for he was entirely ignorant of all worldly customs. But when he entered the room and saw for the first time His Majesty the Scarecrow seated upon his glittering throne, he stopped short in amazement.

Chapter 7

HIS MAJESTY THE SCARECROW

I suppose every reader of this book knows what a scarecrow is; but Jack Pumpkinhead, never having seen such a creation, was more surprised at meeting the remarkable King of the Emerald City than by any other one experience of his brief life.

His Majesty the Scarecrow was dressed in a suit of faded blue clothes, and his head was merely a small sack stuffed with straw, upon which eyes, ears, a nose and a mouth had been rudely painted to represent a face. The clothes were also stuffed with straw, and that so unevenly or carelessly that his Majesty's legs and arms seemed more bumpy than was necessary. Upon his hands were gloves with long fingers, and these were padded with cotton. Wisps of straw stuck out from the monarch's coat and also from his neck and boot-tops. Upon his head he wore a heavy golden crown set thick with sparkling jewels, and the weight of this crown caused his brow to sag in wrinkles, giving a thoughtful expression to the painted face. Indeed, the crown alone betokened majesty; in all else the, Scarecrow King was but a simple scarecrow—flimsy, awkward, and unsubstantial.

But if the strange appearance of his Majesty the Scarecrow seemed startling to Jack, no less wonderful was the form of the Pumpkinhead to the Scarecrow. The purple trousers and pink waistcoat and red shirt hung loosely over the wooden joints Tip had manufactured, and the carved face on the pumpkin grinned perpetually, as if its wearer considered life the jolliest thing imaginable.

At first, indeed, His Majesty thought his queer visitor was laughing at him, and was inclined to resent such a liberty; but it was not without reason that the Scarecrow had attained the reputation of being the wisest personage in the Land of Oz. He made a more careful examination of his visitor, and soon discovered that Jack's features were carved into a smile and that he could not look grave if he wished to.

The King was the first to speak. After regarding Jack for some minutes he said, in a tone of wonder:

"Where on earth did you come from, and how do you happen to be alive?"

"I beg your Majesty's pardon," returned the Pumpkinhead; "but I do not understand you."

"What don't you understand?" asked the Scarecrow.

"Why, I don't understand your language. You see, I came from the Country of the Gillikins, so that I am a foreigner."

"Ah, to be sure!" exclaimed the Scarecrow. "I myself speak the language of the Munchkins, which is also the language of the Emerald City. But you, I suppose, speak the language of the Pumpkinheads?"

"Exactly so, your Majesty" replied the other, bowing; "so it will be impossible for us to understand one another."

"That is unfortunate, certainly," said the Scarecrow, thoughtfully. "We must have an interpreter."

"What is an interpreter?" asked Jack.

"A person who understands both my language and your own. When I say anything, the interpreter can tell you what I mean; and when you say anything the interpreter can tell me what *you* mean. For the interpreter can speak both languages as well as understand them."

"That is certainly clever," said Jack, greatly pleased at finding so simple a way out of the difficulty.

So the Scarecrow commanded the Soldier with the Green Whiskers to search among his people until he found one who understood the language of the Gillikins as well as the language of the Emerald City, and to bring that person to him at once.

When the Soldier had departed the Scarecrow said:

"Won't you take a chair while we are waiting?"

"Your Majesty forgets that I cannot understand you," replied the Pumpkinhead. "If you wish me to sit down you must make a sign for me to do so." The Scarecrow came down from his throne and rolled an armchair to a position behind the Pumpkinhead. Then he gave Jack a sudden push that sent him sprawling upon the cushions in so awkward a fashion that he doubled up like a jackknife, and had hard work to untangle himself.

"Did you understand that sign?" asked His Majesty, politely.

"Perfectly," declared Jack, reaching up his arms to turn his head to the front, the pumpkin having twisted around upon the stick that supported it.

"You seem hastily made," remarked the Scarecrow, watching Jack's efforts to straighten himself.

"Not more so than your Majesty," was the frank reply.

"There is this difference between us," said the Scarecrow, "that whereas I will bend, but not break, you will break, but not bend."

At this moment the soldier returned leading a young girl by the hand. She seemed very sweet and modest, having a pretty face and beautiful green eyes and hair. A dainty green silk skirt reached to her knees, showing silk stockings embroidered with pea-pods, and green satin slippers with bunches of lettuce for decorations instead of bows or buckles. Upon her silken waist clover leaves were embroidered, and she wore a jaunty little jacket trimmed with sparkling emeralds of a uniform size.

"Why, it's little Jellia Jamb!" exclaimed the Scarecrow, as the green maiden bowed her pretty head before him. "Do you understand the language of the Gillikins, my dear?"

"Yes, your Majesty," she answered, "for I was born in the North Country."

"Then you shall be our interpreter," said the Scarecrow, "and explain to this Pumpkinhead all that I say, and also explain to me all that *he* says. Is this arrangement satisfactory?" he asked, turning toward his guest.

"Very satisfactory indeed," was the reply.

"Then ask him, to begin with," resumed the Scarecrow, turning to Jellia, "what brought him to the Emerald City"

But instead of this the girl, who had been staring at Jack, said to him:

"You are certainly a wonderful creature. Who made you?"

"A boy named Tip," answered Jack.

"What does he say?" inquired the Scarecrow. "My ears must have deceived me. What did he say?"

"He says that your Majesty's brains seem to have come loose," replied the girl, demurely.

The Scarecrow moved uneasily upon his throne, and felt of his head with his left hand.

"What a fine thing it is to understand two different languages," he said, with a perplexed sigh. "Ask him, my dear, if he has any objection to being put in jail for insulting the ruler of the Emerald City."

"I didn't insult you!" protested Jack, indignantly.

"Tut—tut!" cautioned the Scarecrow "wait, until Jellia translates my speech. What have we got an interpreter for, if you break out in this rash way?"

"All right, I'll wait," replied the Pumpkinhead, in a surly tone—although his face smiled as genially as ever. "Translate the speech, young woman."

"His Majesty inquires if you are hungry," said Jellia.

"Oh, not at all!" answered Jack, more pleasantly, "for it is impossible for me to eat."

"It's the same way with me," remarked the Scarecrow. "What did he say, Jellia, my dear?"

"He asked if you were aware that one of your eyes is painted larger than the other," said the girl, mischievously.

"Don't you believe her, your Majesty," cried Jack.

"Oh, I don't," answered the Scarecrow, calmly. Then, casting a sharp look at the girl, he asked:

"Are you quite certain you understand the languages of both the Gillikins and the Munchkins?"

"Quite certain, your Majesty," said Jellia Jamb, trying hard not to laugh in the face of royalty.

"Then how is it that I seem to understand them myself?" inquired the Scarecrow.

"Because they are one and the same!" declared the girl, now laughing merrily. "Does not your Majesty know that in all the land of Oz but one language is spoken?"

"Is it indeed so?" cried the Scarecrow, much relieved to hear this; "then I might easily have been my own interpreter!"

"It was all my fault, your Majesty," said Jack, looking rather foolish, "I thought we must surely speak different languages, since we came from different countries."

"This should be a warning to you never to think," returned the Scarecrow, severely. "For unless one can think wisely it is better to remain a dummy—which you most certainly are."

"I am!—I surely am!" agreed the Pumpkinhead.

"It seems to me," continued the Scarecrow, more mildly, "that your manufacturer spoiled some good pies to create an indifferent man."

"I assure your Majesty that I did not ask to be created," answered Jack.

"Ah! It was the same in my case," said the King, pleasantly. "And so, as we differ from all ordinary people, let us become friends."

"With all my heart!" exclaimed Jack.

"What! Have you a heart?" asked the Scarecrow, surprised.

"No; that was only imaginative—I might say, a figure of speech," said the other.

"Well, your most prominent figure seems to be a figure of wood; so I must beg you to restrain an imagination which, having no brains, you have no right to exercise," suggested the Scarecrow, warningly.

"To be sure!" said Jack, without in the least comprehending.

His Majesty then dismissed Jellia Jamb and the Soldier with the Green Whiskers, and when they were gone he took his new friend by the arm and led him into the courtyard to play a game of quoits.

Chapter 8

GEN. JINJUR'S ARMY OF REVOLT

T<small>IP</small> was so anxious to rejoin his man Jack and the Saw-Horse that he walked a full half the distance to the Emerald City without stopping to rest. Then he discovered that he was hungry and the crackers and cheese he had provided for the Journey had all been eaten.

While wondering what he should do in this emergency he came upon a girl sitting by the roadside. She wore a costume that struck the boy as being remarkably brilliant: her silken waist being of emerald green and her skirt of four distinct colors—blue in front, yellow at the left side, red at the back and purple at the right side. Fastening the waist in front were four buttons—the top one blue, the next yellow, a third red and the last purple.

The splendor of this dress was almost barbaric; so Tip was fully justified in staring at the gown for some moments before his eyes were attracted by the pretty face above it. Yes, the face was pretty enough, he decided; but it wore an expression of discontent coupled to a shade of defiance or audacity.

While the boy stared the girl looked upon him calmly. A lunch basket stood beside her, and she held a dainty sandwich in one hand and a hard-boiled egg in the other, eating with an evident appetite that aroused Tip's sympathy.

He was just about to ask a share of the luncheon when the girl stood up and brushed the crumbs from her lap.

"There!" said she; "it is time for me to go. Carry that basket for me and help yourself to its contents if you are hungry."

Tip seized the basket eagerly and began to eat, following for a time the strange girl without bothering to ask questions. She walked along before him with swift strides, and there was about her an air of decision and importance that led him to suspect she was some great personage.

Finally, when he had satisfied his hunger, he ran up beside her and tried to keep pace with her swift footsteps—a very difficult feat, for she was much taller than he, and evidently in a hurry.

"Thank you very much for the sandwiches," said Tip, as he trotted along. "May I ask your name?"

"I am General Jinjur," was the brief reply.

"Oh!" said the boy surprised. "What sort of a General?"

"I command the Army of Revolt in this war," answered the General, with unnecessary sharpness.

"Oh!" he again exclaimed. "I didn't know there was a war."

"You were not supposed to know it," she returned, "for we have kept it a secret; and considering that our army is composed entirely of girls," she added, with some pride, "it is surely a remarkable thing that our Revolt is not yet discovered."

"It is, indeed," acknowledged Tip. "But where is your army?"

"About a mile from here," said General Jinjur. "The forces have assembled from all parts of the Land of Oz, at my express command. For this is the day we are to conquer His Majesty the Scarecrow, and wrest from him the throne. The Army of Revolt only awaits my coming to march upon the Emerald City."

"Well!" declared Tip, drawing a long breath, "this is certainly a surprising thing! May I ask why you wish to conquer His Majesty the Scarecrow?"

"Because the Emerald City has been ruled by men long enough, for one reason," said the girl.

"Moreover, the City glitters with beautiful gems, which might far better be used for rings, bracelets and necklaces; and there is enough money in the King's treasury to buy every girl in our Army a dozen new gowns. So we intend to conquer the City and run the government to suit ourselves."

Jinjur spoke these words with an eagerness and decision that proved she was in earnest.

"But war is a terrible thing," said Tip, thoughtfully.

"This war will be pleasant," replied the girl, cheerfully.

"Many of you will be slain!" continued the boy, in an awed voice.

"Oh, no", said Jinjur. "What man would oppose a girl, or dare to harm her? And there is not an ugly face in my entire Army."

Tip laughed.

"Perhaps you are right," said he. "But the Guardian of the Gate is considered a faithful Guardian, and the King's Army will not let the City be conquered without a struggle."

"The Army is old and feeble," replied General Jinjur, scornfully. "His strength has all been used to grow whiskers, and his wife has such a temper that she has already pulled more than half of them out by the roots. When the Wonderful Wizard reigned the Soldier with the Green Whiskers was a very good Royal Army, for people feared the Wizard. But no one is afraid of the Scarecrow, so his Royal Army don't count for much in time of war."

After this conversation they proceeded some distance in silence, and before long reached a large clearing in the forest where fully four hundred young women were assembled. These were laughing and talking together as gaily as if they had gathered for a picnic instead of a war of conquest.

They were divided into four companies, and Tip noticed that all were dressed in costumes similar to that worn by General Jinjur. The only real difference was that while those girls from the Munchkin country had the blue strip in front of their skirts, those from the country of the Quadlings had the red strip in front; and those from the country of the Winkies had the yellow strip in front, and the Gillikin girls wore the purple strip in front. All had green waists, representing the Emerald City they intended to conquer, and the top button on each waist indicated by its color which country the wearer came from. The uniforms were Jaunty and becoming, and quite effective when massed together.

Tip thought this strange Army bore no weapons whatever; but in this he was wrong. For each girl had stuck through the knot of her back hair two long, glittering knitting-needles.

General Jinjur immediately mounted the stump of a tree and addressed her army.

"Friends, fellow-citizens, and girls!" she said; "we are about to begin our great Revolt against the men of Oz! We march to conquer the Emerald City—to dethrone the Scarecrow King—to acquire thousands of gorgeous gems—to rifle the royal treasury—and to obtain power over our former oppressors!"

"Hurrah!" said those who had listened; but Tip thought most of the Army was too much engaged in chattering to pay attention to the words of the General.

The command to march was now given, and the girls formed themselves into four bands, or companies, and set off with eager strides toward the Emerald City.

The boy followed after them, carrying several baskets and wraps and packages which various members of the Army of Revolt had placed in his care. It was not long before they came to the green granite walls of the City and halted before the gateway.

The Guardian of the Gate at once came out and looked at them curiously, as if a circus had come to town. He carried a bunch of keys swung round his neck by a golden chain; his hands were thrust carelessly into his pockets, and he seemed to have no idea at all that the City was threatened by rebels. Speaking pleasantly to the girls, he said:

"Good morning, my dears! What can I do for you?"

"Surrender instantly!" answered General Jinjur, standing before him and frowning as terribly as her pretty face would allow her to.

"Surrender!" echoed the man, astounded. "Why, it's impossible. It's against the law! I never heard of such a thing in my life."

"Still, you must surrender!" exclaimed the General, fiercely. "We are revolting!"

"You don't look it," said the Guardian, gazing from one to another, admiringly.

"But we are!" cried Jinjur, stamping her foot, impatiently; "and we mean to conquer the Emerald City!"

"Good gracious!" returned the surprised Guardian of the Gates; "what a nonsensical idea! Go home to your mothers, my good girls, and milk the cows and bake the bread. Don't you know it's a dangerous thing to conquer a city?"

"We are not afraid!" responded the General; and she looked so determined that it made the Guardian uneasy.

So he rang the bell for the Soldier with the Green Whiskers, and the next minute was sorry he had done so. For immediately he was surrounded by a crowd of girls who drew the knitting-needles from their hair and began Jabbing them at the Guardian with the sharp points dangerously near his fat cheeks and blinking eyes.

The poor man howled loudly for mercy and made no resistance when Jinjur drew the bunch of keys from around his neck.

Followed by her Army the General now rushed to the gateway, where she was confronted by the Royal Army of Oz—which was the other name for the Soldier with the Green Whiskers.

"Halt!" he cried, and pointed his long gun full in the face of the leader.

Some of the girls screamed and ran back, but General Jinjur bravely stood her ground and said, reproachfully:

"Why, how now? Would you shoot a poor, defenceless girl?"

"No," replied the soldier. "for my gun isn't loaded."

"Not loaded?"

"No; for fear of accidents. And I've forgotten where I hid the powder and shot to load it with. But if you'll wait a short time I'll try to hunt them up."

"Don't trouble yourself," said Jinjur, cheerfully. Then she turned to her Army and cried:

"Girls, the gun isn't loaded!"

"Hooray," shrieked the rebels, delighted at this good news, and they proceeded to rush upon the Soldier with the Green Whiskers in such a crowd that it was a wonder they didn't stick the knitting-needles into one another.

But the Royal Army of Oz was too much afraid of women to meet the onslaught. He simply turned about and ran with all his might through the gate and toward the royal palace, while General Jinjur and her mob flocked into the unprotected City.

In this way was the Emerald City captured without a drop of blood being spilled. The Army of Revolt had become an Army of Conquerors!

Chapter 9

THE SCARECROW PLANS AN ESCAPE

Tip slipped away from the girls and followed swiftly after the Soldier with the Green Whiskers. The invading army entered the City more slowly, for they stopped to dig emeralds out of the walls and paving-stones with the points of their knitting-needles. So the Soldier and the boy reached the palace before the news had spread that the City was conquered.

The Scarecrow and Jack Pumpkinhead were still playing at quoits in the courtyard when the game was interrupted by the abrupt entrance of the Royal Army of Oz, who came flying in without his hat or gun, his clothes in sad disarray and his long beard floating a yard behind him as he ran.

"Tally one for me," said the Scarecrow, calmly "What's wrong, my man?" he added, addressing the Soldier.

"Oh! your Majesty—your Majesty! The City is conquered!" gasped the Royal Army, who was all out of breath.

"This is quite sudden," said the Scarecrow. "But please go and bar all the doors and windows of the palace, while I show this Pumpkinhead how to throw a quoit."

The Soldier hastened to do this, while Tip, who had arrived at his heels, remained in the courtyard to look at the Scarecrow with wondering eyes.

His Majesty continued to throw the quoits as coolly as if no danger threatened his throne, but the Pumpkinhead, having caught sight of Tip, ambled toward the boy as fast as his wooden legs would go.

"Good afternoon, noble parent!" he cried, delightedly. "I'm glad to see you are here. That terrible Saw-Horse ran away with me."

"I suspected it," said Tip. "Did you get hurt? Are you cracked at all?"

"No, I arrived safely," answered Jack, "and his Majesty has been very kind indeed to me."

At this moment the Soldier with the Green Whiskers returned, and the Scarecrow asked:

"By the way, who has conquered me?"

"A regiment of girls, gathered from the four corners of the Land of Oz," replied the Soldier, still pale with fear.

"But where was my Standing Army at the time?" inquired his Majesty, looking at the Soldier, gravely.

"Your Standing Army was running," answered the fellow, honestly; "for no man could face the terrible weapons of the invaders."

"Well," said the Scarecrow, after a moment's thought, "I don't mind much the loss of my throne, for it's a tiresome job to rule over the Emerald City. And this crown is so heavy that it makes my head ache. But I hope the Conquerors have no intention of injuring me, just because I happen to be the King."

"I heard them, say" remarked Tip, with some hesitation, "that they intend to make a rag carpet of your outside and stuff their sofa-cushions with your inside."

"Then I am really in danger," declared his Majesty, positively, "and it will be wise for me to consider a means to escape."

"Where can you go?" asked Jack Pumpkinhead.

"Why, to my friend the Tin Woodman, who rules over the Winkies, and calls himself their Emperor," was the answer. "I am sure he will protect me."

Tip was looking out the window.

"The palace is surrounded by the enemy," said he. "It is too late to escape. They would soon tear you to pieces."

The Scarecrow sighed.

"In an emergency," he announced, "it is always a good thing to pause and reflect. Please excuse me while I pause and reflect."

"But we also are in danger," said the Pumpkinhead, anxiously. "If any of these girls understand cooking, my end is not far off!"

"Nonsense!" exclaimed the Scarecrow. "they're too busy to cook, even if they know how!"

"But should I remain here a prisoner for any length of time," protested Jack, "I'm liable to spoil."

"Ah! then you would not be fit to associate with," returned the Scarecrow. "The matter is more serious than I suspected."

"You," said the Pumpkinhead, gloomily, "are liable to live for many years. My life is necessarily short. So I must take advantage of the few days that remain to me."

"There, there! Don't worry," answered the Scarecrow soothingly; "if you'll keep quiet long enough for me to think, I'll try to find some way for us all to escape."

So the others waited in patient silence while the Scarecrow walked to a corner and stood with his face to the wall for a good five minutes. At the end of that time he faced them with a more cheerful expression upon his painted face.

"Where is the Saw-Horse you rode here?" he asked the Pumpkinhead.

"Why, I said he was a jewel, and so your man locked him up in the royal treasury," said Jack.

"It was the only place I could think of your Majesty," added the Soldier, fearing he had made a blunder.

"It pleases me very much," said the Scarecrow. "Has the animal been fed?"

"Oh, yes; I gave him a heaping peck of sawdust."

"Excellent!" cried the Scarecrow. "Bring the horse here at once."

The Soldier hastened away, and presently they heard the clattering of the horse's wooden legs upon the pavement as he was led into the courtyard.

His Majesty regarded the steed critically. "He doesn't seem especially graceful!" he remarked, musingly. "but I suppose he can run?"

"He can, indeed," said Tip, gazing upon the Saw-Horse admiringly.

"Then, bearing us upon his back, he must make a dash through the ranks of the rebels and carry us to my friend the Tin Woodman," announced the Scarecrow.

"He can't carry four!" objected Tip.

"No, but he may be induced to carry three," said his Majesty. "I shall therefore leave my Royal Army Behind. For, from the ease with which he was conquered, I have little confidence in his powers."

"Still, he can run," declared Tip, laughing.

"I expected this blow" said the Soldier, sulkily; "but I can bear it. I shall disguise myself by cutting off my lovely green whiskers. And, after all, it is no more dangerous to face those reckless girls than to ride this fiery, untamed wooden horse!"

"Perhaps you are right," observed his Majesty. "But, for my part, not being a soldier, I am fond of danger. Now, my boy, you must mount first. And please sit as close to the horse's neck as possible."

Tip climbed quickly to his place, and the Soldier and the Scarecrow managed to hoist the Pumpkinhead to a seat just behind him. There remained so little space for the King that he was liable to fall off as soon as the horse started.

"Fetch a clothesline," said the King to his Army, "and tie us all together. Then if one falls off we will all fall off."

And while the Soldier was gone for the clothesline his Majesty continued, "it is well for me to be careful, for my very existence is in danger."

"I have to be as careful as you do," said Jack.

"Not exactly," replied the Scarecrow. "for if anything happened to me, that would be the end of me. But if anything happened to you, they could use you for seed."

The Soldier now returned with a long line and tied all three firmly together, also lashing them to the body of the Saw-Horse; so there seemed little danger of their tumbling off.

"Now throw open the gates," commanded the Scarecrow, "and we will make a dash to liberty or to death."

The courtyard in which they were standing was located in the center of the great palace, which surrounded it on all sides. But in one place a passage led to an outer gateway, which the Soldier had barred by order of his sovereign. It was through this gateway his Majesty proposed to escape, and the Royal Army now led the Saw-Horse along the passage and unbarred the gate, which swung backward with a loud crash.

"Now," said Tip to the horse, "you must save us all. Run as fast as you can for the gate of the City, and don't let anything stop you."

"All right!" answered the Saw-Horse, gruffly, and dashed away so suddenly that Tip had to gasp for breath and hold firmly to the post he had driven into the creature's neck.

Several of the girls, who stood outside guarding the palace, were knocked over by the Saw-Horse's mad rush. Others ran screaming out of the way, and only one or two jabbed their knitting-needles frantically at the escaping prisoners. Tip got one small prick in his left arm, which smarted for an hour afterward; but the needles had no effect upon the Scarecrow or Jack Pumpkinhead, who never even suspected they were being prodded.

As for the Saw-Horse, he made a wonderful record upsetting a fruit cart, overturning several meek looking men, and finally bowling over the new Guardian of the Gate—a fussy little fat woman appointed by General Jinjur.

Nor did the impetuous charger stop then. Once outside the walls of the Emerald City he dashed along the road to the West with fast and violent leaps that shook the breath out of the boy and filled the Scarecrow with wonder.

Jack had ridden at this mad rate once before, so he devoted every effort to holding, with both hands, his pumpkin head upon its stick, enduring meantime the dreadful jolting with the courage of a philosopher.

"Slow him up! Slow him up!" shouted the Scarecrow. "My straw is all shaking down into my legs."

But Tip had no breath to speak, so the Saw-Horse continued his wild career unchecked and with unabated speed.

Presently they came to the banks of a wide river, and without a pause the wooden steed gave one final leap and launched them all in mid-air.

A second later they were rolling, splashing and bobbing about in the water, the horse struggling frantically to find a rest for its feet and its riders being first plunged beneath the rapid current and then floating upon the surface like corks.

⊶━━━━━━━⊷

Chapter 10

THE JOURNEY TO THE TIN WOODMAN

Tip was well soaked and dripping water from every angle of his body. But he managed to lean forward and shout in the ear of the Saw-Horse:

"Keep still, you fool! Keep still!"

The horse at once ceased struggling and floated calmly upon the surface, its wooden body being as buoyant as a raft.

"What does that word 'fool' mean?" enquired the horse.

"It is a term of reproach," answered Tip, somewhat ashamed of the expression. "I only use it when I am angry."

"Then it pleases me to be able to call you a fool, in return," said the horse. "For I did not make the river, nor put it in our way; so only a term of, reproach is fit for one who becomes angry with me for falling into the water."

"That is quite evident," replied Tip; "so I will acknowledge myself in the wrong." Then he called out to the Pumpkinhead: "are you all right, Jack?"

There was no reply. So the boy called to the King "are you all right, your majesty?"

The Scarecrow groaned.

"I'm all wrong, somehow," he said, in a weak voice. "How very wet this water is!"

Tip was bound so tightly by the cord that he could not turn his head to look at his companions; so he said to the Saw-Horse:

"Paddle with your legs toward the shore."

The horse obeyed, and although their progress was slow they finally reached the opposite river bank at a place where it was low enough to enable the creature to scramble upon dry land.

With some difficulty the boy managed to get his knife out of his pocket and cut the cords that bound the riders to one another and to the wooden horse. He heard the Scarecrow fall to the ground with a mushy sound, and then he himself quickly dismounted and looked at his friend Jack.

The wooden body, with its gorgeous clothing, still sat upright upon the horse's back; but the pumpkin head was gone, and only the sharpened stick that served for a neck was visible. As for the Scarecrow, the straw in his body had shaken down with the jolting and packed itself into his legs and the lower part of his body—which appeared very plump and round while his upper half seemed like an empty sack. Upon his head the Scarecrow still wore the heavy crown, which had been sewed on to prevent his losing it; but the head was now so damp and limp that the weight of the gold and jewels sagged forward and crushed the painted face into a mass of wrinkles that made him look exactly like a Japanese pug dog.

Tip would have laughed—had he not been so anxious about his man Jack. But the Scarecrow, however damaged, was all there, while the pumpkin head that was so necessary to Jack's existence was missing; so the boy seized a long pole that fortunately lay near at hand and anxiously turned again toward the river.

Far out upon the waters he sighted the golden hue of the pumpkin, which gently bobbed up and down with the motion of the waves. At that moment it was quite out of Tip's reach, but after a time it floated nearer and still nearer until the boy was able to reach it with his pole and draw it to the shore. Then he brought it to the top of the bank, carefully wiped the water from its pumpkin face with his handkerchief, and ran with it to Jack and replaced the head upon the man's neck.

"Dear me!" were Jack's first words. "What a dreadful experience! I wonder if water is liable to spoil pumpkins?"

Tip did not think a reply was necessary, for he knew that the Scarecrow also stood in need of his help. So he carefully removed the straw from the King's body and legs, and spread it out in the sun to dry. The wet clothing he hung over the body of the Saw-Horse.

"If water spoils pumpkins," observed Jack, with a deep sigh, "then my days are numbered."

"I've never noticed that water spoils pumpkins," returned Tip; "unless the water happens to be boiling. If your head isn't cracked, my friend, you must be in fairly good condition."

"Oh, my head isn't cracked in the least," declared Jack, more cheerfully.

"Then don't worry," retorted the boy. "Care once killed a cat."

"Then," said Jack, seriously, "I am very glad indeed that I am not a cat."

The sun was fast drying their clothing, and Tip stirred up his Majesty's straw so that the warm rays might absorb the moisture and make it as crisp and dry as ever. When this had been accomplished he stuffed the Scarecrow into symmetrical shape and smoothed out his face so that he wore his usual gay and charming expression.

"Thank you very much," said the monarch, brightly, as he walked about and found himself to be well balanced. "There are several distinct advantages in being a Scarecrow. For if one has friends near at hand to repair damages, nothing very serious can happen to you."

"I wonder if hot sunshine is liable to crack pumpkins," said Jack, with an anxious ring in his voice.

"Not at all—not at all!" replied the Scarecrow, gaily. "All you need fear, my boy, is old age. When your golden youth has decayed we shall quickly part company—but you needn't look forward to it; we'll discover the fact ourselves, and notify you. But come! Let us resume our journey. I am anxious to greet my friend the Tin Woodman."

So they remounted the Saw-Horse, Tip holding to the post, the Pumpkinhead clinging to Tip, and the Scarecrow with both arms around the wooden form of Jack.

"Go slowly, for now there is no danger of pursuit," said Tip to his steed.

"All right!" responded the creature, in a voice rather gruff.

"Aren't you a little hoarse?" asked the Pumpkinhead politely.

The Saw-Horse gave an angry prance and rolled one knotty eye backward toward Tip.

"See here," he growled, "can't you protect me from insult?"

"To be sure!" answered Tip, soothingly. "I am sure Jack meant no harm. And it will not do for us to quarrel, you know; we must all remain good friends."

"I'll have nothing more to do with that Pumpkinhead," declared the Saw-Horse, viciously. "he loses his head too easily to suit me."

There seemed no fitting reply to this speech, so for a time they rode along in silence.

After a while the Scarecrow remarked:

"This reminds me of old times. It was upon this grassy knoll that I once saved Dorothy from the Stinging Bees of the Wicked Witch of the West."

"Do Stinging Bees injure pumpkins?" asked Jack, glancing around fearfully.

"They are all dead, so it doesn't matter," replied the Scarecrow. "And here is where Nick Chopper destroyed the Wicked Witch's Grey Wolves."

"Who was Nick Chopper?" asked Tip.

"That is the name of my friend the Tin Woodman, answered his Majesty. And here is where the Winged Monkeys captured and bound us, and flew away with little Dorothy," he continued, after they had traveled a little way farther.

"Do Winged Monkeys ever eat pumpkins?" asked Jack, with a shiver of fear.

"I do not know; but you have little cause to, worry, for the Winged Monkeys are now the slaves of Glinda the Good, who owns the Golden Cap that commands their services," said the Scarecrow, reflectively.

Then the stuffed monarch became lost in thought recalling the days of past adventures. And the Saw-Horse rocked and rolled over the flower-strewn fields and carried its riders swiftly upon their way.

Twilight fell, bye and bye, and then the dark shadows of night. So Tip stopped the horse and they all proceeded to dismount.

"I'm tired out," said the boy, yawning wearily; "and the grass is soft and cool. Let us lie down here and sleep until morning."

"I can't sleep," said Jack.

"I never do," said the Scarecrow.

"I do not even know what sleep is," said the Saw-Horse.

"Still, we must have consideration for this poor boy, who is made of flesh and blood and bone, and gets tired," suggested the Scarecrow, in his usual thoughtful manner. "I remember it was the same way with little Dorothy. We always had to sit through the night while she slept."

"I'm sorry," said Tip, meekly, "but I can't help it. And I'm dreadfully hungry, too!"

"Here is a new danger!" remarked Jack, gloomily. "I hope you are not fond of eating pumpkins."

"Not unless they're stewed and made into pies," answered the boy, laughing. "So have no fears of me, friend Jack."

"What a coward that Pumpkinhead is!" said the Saw-Horse, scornfully.

"You might be a coward yourself, if you knew you were liable to spoil!" retorted Jack, angrily.

"There!—there!" interrupted the Scarecrow; "don't let us quarrel. We all have our weaknesses, dear friends; so we must strive to be considerate of one another. And since this poor boy is hungry and has nothing whatever to eat, let us all remain quiet and allow him to sleep; for it is said that in sleep a mortal may forget even hunger."

"Thank you!" exclaimed Tip, gratefully. "Your Majesty is fully as good as you are wise—and that is saying a good deal!"

He then stretched himself upon the grass and, using the stuffed form of the Scarecrow for a pillow, was presently fast asleep.

Chapter 11

A NICKEL-PLATED EMPEROR

Tip awoke soon after dawn, but the Scarecrow had already risen and plucked, with his clumsy fingers, a double-handful of ripe berries from some bushes near by. These the boy ate greedily, finding them an ample breakfast, and afterward the little party resumed its Journey.

After an hour's ride they reached the summit of a hill from whence they espied the City of the Winkies and noted the tall domes of the Emperor's palace rising from the clusters of more modest dwellings.

The Scarecrow became greatly animated at this sight, and exclaimed:

"How delighted I shall be to see my old friend the Tin Woodman again! I hope that he rules his people more successfully than I have ruled mine!"

"Is the Tin Woodman the Emperor of the Winkies?" asked the horse.

"Yes, indeed. They invited him to rule over them soon after the Wicked Witch was destroyed; and as Nick Chopper has the best heart in all the world I am sure he has proved an excellent and able emperor."

"I thought that 'Emperor' was the title of a person who rules an empire," said Tip, "and the Country of the Winkies is only a Kingdom."

"Don't mention that to the Tin Woodman!" exclaimed the Scarecrow, earnestly. "You would hurt his feelings terribly. He is a proud man, as he has every reason to be, and it pleases him to be termed Emperor rather than King."

"I'm sure it makes no difference to me," replied the boy.

The Saw-Horse now ambled forward at a pace so fast that its riders had hard work to stick upon its back; so there was little further conversation until they drew up beside the palace steps.

An aged Winkie, dressed in a uniform of silver cloth, came forward to assist them to alight. Said the Scarecrow to his personage:

"Show us at once to your master, the Emperor."

The man looked from one to another of the party in an embarrassed way, and finally answered:

"I fear I must ask you to wait for a time. The Emperor is not receiving this morning."

"How is that?" enquired the Scarecrow, anxiously. "I hope nothing has happened to him."

"Oh, no; nothing serious," returned the man. "But this is his Majesty's day for being polished; and just now his august presence is thickly smeared with putz-pomade."

"Oh, I see!" cried the Scarecrow, greatly reassured. "My friend was ever inclined to be a dandy, and I suppose he is now more proud than ever of his personal appearance."

"He is, indeed," said the man, with a polite bow. "Our mighty Emperor has lately caused himself to be nickel-plated."

"Good Gracious!" the Scarecrow exclaimed at hearing this. "If his wit bears the same polish, how sparkling it must be! But show us in—I'm sure the Emperor will receive us, even in his present state"

"The Emperor's state is always magnificent," said the man. "But I will venture to tell him of your arrival, and will receive his commands concerning you."

So the party followed the servant into a splendid ante-room, and the Saw-Horse ambled awkwardly after them, having no knowledge that a horse might be expected to remain outside.

The travelers were at first somewhat awed by their surroundings, and even the Scarecrow seemed impressed as he examined the rich hangings of silver cloth caught up into knots and fastened with tiny silver axes. Upon a handsome center-table stood a large silver oil-can, richly engraved with scenes from the past adventures of the Tin Woodman, Dorothy, the Cowardly Lion and the Scarecrow: the lines of the engraving being traced upon the silver in yellow gold. On the walls hung several portraits, that of the Scarecrow seeming to be the most prominent and carefully executed, while a the large painting of the famous Wizard of Oz, in act of presenting the Tin Woodman with a heart, covered almost one entire end of the room.

While the visitors gazed at these things in silent admiration they suddenly heard a loud voice in the next room exclaim:

"Well! well! well! What a great surprise!"

And then the door burst open and Nick Chopper rushed into their midst and caught the Scarecrow in a close and loving embrace that creased him into many folds and wrinkles.

"My dear old friend! My noble comrade!" cried the Tin Woodman, joyfully. "how delighted! I am to meet you once again."

And then he released the Scarecrow and held him at arms' length while he surveyed the beloved, painted features.

But, alas! the face of the Scarecrow and many portions of his body bore great blotches of putz-pomade; for the Tin Woodman, in his eagerness to welcome his friend, had quite forgotten the condition of his toilet and had rubbed the thick coating of paste from his own body to that of his comrade.

"Dear me!" said the Scarecrow dolefully. "What a mess I'm in!"

"Never mind, my friend," returned the Tin Woodman, "I'll send you to my Imperial Laundry, and you'll come out as good as new."

"Won't I be mangled?" asked the Scarecrow.

"No, indeed!" was the reply. "But tell me, how came your Majesty here? and who are your companions?"

The Scarecrow, with great politeness, introduced Tip and Jack Pumpkinhead, and the latter personage seemed to interest the Tin Woodman greatly.

"You are not very substantial, I must admit," said the Emperor. "but you are certainly unusual, and therefore worthy to become a member of our select society."

"I thank your Majesty," said Jack, humbly.

"I hope you are enjoying good health?" continued the Woodman.

"At present, yes;" replied the Pumpkinhead, with a sigh; "but I am in constant terror of the day when I shall spoil."

"Nonsense!" said the Emperor—but in a kindly, sympathetic tone. "Do not, I beg of you, dampen today's sun with the showers of tomorrow. For before your head has time to spoil you can have it canned, and in that way it may be preserved indefinitely."

Tip, during this conversation, was looking at the Woodman with undisguised amazement, and noticed that the celebrated Emperor of the Winkies was composed entirely of pieces of tin, neatly soldered and riveted together into the form of a man. He rattled and clanked a little, as he moved, but in the main he seemed to be most cleverly constructed, and his appearance was only marred by the thick coating of polishing-paste that covered him from head to foot.

The boy's intent gaze caused the Tin Woodman to remember that he was not in the most presentable condition, so he begged his friends to excuse him while he retired to his private apartment and allowed his servants to polish him. This was accomplished in a short time, and when the emperor returned his nickel-plated body shone so magnificently that the Scarecrow heartily congratulated him on his improved appearance.

"That nickel-plate was, I confess, a happy thought," said Nick; "and it was the more necessary because I had become somewhat scratched during my adventurous experiences. You will observe this engraved star upon my left breast. It not only indicates where my excellent heart lies, but covers very neatly the patch made by the Wonderful Wizard when he placed that valued organ in my breast with his own skillful hands."

"Is your heart, then, a hand-organ?" asked the Pumpkinhead, curiously.

"By no means," responded the emperor, with dignity. "It is, I am convinced, a strictly orthodox heart, although somewhat larger and warmer than most people possess."

Then he turned to the Scarecrow and asked:

"Are your subjects happy and contented, my dear friend?"

"I cannot, say" was the reply. "for the girls of Oz have risen in revolt and driven me out of the emerald City."

"Great Goodness!" cried the Tin Woodman, "What a calamity! They surely do not complain of your wise and gracious rule?"

"No; but they say it is a poor rule that don't work both ways," answered the Scarecrow; "and these females are also of the opinion that men have ruled the land long enough. So they have captured my city, robbed the treasury of all its jewels, and are running things to suit themselves."

"Dear me! What an extraordinary idea!" cried the Emperor, who was both shocked and surprised.

"And I heard some of them say," said Tip, "that they intend to march here and capture the castle and city of the Tin Woodman."

"Ah! we must not give them time to do that," said the Emperor, quickly; "we will go at once and recapture the Emerald City and place the Scarecrow again upon his throne."

"I was sure you would help me," remarked the Scarecrow in a pleased voice. "How large an army can you assemble?"

"We do not need an army," replied the Woodman. "We four, with the aid of my gleaming axe, are enough to strike terror into the hearts of the rebels."

"We five," corrected the Pumpkinhead.

"Five?" repeated the Tin Woodman.

"Yes; the Saw-Horse is brave and fearless," answered Jack, forgetting his recent quarrel with the quadruped.

The Tin Woodman looked around him in a puzzled way, for the Saw-Horse had until now remained quietly standing in a corner, where the Emperor had not noticed him. Tip immediately called the odd-looking creature to them, and it approached so awkwardly that it nearly upset the beautiful center-table and the engraved oil-can.

"I begin to think," remarked the Tin Woodman as he looked earnestly at the Saw-Horse, "that wonders will never cease! How came this creature alive?"

"I did it with a magic powder," modestly asserted the boy. "and the Saw-Horse has been very useful to us."

"He enabled us to escape the rebels," added the Scarecrow.

"Then we must surely accept him as a comrade," declared the emperor. "A live Saw-Horse is a distinct novelty, and should prove an interesting study. Does he know anything?"

"Well, I cannot claim any great experience in life," the Saw-Horse answered for himself. "but I seem to learn very quickly, and often it occurs to me that I know more than any of those around me."

"Perhaps you do," said the emperor; "for experience does not always mean wisdom. But time is precious just now, so let us quickly make preparations to start upon our Journey."

The emperor called his Lord High Chancellor and instructed him how to run the kingdom during his absence. Meanwhile the Scarecrow was taken apart and the painted sack that served him for a head was carefully laundered and restuffed with the brains originally given him by the great Wizard. His clothes were also cleaned and pressed by the Imperial tailors, and his crown polished and again sewed upon his head, for the Tin Woodman insisted he should not renounce this badge of royalty. The Scarecrow now presented a very respectable appearance, and although in no way addicted to vanity he was quite pleased with himself and strutted a trifle as he walked. While this was being done Tip mended the wooden limbs of Jack Pumpkinhead and made them stronger than before, and the Saw-Horse was also inspected to see if he was in good working order.

Then bright and early the next morning they set out upon the return Journey to the emerald City, the Tin Woodman bearing upon his shoulder a gleaming axe and leading the way, while the Pumpkinhead rode upon the Saw-Horse and Tip and the Scarecrow walked upon either side to make sure that he didn't fall off or become damaged.

Chapter 12

MR. H. M. WOGGLE-BUG, T. E.

Now, General Jinjur—who, you will remember, commanded the Army of Revolt—was rendered very uneasy by the escape of the Scarecrow from the Emerald City. She feared, and with good reason, that if his Majesty and the Tin Woodman Joined forces, it would mean danger to her and her entire army; for the people of Oz had not yet forgotten the deeds of these famous heroes, who had passed successfully through so many startling adventures.

So Jinjur sent post-haste for old Mombi, the witch, and promised her large rewards if she would come to the assistance of the rebel army.

Mombi was furious at the trick Tip had played upon her as well as at his escape and the theft of the precious Powder of Life; so she needed no urging to induce her to travel to the Emerald City to assist Jinjur in defeating the Scarecrow and the Tin Woodman, who had made Tip one of their friends.

Mombi had no sooner arrived at the royal palace than she discovered, by means of her secret magic, that the adventurers were starting upon their Journey to the Emerald City; so she retired to a small room high up in a tower and locked herself in while she practised such arts as she could command to prevent the return of the Scarecrow and his companions.

That was why the Tin Woodman presently stopped and said:

"Something very curious has happened. I ought to know by heart and every step of this Journey, yet I fear we have already lost our way."

"That is quite impossible!" protested the Scarecrow. "Why do you think, my dear friend, that we have gone astray?"

"Why, here before us is a great field of sunflowers—and I never saw this field before in all my life."

At these words they all looked around, only to find that they were indeed surrounded by a field of tall stalks, every stalk bearing at its top a gigantic sunflower. And not only were these flowers almost blinding in their vivid hues of red and gold, but each one whirled around upon its stalk like a miniature wind-mill, completely dazzling the vision of the beholders and so mystifying them that they knew not which way to turn.

"It's witchcraft!" exclaimed Tip.

While they paused, hesitating and wondering, the Tin Woodman uttered a cry of impatience and advanced with swinging axe to cut down the stalks before him. But now the sunflowers suddenly stopped their rapid whirling, and the travelers plainly saw a girl's face appear in the center of each flower. These lovely faces looked upon the astonished band with mocking smiles, and then burst into a chorus of merry laughter at the dismay their appearance caused.

"Stop! stop!" cried Tip, seizing the Woodman's arm; "they're alive! they're girls!"

At that moment the flowers began whirling again, and the faces faded away and were lost in the rapid revolutions.

The Tin Woodman dropped his axe and sat down upon the ground.

"It would be heartless to chop down those pretty creatures," said he, despondently. "and yet I do not know how else we can proceed upon our way"

"They looked to me strangely like the faces of the Army of Revolt," mused the Scarecrow. "But I cannot conceive how the girls could have followed us here so quickly."

"I believe it's magic," said Tip, positively, "and that someone is playing a trick upon us. I've known old Mombi do things like that before. Probably it's nothing more than an illusion, and there are no sunflowers here at all."

"Then let us shut our eyes and walk forward," suggested the Woodman.

"Excuse me," replied the Scarecrow. "My eyes are not painted to shut. Because you happen to have tin eyelids, you must not imagine we are all built in the same way."

"And the eyes of the Saw-Horse are knot eyes," said Jack, leaning forward to examine them.

"Nevertheless, you must ride quickly forward," commanded Tip, "and we will follow after you and so try to escape. My eyes are already so dazzled that I can scarcely see."

So the Pumpkinhead rode boldly forward, and Tip grasped the stub tail of the Saw-Horse and followed with closed eyes. The Scarecrow and the Tin Woodman brought up the rear, and before they had gone many yards a joyful shout from Jack announced that the way was clear before them.

Then all paused to look backward, but not a trace of the field of sunflowers remained.

More cheerfully, now they proceeded upon their Journey; but old Mombi had so changed the appearance of the landscape that they would surely have been lost had not the Scarecrow wisely concluded to take their direction from the sun. For no witchcraft could change the course of the sun, and it was therefore a safe guide.

However, other difficulties lay before them. The Saw-Horse stepped into a rabbit hole and fell to the ground. The Pumpkinhead was pitched high into the air, and his history would probably have ended at that exact moment had not the Tin Woodman skillfully caught the pumpkin as it descended and saved it from injury.

Tip soon had it fitted to the neck again and replaced Jack upon his feet. But the Saw-Horse did not escape so easily. For when his leg was pulled from the rabbit hole it was found to be broken short off, and must be replaced or repaired before he could go a step farther.

"This is quite serious," said the Tin Woodman. "If there were trees near by I might soon manufacture another leg for this animal; but I cannot see even a shrub for miles around."

"And there are neither fences nor houses in this part of the land of Oz," added the Scarecrow, disconsolately.

"Then what shall we do?" enquired the boy.

"I suppose I must start my brains working," replied his Majesty the Scarecrow; "for experience has, taught me that I can do anything if I but take time to think it out."

"Let us all think," said Tip; "and perhaps we shall find a way to repair the Saw-Horse."

So they sat in a row upon the grass and began to think, while the Saw-Horse occupied itself by gazing curiously upon its broken limb.

"Does it hurt?" asked the Tin Woodman, in a soft, sympathetic voice.

"Not in the least," returned the Saw-Horse; "but my pride is injured to find that my anatomy is so brittle."

For a time the little group remained in silent thought. Presently the Tin Woodman raised his head and looked over the fields.

"What sort of creature is that which approaches us?" he asked, wonderingly.

The others followed his gaze, and discovered coming toward them the most extraordinary object they had ever beheld. It advanced quickly and noiselessly over the soft grass and in a few minutes stood before the adventurers and regarded them with an astonishment equal to their own.

The Scarecrow was calm under all circumstances.

"Good morning!" he said, politely.

The stranger removed his hat with a flourish, bowed very low, and then responded:

"Good morning, one and all. I hope you are, as an aggregation, enjoying excellent health. Permit me to present my card."

With this courteous speech it extended a card toward the Scarecrow, who accepted it, turned it over and over, and handed it with a shake of his head to Tip.

The boy read aloud:

"MR. H. M. WOGGLE-BUG, T. E."

"Dear me!" ejaculated the Pumpkinhead, staring somewhat intently.

"How very peculiar!" said the Tin Woodman.

Tip's eyes were round and wondering, and the Saw-Horse uttered a sigh and turned away its head.

"Are you really a Woggle-Bug?" enquired the Scarecrow.

"Most certainly, my dear sir!" answered the stranger, briskly. "Is not my name upon the card?"

"It is," said the Scarecrow. "But may I ask what 'H. M.' stands for?"

"'H. M.' means Highly Magnified," returned the Woggle-Bug, proudly.

"Oh, I see." The Scarecrow viewed the stranger critically. "And are you, in truth, highly magnified?"

"Sir," said the Woggle-Bug, "I take you for a gentleman of judgment and discernment. Does it not occur to you that I am several thousand times greater than any Woggle-Bug you ever saw before? Therefore it is plainly evident that I am Highly Magnified, and there is no good reason why you should doubt the fact."

"Pardon me," returned the Scarecrow. "My brains are slightly mixed since I was last laundered. Would it be improper for me to ask, also, what the 'T.E.' at the end of your name stands for?"

"Those letters express my degree," answered the Woggle-Bug, with a condescending smile. "To be more explicit, the initials mean that I am Thoroughly Educated."

"Oh!" said the Scarecrow, much relieved.

Tip had not yet taken his eyes off this wonderful personage. What he saw was a great, round, buglike body supported upon two slender legs which ended in delicate feet—the toes curling upward. The body of the Woggle-Bug was rather flat, and judging from what could be seen of it was of a glistening dark brown color upon the back, while the front was striped with alternate bands of light brown and white, blending together at the edges. Its arms were fully as slender as its legs, and upon a rather long neck was perched its head—not unlike the head of a man, except that its nose ended in a curling antenna, or "feeler," and its ears from the upper points bore antennae that decorated the sides of its head like two miniature, curling pig tails. It must be admitted that the round, black eyes were rather bulging in appearance; but the expression upon the Woggle-Bug's face was by no means unpleasant.

For dress the insect wore a dark-blue swallowtail coat with a yellow silk lining and a flower in the button-hole; a vest of white duck that stretched tightly across the wide body; knickerbockers of fawn-colored plush, fastened at the knees with gilt buckles; and, perched upon its small head, was jauntily set a tall silk hat.

Standing upright before our amazed friends the Woggle-Bug appeared to be fully as tall as the Tin Woodman; and surely no bug in all the Land of Oz had ever before attained so enormous a size.

"I confess," said the Scarecrow, "that your abrupt appearance has caused me surprise, and no doubt has startled my companions. I hope, however, that this circumstance will not distress you. We shall probably get used to you in time."

"Do not apologize, I beg of you!" returned the Woggle-Bug, earnestly. "It affords me great pleasure to surprise people; for surely I cannot be classed with ordinary insects and am entitled to both curiosity and admiration from those I meet."

"You are, indeed," agreed his Majesty.

"If you will permit me to seat myself in your august company," continued the stranger, "I will gladly relate my history, so that you will be better able to comprehend my unusual—may I say remarkable?—appearance."

"You may say what you please," answered the Tin Woodman, briefly.

So the Woggle-Bug sat down upon the grass, facing the little group of wanderers, and told them the following story:

Chapter 13

A HIGHLY MAGNIFIED HISTORY

"It is but honest that I should acknowledge at the beginning of my recital that I was born an ordinary Woggle-Bug," began the creature, in a frank and friendly tone. "Knowing no better, I used my arms as well as my legs for walking, and crawled under the edges of stones or hid among the roots of grasses with no thought beyond finding a few insects smaller than myself to feed upon.

"The chill nights rendered me stiff and motionless, for I wore no clothing, but each morning the warm rays of the sun gave me new life and restored me to activity. A horrible existence is this, but you must remember it is the regular ordained existence of Woggle-Bugs, as well as of many other tiny creatures that inhabit the earth.

"But Destiny had singled me out, humble though I was, for a grander fate! One day I crawled near to a country school house, and my curiosity being excited by the monotonous hum of the students within, I made bold to enter and creep along a crack between two boards until I reached the far end, where, in front of a hearth of glowing embers, sat the master at his desk.

"No one noticed so small a creature as a Woggle-Bug, and when I found that the hearth was even warmer and more comfortable than the sunshine, I resolved to establish my future home beside it. So I found a charming nest between two bricks and hid myself therein for many, many months.

"Professor Nowitall is, doubtless, the most famous scholar in the land of Oz, and after a few days I began to listen to the lectures and discourses he gave his pupils. Not one of them was more attentive than the humble, unnoticed Woggle-Bug, and

I acquired in this way a fund of knowledge that I will myself confess is simply marvelous. That is why I place 'T.E.' Thoroughly Educated upon my cards; for my greatest pride lies in the fact that the world cannot produce another Woggle-Bug with a tenth part of my own culture and erudition."

"I do not blame you," said the Scarecrow. "Education is a thing to be proud of. I'm educated myself. The mess of brains given me by the Great Wizard is considered by my friends to be unexcelled."

"Nevertheless," interrupted the Tin Woodman, "a good heart is, I believe, much more desirable than education or brains."

"To me," said the Saw-Horse, "a good leg is more desirable than either."

"Could seeds be considered in the light of brains?" enquired the Pumpkinhead, abruptly.

"Keep quiet!" commanded Tip, sternly.

"Very well, dear father," answered the obedient Jack.

The Woggle-Bug listened patiently—even respectfully—to these remarks, and then resumed his story.

"I must have lived fully three years in that secluded school-house hearth," said he, "drinking thirstily of the ever-flowing fount of limpid knowledge before me."

"Quite poetical," commented the Scarecrow, nodding his head approvingly.

"But one, day" continued the Bug, "a marvelous circumstance occurred that altered my very existence and brought me to my present pinnacle of greatness. The Professor discovered me in the act of crawling across the hearth, and before I could escape he had caught me between his thumb and forefinger.

"'My dear children,' said he, 'I have captured a Woggle-Bug—a very rare and interesting specimen. Do any of you know what a Woggle-Bug is?'

"'No!' yelled the scholars, in chorus.

"'Then,' said the Professor, 'I will get out my famous magnifying-glass and throw the insect upon a screen in a highly-magnified condition, that you may all study carefully its peculiar construction and become acquainted with its habits and manner of life.'

"He then brought from a cupboard a most curious instrument, and before I could realize what had happened I found myself thrown upon a screen in a highly-magnified state—even as you now behold me.

"The students stood up on their stools and craned their heads forward to get a better view of me, and two little girls jumped upon the sill of an open window where they could see more plainly.

"'Behold!' cried the Professor, in a loud voice, 'this highly-magnified Woggle-Bug; one of the most curious insects in existence!'

"Being Thoroughly Educated, and knowing what is required of a cultured gentleman, at this juncture I stood upright and, placing my hand upon my bosom, made a very polite bow. My action, being unexpected, must have startled them, for one of the little girls perched upon the window-sill gave a scream and fell backward out the window, drawing her companion with her as she disappeared.

"The Professor uttered a cry of horror and rushed away through the door to see if the poor children were injured by the fall. The scholars followed after him in a wild mob, and I was left alone in the school-room, still in a Highly-Magnified state and free to do as I pleased.

"It immediately occurred to me that this was a good opportunity to escape. I was proud of my great size, and realized that now I could safely travel anywhere in the world, while my superior culture would make me a fit associate for the most learned person I might chance to meet.

"So, while the Professor picked the little girls—who were more frightened than hurt—off the ground, and the pupils clustered around him closely grouped, I calmly walked out of the school-house, turned a corner, and escaped unnoticed to a grove of trees that stood near"

"Wonderful!" exclaimed the Pumpkinhead, admiringly.

"It was, indeed," agreed the Woggle-Bug. "I have never ceased to congratulate myself for escaping while I was Highly Magnified; for even my excessive knowledge would have proved of little use to me had I remained a tiny, insignificant insect."

"I didn't know before," said Tip, looking at the Woggle-Bug with a puzzled expression, "that insects wore clothes."

"Nor do they, in their natural state," returned the stranger. "But in the course of my wanderings I had the good fortune to save the ninth life of a tailor—tailors having, like cats, nine lives, as you probably know. The fellow was exceedingly grateful, for had he lost that ninth life it would have been the end of him; so he begged permission to furnish me with the stylish costume I now wear. It fits very nicely, does it not?" and the Woggle-Bug stood up and turned himself around slowly, that all might examine his person.

"He must have been a good tailor," said the Scarecrow, somewhat enviously.

"He was a good-hearted tailor, at any rate," observed Nick Chopper.

"But where were you going, when you met us?" Tip asked the Woggle-Bug.

"Nowhere in particular," was the reply, "although it is my intention soon to visit the Emerald City and arrange to give a course of lectures to select audiences on the 'Advantages of Magnification.'"

"We are bound for the Emerald City now," said the Tin Woodman; "so, if it pleases you to do so, you are welcome to travel in our company."

The Woggle-Bug bowed with profound grace.

"It will give me great pleasure," said he "to accept your kind invitation; for nowhere in the Land of Oz could I hope to meet with so congenial a company."

"That is true," acknowledged the Pumpkinhead. "We are quite as congenial as flies and honey."

"But—pardon me if I seem inquisitive—are you not all rather—ahem! rather unusual?" asked the Woggle-Bug, looking from one to another with unconcealed interest.

"Not more so than yourself," answered the Scarecrow. "Everything in life is unusual until you get accustomed to it."

"What rare philosophy!" exclaimed the Woggle-Bug, admiringly.

"Yes; my brains are working well today," admitted the Scarecrow, an accent of pride in his voice.

"Then, if you are sufficiently rested and refreshed, let us bend our steps toward the Emerald City," suggested the magnified one.

"We can't," said Tip. "The Saw-Horse has broken a leg, so he can't bend his steps. And there is no wood around to make him a new limb from. And we can't leave the horse behind because the Pumpkinhead is so stiff in his Joints that he has to ride."

"How very unfortunate!" cried the Woggle-Bug. Then he looked the party over carefully and said:

"If the Pumpkinhead is to ride, why not use one of his legs to make a leg for the horse that carries him? I judge that both are made of wood."

"Now, that is what I call real cleverness," said the Scarecrow, approvingly. "I wonder my brains did not think of that long ago! Get to work, my dear Nick, and fit the Pumpkinhead's leg to the Saw-Horse."

Jack was not especially pleased with this idea; but he submitted to having his left leg amputated by the Tin Woodman and whittled down to fit the left leg of the Saw-Horse. Nor was the Saw-Horse especially pleased with the operation, either; for he growled a good deal about being "butchered," as he called it, and afterward declared that the new leg was a disgrace to a respectable Saw-Horse.

"I beg you to be more careful in your speech," said the Pumpkinhead, sharply. "Remember, if you please, that it is my leg you are abusing."

"I cannot forget it," retorted the Saw-Horse, "for it is quite as flimsy as the rest of your person."

"Flimsy! me flimsy!" cried Jack, in a rage. "How dare you call me flimsy?"

"Because you are built as absurdly as a jumping-jack," sneered the horse, rolling his knotty eyes in a vicious manner. "Even your head won't stay straight, and you never can tell whether you are looking backwards or forwards!"

"Friends, I entreat you not to quarrel!" pleaded the Tin Woodman, anxiously. "As a matter of fact, we are none of us above criticism; so let us bear with each others' faults."

"An excellent suggestion," said the Woggle-Bug, approvingly. "You must have an excellent heart, my metallic friend."

"I have," returned Nick, well pleased. "My heart is quite the best part of me. But now let us start upon our Journey.

They perched the one-legged Pumpkinhead upon the Saw-Horse, and tied him to his seat with cords, so that he could not possibly fall off.

And then, following the lead of the Scarecrow, they all advanced in the direction of the Emerald City.

Chapter 14

OLD MOMBI INDULGES IN WITCHCRAFT

THEY soon discovered that the Saw-Horse limped, for his new leg was a trifle too long. So they were obliged to halt while the Tin Woodman chopped it down with his axe, after which the wooden steed paced along more comfortably. But the Saw-Horse was not entirely satisfied, even yet.

"It was a shame that I broke my other leg!" it growled.

"On the contrary," airily remarked the Woggle-Bug, who was walking alongside, "you should consider the accident most fortunate. For a horse is never of much use until he has been broken."

"I beg your pardon," said Tip, rather provoked, for he felt a warm interest in both the Saw-Horse and his man Jack; "but permit me to say that your joke is a poor one, and as old as it is poor."

"Still, it is a Joke," declared the Woggle-Bug; firmly, "and a Joke derived from a play upon words is considered among educated people to be eminently proper."

"What does that mean?" enquired the Pumpkinhead, stupidly.

"It means, my dear friend," explained the Woggle-Bug, "that our language contains many words having a double meaning; and that to pronounce a joke that allows both meanings of a certain word, proves the joker a person of culture and refinement, who has, moreover, a thorough command of the language."

"I don't believe that," said Tip, plainly; "anybody can make a pun."

"Not so," rejoined the Woggle-Bug, stiffly. "It requires education of a high order. Are you educated, young sir?"

"Not especially," admitted Tip.

"Then you cannot judge the matter. I myself am Thoroughly Educated, and I say that puns display genius. For instance, were I to ride upon this Saw-Horse, he would not only be an animal he would become an equipage. For he would then be a horse-and-buggy."

At this the Scarecrow gave a gasp and the Tin Woodman stopped short and looked reproachfully at the Woggle-Bug. At the same time the Saw-Horse loudly snorted his derision; and even the Pumpkinhead put up his hand to hide the smile which, because it was carved upon his face, he could not change to a frown.

But the Woggle-Bug strutted along as if he had made some brilliant remark, and the Scarecrow was obliged to say:

"I have heard, my dear friend, that a person can become over-educated; and although I have a high respect for brains, no matter how they may be arranged or classified, I begin to suspect that yours are slightly tangled. In any event, I must beg you to restrain your superior education while in our society."

"We are not very particular," added the Tin Woodman; "and we are exceedingly kind hearted. But if your superior culture gets leaky again—" He did not complete the sentence, but he twirled his gleaming axe so carelessly that the Woggle-Bug looked frightened, and shrank away to a safe distance.

The others marched on in silence, and the Highly Magnified one, after a period of deep thought, said in an humble voice:

"I will endeavor to restrain myself."

"That is all we can expect," returned the Scarecrow pleasantly; and good nature being thus happily restored to the party, they proceeded upon their way.

When they again stopped to allow Tip to rest—the boy being the only one that seemed to tire—the Tin Woodman noticed many small, round holes in the grassy meadow.

"This must be a village of the Field Mice," he said to the Scarecrow. "I wonder if my old friend, the Queen of the Mice, is in this neighborhood."

"If she is, she may be of great service to us," answered the Scarecrow, who was impressed by a sudden thought. "See if you can call her, my dear Nick."

So the Tin Woodman blew a shrill note upon a silver whistle that hung around his neck, and presently a tiny grey mouse popped from a near-by hole and advanced fearlessly toward them. For the Tin Woodman had once saved her life, and the Queen of the Field Mice knew he was to be trusted.

"Good day, your Majesty," said Nick, politely addressing the mouse; "I trust you are enjoying good health?"

"Thank you, I am quite well," answered the Queen, demurely, as she sat up and displayed the tiny golden crown upon her head. "Can I do anything to assist my old friends?"

"You can, indeed," replied the Scarecrow, eagerly. "Let me, I intreat you, take a dozen of your subjects with me to the Emerald City."

"Will they be injured in any way?" asked the Queen, doubtfully.

"I think not," replied the Scarecrow. "I will carry them hidden in the straw which stuffs my body, and when I give them the signal by unbuttoning my jacket, they have only to rush out and scamper home again as fast as they can. By doing this they will assist me to regain my throne, which the Army of Revolt has taken from me."

"In that case," said the Queen, "I will not refuse your request. Whenever you are ready, I will call twelve of my most intelligent subjects."

"I am ready now" returned the Scarecrow. Then he lay flat upon the ground and unbuttoned his jacket, displaying the mass of straw with which he was stuffed.

The Queen uttered a little piping call, and in an instant a dozen pretty field mice had emerged from their holes and stood before their ruler, awaiting her orders.

What the Queen said to them none of our travelers could understand, for it was in the mouse language; but the field mice obeyed without hesitation, running one after the other to the Scarecrow and hiding themselves in the straw of his breast.

When all of the twelve mice had thus concealed themselves, the Scarecrow buttoned his Jacket securely and then arose and thanked the Queen for her kindness.

"One thing more you might do to serve us," suggested the Tin Woodman; "and that is to run ahead and show us the way to the Emerald City. For some enemy is evidently trying to prevent us from reaching it."

"I will do that gladly," returned the Queen. "Are you ready?"

The Tin Woodman looked at Tip.

"I'm rested," said the boy. "Let us start."

Then they resumed their journey, the little grey Queen of the Field Mice running swiftly ahead and then pausing until the travelers drew near, when away she would dart again.

Without this unerring guide the Scarecrow and his comrades might never have gained the Emerald City; for many were the obstacles thrown in their way by the arts of old Mombi. Yet not one of the obstacles really existed—all were cleverly contrived deceptions. For when they came to the banks of a rushing river that threatened to bar their way the little Queen kept steadily on, passing through the seeming flood in safety; and our travelers followed her without encountering a single drop of water.

Again, a high wall of granite towered high above their heads and opposed their advance. But the grey Field Mouse walked straight through it, and the others did the same, the wall melting into mist as they passed it.

Afterward, when they had stopped for a moment to allow Tip to rest, they saw forty roads branching off from their feet in forty different directions; and soon these forty roads began whirling around like a mighty wheel, first in one direction and then in the other, completely bewildering their vision.

But the Queen called for them to follow her and darted off in a straight line; and when they had gone a few paces the whirling pathways vanished and were seen no more.

Mombi's last trick was the most fearful of all. She sent a sheet of crackling flame rushing over the meadow to consume them; and for the first time the Scarecrow became afraid and turned to fly.

"If that fire reaches me I will be gone in no time!" said he, trembling until his straw rattled. "It's the most dangerous thing I ever encountered."

"I'm off, too!" cried the Saw-Horse, turning and prancing with agitation; "for my wood is so dry it would burn like kindlings."

"Is fire dangerous to pumpkins?" asked Jack, fearfully.

"You'll be baked like a tart—and so will I!" answered the Woggle-Bug, getting down on all fours so he could run the faster.

But the Tin Woodman, having no fear of fire, averted the stampede by a few sensible words.

"Look at the Field Mouse!" he shouted. "The fire does not burn her in the least. In fact, it is no fire at all, but only a deception."

Indeed, to watch the little Queen march calmly through the advancing flames restored courage to every member of the party, and they followed her without being even scorched.

"This is surely a most extraordinary adventure," said the Woggle-Bug, who was greatly amazed; "for it upsets all the Natural Laws that I heard Professor Nowitall teach in the school-house."

"Of course it does," said the Scarecrow, wisely. "All magic is unnatural, and for that reason is to be feared and avoided. But I see before us the gates of the Emerald City, so I imagine we have now overcome all the magical obstacles that seemed to oppose us."

Indeed, the walls of the City were plainly visible, and the Queen of the Field Mice, who had guided them so faithfully, came near to bid them good-bye.

"We are very grateful to your Majesty for your kind assistance," said the Tin Woodman, bowing before the pretty creature.

"I am always pleased to be of service to my friends," answered the Queen, and in a flash she had darted away upon her journey home.

Chapter 15

THE PRISONERS OF THE QUEEN

APPROACHING the gateway of the Emerald City the travelers found it guarded by two girls of the Army of Revolt, who opposed their entrance by drawing the knitting-needles from their hair and threatening to prod the first that came near.

But the Tin Woodman was not afraid.

"At the worst they can but scratch my beautiful nickel-plate," he said. "But there will be no 'worst,' for I think I can manage to frighten these absurd soldiers very easily. Follow me closely, all of you!"

Then, swinging his axe in a great circle to right and left before him, he advanced upon the gate, and the others followed him without hesitation.

The girls, who had expected no resistance whatever, were terrified by the sweep of the glittering axe and fled screaming into the city; so that our travelers passed the gates in safety and marched down the green marble pavement of the wide street toward the royal palace.

"At this rate we will soon have your Majesty upon the throne again," said the Tin Woodman, laughing at his easy conquest of the guards.

"Thank you, friend Nick," returned the Scarecrow, gratefully. "Nothing can resist your kind heart and your sharp axe."

As they passed the rows of houses they saw through the open doors that men were sweeping and dusting and washing dishes, while the women sat around in groups, gossiping and laughing.

"What has happened?" the Scarecrow asked a sad-looking man with a bushy beard, who wore an apron and was wheeling a baby-carriage along the sidewalk.

"Why, we've had a revolution, your Majesty as you ought to know very well," replied the man; "and since you went away the women have been running things to suit themselves. I'm glad you have decided to come back and restore order, for doing housework and minding the children is wearing out the strength of every man in the Emerald City."

"Hm!" said the Scarecrow, thoughtfully. "If it is such hard work as you say, how did the women manage it so easily?"

"I really do not know" replied the man, with a deep sigh. "Perhaps the women are made of castiron."

No movement was made, as they passed along the street, to oppose their progress. Several of the women stopped their gossip long enough to cast curious looks upon our friends, but immediately they would turn away with a laugh or a sneer and resume their chatter. And when they met with several girls belonging to the Army of Revolt, those soldiers, instead of being alarmed or appearing surprised, merely stepped out of the way and allowed them to advance without protest.

This action rendered the Scarecrow uneasy.

"I'm afraid we are walking into a trap," said he.

"Nonsense!" returned Nick Chopper, confidently; "the silly creatures are conquered already!"

But the Scarecrow shook his head in a way that expressed doubt, and Tip said:

"It's too easy, altogether. Look out for trouble ahead."

"I will," returned his Majesty. Unopposed they reached the royal palace and marched up the marble steps, which had once been thickly crusted with emeralds but were now filled with tiny holes where the jewels had been ruthlessly torn from their settings by the Army of Revolt. And so far not a rebel barred their way.

Through the arched hallways and into the magnificent throne room marched the Tin Woodman and his followers, and here, when the green silken curtains fell behind them, they saw a curious sight.

Seated within the glittering throne was General Jinjur, with the Scarecrow's second-best crown upon her head, and the royal sceptre in her right hand. A box of caramels, from which she was eating, rested in her lap, and the girl seemed entirely at ease in her royal surroundings.

The Scarecrow stepped forward and confronted her, while the Tin Woodman leaned upon his axe and the others formed a half-circle back of his Majesty's person.

"How dare you sit in my throne?" demanded the Scarecrow, sternly eyeing the intruder. "Don't you know you are guilty of treason, and that there is a law against treason?"

"The throne belongs to whoever is able to take it," answered Jinjur, as she slowly ate another caramel. "I have taken it, as you see; so just now I am the Queen, and all who oppose me are guilty of treason, and must be punished by the law you have just mentioned."

This view of the case puzzled the Scarecrow.

"How is it, friend Nick?" he asked, turning to the Tin Woodman.

"Why, when it comes to Law, I have nothing to, say" answered that personage. "for laws were never meant to be understood, and it is foolish to make the attempt."

"Then what shall we do?" asked the Scarecrow, in dismay.

"Why don't you marry the Queen? And then you can both rule," suggested the Woggle-Bug.

Jinjur glared at the insect fiercely. "Why don't you send her back to her mother, where she belongs?" asked Jack Pumpkinhead.

Jinjur frowned.

"Why don't you shut her up in a closet until she behaves herself, and promises to be good?" enquired Tip. Jinjur's lip curled scornfully.

"Or give her a good shaking!" added the Saw-Horse.

"No," said the Tin Woodman, "we must treat the poor girl with gentleness. Let us give her all the Jewels she can carry, and send her away happy and contented."

At this Queen Jinjur laughed aloud, and the next minute clapped her pretty hands together thrice, as if for a signal.

"You are very absurd creatures," said she; "but I am tired of your nonsense and have no time to bother with you longer."

While the monarch and his friends listened in amazement to this impudent speech, a startling thing happened. The Tin Woodman's axe was snatched from his grasp by some person behind him, and he found himself disarmed and helpless. At the same instant a shout of laughter rang in the ears of the devoted band, and turning to see whence this came they found themselves surrounded by the Army of Revolt, the girls bearing in either hand their glistening knitting-needles. The entire throne room seemed to be filled with the rebels, and the Scarecrow and his comrades realized that they were prisoners.

"You see how foolish it is to oppose a woman's wit," said Jinjur, gaily; "and this event only proves that I am more fit to rule the Emerald City than a Scarecrow. I bear you no ill will, I assure you; but lest you should prove troublesome to me in the future I shall order you all to be destroyed. That is, all except the boy, who belongs to old Mombi and must be restored to her keeping. The rest of you are not human, and therefore it will not be wicked to demolish you. The Saw-Horse and the Pumpkinhead's body I will have chopped up for kindling-wood; and the pumpkin shall be made into tarts. The Scarecrow will do nicely to start a bonfire, and the tin man can be cut into small pieces and fed to the goats. As for this immense Woggle-Bug—"

"Highly Magnified, if you please!" interrupted the insect.

"I think I will ask the cook to make green-turtle soup of you," continued the Queen, reflectively.

The Woggle-Bug shuddered.

"Or, if that won't do, we might use you for a Hungarian goulash, stewed and highly spiced," she added, cruelly.

This programme of extermination was so terrible that the prisoners looked upon one another in a panic of fear. The Scarecrow alone did not give way to despair. He stood quietly before the Queen and his brow was wrinkled in deep thought as he strove to find some means to escape.

While thus engaged he felt the straw within his breast move gently. At once his expression changed from sadness to joy, and raising his hand he quickly unbuttoned the front of his jacket.

This action did not pass unnoticed by the crowd of girls clustering about him, but none of them suspected what he was doing until a tiny grey mouse leaped from his bosom to the floor and scampered away between the feet of the Army of Revolt. Another mouse quickly followed; then another and another, in rapid succession. And suddenly such a scream of terror went up from the Army that it might easily have filled the stoutest heart with consternation. The flight that ensued turned to a stampede, and the stampede to a panic.

For while the startled mice rushed wildly about the room the Scarecrow had only time to note a whirl of skirts and a twinkling of feet as the girls disappeared from the palace—pushing and crowding one another in their mad efforts to escape.

The Queen, at the first alarm, stood up on the cushions of the throne and began to dance frantically upon her tiptoes. Then a mouse ran up the cushions, and with a terrified leap poor Jinjur shot clear over the head of the Scarecrow and escaped through an archway—never pausing in her wild career until she had reached the city gates.

So, in less time than I can explain, the throne room was deserted by all save the Scarecrow and his friends, and the Woggle-Bug heaved a deep sigh of relief as he exclaimed:

"Thank goodness, we are saved!"

"For a time, yes;" answered the Tin Woodman. "But the enemy will soon return, I fear."

"Let us bar all the entrances to the palace!" said the Scarecrow. "Then we shall have time to think what is best to be done."

So all except Jack Pumpkinhead, who was still tied fast to the Saw-Horse, ran to the various entrances of the royal palace and closed the heavy doors, bolting and locking them securely. Then, knowing that the Army of Revolt could not batter down the barriers in several days, the adventurers gathered once more in the throne room for a council of war.

Chapter 16

SCARECROW TAKES TIME TO THINK

"IT seems to me," began the Scarecrow, when all were again assembled in the throne room, "that the girl Jinjur is quite right in claiming to be Queen. And if she is right, then I am wrong, and we have no business to be occupying her palace."

"But you were the King until she came," said the Woggle-Bug, strutting up and down with his hands in his pockets; "so it appears to me that she is the interloper instead of you."

"Especially as we have just conquered her and put her to flight," added the Pumpkinhead, as he raised his hands to turn his face toward the Scarecrow.

"Have we really conquered her?" asked the Scarecrow, quietly. "Look out of the window, and tell me what you see."

Tip ran to the window and looked out.

"The palace is surrounded by a double row of girl soldiers," he announced.

"I thought so," returned the Scarecrow. "We are as truly their prisoners as we were before the mice frightened them from the palace."

"My friend is right," said Nick Chopper, who had been polishing his breast with a bit of chamois-leather. "Jinjur is still the Queen, and we are her prisoners."

"But I hope she cannot get at us," exclaimed the Pumpkinhead, with a shiver of fear. "She threatened to make tarts of me, you know."

"Don't worry," said the Tin Woodman. "It cannot matter greatly. If you stay shut up here you will spoil in time, anyway. A good tart is far more admirable than a decayed intellect."

"Very true," agreed the Scarecrow.

"Oh, dear!" moaned Jack; "what an unhappy lot is mine! Why, dear father, did you not make me out of tin—or even out of straw—so that I would keep indefinitely."

"Shucks!" returned Tip, indignantly. "You ought to be glad that I made you at all." Then he added, reflectively, "everything has to come to an end, some time."

"But I beg to remind you," broke in the Woggle-Bug, who had a distressed look in his bulging, round eyes, "that this terrible Queen Jinjur suggested making a goulash of me—Me! the only Highly Magnified and Thoroughly Educated Woggle-Bug in the wide, wide world!"

"I think it was a brilliant idea," remarked the Scarecrow, approvingly.

"Don't you imagine he would make a better soup?" asked the Tin Woodman, turning toward his friend.

"Well, perhaps," acknowledged the Scarecrow.

The Woggle-Bug groaned.

"I can see, in my mind's eye," said he, mournfully, "the goats eating small pieces of my dear comrade, the Tin Woodman, while my soup is being cooked on a bonfire built of the Saw-Horse and Jack Pumpkinhead's body, and Queen Jinjur watches me boil while she feeds the flames with my friend the Scarecrow!"

This morbid picture cast a gloom over the entire party, making them restless and anxious.

"It can't happen for some time," said the Tin Woodman, trying to speak cheerfully; "for we shall be able to keep Jinjur out of the palace until she manages to break down the doors."

"And in the meantime I am liable to starve to death, and so is the Woggle-Bug," announced Tip.

"As for me," said the Woggle-Bug, "I think that I could live for some time on Jack Pumpkinhead. Not that I prefer pumpkins for food; but I believe they are somewhat nutritious, and Jack's head is large and plump."

"How heartless!" exclaimed the Tin Woodman, greatly shocked. "Are we cannibals, let me ask? Or are we faithful friends?"

"I see very clearly that we cannot stay shut up in this palace," said the Scarecrow, with decision. "So let us end this mournful talk and try to discover a means to escape."

At this suggestion they all gathered eagerly around the throne, wherein was seated the Scarecrow, and as Tip sat down upon a stool there fell from his pocket a pepper-box, which rolled upon the floor.

"What is this?" asked Nick Chopper, picking up the box.

"Be careful!" cried the boy. "That's my Powder of Life. Don't spill it, for it is nearly gone."

"And what is the Powder of Life?" enquired the Scarecrow, as Tip replaced the box carefully in his pocket.

"It's some magical stuff old Mombi got from a crooked sorcerer," explained the boy. "She brought Jack to life with it, and afterward I used it to bring the Saw-Horse to life. I guess it will make anything live that is sprinkled with it; but there's only about one dose left."

"Then it is very precious," said the Tin Woodman.

"Indeed it is," agreed the Scarecrow. "It may prove our best means of escape from our difficulties. I believe I will think for a few minutes; so I will thank you, friend Tip, to get out your knife and rip this heavy crown from my forehead."

Tip soon cut the stitches that had fastened the crown to the Scarecrow's head, and the former monarch of the Emerald City removed it with a sigh of relief and hung it on a peg beside the throne.

"That is my last memento of royalty" said he; "and I'm glad to get rid of it. The former King of this City, who was named Pastoria, lost the crown to the Wonderful Wizard, who passed it on to me. Now the girl Jinjur claims it, and I sincerely hope it will not give her a headache."

"A kindly thought, which I greatly admire," said the Tin Woodman, nodding approvingly.

"And now I will indulge in a quiet think," continued the Scarecrow, lying back in the throne.

The others remained as silent and still as possible, so as not to disturb him; for all had great confidence in the extraordinary brains of the Scarecrow.

And, after what seemed a very long time indeed to the anxious watchers, the thinker sat up, looked upon his friends with his most whimsical expression, and said:

"My brains work beautifully today. I'm quite proud of them. Now, listen! If we attempt to escape through the doors of the palace we shall surely be captured. And, as we can't escape through the ground, there is only one other thing to be done. We must escape through the air!"

He paused to note the effect of these words; but all his hearers seemed puzzled and unconvinced.

"The Wonderful Wizard escaped in a balloon," he continued. "We don't know how to make a balloon, of course; but any sort of thing that can fly through the air can carry us easily. So I suggest that my friend the Tin Woodman, who is a skillful mechanic, shall build some sort of a machine, with good strong wings, to carry us; and our friend Tip can then bring the Thing to life with his magical powder."

"Bravo!" cried Nick Chopper.

"What splendid brains!" murmured Jack.

"Really quite clever!" said the Educated Woggle-Bug.

"I believe it can be done," declared Tip; "that is, if the Tin Woodman is equal to making the Thing."

"I'll do my best," said Nick, cheerily; "and, as a matter of fact, I do not often fail in what I attempt. But the Thing will have to be built on the roof of the palace, so it can rise comfortably into the air."

"To be sure," said the Scarecrow.

"Then let us search through the palace," continued the Tin Woodman, "and carry all the material we can find to the roof, where I will begin my work."

"First, however," said the Pumpkinhead, "I beg you will release me from this horse, and make me another leg to walk with. For in my present condition I am of no use to myself or to anyone else."

So the Tin Woodman knocked a mahogany center-table to pieces with his axe and fitted one of the legs, which was beautifully carved, on to the body of Jack Pumpkinhead, who was very proud of the acquisition.

"It seems strange," said he, as he watched the Tin Woodman work, "that my left leg should be the most elegant and substantial part of me."

"That proves you are unusual," returned the Scarecrow. "and I am convinced that the only people worthy of consideration in this world are the unusual ones. For the common folks are like the leaves of a tree, and live and die unnoticed."

"Spoken like a philosopher!" cried the Woggle-Bug, as he assisted the Tin Woodman to set Jack upon his feet.

"How do you feel now?" asked Tip, watching the Pumpkinhead stump around to try his new leg.

"As good as new" answered Jack, joyfully, "and quite ready to assist you all to escape."

"Then let us get to work," said the Scarecrow, in a business-like tone.

So, glad to be doing anything that might lead to the end of their captivity, the friends separated to wander over the palace in search of fitting material to use in the construction of their aerial machine.

Chapter 17

THE ASTONISHING FLIGHT
OF THE GUMP

WHEN the adventurers reassembled upon the roof it was found that a remarkably queer assortment of articles had been selected by the various members of the party. No one seemed to have a very clear idea of what was required, but all had brought something.

The Woggle-Bug had taken from its position over the mantle-piece in the great hallway the head of a Gump, which was adorned with wide-spreading antlers; and this, with great care and greater difficulty, the insect had carried up the stairs to the roof. This Gump resembled an Elk's head, only the nose turned upward in a saucy manner and there were whiskers upon its chin, like those of a billy-goat. Why the Woggle-Bug selected this article he could not have explained, except that it had aroused his curiosity.

Tip, with the aid of the Saw-Horse, had brought a large, upholstered sofa to the roof. It was an oldfashioned piece of furniture, with high back and ends, and it was so heavy that even by resting the greatest weight upon the back of the Saw-Horse, the boy found himself out of breath when at last the clumsy sofa was dumped upon the roof.

The Pumpkinhead had brought a broom, which was the first thing he saw. The Scarecrow arrived with a coil of clothes-lines and ropes which he had taken from the courtyard, and in his trip up the stairs he had become so entangled in the loose ends of the ropes that both he and his burden tumbled in a heap upon the roof and might have rolled off if Tip had not rescued him.

The Tin Woodman appeared last. He also had been to the courtyard, where he had cut four great, spreading leaves from a huge palm-tree that was the pride of all the inhabitants of the Emerald City.

"My dear Nick!" exclaimed the Scarecrow, seeing what his friend had done; "you have been guilty of the greatest crime any person can commit in the Emerald City. If I remember rightly, the penalty for chopping leaves from the royal palm-tree is to be killed seven times and afterward imprisoned for life."

"It cannot be helped now" answered the Tin Woodman, throwing down the big leaves upon the roof. "But it may be one more reason why it is necessary for us to escape. And now let us see what you have found for me to work with."

Many were the doubtful looks cast upon the heap of miscellaneous material that now cluttered the roof, and finally the Scarecrow shook his head and remarked:

"Well, if friend Nick can manufacture, from this mess of rubbish, a Thing that will fly through the air and carry us to safety, then I will acknowledge him to be a better mechanic than I suspected."

But the Tin Woodman seemed at first by no means sure of his powers, and only after polishing his forehead vigorously with the chamois-leather did he resolve to undertake the task.

"The first thing required for the machine," said he, "is a body big enough to carry the entire party. This sofa is the biggest thing we have, and might be used for a body. But, should the machine ever tip sideways, we would all slide off and fall to the ground."

"Why not use two sofas?" asked Tip. "There's another one just like this down stairs."

"That is a very sensible suggestion," exclaimed the Tin Woodman. "You must fetch the other sofa at once."

So Tip and the Saw-Horse managed, with much labor, to get the second sofa to the roof; and when the two were placed together, edge to edge, the backs and ends formed a protecting rampart all around the seats.

"Excellent!" cried the Scarecrow. "We can ride within this snug nest quite at our ease."

The two sofas were now bound firmly together with ropes and clothes-lines, and then Nick Chopper fastened the Gump's head to one end.

"That will show which is the front end of the Thing," said he, greatly pleased with the idea. "And, really, if you examine it critically, the Gump looks very well as a figure-head. These great palm-leaves, for which I have endangered my life seven times, must serve us as wings."

"Are they strong enough?" asked the boy.

"They are as strong as anything we can get," answered the Woodman; "and although they are not in proportion to the Thing's body, we are not in a position to be very particular."

So he fastened the palm-leaves to the sofas, two on each side.

Said the Woggle-Bug, with considerable admiration:

"The Thing is now complete, and only needs to be brought to life."

"Stop a moment!" exclaimed Jack. "Are you not going to use my broom?"

"What for?" asked the Scarecrow.

"Why, it can be fastened to the back end for a tail," answered the Pumpkinhead. "Surely you would not call the Thing complete without a tail."

"Hm!" said the Tin Woodman, "I do not see the use of a tail. We are not trying to copy a beast, or a fish, or a bird. All we ask of the Thing is to carry us through the air."

"Perhaps, after the Thing is brought to life, it can use a tail to steer with," suggested the Scarecrow. "For if it flies through the air it will not be unlike a bird, and I've noticed that all birds have tails, which they use for a rudder while flying."

"Very well," answered Nick, "the broom shall be used for a tail," and he fastened it firmly to the back end of the sofa body.

Tip took the pepper-box from his pocket.

"The Thing looks very big," said he, anxiously; "and I am not sure there is enough powder left to bring all of it to life. But I'll make it go as far as possible."

"Put most on the wings," said Nick Chopper; "for they must be made as strong as possible."

"And don't forget the head!" exclaimed the Woggle-Bug.

"Or the tail!" added Jack Pumpkinhead.

"Do be quiet," said Tip, nervously; "you must give me a chance to work the magic charm in the proper manner."

Very carefully he began sprinkling the Thing with the precious powder. Each of the four wings was first lightly covered with a layer, then the sofas were sprinkled, and the broom given a slight coating.

"The head! The head! Don't, I beg of you, forget the head!" cried the Woggle-Bug, excitedly.

"There's only a little of the powder left," announced Tip, looking within the box. "And it seems to me it is more important to bring the legs of the sofas to life than the head."

"Not so," decided the Scarecrow. "Every thing must have a head to direct it; and since this creature is to fly, and not walk, it is really unimportant whether its legs are alive or not."

So Tip abided by this decision and sprinkled the Gump's head with the remainder of the powder.

"Now" said he, "keep silence while I work the, charm!"

Having heard old Mombi pronounce the magic words, and having also succeeded in bringing the Saw-Horse to life, Tip did not hesitate an instant in speaking the three cabalistic words, each accompanied by the peculiar gesture of the hands.

It was a grave and impressive ceremony.

As he finished the incantation the Thing shuddered throughout its huge bulk, the Gump gave the screeching cry that is familiar to those animals, and then the four wings began flopping furiously.

Tip managed to grasp a chimney, else he would have been blown off the roof by the terrible breeze raised by the wings. The Scarecrow, being light in weight, was caught up bodily and borne through the air until Tip luckily seized him by one leg and held him fast. The Woggle-Bug lay flat upon the roof and so escaped harm, and the Tin Woodman, whose weight of tin anchored him firmly, threw both arms around Jack Pumpkinhead and managed to save him. The Saw-Horse toppled over upon his back and lay with his legs waving helplessly above him.

And now, while all were struggling to recover themselves, the Thing rose slowly from the roof and mounted into the air.

"Here! Come back!" cried Tip, in a frightened voice, as he clung to the chimney with one hand and the Scarecrow with the other. "Come back at once, I command you!"

It was now that the wisdom of the Scarecrow, in bringing the head of the Thing to life instead of the legs, was proved beyond a doubt. For the Gump, already high in the air, turned its head at Tip's command and gradually circled around until it could view the roof of the palace.

"Come back!" shouted the boy, again.

And the Gump obeyed, slowly and gracefully waving its four wings in the air until the Thing had settled once more upon the roof and become still.

Chapter 18

IN THE JACKDAW'S NEST

"This," said the Gump, in a squeaky voice not at all proportioned to the size of its great body, "is the most novel experience I ever heard of. The last thing I remember distinctly is walking through the forest and hearing a loud noise. Something probably killed me then, and it certainly ought to have been the end of me. Yet here I am, alive again, with four monstrous wings and a body which I venture to say would make any respectable animal or fowl weep with shame to own. What does it all mean? Am I a Gump, or am I a juggernaut?" The creature, as it spoke, wiggled its chin whiskers in a very comical manner.

"You're just a Thing," answered Tip, "with a Gump's head on it. And we have made you and brought you to life so that you may carry us through the air wherever we wish to go."

"Very good!" said the Thing. "As I am not a Gump, I cannot have a Gump's pride or independent spirit. So I may as well become your servant as anything else. My only satisfaction is that I do not seem to have a very strong constitution, and am not likely to live long in a state of slavery."

"Don't say that, I beg of you!" cried the Tin Woodman, whose excellent heart was strongly affected by this sad speech. "Are you not feeling well today?"

"Oh, as for that," returned the Gump, "it is my first day of existence; so I cannot Judge whether I am feeling well or ill." And it waved its broom tail to and fro in a pensive manner.

"Come, come!" said the Scarecrow, kindly. "do try, to be more cheerful and take life as you find it. We shall be kind masters, and will strive to render your existence as pleasant as possible. Are you willing to carry us through the air wherever we wish to go?"

"Certainly," answered the Gump. "I greatly prefer to navigate the air. For should I travel on the earth and meet with one of my own species, my embarrassment would be something awful!"

"I can appreciate that," said the Tin Woodman, sympathetically.

"And yet," continued the Thing, "when I carefully look you over, my masters, none of you seems to be constructed much more artistically than I am."

"Appearances are deceitful," said the Woggle-Bug, earnestly. "I am both Highly Magnified and Thoroughly Educated."

"Indeed!" murmured the Gump, indifferently.

"And my brains are considered remarkably rare specimens," added the Scarecrow, proudly.

"How strange!" remarked the Gump.

"Although I am of tin," said the Woodman, "I own a heart altogether the warmest and most admirable in the whole world."

"I'm delighted to hear it," replied the Gump, with a slight cough.

"My smile," said Jack Pumpkinhead, "is worthy your best attention. It is always the same."

"*Semper idem*," explained the Woggle-Bug, pompously; and the Gump turned to stare at him.

"And I," declared the Saw-Horse, filling in an awkward pause, "am only remarkable because I can't help it."

"I am proud, indeed, to meet with such exceptional masters," said the Gump, in a careless tone. "If I could but secure so complete an introduction to myself, I would be more than satisfied."

"That will come in time," remarked the Scarecrow. "To 'Know Thyself' is considered quite an accomplishment, which it has taken us, who are your elders, months to perfect. But now," he added, turning to the others, "let us get aboard and start upon our journey."

"Where shall we go?" asked Tip, as he clambered to a seat on the sofas and assisted the Pumpkinhead to follow him.

"In the South Country rules a very delightful Queen called Glinda the Good, who I am sure will gladly receive us," said the Scarecrow, getting into the Thing clumsily. "Let us go to her and ask her advice."

"That is cleverly thought of," declared Nick Chopper, giving the Woggle-Bug a boost and then toppling the Saw-Horse into the rear end of the cushioned seats. "I know Glinda the Good, and believe she will prove a friend indeed."

"Are we all ready?" asked the boy.

"Yes," announced the Tin Woodman, seating himself beside the Scarecrow.

"Then," said Tip, addressing the Gump, "be kind enough to fly with us to the Southward; and do not go higher than to escape the houses and trees, for it makes me dizzy to be up so far."

"All right," answered the Gump, briefly.

It flopped its four huge wings and rose slowly into the air; and then, while our little band of adventurers clung to the backs and sides of the sofas for support, the Gump turned toward the South and soared swiftly and majestically away.

"The scenic effect, from this altitude, is marvelous," commented the educated Woggle-Bug, as they rode along.

"Never mind the scenery," said the Scarecrow. "Hold on tight, or you may get a tumble. The Thing seems to rock badly."

"It will be dark soon," said Tip, observing that the sun was low on the horizon. "Perhaps we should have waited until morning. I wonder if the Gump can fly in the night."

"I've been wondering that myself," returned the Gump quietly. "You see, this is a new experience to me. I used to have legs that carried me swiftly over the ground. But now my legs feel as if they were asleep."

"They are," said Tip. "We didn't bring 'em to life."

"You're expected to fly," explained the Scarecrow. "not to walk."

"We can walk ourselves," said the Woggle-Bug.

"I begin to understand what is required of me," remarked the Gump; "so I will do my best to please you," and he flew on for a time in silence.

Presently Jack Pumpkinhead became uneasy.

"I wonder if riding through the air is liable to spoil pumpkins," he said.

"Not unless you carelessly drop your head over the side," answered the Woggle-Bug. "In that event your head would no longer be a pumpkin, for it would become a squash."

"Have I not asked you to restrain these unfeeling jokes?" demanded Tip, looking at the Woggle-Bug with a severe expression.

"You have; and I've restrained a good many of them," replied the insect. "But there are opportunities for so many excellent puns in our language that, to an educated person like myself, the temptation to express them is almost irresistible."

"People with more or less education discovered those puns centuries ago," said Tip.

"Are you sure?" asked the Woggle-Bug, with a startled look.

"Of course I am," answered the boy. "An educated Woggle-Bug may be a new thing; but a Woggle-Bug education is as old as the hills, judging from the display you make of it."

The insect seemed much impressed by this remark, and for a time maintained a meek silence.

The Scarecrow, in shifting his seat, saw upon the cushions the pepper-box which Tip had cast aside, and began to examine it.

"Throw it overboard," said the boy; "it's quite empty now, and there's no use keeping it."

"Is it really empty?" asked the Scarecrow, looking curiously into the box.

"Of course it is," answered Tip. "I shook out every grain of the powder."

"Then the box has two bottoms," announced the Scarecrow, "for the bottom on the inside is fully an inch away from the bottom on the outside."

"Let me see," said the Tin Woodman, taking the box from his friend. "Yes," he declared, after looking it over, "the thing certainly has a false bottom. Now, I wonder what that is for?"

"Can't you get it apart, and find out?" enquired Tip, now quite interested in the mystery.

"Why, yes; the lower bottom unscrews," said the Tin Woodman. "My fingers are rather stiff; please see if you can open it."

He handed the pepper-box to Tip, who had no difficulty in unscrewing the bottom. And in the cavity below were three silver pills, with a carefully folded paper lying underneath them.

This paper the boy proceeded to unfold, taking care not to spill the pills, and found several lines clearly written in red ink.

"Read it aloud," said the Scarecrow. so Tip read, as follows:

"DR. NIKIDIK'S CELEBRATED WISHING PILLS.

"*Directions for Use:* Swallow one pill; count seventeen by twos; then make a Wish. The Wish will immediately be granted.

CAUTION: Keep in a Dry and Dark Place."

"Why, this is a very valuable discovery!" cried the Scarecrow.

"It is, indeed," replied Tip, gravely. "These pills may be of great use to us. I wonder if old Mombi knew they were in the bottom of the pepper-box. I remember hearing her say that she got the Powder of Life from this same Nikidik."

"He must be a powerful Sorcerer!" exclaimed the Tin Woodman; "and since the powder proved a success we ought to have confidence in the pills."

"But how," asked the Scarecrow, "can anyone count seventeen by twos? Seventeen is an odd number."

"That is true," replied Tip, greatly disappointed. "No one can possibly count seventeen by twos."

"Then the pills are of no use to us," wailed the Pumpkinhead; "and this fact overwhelms me with grief. For I had intended wishing that my head would never spoil."

"Nonsense!" said the Scarecrow, sharply. "If we could use the pills at all we would make far better wishes than that."

"I do not see how anything could be better," protested poor Jack. "If you were liable to spoil at any time you could understand my anxiety."

"For my part," said the Tin Woodman, "I sympathize with you in every respect. But since we cannot count seventeen by twos, sympathy is all you are liable to get."

By this time it had become quite dark, and the voyagers found above them a cloudy sky, through which the rays of the moon could not penetrate.

The Gump flew steadily on, and for some reason the huge sofa-body rocked more and more dizzily every hour.

The Woggle-Bug declared he was sea-sick; and Tip was also pale and somewhat distressed. But the others clung to the backs of the sofas and did not seem to mind the motion as long as they were not tipped out.

Darker and darker grew the night, and on and on sped the Gump through the black heavens. The travelers could not even see one another, and an oppressive silence settled down upon them.

After a long time Tip, who had been thinking deeply, spoke.

"How are we to know when we come to the pallace of Glinda the Good?" he asked.

"It's a long way to Glinda's palace," answered the Woodman; "I've traveled it."

"But how are we to know how fast the Gump is flying?" persisted the boy. "We cannot see a single thing down on the earth, and before morning we may be far beyond the place we want to reach."

"That is all true enough," the Scarecrow replied, a little uneasily. "But I do not see how we can stop just now; for we might alight in a river, or on, the top of a steeple; and that would be a great disaster."

So they permitted the Gump to fly on, with regular flops of its great wings, and waited patiently for morning.

Then Tip's fears were proven to be well founded; for with the first streaks of gray dawn they looked over the sides of the sofas and discovered rolling plains dotted with queer villages, where the houses, instead of being dome-shaped—as they all are in the Land of Oz—had slanting roofs that rose to a peak in the center. Odd looking animals were also moving about upon the open plains, and the country was unfamiliar to both the Tin Woodman and the Scarecrow, who had formerly visited Glinda the Good's domain and knew it well.

"We are lost!" said the Scarecrow, dolefully. "The Gump must have carried us entirely out of the Land of Oz and over the sandy deserts and into the terrible outside world that Dorothy told us about."

"We must get back," exclaimed the Tin Woodman, earnestly. "we must get back as soon as possible!"

"Turn around!" cried Tip to the Gump. "turn as quickly as you can!"

"If I do I shall upset," answered the Gump. "I'm not at all used to flying, and the best plan would be for me to alight in some place, and then I can turn around and take a fresh start."

Just then, however, there seemed to be no stopping-place that would answer their purpose. They flew over a village so big that the Woggle-Bug declared it was a city, and then they came to a range of high mountains with many deep gorges and steep cliffs showing plainly.

"Now is our chance to stop," said the boy, finding they were very close to the mountain tops. Then he turned to the Gump and commanded: "Stop at the first level place you see!"

"Very well," answered the Gump, and settled down upon a table of rock that stood between two cliffs.

But not being experienced in such matters, the Gump did not judge his speed correctly; and instead of coming to a stop upon the flat rock he missed it by half the width of his body, breaking off both his right wings against the sharp edge of the rock and then tumbling over and over down the cliff.

Our friends held on to the sofas as long as they could, but when the Gump caught on a projecting rock the Thing stopped suddenly—bottom side up—and all were immediately dumped out.

By good fortune they fell only a few feet; for underneath them was a monster nest, built by a colony of Jackdaws in a hollow ledge of rock; so none of them—not even the Pumpkinhead— was injured by the fall. For Jack found his precious head resting on the soft breast of the Scarecrow, which made an excellent cushion; and Tip fell on a mass of leaves and papers, which saved him from injury. The Woggle-Bug had bumped his round head against the Saw-Horse, but without causing him more than a moment's inconvenience.

The Tin Woodman was at first much alarmed; but finding he had escaped without even a scratch upon his beautiful nickle-plate he at once regained his accustomed cheerfulness and turned to address his comrades.

"Our Journey had ended rather suddenly," said he; "and we cannot justly blame our friend the Gump for our accident, because he did the best he could under the circumstances. But how we are ever to escape from this nest I must leave to someone with better brains than I possess."

Here he gazed at the Scarecrow; who crawled to the edge of the nest and looked over. Below them was a sheer precipice several hundred feet in depth. Above them was a smooth cliff unbroken save by the point of rock where the wrecked body of the Gump still hung suspended from the end of one of the sofas. There really seemed to be no means of escape, and as they realized their helpless plight the little band of adventurers gave way to their bewilderment.

"This is a worse prison than the palace," sadly remarked the Woggle-Bug.

"I wish we had stayed there," moaned Jack.

"I'm afraid the mountain air isn't good for pumpkins."

"It won't be when the Jackdaws come back," growled the Saw-Horse, which lay waving its legs in a vain endeavor to get upon its feet again. "Jackdaws are especially fond of pumpkins."

"Do you think the birds will come here?" asked Jack, much distressed.

"Of course they will," said Tip; "for this is their nest. And there must be hundreds of them," he continued, "for see what a lot of things they have brought here!"

Indeed, the nest was half filled with a most curious collection of small articles for which the birds could have no use, but which the thieving Jackdaws had stolen during many years from the homes of men. And as the nest was safely hidden where no human being could reach it, this lost property would never be recovered.

The Woggle-Bug, searching among the rubbish—for the Jackdaws stole useless things as well as valuable ones—turned up with his foot a beautiful diamond necklace. This was so greatly admired by the Tin Woodman that the Woggle-Bug presented it to him with a graceful speech, after which the Woodman hung it around his neck with much pride, rejoicing exceedingly when the big diamonds glittered in the sun's rays.

But now they heard a great jabbering and flopping of wings, and as the sound grew nearer to them Tip exclaimed:

"The Jackdaws are coming! And if they find us here they will surely kill us in their anger."

"I was afraid of this!" moaned the Pumpkinhead. "My time has come!"

"And mine, also!" said the Woggle-Bug; "for Jackdaws are the greatest enemies of my race."

The others were not at all afraid; but the Scarecrow at once decided to save those of the party who were liable to be injured by the angry birds. So he commanded Tip to take off Jack's head and lie down with it in the bottom of the nest, and when this was done he ordered the Woggle-Bug to lie beside Tip. Nick Chopper, who knew from past experience Just what to do, then took the Scarecrow to pieces (all except his head) and scattered the straw over Tip and the Woggle-Bug, completely covering their bodies.

Hardly had this been accomplished when the flock of Jackdaws reached them. Perceiving the intruders in their nest the birds flew down upon them with screams of rage.

Chapter 19

DR. NIKIDIK'S FAMOUS WISHING PILLS

THE Tin Woodman was usually a peaceful man, but when occasion required he could fight as fiercely as a Roman gladiator. So, when the Jackdaws nearly knocked him down in their rush of wings, and their sharp beaks and claws threatened to damage his brilliant plating, the Woodman picked up his axe and made it whirl swiftly around his head.

But although many were beaten off in this way, the birds were so numerous and so brave that they continued the attack as furiously as before. Some of them pecked at the eyes of the Gump, which hung over the nest in a helpless condition; but the Gump's eyes were of glass and could not be injured. Others of the Jackdaws rushed at the Saw-Horse; but that animal, being still upon his back, kicked out so viciously with his wooden legs that he beat off as many assailants as did the Woodman's axe.

Finding themselves thus opposed, the birds fell upon the Scarecrow's straw, which lay at the center of the nest, covering Tip and the Woggle-Bug and Jack's pumpkin head, and began tearing it away and flying off with it, only to let it drop, straw by straw into the great gulf beneath.

The Scarecrow's head, noting with dismay this wanton destruction of his interior, cried to the Tin Woodman to save him; and that good friend responded with renewed energy. His axe fairly flashed among the Jackdaws, and fortunately the Gump began wildly waving the two wings remaining on the left side of its body. The flutter of these great wings filled the Jackdaws with terror, and when the Gump by its exertions freed itself from the peg of rock on which it hung, and sank flopping into the nest, the alarm of the birds knew no bounds and they fled screaming over the mountains.

When the last foe had disappeared, Tip crawled from under the sofas and assisted the Woggle-Bug to follow him.

"We are saved!" shouted the boy, delightedly.

"We are, indeed!" responded the Educated Insect, fairly hugging the stiff head of the Gump in his joy. "and we owe it all to the flopping of the Thing, and the good axe of the Woodman!"

"If I am saved, get me out of here!" called Jack; whose head was still beneath the sofas; and Tip managed to roll the pumpkin out and place it upon its neck again. He also set the Saw-Horse upright, and said to it:

"We owe you many thanks for the gallant fight you made."

"I really think we have escaped very nicely," remarked the Tin Woodman, in a tone of pride.

"Not so!" exclaimed a hollow voice.

At this they all turned in surprise to look at the Scarecrow's head, which lay at the back of the nest.

"I am completely ruined!" declared the Scarecrow, as he noted their astonishment. "For where is the straw that stuffs my body?"

The awful question startled them all. They gazed around the nest with horror, for not a vestige of straw remained. The Jackdaws had stolen it to the last wisp and flung it all into the chasm that yawned for hundreds of feet beneath the nest.

"My poor, poor friend!" said the Tin Woodman, taking up the Scarecrow's head and caressing it tenderly; "whoever could imagine you would come to this untimely end?"

"I did it to save my friends," returned the head; "and I am glad that I perished in so noble and unselfish a manner."

"But why are you all so despondent?" inquired the Woggle-Bug. "The Scarecrow's clothing is still safe."

"Yes," answered the Tin Woodman; "but our friend's clothes are useless without stuffing."

"Why not stuff him with money?" asked Tip.

"Money!" they all cried, in an amazed chorus.

"To be sure," said the boy. "In the bottom of the nest are thousands of dollar bills—and two-dollar bills—and five-dollar bills—and tens, and twenties, and fifties. There are enough of them to stuff a dozen Scarecrows. Why not use the money?"

The Tin Woodman began to turn over the rubbish with the handle of his axe; and, sure enough, what they had first thought only worthless papers were found to be all bills of various denominations, which the mischievous Jackdaws had for years been engaged in stealing from the villages and cities they visited.

There was an immense fortune lying in that inaccessible nest; and Tip's suggestion was, with the Scarecrow's consent, quickly acted upon.

They selected all the newest and cleanest bills and assorted them into various piles. The Scarecrow's left leg and boot were stuffed with five-dollar bills; his right leg was stuffed with ten-dollar bills, and his body so closely filled with fifties, one-hundreds and one-thousands that he could scarcely button his jacket with comfort.

"You are now" said the Woggle-Bug, impressively, when the task had been completed, "the most valuable member of our party; and as you are among faithful friends there is little danger of your being spent."

"Thank you," returned the Scarecrow, gratefully. "I feel like a new man; and although at first glance I might be mistaken for a Safety Deposit Vault, I beg you to remember that my Brains are still composed of the same old material. And these are the possessions that have always made me a person to be depended upon in an emergency."

"Well, the emergency is here," observed Tip; "and unless your brains help us out of it we shall be compelled to pass the remainder of our lives in this nest."

"How about these wishing pills?" enquired the Scarecrow, taking the box from his jacket pocket. "Can't we use them to escape?"

"Not unless we can count seventeen by twos," answered the Tin Woodman. "But our friend the Woggle-Bug claims to be highly educated, so he ought easily to figure out how that can be done."

"It isn't a question of education," returned the Insect; "it's merely a question of mathematics. I've seen the professor work lots of sums on the blackboard, and he claimed anything could be done with x's and y's and a's, and such things, by mixing them up with plenty of plusses and minuses and equals, and so forth. But he never said anything, so far as I can remember, about counting up to the odd number of seventeen by the even numbers of twos."

"Stop! stop!" cried the Pumpkinhead. "You're making my head ache."

"And mine," added the Scarecrow. "Your mathematics seem to me very like a bottle of mixed pickles the more you fish for what you want the less chance you have of getting it. I am certain that if the thing can be accomplished at all, it is in a very simple manner."

"Yes," said Tip. "old Mombi couldn't use x's and minuses, for she never went to school."

"Why not start counting at a half of one?" asked the Saw-Horse, abruptly. "Then anyone can count up to seventeen by twos very easily."

They looked at each other in surprise, for the Saw-Horse was considered the most stupid of the entire party.

"You make me quite ashamed of myself," said the Scarecrow, bowing low to the Saw-Horse.

"Nevertheless, the creature is right," declared the Woggle-Bug; "for twice one-half is one, and if you get to one it is easy to count from one up to seventeen by twos."

"I wonder I didn't think of that myself," said the Pumpkinhead.

"I don't," returned the Scarecrow. "You're no wiser than the rest of us, are you? But let us make a wish at once. Who will swallow the first pill?"

"Suppose you do it," suggested Tip.

"I can't," said the Scarecrow.

"Why not? You've a mouth, haven't you?" asked the boy.

"Yes; but my mouth is painted on, and there's no swallow connected with it," answered the Scarecrow. "In fact," he continued, looking from one to another critically, "I believe the boy and the Woggle-Bug are the only ones in our party that are able to swallow."

Observing the truth of this remark, Tip said:

"Then I will undertake to make the first wish. Give me one of the Silver Pills."

This the Scarecrow tried to do; but his padded gloves were too clumsy to clutch so small an object, and he held the box toward the boy while Tip selected one of the pills and swallowed it.

"Count!" cried the Scarecrow.

"One-half, one, three, five, seven, nine, eleven," counted Tip. "thirteen, fifteen, seventeen."

"Now wish!" said the Tin Woodman anxiously:

But Just then the boy began to suffer such fearful pains that he became alarmed.

"The pill has poisoned me!" he gasped; "O—h! O-o-o-o-o! Ouch! Murder! Fire! O-o-h!" and here he rolled upon the bottom of the nest in such contortions that he frightened them all.

"What can we do for you. Speak, I beg!" entreated the Tin Woodman, tears of sympathy running down his nickel cheeks.

"I—I don't know!" answered Tip. "O—h! I wish I'd never swallowed that pill!"

Then at once the pain stopped, and the boy rose to his feet again and found the Scarecrow looking with amazement at the end of the pepper-box.

"What's happened?" asked the boy, a little ashamed of his recent exhibition.

"Why, the three pills are in the box again!" said the Scarecrow.

"Of course they are," the Woggle-Bug declared. "Didn't Tip wish that he'd never swallowed one of them? Well, the wish came true, and he *didn't* swallow one of them. So of course they are all three in the box."

"That may be; but the pill gave me a dreadful pain, just the same," said the boy.

"Impossible!" declared the Woggle-Bug. "If you have never swallowed it, the pill can not have given you a pain. And as your wish, being granted, proves you did not swallow the pill, it is also plain that you suffered no pain."

"Then it was a splendid imitation of a pain," retorted Tip, angrily. "Suppose you try the next pill yourself. We've wasted one wish already."

"Oh, no, we haven't!" protested the Scarecrow. "Here are still three pills in the box, and each pill is good for a wish."

"Now you're making *my* head ache," said Tip. "I can't understand the thing at all. But I won't take another pill, I promise you!" and with this remark he retired sulkily to the back of the nest.

"Well," said the Woggle-Bug, "it remains for me to save us in my most Highly Magnified and Thoroughly Educated manner; for I seem to be the only one able and willing to make a wish. Let me have one of the pills."

He swallowed it without hesitation, and they all stood admiring his courage while the Insect counted seventeen by twos in the same way that Tip had done. And for some reason—perhaps because Woggle-Bugs have stronger stomachs than boys—the silver pellet caused it no pain whatever.

"I wish the Gump's broken wings mended, and as good as new!" said the Woggle-Bug, in a slow; impressive voice.

All turned to look at the Thing, and so quickly had the wish been granted that the Gump lay before them in perfect repair, and as well able to fly through the air as when it had first been brought to life on the roof of the palace.

<hr/>

Chapter 20

THE SCARECROW APPEALS
TO GLINDA

"Hooray!" shouted the Scarecrow, gaily. "We can now leave this miserable Jackdaws' nest whenever we please."

"But it is nearly dark," said the Tin Woodman; "and unless we wait until morning to make our flight we may get into more trouble. I don't like these night trips, for one never knows what will happen."

So it was decided to wait until daylight, and the adventurers amused themselves in the twilight by searching the Jackdaws' nest for treasures.

The Woggle-Bug found two handsome bracelets of wrought gold, which fitted his slender arms very well. The Scarecrow took a fancy for rings, of which there were many in the nest. Before long he had fitted a ring to each finger of his padded gloves, and not being content with that display he added one more to each thumb. As he carefully chose those rings set with sparkling stones, such as rubies, amethysts and sapphires, the Scarecrow's hands now presented a most brilliant appearance.

"This nest would be a picnic for Queen Jinjur," said he, musingly. "for as nearly as I can make out she and her girls conquered me merely to rob my city of its emeralds."

The Tin Woodman was content with his diamond necklace and refused to accept any additional decorations; but Tip secured a fine gold watch, which was attached to a heavy fob, and placed it in his pocket with much pride. He also pinned several jeweled brooches to Jack Pumpkinhead's red waistcoat, and attached a lorgnette, by means of a fine chain, to the neck of the Saw-Horse.

"It's very pretty," said the creature, regarding the lorgnette approvingly; "but what is it for?"

None of them could answer that question, however; so the Saw-Horse decided it was some rare decoration and became very fond of it.

That none of the party might be slighted, they ended by placing several large seal rings upon the points of the Gump's antlers, although that odd personage seemed by no means gratified by the attention.

Darkness soon fell upon them, and Tip and the Woggle-Bug went to sleep while the others sat down to wait patiently for the day.

Next morning they had cause to congratulate themselves upon the useful condition of the Gump; for with daylight a great flock of Jackdaws approached to engage in one more battle for the possession of the nest.

But our adventurers did not wait for the assault. They tumbled into the cushioned seats of the sofas as quickly as possible, and Tip gave the word to the Gump to start.

At once it rose into the air, the great wings flopping strongly and with regular motions, and in a few moments they were so far from the nest that the chattering Jackdaws took possession without any attempt at pursuit.

The Thing flew due North, going in the same direction from whence it had come. At least, that was the Scarecrow's opinion, and the others agreed that the Scarecrow was the best judge of direction. After passing over several cities and villages the Gump carried them high above a broad plain where houses became more and more scattered until they disappeared altogether. Next came the wide, sandy desert separating the rest of the world from the Land of Oz, and before noon they saw the dome-shaped houses that proved they were once more within the borders of their native land.

"But the houses and fences are blue," said the Tin Woodman, "and that indicates we are in the land of the Munchkins, and therefore a long distance from Glinda the Good."

"What shall we do?" asked the boy, turning to their guide.

"I don't know" replied the Scarecrow, frankly. "If we were at the Emerald City we could then move directly southward, and so reach our destination. But we dare not go to the Emerald City, and the Gump is probably carrying us further in the wrong direction with every flop of its wings."

"Then the Woggle-Bug must swallow another pill," said Tip, decidedly, "and wish us headed in the right direction."

"Very well," returned the Highly Magnified one; "I'm willing."

But when the Scarecrow searched in his pocket for the pepper-box containing the two silver Wishing Pills, it was not to be found. Filled with anxiety, the voyagers hunted throughout every inch of the Thing for the precious box; but it had disappeared entirely.

And still the Gump flew onward, carrying them they knew not where.

"I must have left the pepper-box in the Jackdaws' nest," said the Scarecrow, at length.

"It is a great misfortune," the Tin Woodman declared. "But we are no worse off than before we discovered the Wishing Pills."

"We are better off," replied Tip. "for the one pill we used has enabled us to escape from that horrible nest."

"Yet the loss of the other two is serious, and I deserve a good scolding for my carelessness," the Scarecrow rejoined, penitently.

"For in such an unusual party as this accidents are liable to happen any moment, and even now we may be approaching a new danger."

No one dared contradict this, and a dismal silence ensued.

The Gump flew steadily on.

Suddenly Tip uttered an exclamation of surprise. "We must have reached the South Country," he cried, "for below us everything is red!"

Immediately they all leaned over the backs of the sofas to look—all except Jack, who was too careful of his pumpkin head to risk its slipping off his neck. Sure enough; the red houses and fences and trees indicated they were within the domain of Glinda the Good; and presently, as they glided rapidly on, the Tin Woodman recognized the roads and buildings they passed, and altered slightly the flight of the Gump so that they might reach the palace of the celebrated Sorceress.

"Good!" cried the Scarecrow, delightedly. "We do not need the lost Wishing Pills now, for we have arrived at our destination."

Gradually the Thing sank lower and nearer to the ground until at length it came to rest within the beautiful gardens of Glinda, settling upon a velvety green lawn close by a fountain which sent sprays of flashing gems, instead of water, high into the air, whence they fell with a soft, tinkling sound into the carved marble basin placed to receive them.

Everything was very gorgeous in Glinda's gardens, and while our voyagers gazed about with admiring eyes a company of soldiers silently appeared and surrounded them. But these soldiers of the great Sorceress were entirely different from those of Jinjur's Army of Revolt, although they were likewise girls. For Glinda's soldiers wore neat uniforms and bore swords and spears; and they marched with a skill and precision that proved them well trained in the arts of war.

The Captain commanding this troop—which was Glinda's private Body Guard—recognized the Scarecrow and the Tin Woodman at once, and greeted them with respectful salutations.

"Good day!" said the Scarecrow, gallantly removing his hat, while the Woodman gave a soldierly salute; "we have come to request an audience with your fair Ruler."

"Glinda is now within her palace, awaiting you," returned the Captain; "for she saw you coming long before you arrived."

"That is strange!" said Tip, wondering.

"Not at all," answered the Scarecrow, "for Glinda the Good is a mighty Sorceress, and nothing that goes on in the Land of Oz escapes her notice. I suppose she knows why we came as well as we do ourselves."

"Then what was the use of our coming?" asked Jack, stupidly.

"To prove you are a Pumpkinhead!" retorted the Scarecrow. "But, if the Sorceress expects us, we must not keep her waiting."

So they all clambered out of the sofas and followed the Captain toward the palace—even the Saw-Horse taking his place in the queer procession.

Upon her throne of finely wrought gold sat Glinda, and she could scarcely repress a smile as her peculiar visitors entered and bowed before her. Both the Scarecrow and the Tin Woodman she knew and liked; but the awkward Pumpkinhead and Highly Magnified Woggle-Bug were creatures she had never seen before, and they seemed even more curious than the others. As for the Saw-Horse, he looked to be nothing more than an animated chunk of wood; and he bowed so stiffly that his head bumped against the floor, causing a ripple of laughter among the soldiers, in which Glinda frankly joined.

"I beg to announce to your glorious highness," began the Scarecrow, in a solemn voice, "that my Emerald City has been overrun by a crowd of impudent girls with knitting-needles, who have enslaved all the men, robbed the streets and public buildings of all their emerald jewels, and usurped my throne."

"I know it," said Glinda.

"They also threatened to destroy me, as well as all the good friends and allies you see before you," continued the Scarecrow. "and had we not managed to escape their clutches our days would long since have ended."

"I know it," repeated Glinda.

"Therefore I have come to beg your assistance," resumed the Scarecrow, "for I believe you are always glad to succor the unfortunate and oppressed."

"That is true," replied the Sorceress, slowly. "But the Emerald City is now ruled by General Jinjur, who has caused herself to be proclaimed Queen. What right have I to oppose her?"

"Why, she stole the throne from me," said the Scarecrow.

"And how came you to possess the throne?" asked Glinda.

"I got it from the Wizard of Oz, and by the choice of the people," returned the Scarecrow, uneasy at such questioning.

"And where did the Wizard get it?" she continued gravely.

"I am told he took it from Pastoria, the former King," said the Scarecrow, becoming confused under the intent look of the Sorceress.

"Then," declared Glinda, "the throne of the Emerald City belongs neither to you nor to Jinjur, but to this Pastoria from whom the Wizard usurped it."

"That is true," acknowledged the Scarecrow, humbly; "but Pastoria is now dead and gone, and some one must rule in his place."

"Pastoria had a daughter, who is the rightful heir to the throne of the Emerald City. Did you know that?" questioned the Sorceress.

"No," replied the Scarecrow. "But if the girl still lives I will not stand in her way. It will satisfy me as well to have Jinjur turned out, as an impostor, as to regain the throne myself. In fact, it isn't much fun to be King, especially if one has good brains. I have known for some time that I am fitted to occupy a far more exalted position. But where is the girl who owns the throne, and what is her name?"

"Her name is Ozma," answered Glinda. "But where she is I have tried in vain to discover. For the Wizard of Oz, when he stole the throne from Ozma's father, hid the girl in some secret place; and by means of a magical trick with which I am not familiar he also managed to prevent her being discovered—even by so experienced a Sorceress as myself."

"That is strange," interrupted the Woggle-Bug, pompously. "I have been informed that the Wonderful Wizard of Oz was nothing more than a humbug!"

"Nonsense!" exclaimed the Scarecrow, much provoked by this speech. "Didn't he give me a wonderful set of brains?"

"There's no humbug about my heart," announced the Tin Woodman, glaring indignantly at the Woggle-Bug.

"Perhaps I was misinformed," stammered the Insect, shrinking back; "I never knew the Wizard personally."

"Well, we did," retorted the Scarecrow, "and he was a very great Wizard, I assure you. It is true he was guilty of some slight impostures, but unless he was a great Wizard how—let me ask— could he have hidden this girl Ozma so securely that no one can find her?"

"I—I give it up!" replied the Woggle-Bug, meekly.

"That is the most sensible speech you've made," said the Tin Woodman.

"I must really make another effort to discover where this girl is hidden," resumed the Sorceress, thoughtfully. "I have in my library a book in which is inscribed every action of the Wizard while he was in our land of Oz—or, at least, every action that could be observed by my spies. This book I will read carefully tonight, and try to single out the acts that may guide us in discovering the lost Ozma. In the meantime, pray amuse yourselves in my palace and command my servants as if they were your own. I will grant you another audience tomorrow."

With this gracious speech Glinda dismissed the adventurers, and they wandered away through the beautiful gardens, where they passed several hours enjoying all the delightful things with which the Queen of the Southland had surrounded her royal palace.

On the following morning they again appeared before Glinda, who said to them:

"I have searched carefully through the records of the Wizard's actions, and among them I can find but three that appear to have been suspicious. He ate beans with a knife, made three secret visits to old Mombi, and limped slightly on his left foot."

"Ah! that last is certainly suspicious!" exclaimed the Pumpkinhead.

"Not necessarily," said the Scarecrow. "he may, have had corns. Now, it seems to me his eating beans with a knife is more suspicious."

"Perhaps it is a polite custom in Omaha, from which great country the Wizard originally came," suggested the Tin Woodman.

"It may be," admitted the Scarecrow.

"But why," asked Glinda, "did he make three secret visits to old Mombi?"

"Ah! Why, indeed!" echoed the Woggle-Bug, impressively.

"We know that the Wizard taught the old woman many of his tricks of magic," continued Glinda; "and this he would not have done had she not assisted him in some way. So we may suspect with good reason that Mombi aided him to hide the girl Ozma, who was the real heir to the throne of the Emerald City, and a constant danger to the usurper. For, if the people knew that she lived, they would quickly make her their Queen and restore her to her rightful position."

"An able argument!" cried the Scarecrow. "I have no doubt that Mombi was mixed up in this wicked business. But how does that knowledge help us?"

"We must find Mombi," replied Glinda, "and force her to tell where the girl is hidden."

"Mombi is now with Queen Jinjur, in the Emerald, City" said Tip. "It was she who threw so many obstacles in our pathway, and made Jinjur threaten to destroy my friends and give me back into the old witch's power."

"Then," decided Glinda, "I will march with my army to the Emerald City, and take Mombi prisoner. After that we can, perhaps, force her to tell the truth about Ozma."

"She is a terrible old woman!" remarked Tip, with a shudder at the thought of Mombi's black kettle; "and obstinate, too."

"I am quite obstinate myself," returned the Sorceress, with a sweet smile. "so I do not fear Mombi in the least. Today I will make all necessary preparations, and we will march upon the Emerald City at daybreak tomorrow."

Chapter 21

THE TIN-WOODMAN PLUCKS A ROSE

THE Army of Glinda the Good looked very grand and imposing when it assembled at daybreak before the palace gates. The uniforms of the girl soldiers were pretty and of gay colors, and their silver-tipped spears were bright and glistening, the long shafts being inlaid with mother-of-pearl. All the officers wore sharp, gleaming swords, and shields edged with peacock-feathers; and it really seemed that no foe could by any possibility defeat such a brilliant army.

The Sorceress rode in a beautiful palanquin which was like the body of a coach, having doors and windows with silken curtains; but instead of wheels, which a coach has, the palanquin rested upon two long, horizontal bars, which were borne upon the shoulders of twelve servants.

The Scarecrow and his comrades decided to ride in the Gump, in order to keep up with the swift march of the army; so, as soon as Glinda had started and her soldiers had marched away to the inspiring strains of music played by the royal band, our friends climbed into the sofas and followed. The Gump flew along slowly at a point directly over the palanquin in which rode the Sorceress.

"Be careful," said the Tin Woodman to the Scarecrow, who was leaning far over the side to look at the army below. "You might fall."

"It wouldn't matter," remarked the educated Woggle-Bug. "he can't get broke so long as he is stuffed with money."

"Didn't I ask you" began Tip, in a reproachful voice.

"You did!" said the Woggle-Bug, promptly. "And I beg your pardon. I will really try to restrain myself."

"You'd better," declared the boy. "That is, if you wish to travel in our company."

"Ah! I couldn't bear to part with you now," murmured the Insect, feelingly; so Tip let the subject drop.

The army moved steadily on, but night had fallen before they came to the walls of the Emerald City. By the dim light of the new moon, however, Glinda's forces silently surrounded the city and pitched their tents of scarlet silk upon the greensward. The tent of the Sorceress was larger than the others, and was composed of pure white silk, with scarlet banners flying above it. A tent was also pitched for the Scarecrow's party; and when these preparations had been made, with military precision and quickness, the army retired to rest.

Great was the amazement of Queen Jinjur next morning when her soldiers came running to inform her of the vast army surrounding them. She at once climbed to a high tower of the royal palace and saw banners waving in every direction and the great white tent of Glinda standing directly before the gates.

"We are surely lost!" cried Jinjur, in despair; "for how can our knitting-needles avail against the long spears and terrible swords of our foes?"

"The best thing we can do," said one of the girls, "is to surrender as quickly as possible, before we get hurt."

"Not so," returned Jinjur, more bravely. "The enemy is still outside the walls, so we must try to gain time by engaging them in parley. Go you with a flag of truce to Glinda and ask her why she has dared to invade my dominions, and what are her demands."

So the girl passed through the gates, bearing a white flag to show she was on a mission of peace, and came to Glinda's tent. "Tell your Queen," said the Sorceress to the girl, "that she must deliver up to me old Mombi, to be my prisoner. If this is done I will not molest her farther."

Now when this message was delivered to the Queen it filled her with dismay, for Mombi was her chief counsellor, and Jinjur was terribly afraid of the old hag. But she sent for Mombi, and told her what Glinda had said.

"I see trouble ahead for all of us," muttered the old witch, after glancing into a magic mirror she carried in her pocket. "But we may even yet escape by deceiving this sorceress, clever as she thinks herself."

"Don't you think it will be safer for me to deliver you into her hands?" asked Jinjur, nervously.

"If you do, it will cost you the throne of the Emerald City!" answered the witch, positively. "But if you will let me have my own way, I can save us both very easily."

"Then do as you please," replied Jinjur, "for it is so aristocratic to be a Queen that I do not wish to be obliged to return home again, to make beds and wash dishes for my mother."

So Mombi called Jellia Jamb to her, and performed a certain magical rite with which she was familiar. As a result of the enchantment Jellia took on the form and features of Mombi, while the old witch grew to resemble the girl so closely that it seemed impossible anyone could guess the deception.

"Now," said old Mombi to the Queen, "let your soldiers deliver up this girl to Glinda. She will think she has the real Mombi in her power, and so will return immediately to her own country in the South."

Therefore Jellia, hobbling along like an aged woman, was led from the city gates and taken before Glinda.

"Here is the person you demanded," said one of the guards, "and our Queen now begs you will go away, as you promised, and leave us in peace."

"That I will surely do," replied Glinda, much pleased; "if this is really the person she seems to be."

"It is certainly old Mombi," said the guard, who believed she was speaking the truth; and then Jinjur's soldiers returned within the city's gates.

The Sorceress quickly summoned the Scarecrow and his friends to her tent, and began to question the supposed Mombi about the lost girl Ozma. But Jellia knew nothing at all of this affair, and presently she grew so nervous under the questioning that she gave way and began to weep, to Glinda's great astonishment.

"Here is some foolish trickery!" said the Sorceress, her eyes flashing with anger. "This is not Mombi at all, but some other person who has been made to resemble her! Tell me," she demanded, turning to the trembling girl, "what is your name?"

This Jellia dared not tell, having been threatened with death by the witch if she confessed the fraud. But Glinda, sweet and fair though she was, understood magic better than any other person in the Land of Oz. So, by uttering a few potent words and making a peculiar gesture, she quickly transformed the girl into her proper shape, while at the same time old Mombi, far away in Jinjur's palace, suddenly resumed her own crooked form and evil features.

"Why, it's Jellia Jamb!" cried the Scarecrow, recognizing in the girl one of his old friends.

"It's our interpreter!" said the Pumpkinhead, smiling pleasantly.

Then Jellia was forced to tell of the trick Mombi had played and she also begged Glinda's protection, which the Sorceress readily granted. But Glinda was now really angry, and sent word to Jinjur that the fraud was discovered and she must deliver up the real Mombi or suffer terrible consequences. Jinjur was prepared for this message, for the witch well understood, when her natural form was thrust upon her, that Glinda had discovered her trickery. But the wicked old creature had already thought up a new deception, and had made Jinjur promise to carry it out. So the Queen said to Glinda's messenger:

"Tell your mistress that I cannot find Mombi anywhere, but that Glinda is welcome to enter the city and search herself for the old woman. She may also bring her friends with her, if she likes; but if she does not find Mombi by sundown, the Sorceress must promise to go away peaceably and bother us no more."

Glinda agreed to these terms, well knowing that Mombi was somewhere within the city walls. So Jinjur caused the gates to be thrown open, and Glinda marched in at the head of a company of soldiers, followed by the Scarecrow and the Tin Woodman, while Jack Pumpkinhead rode astride the Saw-Horse, and the Educated, Highly Magnified Woggle-Bug sauntered behind in a dignified manner. Tip walked by the side of the Sorceress, for Glinda had conceived a great liking for the boy.

Of course old Mombi had no intention of being found by Glinda; so, while her enemies were marching up the street, the witch transformed herself into a red rose growing upon a bush in the garden of the palace. It was a clever idea, and a trick Glinda did not suspect; so several precious hours were spent in a vain search for Mombi.

As sundown approached the Sorceress realized she had been defeated by the superior cunning of the aged witch; so she gave the command to her people to march out of the city and back to their tents.

The Scarecrow and his comrades happened to be searching in the garden of the palace just then, and they turned with disappointment to obey Glinda's command. But before they left the garden the Tin Woodman, who was fond of flowers, chanced to espy a big red rose growing upon a bush; so he plucked the flower and fastened it securely in the tin buttonhole of his tin bosom.

As he did this he fancied he heard a low moan proceed from the rose; but he paid no attention to the sound, and Mombi was thus carried out of the city and into Glinda's camp without anyone having a suspicion that they had succeeded in their quest.

Chapter 22

THE TRANSFORMATION OF
OLD MOMBI

THE Witch was at first frightened at finding herself captured by the enemy; but soon she decided that she was exactly as safe in the Tin Woodman's button-hole as growing upon the bush. For no one knew the rose and Mombi to be one, and now that she was without the gates of the City her chances of escaping altogether from Glinda were much improved.

"But there is no hurry," thought Mombi. "I will wait awhile and enjoy the humiliation of this Sorceress when she finds I have outwitted her." So throughout the night the rose lay quietly on the Woodman's bosom, and in the morning, when Glinda summoned our friends to a consultation, Nick Chopper carried his pretty flower with him to the white silk tent.

"For some reason," said Glinda, "we have failed to find this cunning old Mombi; so I fear our expedition will prove a failure. And for that I am sorry, because without our assistance little Ozma will never be rescued and restored to her rightful position as Queen of the Emerald City"

"Do not let us give up so easily," said the Pumpkinhead. "Let us do something else."

"Something else must really be done," replied Glinda, with a smile. "yet I cannot understand how I have been defeated so easily by an old Witch who knows far less of magic than I do myself."

"While we are on the ground I believe it would be wise for us to conquer the Emerald City for Princess Ozma, and find the girl afterward," said the Scarecrow. "And while the girl remains hidden I will gladly rule in her place, for I understand the business of ruling much better than Jinjur does."

"But I have promised not to molest Jinjur," objected Glinda.

"Suppose you all return with me to my kingdom—or Empire, rather," said the Tin Woodman, politely including the entire party in a royal wave of his arm. "It will give me great pleasure to entertain you in my castle, where there is room enough and to spare. And if any of you wish to be nickel-plated, my valet will do it free of all expense."

While the Woodman was speaking Glinda's eyes had been noting the rose in his button-hole, and now she imagined she saw the big red leaves of the flower tremble slightly. This quickly aroused her suspicions, and in a moment more the Sorceress had decided that the seeming rose was nothing else than a transformation of old Mombi. At the same instant Mombi knew she was discovered and must quickly plan an escape, and as transformations were easy to her she immediately took the form of a Shadow and glided along the wall of the tent toward the entrance, thinking thus to disappear.

But Glinda had not only equal cunning, but far more experience than the Witch. So the Sorceress reached the opening of the tent before the Shadow, and with a wave of her hand closed the entrance so securely that Mombi could not find a crack big enough to creep through. The Scarecrow and his friends were greatly surprised at Glinda's actions; for none of them had noted the Shadow. But the Sorceress said to them:

"Remain perfectly quiet, all of you! For the old Witch is even now with us in this tent, and I hope to capture her."

These words so alarmed Mombi that she quickly transformed herself from a shadow to a Black Ant, in which shape she crawled along the ground, seeking a crack or crevice in which to hide her tiny body.

Fortunately, the ground where the tent had been pitched, being Just before the city gates, was hard and smooth; and while the Ant still crawled about, Glinda discovered it and ran quickly forward to effect its capture But, Just as her hand was descending, the Witch, now fairly frantic with fear, made her last transformation, and in the form of a huge Griffin sprang through the wall of the tent—tearing the silk asunder in her rush—and in a moment had darted away with the speed of a whirlwind.

Glinda did not hesitate to follow. She sprang upon the back of the Saw-Horse and cried:

"Now you shall prove that you have a right to be alive! Run—run—run!"

The Saw-Horse ran. Like a flash he followed the Griffin, his wooden legs moving so fast that they twinkled like the rays of a star. Before our friends could recover from their surprise both the Griffin and the Saw-Horse had dashed out of sight.

"Come! Let us follow!" cried the Scarecrow.

They ran to the place where the Gump was lying and quickly tumbled aboard.

"Fly!" commanded Tip, eagerly.

"Where to?" asked the Gump, in its calm voice.

"I don't know," returned Tip, who was very nervous at the delay; "but if you will mount into the air I think we can discover which way Glinda has gone."

"Very well," returned the Gump, quietly; and it spread its great wings and mounted high into the air.

Far away, across the meadows, they could now see two tiny specks, speeding one after the other; and they knew these specks must be the Griffin and the Saw-Horse. So Tip called the Gump's attention to them and bade the creature try to overtake the Witch and the Sorceress. But, swift as was the Gump's flight, the pursued and pursuer moved more swiftly yet, and within a few moments were blotted out against the dim horizon.

"Let us continue to follow them, nevertheless," said the Scarecrow. "for the Land of Oz is of small extent, and sooner or later they must both come to a halt."

Old Mombi had thought herself very wise to choose the form of a Griffin, for its legs were exceedingly fleet and its strength more enduring than that of other animals. But she had not reckoned on the untiring energy of the Saw-Horse, whose wooden limbs could run for days without slacking their speed. Therefore, after an hour's hard running, the Griffin's breath began to fail, and it panted and gasped painfully, and moved more slowly than before. Then it reached the edge of the desert and began racing across the deep sands. But its tired feet sank far into the sand, and in a few minutes the Griffin fell forward, completely exhausted, and lay still upon the desert waste.

Glinda came up a moment later, riding the still vigorous Saw-Horse; and having unwound a slender golden thread from her girdle the Sorceress threw it over the head of the panting and helpless Griffin, and so destroyed the magical power of Mombi's transformation.

For the animal, with one fierce shudder, disappeared from view, while in its place was discovered the form of the old Witch, glaring savagely at the serene and beautiful face of the Sorceress.

Chapter 23

PRINCESS OZMA OF OZ

"You are my prisoner, and it is useless for you to struggle any longer," said Glinda, in her soft, sweet voice. "Lie still a moment, and rest yourself, and then I will carry you back to my tent."

"Why do you seek me?" asked Mombi, still scarce able to speak plainly for lack of breath. "What have I done to you, to be so persecuted?"

"You have done nothing to me," answered the gentle Sorceress; "but I suspect you have been guilty of several wicked actions; and if I find it is true that you have so abused your knowledge of magic, I intend to punish you severely."

"I defy you!" croaked the old hag. "You dare not harm me!"

Just then the Gump flew up to them and alighted upon the desert sands beside Glinda. Our friends were delighted to find that Mombi had finally been captured, and after a hurried consultation it was decided they should all return to the camp in the Gump. So the Saw-Horse was tossed aboard, and then Glinda still holding an end of the golden thread that was around Mombi's neck, forced her prisoner to climb into the sofas. The others now followed, and Tip gave the word to the Gump to return.

The Journey was made in safety, Mombi sitting in her place with a grim and sullen air; for the old hag was absolutely helpless so long as the magical thread encircled her throat. The army hailed Glinda's return with loud cheers, and the party of friends soon gathered again in the royal tent, which had been neatly repaired during their absence.

"Now," said the Sorceress to Mombi, "I want you to tell us why the Wonderful Wizard of Oz paid you three visits, and what became of the child, Ozma, which so curiously disappeared."

The Witch looked at Glinda defiantly, but said not a word.

"Answer me!" cried the Sorceress.

But still Mombi remained silent.

"Perhaps she doesn't know," remarked Jack.

"I beg you will keep quiet," said Tip. "You might spoil everything with your foolishness."

"Very well, dear father!" returned the Pumpkinhead, meekly.

"How glad I am to be a Woggle-Bug!" murmured the Highly Magnified Insect, softly. "No one can expect wisdom to flow from a pumpkin."

"Well," said the Scarecrow, "what shall we do to make Mombi speak? Unless she tells us what we wish to know her capture will do us no good at all."

"Suppose we try kindness," suggested the Tin Woodman. "I've heard that anyone can be conquered with kindness, no matter how ugly they may be."

At this the Witch turned to glare upon him so horribly that the Tin Woodman shrank back abashed.

Glinda had been carefully considering what to do, and now she turned to Mombi and said:

"You will gain nothing, I assure you, by thus defying us. For I am determined to learn the truth about the girl Ozma, and unless you tell me all that you know, I will certainly put you to death."

"Oh, no! Don't do that!" exclaimed the Tin Woodman. "It would be an awful thing to kill anyone—even old Mombi!"

"But it is merely a threat," returned Glinda. "I shall not put Mombi to death, because she will prefer to tell me the truth."

"Oh, I see!" said the tin man, much relieved.

"Suppose I tell you all that you wish to know,". said Mombi, speaking so suddenly that she startled them all. "What will you do with me then?"

"In that case," replied Glinda, "I shall merely ask you to drink a powerful draught which will cause you to forget all the magic you have ever learned."

"Then I would become a helpless old woman!"

"But you would be alive," suggested the Pumpkinhead, consolingly.

"Do try to keep silent!" said Tip, nervously.

"I'll try," responded Jack; "but you will admit that it's a good thing to be alive."

"Especially if one happens to be Thoroughly Educated," added the Woggle-Bug, nodding approval.

"You may make your choice," Glinda said to old Mombi, "between death if you remain silent, and the loss of your magical powers if you tell me the truth. But I think you will prefer to live."

Mombi cast an uneasy glance at the Sorceress, and saw that she was in earnest, and not to be trifled with. So she replied, slowly:

"I will answer your questions."

"That is what I expected," said Glinda, pleasantly. "You have chosen wisely, I assure you."

She then motioned to one of her Captains, who brought her a beautiful golden casket. From this the Sorceress drew an immense white pearl, attached to a slender chain which she placed around her neck in such a way that the pearl rested upon her bosom, directly over her heart.

"Now," said she, "I will ask my first question: Why did the Wizard pay you three visits?"

"Because I would not come to him," answered Mombi.

"That is no answer," said Glinda, sternly. "Tell me the truth."

"Well," returned Mombi, with downcast eyes, "he visited me to learn the way I make tea-biscuits."

"Look up!" commanded the Sorceress.

Mombi obeyed.

"What is the color of my pearl?" demanded Glinda.

"Why—it is black!" replied the old Witch, in a tone of wonder.

"Then you have told me a falsehood!" cried Glinda, angrily. "Only when the truth is spoken will my magic pearl remain a pure white in color."

Mombi now saw how useless it was to try to deceive the Sorceress; so she said, meanwhile scowling at her defeat:

"The Wizard brought to me the girl Ozma, who was then no more than a baby, and begged me to conceal the child."

"That is what I thought," declared Glinda, calmly. "What did he give you for thus serving him?"

"He taught me all the magical tricks he knew. Some were good tricks, and some were only frauds; but I have remained faithful to my promise."

"What did you do with the girl?" asked Glinda; and at this question everyone bent forward and listened eagerly for the reply.

"I enchanted her," answered Mombi.

"In what way?"

"I transformed her into—into—"

"Into what?" demanded Glinda, as the Witch hesitated.

"*Into a boy!*" said Mombi, in a low tone.

"A boy!" echoed every voice; and then, because they knew that this old woman had reared Tip from childhood, all eyes were turned to where the boy stood.

"Yes," said the old Witch, nodding her head; "that is the Princess Ozma—the child brought to me by the Wizard who stole her father's throne. That is the rightful ruler of the Emerald City!" and she pointed her long bony finger straight at the boy.

"I!" cried Tip, in amazement. "Why, I'm no Princess Ozma— I'm not a girl!"

Glinda smiled, and going to Tip she took his small brown hand within her dainty white one.

"You are not a girl just now" said she, gently, "because Mombi transformed you into a boy. But you were born a girl, and also a Princess; so you must resume your proper form, that you may become Queen of the Emerald City."

"Oh, let Jinjur be the Queen!" exclaimed Tip, ready to cry. "I want to stay a boy, and travel with the Scarecrow and the Tin Woodman, and the Woggle-Bug, and Jack—yes! and my friend the Saw-Horse—and the Gump! I don't want to be a girl!"

"Never mind, old chap," said the Tin Woodman, soothingly; "it don't hurt to be a girl, I'm told; and we will all remain your faithful friends just the same. And, to be honest with you, I've always considered girls nicer than boys."

"They're just as nice, anyway," added the Scarecrow, patting Tip affectionately upon the head.

"And they are equally good students," proclaimed the Woggle-Bug. "I should like to become your tutor, when you are transformed into a girl again."

"But—see here!" said Jack Pumpkinhead, with a gasp: "if you become a girl, you can't be my dear father any more!"

"No," answered Tip, laughing in spite of his anxiety. "and I shall not be sorry to escape the relationship." Then he added, hesitatingly, as he turned to Glinda: "I might try it for awhile,-just to see how it seems, you know. But if I don't like being a girl you must promise to change me into a boy again."

"Really," said the Sorceress, "that is beyond my magic. I never deal in transformations, for they are not honest, and no respectable sorceress likes to make things appear to be what they are not. Only unscrupulous witches use the art, and therefore I must ask Mombi to effect your release from her charm, and restore you to your proper form. It will be the last opportunity she will have to practice magic."

Now that the truth about Princes Ozma had been discovered, Mombi did not care what became of Tip; but she feared Glinda's anger, and the boy generously promised to provide for Mombi in her old age if he became the ruler of the Emerald City. So the Witch consented to effect the transformation, and preparations for the event were at once made.

Glinda ordered her own royal couch to be placed in the center of the tent. It was piled high with cushions covered with rose-colored silk, and from a golden railing above hung many folds of pink gossamer, completely concealing the interior of the couch.

The first act of the Witch was to make the boy drink a potion which quickly sent him into a deep and dreamless sleep. Then the Tin Woodman and the Woggle-Bug bore him gently to the couch, placed him upon the soft cushions, and drew the gossamer hangings to shut him from all earthly view.

The Witch squatted upon the ground and kindled a tiny fire of dried herbs, which she drew from her bosom. When the blaze shot up and burned clearly old Mombi scattered a handful of magical powder over the fire, which straightway gave off a rich violet vapor, filling all the tent with its fragrance and forcing the Saw-Horse to sneeze—although he had been warned to keep quiet.

Then, while the others watched her curiously, the hag chanted a rhythmical verse in words which no one understood, and bent her lean body seven times back and forth over the fire. And now the incantation seemed complete, for the Witch stood upright and cried the one word "Yeowa!" in a loud voice.

The vapor floated away; the atmosphere became, clear again; a whiff of fresh air filled the tent, and the pink curtains of the couch trembled slightly, as if stirred from within.

Glinda walked to the canopy and parted the silken hangings. Then she bent over the cushions, reached out her hand, and from the couch arose the form of a young girl, fresh and beautiful as a May morning. Her eyes sparkled as two diamonds, and her lips were tinted like a tourmaline. All adown her back floated tresses of ruddy gold, with a slender jeweled circlet confining them at the brow. Her robes of silken gauze floated around her like a cloud, and dainty satin slippers shod her feet.

At this exquisite vision Tip's old comrades stared in wonder for the space of a full minute, and then every head bent low in honest admiration of the lovely Princess Ozma. The girl herself cast one look into Glinda's bright face, which glowed with pleasure and satisfaction, and then turned upon the others. Speaking the words with sweet diffidence, she said:

"I hope none of you will care less for me than you did before. I'm just the same Tip, you know; only—only—"

"Only you're different!" said the Pumpkinhead; and everyone thought it was the wisest speech he had ever made.

Chapter 24

THE RICHES OF CONTENT

WHEN the wonderful tidings reached the ears of Queen Jinjur—how Mombi the Witch had been captured; how she had confessed her crime to Glinda; and how the long-lost Princess Ozma had been discovered in no less a personage than the boy Tip—she wept real tears of grief and despair.

"To think," she moaned, "that after having ruled as Queen, and lived in a palace, I must go back to scrubbing floors and churning butter again! It is too horrible to think of! I will never consent!"

So when her soldiers, who spent most of their time making fudge in the palace kitchens, counseled Jinjur to resist, she listened to their foolish prattle and sent a sharp defiance to Glinda the Good and the Princess Ozma. The result was a declaration of war, and the very next day Glinda marched upon the Emerald City with pennants flying and bands playing, and a forest of shining spears, sparkling brightly beneath the sun's rays.

But when it came to the walls this brave assembly made a sudden halt; for Jinjur had closed and barred every gateway, and the walls of the Emerald City were builded high and thick with many blocks of green marble. Finding her advance thus baffled, Glinda bent her brows in deep thought, while the Woggle-Bug said, in his most positive tone:

"We must lay siege to the city, and starve it into submission. It is the only thing we can do."

"Not so," answered the Scarecrow. "We still have the Gump, and the Gump can still fly"

The Sorceress turned quickly at this speech, and her face now wore a bright smile.

"You are right," she exclaimed, "and certainly have reason to be proud of your brains. Let us go to the Gump at once!"

So they passed through the ranks of the army until they came to the place, near the Scarecrow's tent, where the Gump lay. Glinda and Princess Ozma mounted first, and sat upon the sofas. Then the Scarecrow and his friends climbed aboard, and still there was room for a Captain and three soldiers, which Glinda considered sufficient for a guard.

Now, at a word from the Princess, the queer Thing they had called the Gump flopped its palm-leaf wings and rose into the air, carrying the party of adventurers high above the walls. They hovered over the palace, and soon perceived Jinjur reclining in a hammock in the courtyard, where she was comfortably reading a novel with a green cover and eating green chocolates, confident that the walls would protect her from her enemies. Obeying a quick command, the Gump alighted safely in this very courtyard, and before Jinjur had time to do more than scream, the Captain and three soldiers leaped out and made the former Queen a prisoner, locking strong chains upon both her wrists.

That act really ended the war; for the Army of Revolt submitted as soon as they knew Jinjur to be a captive, and the Captain marched in safety through the streets and up to the gates of the city, which she threw wide open. Then the bands played their most stirring music while Glinda's army marched into the city, and heralds proclaimed the conquest of the audacious Jinjur and the accession of the beautiful Princess Ozma to the throne of her royal ancestors.

At once the men of the Emerald City cast off their aprons. And it is said that the women were so tired eating of their husbands' cooking that they all hailed the conquest of Jinjur with Joy. Certain it is that, rushing one and all to the kitchens of their houses, the good wives prepared so delicious a feast for the weary men that harmony was immediately restored in every family.

Ozma's first act was to oblige the Army of Revolt to return to her every emerald or other gem stolen from the public streets and buildings; and so great was the number of precious stones picked from their settings by these vain girls, that every one of the royal jewelers worked steadily for more than a month to replace them in their settings.

Meanwhile the Army of Revolt was disbanded and the girls sent home to their mothers. On promise of good behavior Jinjur was likewise released.

Ozma made the loveliest Queen the Emerald City had ever known; and, although she was so young and inexperienced, she ruled her people with wisdom and Justice. For Glinda gave her good advice on all occasions; and the Woggle-Bug, who was appointed to the important post of Public Educator, was quite helpful to Ozma when her royal duties grew perplexing.

The girl, in her gratitude to the Gump for its services, offered the creature any reward it might name.

"Then," replied the Gump, "please take me to pieces. I did not wish to be brought to life, and I am greatly ashamed of my conglomerate personality. Once I was a monarch of the forest, as my antlers fully prove; but now, in my present upholstered condition of servitude, I am compelled to fly through the air— my legs being of no use to me whatever. Therefore I beg to be dispersed."

So Ozma ordered the Gump taken apart. The antlered head was again hung over the mantle-piece in the hall, and the sofas were untied and placed in the reception parlors. The broom tail resumed its accustomed duties in the kitchen, and finally, the

Scarecrow replaced all the clotheslines and ropes on the pegs from which he had taken them on the eventful day when the Thing was constructed.

You might think that was the end of the Gump; and so it was, as a flying-machine. But the head over the mantle-piece continued to talk whenever it took a notion to do so, and it frequently startled, with its abrupt questions, the people who waited in the hall for an audience with the Queen.

The Saw-Horse, being Ozma's personal property, was tenderly cared for; and often she rode the queer creature along the streets of the Emerald City. She had its wooden legs shod with gold, to keep them from wearing out, and the tinkle of these golden shoes upon the pavement always filled the Queen's subjects with awe as they thought upon this evidence of her magical powers.

"The Wonderful Wizard was never so wonderful as Queen Ozma," the people said to one another, in whispers; "for he claimed to do many things he could not do; whereas our new Queen does many things no one would ever expect her to accomplish."

Jack Pumpkinhead remained with Ozma to the end of his days; and he did not spoil as soon as he had feared, although he always remained as stupid as ever. The Woggle-Bug tried to teach him several arts and sciences; but Jack was so poor a student that any attempt to educate him was soon abandoned.

After Glinda's army had marched back home, and peace was restored to the Emerald City, the Tin Woodman announced his intention to return to his own Kingdom of the Winkies.

"It isn't a very big Kingdom," said he to Ozma, "but for that very reason it is easier to rule; and I have called myself an Emperor because I am an Absolute Monarch, and no one interferes in any way with my conduct of public or personal affairs. When I get home I shall have a new coat of nickel plate; for I have become somewhat marred and scratched lately; and then I shall be glad to have you pay me a visit."

"Thank you," replied Ozma. "Some day I may accept the invitation. But what is to become of the Scarecrow?"

"I shall return with my friend the Tin Woodman," said the stuffed one, seriously. "We have decided never to be parted in the future."

"And I have made the Scarecrow my Royal Treasurer," explained the Tin Woodman. "For it has occurred to me that it is a good thing to have a Royal Treasurer who is made of money. What do you think?"

"I think," said the little Queen, smiling, "that your friend must be the richest man in all the world."

"I am," returned the Scarecrow. "but not on account of my money. For I consider brains far superior to money, in every way. You may have noticed that if one has money without brains, he cannot use it to advantage; but if one has brains without money, they will enable him to live comfortably to the end of his days."

"At the same time," declared the Tin Woodman, "you must acknowledge that a good heart is a thing that brains can not create, and that money can not buy. Perhaps, after all, it is I who am the richest man in all the world."

"You are both rich, my friends," said Ozma, gently; "and your riches are the only riches worth having—the riches of content!"

THE END

OZMA OF OZ

To all the boys and girls who read my stories—and especially to the Dorothys—this book is lovingly dedicated.

CONTENTS

Chapter 1

THE GIRL IN THE CHICKEN COOP

THE wind blew hard and joggled the water of the ocean, sending ripples across its surface. Then the wind pushed the edges of the ripples until they became waves, and shoved the waves around until they became billows. The billows rolled dreadfully high: higher even than the tops of houses. Some of them, indeed, rolled as high as the tops of tall trees, and seemed like mountains, and the gulfs between the great billows were like deep valleys.

All this mad dashing and splashing of the waters of the big ocean, which the mischievous wind caused without any good reason whatever, resulted in a terrible storm, and a storm on the ocean is liable to cut many queer pranks and do a lot of damage.

At the time the wind began to blow, a ship was sailing far out upon the waters. When the waves began to tumble and toss and to grow bigger and bigger the ship rolled up and down, and tipped sidewise—first one way and then the other—and was jostled around so roughly that even the sailor-men had to hold fast to the ropes and railings to keep themselves from being swept away by the wind or pitched headlong into the sea.

And the clouds were so thick in the sky that the sunlight couldn't get through them; so that the day grew dark as night, which added to the terrors of the storm.

The Captain of the ship was not afraid, because he had seen storms before, and had sailed his ship through them in safety; but he knew that his passengers would be in danger if they tried to stay on deck, so he put them all into the cabin and told them to stay there until after the storm was over, and to keep brave hearts and not be scared, and all would be well with them.

Now, among these passengers was a little Kansas girl named Dorothy Gale, who was going with her Uncle Henry to Australia, to visit some relatives they had never before seen. Uncle Henry, you must know, was not very well, because he had been working so hard on his Kansas farm that his health had given way and left him weak and nervous. So he left Aunt Em at home to watch after the hired men and to take care of the farm, while he traveled far away to Australia to visit his cousins and have a good rest.

Dorothy was eager to go with him on this journey, and Uncle Henry thought she would be good company and help cheer him up; so he decided to take her along. The little girl was quite an experienced traveller, for she had once been carried by a cyclone as far away from home as the marvelous Land of Oz, and she had met with a good many adventures in that strange country before she managed to get back to Kansas again. So she wasn't easily frightened, whatever happened, and when the wind began to howl and whistle, and the waves began to tumble and toss, our little girl didn't mind the uproar the least bit.

"Of course we'll have to stay in the cabin," she said to Uncle Henry and the other passengers, "and keep as quiet as possible until the storm is over. For the Captain says if we go on deck we may be blown overboard."

No one wanted to risk such an accident as that, you may be sure; so all the passengers stayed huddled up in the dark cabin, listening to the shrieking of the storm and the creaking of the masts and rigging and trying to keep from bumping into one another when the ship tipped sidewise.

Dorothy had almost fallen asleep when she was aroused with a start to find that Uncle Henry was missing. She couldn't imagine where he had gone, and as he was not very strong she began to worry about him, and to fear he might have been careless enough to go on deck. In that case he would be in great danger unless he instantly came down again.

The fact was that Uncle Henry had gone to lie down in his little sleeping-berth, but Dorothy did not know that. She only remembered that Aunt Em had cautioned her to take good care of her uncle, so at once she decided to go on deck and find him, in spite of the fact that the tempest was now worse than ever, and the ship was plunging in a really dreadful manner. Indeed, the little girl found it was as much as she could do to mount the stairs to the deck, and as soon as she got there the wind struck her so fiercely that it almost tore away the skirts of her dress. Yet Dorothy felt a sort of joyous excitement in defying the storm, and while she held fast to the railing she peered around through the gloom and thought she saw the dim form of a man clinging to a mast not far away from her. This might be her uncle, so she called as loudly as she could:

"Uncle Henry! Uncle Henry!"

But the wind screeched and howled so madly that she scarce heard her own voice, and the man certainly failed to hear her, for he did not move.

Dorothy decided she must go to him; so she made a dash forward, during a lull in the storm, to where a big square chicken-coop had been lashed to the deck with ropes. She reached this place in safety, but no sooner had she seized fast hold of the slats of the big box in which the chickens were kept than the wind, as if enraged because the little girl dared to resist its power, suddenly redoubled its fury. With a scream like that of an angry giant it tore away the ropes that held the coop and lifted it high into the air, with Dorothy still clinging to the slats. Around and over it whirled, this way and that, and a few moments later the chicken-coop dropped far away into the sea, where the big waves caught it and slid it up-hill to a foaming crest and then downhill into a deep valley, as if it were nothing more than a plaything to keep them amused.

Dorothy had a good ducking, you may be sure, but she didn't loose her presence of mind even for a second. She kept tight hold of the stout slats and as soon as she could get the water out of her eyes she saw that the wind had ripped the cover from the coop, and the poor chickens were fluttering away in every direction, being blown by the wind until they looked like feather dusters without handles. The bottom of the coop was made of thick boards, so Dorothy found she was clinging to a sort of raft, with sides of slats, which readily bore up her weight. After coughing the water out of her throat and getting her breath again, she managed to climb over the slats and stand upon the firm wooden bottom of the coop, which supported her easily enough.

"Why, I've got a ship of my own!" she thought, more amused than frightened at her sudden change of condition; and then, as the coop climbed up to the top of a big wave, she looked eagerly around for the ship from which she had been blown.

It was far, far away, by this time. Perhaps no one on board had yet missed her, or knew of her strange adventure. Down into a valley between the waves the coop swept her, and when she climbed another crest the ship looked like a toy boat, it was such a long way off. Soon it had entirely disappeared in the gloom, and then Dorothy gave a sigh of regret at parting with Uncle Henry and began to wonder what was going to happen to her next.

Just now she was tossing on the bosom of a big ocean, with nothing to keep her afloat but a miserable wooden hen-coop that had a plank bottom and slatted sides, through which the water constantly splashed and wetted her through to the skin! And there was nothing to eat when she became hungry—as she was sure to do before long—and no fresh water to drink and no dry clothes to put on.

"Well, I declare!" she exclaimed, with a laugh. "You're in a pretty fix, Dorothy Gale, I can tell you! and I haven't the least idea how you're going to get out of it!"

As if to add to her troubles the night was now creeping on, and the gray clouds overhead changed to inky blackness. But the wind, as if satisfied at last with its mischievous pranks, stopped blowing this ocean and hurried away to another part of the world to blow something else; so that the waves, not being joggled any more, began to quiet down and behave themselves.

It was lucky for Dorothy, I think, that the storm subsided; otherwise, brave though she was, I fear she might have perished. Many children, in her place, would have wept and given way to despair; but because Dorothy had encountered so many adventures and come safely through them it did not occur to her at this time to be especially afraid. She was wet and uncomfortable, it is true; but, after sighing that one sigh I told you of, she managed to recall some of her customary cheerfulness and decided to patiently await whatever her fate might be.

By and by the black clouds rolled away and showed a blue sky overhead, with a silver moon shining sweetly in the middle of it and little stars winking merrily at Dorothy when she looked their way. The coop did not toss around any more, but rode the waves more gently—almost like a cradle rocking—so that the floor upon which Dorothy stood was no longer swept by water coming through the slats. Seeing this, and being quite exhausted by the excitement of the past few hours, the little girl decided that sleep would be the best thing to restore her strength and the easiest way in which she could pass the time. The floor was damp and she was herself wringing wet, but fortunately this was a warm climate and she did not feel at all cold. So she sat down in a corner of the coop, leaned her back against the slats, nodded at the friendly stars before she closed her eyes, and was asleep in half a minute.

Chapter 2

THE YELLOW HEN

A strange noise awoke Dorothy, who opened her eyes to find that day had dawned and the sun was shining brightly in a clear sky. She had been dreaming that she was back in Kansas again, and playing in the old barn-yard with the calves and pigs and chickens all around her; and at first, as she rubbed the sleep from her eyes, she really imagined she was there.

"Kut-kut-kut, ka-daw-kut! Kut-kut-kut, ka-daw-kut!"

Ah; here again was the strange noise that had awakened her. Surely it was a hen cackling! But her wide-open eyes first saw, through the slats of the coop, the blue waves of the ocean, now calm and placid, and her thoughts flew back to the past night, so full of danger and discomfort. Also she began to remember that she was a waif of the storm, adrift upon a treacherous and unknown sea.

"Kut-kut-kut, ka-daw-w-w—kut!"

"What's that?" cried Dorothy, starting to her feet.

"Why, I've just laid an egg, that's all," replied a small, but sharp and distinct voice, and looking around her the little girl discovered a yellow hen squatting in the opposite corner of the coop.

"Dear me!" she exclaimed, in surprise; "have *you* been here all night, too?"

"Of course," answered the hen, fluttering her wings and yawning. "When the coop blew away from the ship I clung fast to this corner, with claws and beak, for I knew if I fell into the water I'd surely be drowned. Indeed, I nearly drowned, as it was, with all that water washing over me. I never was so wet before in my life!"

"Yes," agreed Dorothy, "it was pretty wet, for a time, I know. But do you feel comfor'ble now?"

"Not very. The sun has helped to dry my feathers, as it has your dress, and I feel better since I laid my morning egg. But what's to become of us, I should like to know, afloat on this big pond?"

"I'd like to know that, too," said Dorothy. "But, tell me; how does it happen that you are able to talk? I thought hens could only cluck and cackle."

"Why, as for that," answered the yellow hen thoughtfully, "I've clucked and cackled all my life, and never spoken a word before this morning, that I can remember. But when you asked a question, a minute ago, it seemed the most natural thing in the world to answer you. So I spoke, and I seem to keep on speaking, just as you and other human beings do. Strange, isn't it?"

"Very," replied Dorothy. "If we were in the Land of Oz, I wouldn't think it so queer, because many of the animals can talk in that fairy country. But out here in the ocean must be a good long way from Oz."

"How is my grammar?" asked the yellow hen, anxiously. "Do I speak quite properly, in your judgment?"

"Yes," said Dorothy, "you do very well, for a beginner."

"I'm glad to know that," continued the yellow hen, in a confidential tone; "because, if one is going to talk, it's best to talk correctly. The red rooster has often said that my cluck and my cackle were quite perfect; and now it's a comfort to know I am talking properly."

"I'm beginning to get hungry," remarked Dorothy. "It's breakfast time; but there's no breakfast."

"You may have my egg," said the yellow hen. "I don't care for it, you know."

"Don't you want to hatch it?" asked the little girl, in surprise.

"No, indeed; I never care to hatch eggs unless I've a nice snug nest, in some quiet place, with a baker's dozen of eggs under me. That's thirteen, you know, and it's a lucky number for hens. So you may as well eat this egg."

"Oh, I couldn't POSS'BLY eat it, unless it was cooked," exclaimed Dorothy. "But I'm much obliged for your kindness, just the same."

"Don't mention it, my dear," answered the hen, calmly, and began pruning her feathers.

For a moment Dorothy stood looking out over the wide sea. She was still thinking of the egg, though; so presently she asked:

"Why do you lay eggs, when you don't expect to hatch them?"

"It's a habit I have," replied the yellow hen. "It has always been my pride to lay a fresh egg every morning, except when I'm moulting. I never feel like having my morning cackle till the egg is properly laid, and without the chance to cackle I would not be happy."

"It's strange," said the girl, reflectively; "But as I'm not a hen I can't be 'spected to understand that."

"Certainly not, my dear."

Then Dorothy fell silent again. The yellow hen was some company, and a bit of comfort, too; but it was dreadfully lonely out on the big ocean, nevertheless.

After a time the hen flew up and perched upon the topmost slat of the coop, which was a little above Dorothy's head when she was sitting upon the bottom, as she had been doing for some moments past.

"Why, we are not far from land!" exclaimed the hen.

"Where? Where is it?" cried Dorothy, jumping up in great excitement.

"Over there a little way," answered the hen, nodding her head in a certain direction. "We seem to be drifting toward it, so that before noon we ought to find ourselves upon dry land again."

"I shall like that!" said Dorothy, with a little sigh, for her feet and legs were still wetted now and then by the sea-water that came through the open slats

"So shall I," answered her companion. "There is nothing in the world so miserable as a wet hen."

The land, which they seemed to be rapidly approaching, since it grew more distinct every minute, was quite beautiful as viewed by the little girl in the floating hen-coop. Next to the water was a broad beach of white sand and gravel, and farther back were several rocky hills, while beyond these appeared a strip of green trees that marked the edge of a forest. But there were no houses to be seen, nor any sign of people who might inhabit this unknown land.

"I hope we shall find something to eat," said Dorothy, looking eagerly at the pretty beach toward which they drifted. "It's long past breakfast time, now."

"I'm a trifle hungry, myself," declared the yellow hen.

"Why don't you eat the egg?" asked the child. "You don't need to have your food cooked, as I do."

"Do you take me for a cannibal?" cried the hen, indignantly. "I do not know what I have said or done that leads you to insult me!"

"I beg your pardon, I'm sure Mrs.—Mrs.—by the way, may I inquire your name, ma'am?" asked the little girl.

"My name is Bill," said the yellow hen, somewhat gruffly.

"Bill! Why, that's a boy's name."

"What difference does that make?"

"You're a lady hen, aren't you?"

"Of course. But when I was first hatched out no one could tell whether I was going to be a hen or a rooster; so the little boy at the farm where I was born called me Bill, and made a pet of me because I was the only yellow chicken in the whole brood. When I grew up, and he found that I didn't crow and fight, as all the roosters do, he did not think to change my name, and every creature in the barn-yard, as well as the people in the house, knew me as 'Bill.' So Bill I've always been called, and Bill is my name."

"But it's all wrong, you know," declared Dorothy, earnestly; "and, if you don't mind, I shall call you 'Billina.' Putting the 'eena' on the end makes it a girl's name, you see."

"Oh, I don't mind it in the least," returned the yellow hen. "It doesn't matter at all what you call me, so long as I know the name means *me*."

"Very well, Billina. *My* name is Dorothy Gale—just Dorothy to my friends and Miss Gale to strangers. You may call me Dorothy, if you like. We're getting very near the shore. Do you suppose it is too deep for me to wade the rest of the way?"

"Wait a few minutes longer. The sunshine is warm and pleasant, and we are in no hurry."

"But my feet are all wet and soggy," said the girl. "My dress is dry enough, but I won't feel real comfor'ble till I get my feet dried."

She waited; however, as the hen advised, and before long the big wooden coop grated gently on the sandy beach and the dangerous voyage was over.

It did not take the castaways long to reach the shore, you may be sure. The yellow hen flew to the sands at once, but Dorothy had to climb over the high slats. Still, for a country girl, that was not much of a feat, and as soon as she was safe ashore Dorothy drew off her wet shoes and stockings and spread them upon the sun-warmed beach to dry.

Then she sat down and watched Billina, who was pick-pecking away with her sharp bill in the sand and gravel, which she scratched up and turned over with her strong claws.

"What are you doing?" asked Dorothy.

"Getting my breakfast, of course," murmured the hen, busily pecking away.

"What do you find?" inquired the girl, curiously.

"Oh, some fat red ants, and some sand-bugs, and once in a while a tiny crab. They are very sweet and nice, I assure you."

"How dreadful!" exclaimed Dorothy, in a shocked voice.

"What is dreadful?" asked the hen, lifting her head to gaze with one bright eye at her companion.

"Why, eating live things, and horrid bugs, and crawly ants. You ought to be *'shamed* of yourself!"

"Goodness me!" returned the hen, in a puzzled tone; "how queer you are, Dorothy! Live things are much fresher and more wholesome than dead ones, and you humans eat all sorts of dead creatures."

"We don't!" said Dorothy.

"You do, indeed," answered Billina. "You eat lambs and sheep and cows and pigs and even chickens."

"But we cook 'em," said Dorothy, triumphantly.

"What difference does that make?"

"A good deal," said the girl, in a graver tone. "I can't just 'splain the diff'rence, but it's there. And, anyhow, we never eat such dreadful things as *bugs*."

"But you eat the chickens that eat the bugs," retorted the yellow hen, with an odd cackle. "So you are just as bad as we chickens are."

This made Dorothy thoughtful. What Billina said was true enough, and it almost took away her appetite for breakfast. As for the yellow hen, she continued to peck away at the sand busily, and seemed quite contented with her bill-of-fare.

Finally, down near the water's edge, Billina stuck her bill deep into the sand, and then drew back and shivered.

"Ow!" she cried. "I struck metal, that time, and it nearly broke my beak."

"It prob'bly was a rock," said Dorothy, carelessly.

"Nonsense. I know a rock from metal, I guess," said the hen. "There's a different feel to it."

"But there couldn't be any metal on this wild, deserted seashore," persisted the girl. "Where's the place? I'll dig it up, and prove to you I'm right."

Billina showed her the place where she had "stubbed her bill," as she expressed it, and Dorothy dug away the sand until she felt something hard. Then, thrusting in her hand, she pulled the thing out, and discovered it to be a large sized golden key—rather old, but still bright and of perfect shape.

"What did I tell you?" cried the hen, with a cackle of triumph. "Can I tell metal when I bump into it, or is the thing a rock?"

"It's metal, sure enough," answered the child, gazing thoughtfully at the curious thing she had found. "I think it is pure gold, and it must have lain hidden in the sand for a long time. How do you suppose it came there, Billina? And what do you suppose this mysterious key unlocks?"

"I can't say," replied the hen. "You ought to know more about locks and keys than I do."

Dorothy glanced around. There was no sign of any house in that part of the country, and she reasoned that every key must fit a lock and every lock must have a purpose. Perhaps the key had been lost by somebody who lived far away, but had wandered on this very shore.

Musing on these things the girl put the key in the pocket of her dress and then slowly drew on her shoes and stockings, which the sun had fully dried.

"I b'lieve, Billina," she said, "I'll have a look 'round, and see if I can find some breakfast."

Chapter 3

LETTERS IN THE SAND

WALKING a little way back from the water's edge, toward the grove of trees, Dorothy came to a flat stretch of white sand that seemed to have queer signs marked upon its surface, just as one would write upon sand with a stick.

"What does it say?" she asked the yellow hen, who trotted along beside her in a rather dignified fashion.

"How should I know?" returned the hen. "I cannot read."

"Oh! Can't you?"

"Certainly not; I've never been to school, you know."

"Well, I have," admitted Dorothy; "but the letters are big and far apart, and it's hard to spell out the words."

But she looked at each letter carefully, and finally discovered that these words were written in the sand:

"BEWARE THE WHEELERS!"

"That's rather strange," declared the hen, when Dorothy had read aloud the words. "What do you suppose the Wheelers are?"

"Folks that wheel, I guess. They must have wheelbarrows, or baby-cabs or hand-carts," said Dorothy.

"Perhaps they're automobiles," suggested the yellow hen. "There is no need to beware of baby-cabs and wheelbarrows; but automobiles are dangerous things. Several of my friends have been run over by them."

"It can't be auto'biles," replied the girl, "for this is a new, wild country, without even trolley-cars or tel'phones. The people here havn't been discovered yet, I'm sure; that is, if there *are* any people. So I don't b'lieve there *can* be any auto'biles, Billina."

"Perhaps not," admitted the yellow hen. "Where are you going now?"

"Over to those trees, to see if I can find some fruit or nuts," answered Dorothy.

She tramped across the sand, skirting the foot of one of the little rocky hills that stood near, and soon reached the edge of the forest.

At first she was greatly disappointed, because the nearer trees were all punita, or cotton-wood or eucalyptus, and bore no fruit or nuts at all. But, bye and bye, when she was almost in despair, the little girl came upon two trees that promised to furnish her with plenty of food.

One was quite full of square paper boxes, which grew in clusters on all the limbs, and upon the biggest and ripest boxes the word "Lunch" could be read, in neat raised letters. This tree seemed to bear all the year around, for there were lunch-box blossoms on some of the branches, and on others tiny little lunch-boxes that were as yet quite green, and evidently not fit to eat until they had grown bigger.

The leaves of this tree were all paper napkins, and it presented a very pleasing appearance to the hungry little girl.

But the tree next to the lunch-box tree was even more wonderful, for it bore quantities of tin dinner-pails, which were so full and heavy that the stout branches bent underneath their weight. Some were small and dark-brown in color; those larger were of a dull tin color; but the really ripe ones were pails of bright tin that shone and glistened beautifully in the rays of sunshine that touched them.

Dorothy was delighted, and even the yellow hen acknowledged that she was surprised.

The little girl stood on tip-toe and picked one of the nicest and biggest lunch-boxes, and then she sat down upon the ground and eagerly opened it. Inside she found, nicely wrapped in white papers, a ham sandwich, a piece of sponge-cake, a pickle, a slice of new cheese and an apple. Each thing had a separate stem, and so had to be picked off the side of the box; but Dorothy found them all to be delicious, and she ate every bit of luncheon in the box before she had finished.

"A lunch isn't zactly breakfast," she said to Billina, who sat beside her curiously watching. "But when one is hungry one can eat even supper in the morning, and not complain."

"I hope your lunch-box was perfectly ripe," observed the yellow hen, in a anxious tone. "So much sickness is caused by eating green things."

"Oh, I'm sure it was ripe," declared Dorothy, "all, that is, 'cept the pickle, and a pickle just *has* to be green, Billina. But everything tasted perfectly splendid, and I'd rather have it than a church picnic. And now I think I'll pick a dinner-pail, to have when I get hungry again, and then we'll start out and 'splore the country, and see where we are."

"Havn't you any idea what country this is?" inquired Billina.

"None at all. But listen: I'm quite sure it's a fairy country, or such things as lunch-boxes and dinner-pails wouldn't be growing upon trees. Besides, Billina, being a hen, you wouldn't be able to talk in any civ'lized country, like Kansas, where no fairies live at all."

"Perhaps we're in the Land of Oz," said the hen, thoughtfully.

"No, that can't be," answered the little girl; "because I've been to the Land of Oz, and it's all surrounded by a horrid desert that no one can cross."

"Then how did you get away from there again?" asked Billina.

"I had a pair of silver shoes, that carried me through the air; but I lost them," said Dorothy.

"Ah, indeed," remarked the yellow hen, in a tone of unbelief.

"Anyhow," resumed the girl, "there is no seashore near the Land of Oz, so this must surely be some other fairy country."

While she was speaking she selected a bright and pretty dinner-pail that seemed to have a stout handle, and picked it from its branch. Then, accompanied by the yellow hen, she walked out of the shadow of the trees toward the sea-shore.

They were part way across the sands when Billina suddenly cried, in a voice of terror:

"What's that?"

Dorothy turned quickly around, and saw coming out of a path that led from between the trees the most peculiar person her eyes had ever beheld.

It had the form of a man, except that it walked, or rather rolled, upon all fours, and its legs were the same length as its arms, giving them the appearance of the four legs of a beast. Yet it was no beast that Dorothy had discovered, for the person was clothed most gorgeously in embroidered garments of many colors, and wore a straw hat perched jauntily upon the side of its head. But it differed from human beings in this respect, that instead of hands and feet there grew at the end of its arms and legs round wheels, and by means of these wheels it rolled very swiftly over the level ground. Afterward Dorothy found that these odd wheels were of the same hard substance that our finger-nails and toe-nails are composed of, and she also learned that creatures of this strange race were born in this queer fashion. But when our little girl first caught sight of the first individual of a race that was destined to cause her a lot of trouble, she had an idea that the brilliantly-clothed personage was on roller-skates, which were attached to his hands as well as to his feet.

"Run!" screamed the yellow hen, fluttering away in great fright. "It's a Wheeler!"

"A Wheeler?" exclaimed Dorothy. "What can that be?"

"Don't you remember the warning in the sand: 'Beware the Wheelers'? Run, I tell you—run!"

So Dorothy ran, and the Wheeler gave a sharp, wild cry and came after her in full chase.

Looking over her shoulder as she ran, the girl now saw a great procession of Wheelers emerging from the forest—dozens and dozens of them—all clad in splendid, tight-fitting garments and all rolling swiftly toward her and uttering their wild, strange cries.

"They're sure to catch us!" panted the girl, who was still carrying the heavy dinner-pail she had picked. "I can't run much farther, Billina."

"Climb up this hill,—quick!" said the hen; and Dorothy found she was very near to the heap of loose and jagged rocks they had passed on their way to the forest. The yellow hen was even now fluttering among the rocks, and Dorothy followed as best she could, half climbing and half tumbling up the rough and rugged steep.

She was none too soon, for the foremost Wheeler reached the hill a moment after her; but while the girl scrambled up the rocks the creature stopped short with howls of rage and disappointment.

Dorothy now heard the yellow hen laughing, in her cackling, henny way.

"Don't hurry, my dear," cried Billina. "They can't follow us among these rocks, so we're safe enough now."

Dorothy stopped at once and sat down upon a broad boulder, for she was all out of breath.

The rest of the Wheelers had now reached the foot of the hill, but it was evident that their wheels would not roll upon the rough and jagged rocks, and therefore they were helpless to follow Dorothy and the hen to where they had taken refuge. But they circled all around the little hill, so the child and Billina were fast prisoners and could not come down without being captured.

Then the creatures shook their front wheels at Dorothy in a threatening manner, and it seemed they were able to speak as well as to make their dreadful outcries, for several of them shouted:

"We'll get you in time, never fear! And when we do get you, we'll tear you into little bits!"

"Why are you so cruel to me?" asked Dorothy. "I'm a stranger in your country, and have done you no harm."

"No harm!" cried one who seemed to be their leader. "Did you not pick our lunch-boxes and dinner-pails? Have you not a stolen dinner-pail still in your hand?"

"I only picked one of each," she answered. "I was hungry, and I didn't know the trees were yours."

"That is no excuse," retorted the leader, who was clothed in a most gorgeous suit. "It is the law here that whoever picks a dinner-pail without our permission must die immediately."

"Don't you believe him," said Billina. "I'm sure the trees do not belong to these awful creatures. They are fit for any mischief, and it's my opinion they would try to kill us just the same if you hadn't picked a dinner-pail."

"I think so, too," agreed Dorothy. "But what shall we do now?"

"Stay where we are," advised the yellow hen. "We are safe from the Wheelers until we starve to death, anyhow; and before that time comes a good many things can happen."

Chapter 4

TIKTOK *THE* MACHINE MAN

AFTER an hour or so most of the band of Wheelers rolled back into the forest, leaving only three of their number to guard the hill. These curled themselves up like big dogs and pretended to go to sleep on the sands; but neither Dorothy nor Billina were fooled by this trick, so they remained in security among the rocks and paid no attention to their cunning enemies.

Finally the hen, fluttering over the mound, exclaimed: "Why, here's a path!"

So Dorothy at once clambered to where Billina sat, and there, sure enough, was a smooth path cut between the rocks. It seemed to wind around the mound from top to bottom, like a cork-screw, twisting here and there between the rough boulders but always remaining level and easy to walk upon.

Indeed, Dorothy wondered at first why the Wheelers did not roll up this path; but when she followed it to the foot of the mound she found that several big pieces of rock had been placed directly across the end of the way, thus preventing any one outside from seeing it and also preventing the Wheelers from using it to climb up the mound.

Then Dorothy walked back up the path, and followed it until she came to the very top of the hill, where a solitary round rock stood that was bigger than any of the others surrounding it. The path came to an end just beside this great rock, and for a moment it puzzled the girl to know why the path had been made at all. But the hen, who had been gravely following her around and was now perched upon a point of rock behind Dorothy, suddenly remarked:

"It looks something like a door, doesn't it?"

"What looks like a door?" enquired the child.

"Why, that crack in the rock, just facing you," replied Billina, whose little round eyes were very sharp and seemed to see everything. "It runs up one side and down the other, and across the top and the bott

"What does?"

"Why, the crack. So I think it must be a door of rock, although I do not see any hinges."

"Oh, yes," said Dorothy, now observing for the first time the crack in the rock. "And isn't this a key-hole, Billina?" pointing to a round, deep hole at one side of the door.

"Of course. If we only had the key, now, we could unlock it and see what is there," replied the yellow hen. "May be it's a treasure chamber full of diamonds and rubies, or heaps of shining gold, or——"

"That reminds me," said Dorothy, "of the golden key I picked up on the shore. Do you think that it would fit this key-hole, Billina?"

"Try it and see," suggested the hen.

So Dorothy searched in the pocket of her dress and found the golden key. And when she had put it into the hole of the rock, and turned it, a sudden sharp snap was heard; then, with a solemn creak that made the shivers run down the child's back, the face of the rock fell outward, like a door on hinges, and revealed a small dark chamber just inside.

"Good gracious!" cried Dorothy, shrinking back as far as the narrow path would let her.

For, standing within the narrow chamber of rock, was the form of a man—or, at least, it seemed like a man, in the dim light. He was only about as tall as Dorothy herself, and his body was round as a ball and made out of burnished copper. Also his head and limbs were copper, and these were jointed or hinged to his body in a peculiar way, with metal caps over the joints, like the armor worn by knights in days of old. He stood perfectly still, and where the light struck upon his form it glittered as if made of pure gold.

"Don't be frightened," called Billina, from her perch. "It isn't alive."

"I see it isn't," replied the girl, drawing a long breath.

"It is only made out of copper, like the old kettle in the barnyard at home," continued the hen, turning her head first to one side and then to the other, so that both her little round eyes could examine the object.

"Once," said Dorothy, "I knew a man made out of tin, who was a woodman named Nick Chopper. But he was as alive as we are, 'cause he was born a real man, and got his tin body a little at a time—first a leg and then a finger and then an ear—for the reason that he had so many accidents with his axe, and cut himself up in a very careless manner."

"Oh," said the hen, with a sniff, as if she did not believe the story.

"But this copper man," continued Dorothy, looking at it with big eyes, "is not alive at all, and I wonder what it was made for, and why it was locked up in this queer place."

"That is a mystery," remarked the hen, twisting her head to arrange her wing-feathers with her bill.

Dorothy stepped inside the little room to get a back view of the copper man, and in this way discovered a printed card that hung between his shoulders, it being suspended from a small copper peg at the back of his neck. She unfastened this card and returned to the path, where the light was better, and sat herself down upon a slab of rock to read the printing.

"What does it say?" asked the hen, curiously.

Dorothy read the card aloud, spelling out the big words with some difficulty; and this is what she read:

SMITH & TINKER'S

Patent Double-Action, Extra-Responsive, Thought-Creating, Perfect-Talking

MECHANICAL MAN

Fitted with our Special Clock-Work Attachment. Thinks, Speaks, Acts, and Does Everything but Live.

Manufactured only at our Works at Evna, Land of Ev.

All infringements will be promptly Prosecuted according to Law.

"How queer!" said the yellow hen. "Do you think that is all true, my dear?"

"I don't know," answered Dorothy, who had more to read. "Listen to this, Billina:"

DIRECTIONS FOR USING:

For THINKING:—Wind the Clock-work Man under his left arm, (marked No. 1.)

For SPEAKING:—Wind the Clock-work Man under his right arm, (marked No.2.)

For WALKING and ACTION:—Wind Clock-work in the middle of his back, (marked No. 3.)

N. B.—This Mechanism is guaranteed to work perfectly for a thousand years.

"Well, I declare!" gasped the yellow hen, in amazement; "if the copper man can do half of these things he is a very wonderful machine. But I suppose it is all humbug, like so many other patented articles."

"We might wind him up," suggested Dorothy, "and see what he'll do."

"Where is the key to the clock-work?" asked Billina.

"Hanging on the peg where I found the card."

"Then," said the hen, "let us try him, and find out if he will go. He is warranted for a thousand years, it seems; but we do not know how long he has been standing inside this rock."

Dorothy had already taken the clock key from the peg.

"Which shall I wind up first?" she asked, looking again at the directions on the card.

"Number One, I should think," returned Billina. "That makes him think, doesn't it?"

"Yes," said Dorothy, and wound up Number One, under the left arm.

"He doesn't seem any different," remarked the hen, critically.

"Why, of course not; he is only thinking, now," said Dorothy.

"I wonder what he is thinking about."

"I'll wind up his talk, and then perhaps he can tell us," said the girl.

So she wound up Number Two, and immediately the clock-work man said, without moving any part of his body except his lips:

"Good morn-ing, lit-tle girl. Good morn-ing, Mrs. Hen."

The words sounded a little hoarse and creakey, and they were uttered all in the same tone, without any change of expression whatever; but both Dorothy and Billina understood them perfectly.

"Good morning, sir," they answered, politely.

"Thank you for res-cu-ing me," continued the machine, in the same monotonous voice, which seemed to be worked by a bellows inside of him, like the little toy lambs and cats the children squeeze so that they will make a noise

"Don't mention it," answered Dorothy. And then, being very curious, she asked: "How did you come to be locked up in this place?"

"It is a long sto-ry," replied the copper man; "but I will tell it to you brief-ly. I was pur-chased from Smith & Tin-ker, my man-u-fac-tur-ers, by a cru-el King of Ev, named Ev-ol-do, who used to beat all his serv-ants un-til they died. How-ev-er, he was not a-ble to kill me, be-cause I was not a-live, and one must first live in or-der to die. So that all his beat-ing did me no harm, and mere-ly kept my cop-per bod-y well pol-ished.

"This cru-el king had a love-ly wife and ten beau-ti-ful chil-dren—five boys and five girls—but in a fit of an-ger he sold them all to the Nome King, who by means of his mag-ic arts changed them all in-to oth-er forms and put them in his un-der-ground pal-ace to or-na-ment the rooms.

"Af-ter-ward the King of Ev re-gret-ted his wick-ed ac-tion, and tried to get his wife and chil-dren a-way from the Nome King, but with-out a-vail. So, in de-spair, he locked me up in this rock, threw the key in-to the o-cean, and then jumped in af-ter it and was drowned."

"How very dreadful!" exclaimed Dorothy.

"It is, in-deed," said the machine. "When I found my-self im-pris-oned I shout-ed for help un-til my voice ran down; and then I walked back and forth in this lit-tle room un-til my ac-tion ran down; and then I stood still and thought un-til my thoughts ran down. Af-ter that I re-mem-ber noth-ing un-til you wound me up a-gain."

"It's a very wonderful story," said Dorothy, "and proves that the Land of Ev is really a fairy land, as I thought it was."

"Of course it is," answered the copper man. "I do not sup-pose such a per-fect ma-chine as I am could be made in an-y place but a fair-y land."

"I've never seen one in Kansas," said Dorothy.

"But where did you get the key to un-lock this door?" asked the clock-work voice.

"I found it on the shore, where it was prob'ly washed up by the waves," she answered. "And now, sir, if you don't mind, I'll wind up your action."

"That will please me ve-ry much," said the machine.

So she wound up Number Three, and at once the copper man in a somewhat stiff and jerky fashion walked out of the rocky cavern, took off his copper hat and bowed politely, and then kneeled before Dorothy. Said he:

"From this time forth I am your o-be-di-ent ser-vant. What-ev-er you com-mand, that I will do will-ing-ly—if you keep me wound up."

"What is your name?" she asked.

"Tik-tok," he replied. "My for-mer mas-ter gave me that name be-cause my clock-work al-ways ticks when it is wound up."

"I can hear it now," said the yellow hen.

"So can I," said Dorothy. And then she added, with some anxiety: "You don't strike, do you?"

"No," answered Tiktok; "and there is no a-larm con-nec-ted with my ma-chin-er-y. I can tell the time, though, by speak-ing, and as I nev-er sleep I can wak-en you at an-y hour you wish to get up in the morn-ing."

"That's nice," said the little girl; "only I never wish to get up in the morning."

"You can sleep until I lay my egg," said the yellow hen. "Then, when I cackle, Tiktok will know it is time to waken you."

"Do you lay your egg very early?" asked Dorothy.

"About eight o'clock," said Billina. "And everybody ought to be up by that time, I'm sure."

Chapter 5

DOROTHY OPENS THE DINNER PAIL

"Now Tiktok," said Dorothy, "the first thing to be done is to find a way for us to escape from these rocks. The Wheelers are down below, you know, and threaten to kill us."

"There is no rea-son to be a-fraid of the Wheel-ers," said Tiktok, the words coming more slowly than before.

"Why not?" she asked.

"Be-cause they are ag-g-g—gr-gr-r-r-"

He gave a sort of gurgle and stopped short, waving his hands frantically until suddenly he became motionless, with one arm in the air and the other held stiffly before him with all the copper fingers of the hand spread out like a fan.

"Dear me!" said Dorothy, in a frightened tone. "What can the matter be?"

"He's run down, I suppose," said the hen, calmly. "You couldn't have wound him up very tight."

"I didn't know how much to wind him," replied the girl; "but I'll try to do better next time."

She ran around the copper man to take the key from the peg at the back of his neck, but it was not there.

"It's gone!" cried Dorothy, in dismay.

"What's gone?" asked Billina.

"The key."

"It probably fell off when he made that low bow to you," returned the hen. "Look around, and see if you cannot find it again."

Dorothy looked, and the hen helped her, and by and by the girl discovered the clock-key, which had fallen into a crack of the rock.

At once she wound up Tiktok's voice, taking care to give the key as many turns as it would go around. She found this quite a task, as you may imagine if you have ever tried to wind a clock, but the machine man's first words were to assure Dorothy that he would now run for at least twenty-four hours.

"You did not wind me much, at first," he calmly said, "and I told you that long sto-ry a-bout King Ev-ol-do; so it is no won-der that I ran down."

She next rewound the action clock-work, and then Billina advised her to carry the key to Tiktok in her pocket, so it would not get lost again.

"And now," said Dorothy, when all this was accomplished, "tell me what you were going to say about the Wheelers."

"Why, they are noth-ing to be fright-en'd at," said the machine. "They try to make folks be-lieve that they are ver-y ter-ri-ble, but as a mat-ter of fact the Wheel-ers are harm-less e-nough to an-y one that dares to fight them. They might try to hurt a lit-tle girl like you, per-haps, be-cause they are ver-y mis-chiev-ous. But if I had a club they would run a-way as soon as they saw me."

"Haven't you a club?" asked Dorothy.

"No," said Tiktok.

"And you won't find such a thing among these rocks, either," declared the yellow hen.

"Then what shall we do?" asked the girl.

"Wind up my think-works tight-ly, and I will try to think of some oth-er plan," said Tiktok.

So Dorothy rewound his thought machinery, and while he was thinking she decided to eat her dinner. Billina was already pecking away at the cracks in the rocks, to find something to eat, so Dorothy sat down and opened her tin dinner-pail.

In the cover she found a small tank that was full of very nice lemonade. It was covered by a cup, which might also, when removed, be used to drink the lemonade from. Within the pail were three slices of turkey, two slices of cold tongue, some lobster salad, four slices of bread and butter, a small custard pie, an orange and nine large strawberries, and some nuts and raisins. Singularly enough, the nuts in this dinner-pail grew already cracked, so that Dorothy had no trouble in picking out their meats to eat.

She spread the feast upon the rock beside her and began her dinner, first offering some of it to Tiktok, who declined because, as he said, he was merely a machine. Afterward she offered to share with Billina, but the hen murmured something about "dead things" and said she preferred her bugs and ants.

"Do the lunch-box trees and the dinner-pail trees belong to the Wheelers?" the child asked Tiktok, while engaged in eating her meal.

"Of course not," he answered. "They be-long to the roy-al fam-il-y of Ev, on-ly of course there is no roy-al fam-il-y just now be-cause King Ev-ol-do jumped in-to the sea and his wife and ten chil-dren have been trans-formed by the Nome King. So there is no one to rule the Land of Ev, that I can think of. Per-haps it is for this rea-son that the Wheel-ers claim the trees for their own, and pick the lunch-eons and din-ners to eat them-selves. But they be-long to the King, and you will find the roy-al "E" stamped up-on the bot-tom of ev-er-y din-ner pail."

Dorothy turned the pail over, and at once discovered the royal mark upon it, as Tiktok had said.

"Are the Wheelers the only folks living in the Land of Ev?" enquired the girl.

"No; they on-ly in-hab-it a small por-tion of it just back of the woods," replied the machine. "But they have al-ways been mis-chiev-ous and im-per-ti-nent, and my old mas-ter, King Ev-ol-do, used to car-ry a whip with him, when he walked out, to keep the crea-tures in or-der. When I was first made the Wheel-ers tried to run o-ver me, and butt me with their heads; but they soon found I was built of too sol-id a ma-ter-i-al for them to in-jure."

"You seem very durable," said Dorothy. "Who made you?"

"The firm of Smith & Tin-ker, in the town of Ev-na, where the roy-al pal-ace stands," answered Tiktok.

"Did they make many of you?" asked the child.

"No; I am the on-ly au-to-mat-ic me-chan-i-cal man they ev-er com-plet-ed," he replied. "They were ver-y won-der-ful in-ven-tors, were my mak-ers, and quite ar-tis-tic in all they did."

"I am sure of that," said Dorothy. "Do they live in the town of Evna now?"

"They are both gone," replied the machine. "Mr. Smith was an art-ist, as well as an in-vent-or, and he paint-ed a pic-ture of a riv-er which was so nat-ur-al that, as he was reach-ing a-cross it to paint some flow-ers on the op-po-site bank, he fell in-to the wa-ter and was drowned."

"Oh, I'm sorry for that!" exclaimed the little girl.

"Mis-ter Tin-ker," continued Tiktok, "made a lad-der so tall that he could rest the end of it a-gainst the moon, while he stood on the high-est rung and picked the lit-tle stars to set in the points of the king's crown. But when he got to the moon Mis-ter Tin-ker found it such a love-ly place that he de-cid-ed to live there, so he pulled up the lad-der af-ter him and we have nev-er seen him since."

"He must have been a great loss to this country," said Dorothy, who was by this time eating her custard pie.

"He was," acknowledged Tiktok. "Also he is a great loss to me. For if I should get out of or-der I do not know of an-y one a-ble to re-pair me, be-cause I am so com-pli-cat-ed. You have no i-de-a how full of ma-chin-er-y I am."

"I can imagine it," said Dorothy, readily.

"And now," continued the machine, "I must stop talk-ing and be-gin think-ing a-gain of a way to es-cape from this rock." So he turned halfway around, in order to think without being disturbed.

"The best thinker I ever knew," said Dorothy to the yellow hen, "was a scarecrow."

"Nonsense!" snapped Billina.

"It is true," declared Dorothy. "I met him in the Land of Oz, and he travelled with me to the city of the great Wizard of Oz, so as to get some brains, for his head was only stuffed with straw. But it seemed to me that he thought just as well before he got his brains as he did afterward."

"Do you expect me to believe all that rubbish about the Land of Oz?" enquired Billina, who seemed a little cross—perhaps because bugs were scarce.

"What rubbish?" asked the child, who was now finishing her nuts and raisins.

"Why, your impossible stories about animals that can talk, and a tin woodman who is alive, and a scarecrow who can think."

"They are all there," said Dorothy, "for I have seen them."

"I don't believe it!" cried the hen, with a toss of her head.

"That's 'cause you're so ign'rant," replied the girl, who was a little offended at her friend Billina's speech.

"In the Land of Oz," remarked Tiktok, turning toward them, "an-y-thing is pos-si-ble. For it is a won-der-ful fair-y coun-try."

"There, Billina! what did I say?" cried Dorothy. And then she turned to the machine and asked in an eager tone: "Do you know the Land of Oz, Tiktok?"

"No; but I have heard a-bout it," said the copper man. "For it is on-ly sep-a-ra-ted from this Land of Ev by a broad des-ert."

Dorothy clapped her hands together delightedly.

"I'm glad of that!" she exclaimed. "It makes me quite happy to be so near my old friends. The scarecrow I told you of, Billina, is the King of the Land of Oz."

"Par-don me. He is not the king now," said Tiktok.

"He was when I left there," declared Dorothy.

"I know," said Tiktok, "but there was a rev-o-lu-tion in the Land of Oz, and the Scare-crow was de-posed by a sol-dier wo-man named Gen-er-al Jin-jur. And then Jin-jur was de-posed by a lit-tle girl named Oz-ma, who was the right-ful heir to the throne and now rules the land un-der the ti-tle of Oz-ma of Oz."

"That is news to me," said Dorothy, thoughtfully. "But I s'pose lots of things have happened since I left the Land of Oz. I wonder what has become of the Scarecrow, and of the Tin Woodman, and the Cowardly Lion. And I wonder who this girl Ozma is, for I never heard of her before."

But Tiktok did not reply to this. He had turned around again to resume his thinking.

Dorothy packed the rest of the food back into the pail, so as not to be wasteful of good things, and the yellow hen forgot her dignity far enough to pick up all of the scattered crumbs, which she ate rather greedily, although she had so lately pretended to despise the things that Dorothy preferred as food.

By this time Tiktok approached them with his stiff bow.

"Be kind e-nough to fol-low me," he said, "and I will lead you a-way from here to the town of Ev-na, where you will be more com-for-ta-ble, and also I will pro-tect you from the Wheel-ers."

"All right," answered Dorothy, promptly. "I'm ready!"

Chapter 6

THE HEADS OF LANGWIDERE

THEY walked slowly down the path between the rocks, Tiktok going first, Dorothy following him, and the yellow hen trotting along last of all.

At the foot of the path the copper man leaned down and tossed aside with ease the rocks that cumbered the way. Then he turned to Dorothy and said:

"Let me car-ry your din-ner-pail."

She placed it in his right hand at once, and the copper fingers closed firmly over the stout handle.

Then the little procession marched out upon the level sands.

As soon as the three Wheelers who were guarding the mound saw them, they began to shout their wild cries and rolled swiftly toward the little group, as if to capture them or bar their way. But when the foremost had approached near enough, Tiktok swung the tin dinner-pail and struck the Wheeler a sharp blow over its head with the queer weapon. Perhaps it did not hurt very much, but it made a great noise, and the Wheeler uttered a howl and tumbled over upon its side. The next minute it scrambled to its wheels and rolled away as fast as it could go, screeching with fear at the same time.

"I told you they were harm-less," began Tiktok; but before he could say more another Wheeler was upon them. Crack! went the dinner-pail against its head, knocking its straw hat a dozen feet away; and that was enough for this Wheeler, also. It rolled away after the first one, and the third did not wait to be pounded with the pail, but joined its fellows as quickly as its wheels would whirl.

The yellow hen gave a cackle of delight, and flying to a perch upon Tiktok's shoulder, she said:

"Bravely done, my copper friend! and wisely thought of, too. Now we are free from those ugly creatures."

But just then a large band of Wheelers rolled from the forest, and relying upon their numbers to conquer, they advanced fiercely upon Tiktok. Dorothy grabbed Billina in her arms and held her tight, and the machine embraced the form of the little girl with his left arm, the better to protect her. Then the Wheelers were upon them.

Rattlety, bang! bang! went the dinner-pail in every direction, and it made so much clatter bumping against the heads of the Wheelers that they were much more frightened than hurt and fled in a great panic. All, that is, except their leader. This Wheeler had stumbled against another and fallen flat upon his back, and before he could get his wheels under him to rise again, Tiktok had fastened his copper fingers into the neck of the gorgeous jacket of his foe and held him fast.

"Tell your peo-ple to go a-way," commanded the machine.

The leader of the Wheelers hesitated to give this order, so Tiktok shook him as a terrier dog does a rat, until the Wheeler's teeth rattled together with a noise like hailstones on a window pane. Then, as soon as the creature could get its breath, it shouted to the others to roll away, which they immediately did.

"Now," said Tiktok, "you shall come with us and tell me what I want to know."

"You'll be sorry for treating me in this way," whined the Wheeler. "I'm a terribly fierce person."

"As for that," answered Tiktok, "I am only a ma-chine, and can-not feel sor-row or joy, no mat-ter what hap-pens. But you are wrong to think your-self ter-ri-ble or fierce."

"Why so?" asked the Wheeler.

"Be-cause no one else thinks as you do. Your wheels make you help-less to in-jure an-y one. For you have no fists and can not scratch or e-ven pull hair. Nor have you an-y feet to kick with. All you can do is to yell and shout, and that does not hurt an-y one at all."

The Wheeler burst into a flood of tears, to Dorothy's great surprise.

"Now I and my people are ruined forever!" he sobbed; "for you have discovered our secret. Being so helpless, our only hope is to make people afraid of us, by pretending we are very fierce and terrible, and writing in the sand warnings to Beware the Wheelers. Until now we have frightened everyone, but since you have discovered our weakness our enemies will fall upon us and make us very miserable and unhappy."

"Oh, no," exclaimed Dorothy, who was sorry to see this beautifully dressed Wheeler so miserable; "Tiktok will keep your secret, and so will Billina and I. Only, you must promise not to try to frighten children any more, if they come near to you."

"I won't—indeed I won't!" promised the Wheeler, ceasing to cry and becoming more cheerful. "I'm not really bad, you know; but we have to pretend to be terrible in order to prevent others from attacking us."

"That is not ex-act-ly true," said Tiktok, starting to walk toward the path through the forest, and still holding fast to his prisoner, who rolled slowly along beside him. "You and your peo-ple are full of mis-chief, and like to both-er those who fear you. And you are of-ten im-pu-dent and dis-a-gree-a-ble, too. But if you will try to cure those faults I will not tell any-one how help-less you are."

"I'll try, of course," replied the Wheeler, eagerly. "And thank you, Mr. Tiktok, for your kindness."

"I am on-ly a ma-chine," said Tiktok. "I can not be kind an-y more than I can be sor-ry or glad. I can on-ly do what I am wound up to do."

"Are you wound up to keep my secret?" asked the Wheeler, anxiously.

"Yes; if you be-have your-self. But tell me: who rules the Land of Ev now?" asked the machine.

"There is no ruler," was the answer, "because every member of the royal family is imprisoned by the Nome King. But the Princess Langwidere, who is a niece of our late King Evoldo, lives in a part of the royal palace and takes as much money out of the royal treasury as she can spend. The Princess Langwidere is not exactly a ruler, you see, because she doesn't rule; but she is the nearest approach to a ruler we have at present."

"I do not re-mem-ber her," said Tiktok. "What does she look like?"

"That I cannot say," replied the Wheeler, "although I have seen her twenty times. For the Princess Langwidere is a different person every time I see her, and the only way her subjects can recognize her at all is by means of a beautiful ruby key which she always wears on a chain attached to her left wrist. When we see the key we know we are beholding the Princess."

"That is strange," said Dorothy, in astonishment. "Do you mean to say that so many different princesses are one and the same person?"

"Not exactly," answered the Wheeler. "There is, of course, but one princess; but she appears to us in many forms, which are all more or less beautiful."

"She must be a witch," exclaimed the girl.

"I do not think so," declared the Wheeler. "But there is some mystery connected with her, nevertheless. She is a very vain creature, and lives mostly in a room surrounded by mirrors, so that she can admire herself whichever way she looks."

No one answered this speech, because they had just passed out of the forest and their attention was fixed upon the scene before them—a beautiful vale in which were many fruit trees and green fields, with pretty farm-houses scattered here and there and broad, smooth roads that led in every direction.

In the center of this lovely vale, about a mile from where our friends were standing, rose the tall spires of the royal palace, which glittered brightly against their background of blue sky. The palace was surrounded by charming grounds, full of flowers and shrubbery. Several tinkling fountains could be seen, and there were pleasant walks bordered by rows of white marble statuary.

All these details Dorothy was, of course, unable to notice or admire until they had advanced along the road to a position quite near to the palace, and she was still looking at the pretty sights when her little party entered the grounds and approached the big front door of the king's own apartments. To their disappointment they found the door tightly closed. A sign was tacked to the panel which read as follows:

OWNER ABSENT.

Please Knock at the Third Door in the Left Wing.

"Now," said Tiktok to the captive Wheeler, "you must show us the way to the Left Wing."

"Very well," agreed the prisoner, "it is around here at the right."

"How can the left wing be at the right?" demanded Dorothy, who feared the Wheeler was fooling them.

"Because there used to be three wings, and two were torn down, so the one on the right is the only one left. It is a trick of the Princess Langwidere to prevent visitors from annoying her."

Then the captive led them around to the wing, after which the machine man, having no further use for the Wheeler, permitted him to depart and rejoin his fellows. He immediately rolled away at a great pace and was soon lost to sight.

Tiktok now counted the doors in the wing and knocked loudly upon the third one.

It was opened by a little maid in a cap trimmed with gay ribbons, who bowed respectfully and asked:

"What do you wish, good people?"

"Are you the Princess Langwidere?" asked Dorothy.

"No, miss; I am her servant," replied the maid.

"May I see the Princess, please?"

"I will tell her you are here, miss, and ask her to grant you an audience," said the maid. "Step in, please, and take a seat in the drawing-room."

So Dorothy walked in, followed closely by the machine. But as the yellow hen tried to enter after them, the little maid cried "Shoo!" and flapped her apron in Billina's face.

"Shoo, yourself!" retorted the hen, drawing back in anger and ruffling up her feathers. "Haven't you any better manners than that?"

"Oh, do you talk?" enquired the maid, evidently surprised.

"Can't you hear me?" snapped Billina. "Drop that apron, and get out of the doorway, so that I may enter with my friends!"

"The Princess won't like it," said the maid, hesitating.

"I don't care whether she likes it or not," replied Billina, and fluttering her wings with a loud noise she flew straight at the maid's face. The little servant at once ducked her head, and the hen reached Dorothy's side, in safety.

"Very well," sighed the maid; "if you are all ruined because of this obstinate hen, don't blame me for it. It isn't safe to annoy the Princess Langwidere."

"Tell her we are waiting, if you please," Dorothy requested, with dignity. "Billina is my friend, and must go wherever I go."

Without more words the maid led them to a richly furnished drawing-room, lighted with subdued rainbow tints that came in through beautiful stained-glass windows.

"Remain here," she said. "What names shall I give the Princess?"

"I am Dorothy Gale, of Kansas," replied the child; "and this gentleman is a machine named Tiktok, and the yellow hen is my friend Billina."

The little servant bowed and withdrew, going through several passages and mounting two marble stairways before she came to the apartments occupied by her mistress.

Princess Langwidere's sitting-room was panelled with great mirrors, which reached from the ceiling to the floor; also the ceiling was composed of mirrors, and the floor was of polished silver that reflected every object upon it. So when Langwidere sat in her easy chair and played soft melodies upon her mandolin, her form was mirrored hundreds of times, in walls and ceiling and floor, and whichever way the lady turned her head she could see and admire her own features. This she loved to do, and just as the maid entered she was saying to herself:

"This head with the auburn hair and hazel eyes is quite attractive. I must wear it more often than I have done of late, although it may not be the best of my collection."

"You have company, Your Highness," announced the maid, bowing low.

"Who is it?" asked Langwidere, yawning.

"Dorothy Gale of Kansas, Mr. Tiktok and Billina," answered the maid.

"What a queer lot of names!" murmured the Princess, beginning to be a little interested. "What are they like? Is Dorothy Gale of Kansas pretty?"

"She might be called so," the maid replied.

"And is Mr. Tiktok attractive?" continued the Princess.

"That I cannot say, Your Highness. But he seems very bright. Will Your Gracious Highness see them?"

"Oh, I may as well, Nanda. But I am tired admiring this head, and if my visitor has any claim to beauty I must take care that she does not surpass me. So I will go to my cabinet and change to No. 17, which I think is my best appearance. Don't you?"

"Your No. 17 is exceedingly beautiful," answered Nanda, with another bow.

Again the Princess yawned. Then she said:

"Help me to rise."

So the maid assisted her to gain her feet, although Langwidere was the stronger of the two; and then the Princess slowly walked across the silver floor to her cabinet, leaning heavily at every step upon Nanda's arm.

Now I must explain to you that the Princess Langwidere had thirty heads—as many as there are days in the month. But of course she could only wear one of them at a time, because she had but one neck. These heads were kept in what she called her "cabinet," which was a beautiful dressing-room that lay just between Langwidere's sleeping-chamber and the mirrored sitting-room. Each head was in a separate cupboard lined with velvet. The cupboards ran all around the sides of the dressing-room, and had elaborately carved doors with gold numbers on the outside and jewelled-framed mirrors on the inside of them.

When the Princess got out of her crystal bed in the morning she went to her cabinet, opened one of the velvet-lined cupboards, and took the head it contained from its golden shelf. Then, by the aid of the mirror inside the open door, she put on the head—as neat and straight as could be—and afterward called her maids to robe her for the day. She always wore a simple white costume, that suited all the heads. For, being able to change her face whenever she liked, the Princess had no interest in wearing a variety of gowns, as have other ladies who are compelled to wear the same face constantly.

Of course the thirty heads were in great variety, no two formed alike but all being of exceeding loveliness. There were heads with golden hair, brown hair, rich auburn hair and black hair; but none with gray hair. The heads had eyes of blue, of gray, of hazel, of brown and of black; but there were no red eyes among them, and all were bright and handsome. The noses were Grecian, Roman, retroussé and Oriental, representing all types of beauty; and the mouths were of assorted sizes and shapes, displaying pearly teeth when the heads smiled. As for dimples, they appeared in cheeks and chins, wherever they might be most charming, and one or two heads had freckles upon the faces to contrast the better with the brilliancy of their complexions.

One key unlocked all the velvet cupboards containing these treasures—a curious key carved from a single blood-red ruby—and this was fastened to a strong but slender chain which the Princess wore around her left wrist.

When Nanda had supported Langwidere to a position in front of cupboard No. 17, the Princess unlocked the door with her ruby key and after handing head No. 9, which she had been wearing, to the maid, she took No. 17 from its shelf and fitted it to her neck. It had black hair and dark eyes and a lovely pearl-and-white complexion, and when Langwidere wore it she knew she was remarkably beautiful in appearance.

There was only one trouble with No. 17; the temper that went with it (and which was hidden somewhere under the glossy black hair) was fiery, harsh and haughty in the extreme, and it often led the Princess to do unpleasant things which she regretted when she came to wear her other heads.

But she did not remember this today, and went to meet her guests in the drawing-room with a feeling of certainty that she would surprise them with her beauty.

However, she was greatly disappointed to find that her visitors were merely a small girl in a gingham dress, a copper man that would only go when wound up, and a yellow hen that was sitting contentedly in Langwidere's best work-basket, where there was a china egg used for darning stockings. (It may surprise you to learn that a princess ever does such a common thing as darn stockings. But, if you will stop to think, you will realize that a princess is sure to wear holes in her stockings, the same as other people; only it isn't considered quite polite to mention the matter.)

"Oh!" said Langwidere, slightly lifting the nose of No. 17. "I thought some one of importance had called."

"Then you were right," declared Dorothy. "I'm a good deal of 'portance myself, and when Billina lays an egg she has the proudest cackle you ever heard. As for Tiktok, he's the——"

"Stop—Stop!" commanded the Princess, with an angry flash of her splendid eyes. "How dare you annoy me with your senseless chatter?"

"Why, you horrid thing!" said Dorothy, who was not accustomed to being treated so rudely.

The Princess looked at her more closely.

"Tell me," she resumed, "are you of royal blood?"

"Better than that, ma'am," said Dorothy. "I came from Kansas."

"Huh!" cried the Princess, scornfully. "You are a foolish child, and I cannot allow you to annoy me. Run away, you little goose, and bother some one else."

Dorothy was so indignant that for a moment she could find no words to reply. But she rose from her chair, and was about to leave the room when the Princess, who had been scanning the girl's face, stopped her by saying, more gently:

"Come nearer to me."

Dorothy obeyed, without a thought of fear, and stood before the Princess while Langwidere examined her face with careful attention.

"You are rather attractive," said the lady, presently. "Not at all beautiful, you understand, but you have a certain style of prettiness that is different from that of any of my thirty heads. So I believe I'll take your head and give you No. 26 for it."

"Well, I b'lieve you won't!" exclaimed Dorothy.

"It will do you no good to refuse," continued the Princess; "for I need your head for my collection, and in the Land of Ev my will is law. I never have cared much for No. 26, and you will find that it is very little worn. Besides, it will do you just as well as the one you're wearing, for all practical purposes."

"I don't know anything about your No. 26, and I don't want to," said Dorothy, firmly. "I'm not used to taking cast-off things, so I'll just keep my own head."

"You refuse?" cried the Princess, with a frown.

"Of course I do," was the reply.

"Then," said Langwidere, "I shall lock you up in a tower until you decide to obey me. Nanda," turning to her maid, "call my army."

Nanda rang a silver bell, and at once a big fat colonel in a bright red uniform entered the room, followed by ten lean soldiers, who all looked sad and discouraged and saluted the princess in a very melancholy fashion.

"Carry that girl to the North Tower and lock her up!" cried the Princess, pointing to Dorothy.

"To hear is to obey," answered the big red colonel, and caught the child by her arm. But at that moment Tiktok raised his dinner-pail and pounded it so forcibly against the colonel's head that the big officer sat down upon the floor with a sudden bump, looking both dazed and very much astonished.

"Help!" he shouted, and the ten lean soldiers sprang to assist their leader.

There was great excitement for the next few moments, and Tiktok had knocked down seven of the army, who were sprawling in every direction upon the carpet, when suddenly the machine paused, with the dinner-pail raised for another blow, and remained perfectly motionless.

"My ac-tion has run down," he called to Dorothy. "Wind me up, quick."

She tried to obey, but the big colonel had by this time managed to get upon his feet again, so he grabbed fast hold of the girl and she was helpless to escape.

"This is too bad," said the machine. "I ought to have run six hours lon-ger, at least, but I sup-pose my long walk and my fight with the Wheel-ers made me run down fast-er than us-u-al."

"Well, it can't be helped," said Dorothy, with a sigh.

"Will you exchange heads with me?" demanded the Princess.

"No, indeed!" cried Dorothy.

"Then lock her up," said Langwidere to her soldiers, and they led Dorothy to a high tower at the north of the palace and locked her securely within. The soldiers afterward tried to lift Tiktok, but they found the machine so solid and heavy that they could not stir it. So they left him standing in the center of the drawing-room.

"People will think I have a new statue," said Langwidere, "so it won't matter in the least, and Nanda can keep him well polished."

"What shall we do with the hen?" asked the colonel, who had just discovered Billina in the work-basket.

"Put her in the chicken-house," answered the Princess. "Some day I'll have her fried for breakfast."

"She looks rather tough, Your Highness," said Nanda, doubtfully.

"That is a base slander!" cried Billina, struggling frantically in the colonel's arms. "But the breed of chickens I come from is said to be poison to all princesses."

"Then," remarked Langwidere, "I will not fry the hen, but keep her to lay eggs; and if she doesn't do her duty I'll have her drowned in the horse trough."

Chapter 7

OZMA *OF* OZ *TO THE* RESCUE

Nanda brought Dorothy bread and water for her supper and she slept upon a hard stone couch with a single pillow and a silken coverlet.

In the morning she leaned out of the window of her prison in the tower to see if there was any way to escape. The room was not so very high up, when compared with our modern buildings, but it was far enough above the trees and farm houses to give her a good view of the surrounding country.

To the east she saw the forest, with the sands beyond it and the ocean beyond that. There was even a dark speck upon the shore that she thought might be the chicken-coop in which she had arrived at this singular country.

Then she looked to the north, and saw a deep but narrow valley lying between two rocky mountains, and a third mountain that shut off the valley at the further end.

Westward the fertile Land of Ev suddenly ended a little way from the palace, and the girl could see miles and miles of sandy desert that stretched further than her eyes could reach. It was this desert, she thought, with much interest, that alone separated her from the wonderful Land of Oz, and she remembered sorrowfully that she had been told no one had ever been able to cross this dangerous waste but herself. Once a cyclone had carried her across it, and a magical pair of silver shoes had carried her back again. But now she had neither a cyclone nor silver shoes to assist her, and her condition was sad indeed. For she had become the prisoner of a disagreeable princess who insisted that she must exchange her head for another one that she was not used to, and which might not fit her at all.

Really, there seemed no hope of help for her from her old friends in the Land of Oz. Thoughtfully she gazed from her narrow window. On all the desert not a living thing was stirring.

Wait, though! Something surely *was* stirring on the desert— something her eyes had not observed at first. Now it seemed like a cloud; now it seemed like a spot of silver; now it seemed to be a mass of rainbow colors that moved swiftly toward her.

What could it be, she wondered?

Then, gradually, but in a brief space of time nevertheless, the vision drew near enough to Dorothy to make out what it was.

A broad green carpet was unrolling itself upon the desert, while advancing across the carpet was a wonderful procession that made the girl open her eyes in amazement as she gazed.

First came a magnificent golden chariot, drawn by a great Lion and an immense Tiger, who stood shoulder to shoulder and trotted along as gracefully as a well-matched team of thoroughbred horses. And standing upright within the chariot was a beautiful girl clothed in flowing robes of silver gauze and wearing a jeweled diadem upon her dainty head. She held in one hand the satin ribbons that guided her astonishing team, and in the other an ivory wand that separated at the top into two prongs, the prongs being tipped by the letters "O" and "Z", made of glistening diamonds set closely together.

The girl seemed neither older nor larger than Dorothy herself, and at once the prisoner in the tower guessed, that the lovely driver of the chariot must be that Ozma of Oz of whom she had so lately heard from Tiktok.

Following close behind the chariot Dorothy saw her old friend the Scarecrow, riding calmly astride a wooden Saw-Horse, which pranced and trotted as naturally as any meat horse could have done.

And then came Nick Chopper, the Tin Woodman, with his funnel-shaped cap tipped carelessly over his left ear, his gleaming axe over his right shoulder, and his whole body sparkling as brightly as it had ever done in the old days when first she knew him.

The Tin Woodman was on foot, marching at the head of a company of twenty-seven soldiers, of whom some were lean and some fat, some short and some tall; but all the twenty-seven were dressed in handsome uniforms of various designs and colors, no two being alike in any respect.

Behind the soldiers the green carpet rolled itself up again, so that there was always just enough of it for the procession to walk upon, in order that their feet might not come in contact with the deadly, life-destroying sands of the desert.

Dorothy knew at once it was a magic carpet she beheld, and her heart beat high with hope and joy as she realized she was soon to be rescued and allowed to greet her dearly beloved friends of Oz—the Scarecrow, the Tin Woodman and the Cowardly Lion.

Indeed, the girl felt herself as good as rescued as soon as she recognized those in the procession, for she well knew the courage and loyalty of her old comrades, and also believed that any others who came from their marvelous country would prove to be pleasant and reliable acquaintances.

As soon as the last bit of desert was passed and all the procession, from the beautiful and dainty Ozma to the last soldier, had reached the grassy meadows of the Land of Ev, the magic carpet rolled itself together and entirely disappeared.

Then the chariot driver turned her Lion and Tiger into a broad roadway leading up to the palace, and the others followed, while Dorothy still gazed from her tower window in eager excitement.

They came quite close to the front door of the palace and then halted, the Scarecrow dismounting from his Saw-Horse to approach the sign fastened to the door, that he might read what it said.

Dorothy, just above him, could keep silent no longer.

"Here I am!" she shouted, as loudly as she could. "Here's Dorothy!"

"Dorothy who?" asked the Scarecrow, tipping his head to look upward until he nearly lost his balance and tumbled over backward.

"Dorothy Gale, of course. Your friend from Kansas," she answered.

"Why, hello, Dorothy!" said the Scarecrow. "What in the world are you doing up there?"

"Nothing," she called down, "because there's nothing to do. Save me, my friend—save me!"

"You seem to be quite safe now," replied the Scarecrow.

"But I'm a prisoner. I'm locked in, so that I can't get out," she pleaded.

"That's all right," said the Scarecrow. "You might be worse off, little Dorothy. Just consider the matter. You can't get drowned, or be run over by a Wheeler, or fall out of an apple-tree. Some folks would think they were lucky to be up there."

"Well, I don't," declared the girl, "and I want to get down immed'i'tly and see you and the Tin Woodman and the Cowardly Lion."

"Very well," said the Scarecrow, nodding. "It shall be just as you say, little friend. Who locked you up?"

"The princess Langwidere, who is a horrid creature," she answered.

At this Ozma, who had been listening carefully to the conversation, called to Dorothy from her chariot, asking:

"Why did the Princess lock you up, my dear?"

"Because," exclaimed Dorothy, "I wouldn't let her have my head for her collection, and take an old, cast-off head in exchange for it."

"I do not blame you," exclaimed Ozma, promptly. "I will see the Princess at once, and oblige her to liberate you."

"Oh, thank you very, very much!" cried Dorothy, who as soon as she heard the sweet voice of the girlish Ruler of Oz knew that she would soon learn to love her dearly.

Ozma now drove her chariot around to the third door of the wing, upon which the Tin Woodman boldly proceeded to knock.

As soon as the maid opened the door Ozma, bearing in her hand her ivory wand, stepped into the hall and made her way at once to the drawing-room, followed by all her company, except the Lion, and the Tiger. And the twenty-seven soldiers made such a noise and a clatter that the little maid Nanda ran away screaming to her mistress, whereupon the Princess Langwidere, roused to great anger by this rude invasion of her palace, came running into the drawing room without any assistance whatever.

There she stood before the slight and delicate form of the little girl from Oz and cried out;—

"How dare you enter my palace unbidden? Leave this room at once, or I will bind you and all your people in chains, and throw you into my darkest dungeons!"

"What a dangerous lady!" murmured the Scarecrow, in a soft voice.

"She seems a little nervous," replied the Tin Woodman.

But Ozma only smiled at the angry Princess.

"Sit down, please," she said, quietly. "I have traveled a long way to see you, and you must listen to what I have to say."

"Must!" screamed the Princess, her black eyes flashing with fury—for she still wore her No. 17 head. "Must, to *me*!"

"To be sure," said Ozma. "I am Ruler of the Land of Oz, and I am powerful enough to destroy all your kingdom, if I so wish. Yet I did not come here to do harm, but rather to free the royal family of Ev from the thrall of the Noma King, the news having reached me that he is holding the Queen and her children prisoners."

Hearing these words, Langwidere suddenly became quiet.

"I wish you could, indeed, free my aunt and her ten royal children," said she, eagerly. "For if they were restored to their proper forms and station they could rule the Kingdom of Ev themselves, and that would save me a lot of worry and trouble. At present there are at least ten minutes every day that I must devote to affairs of state, and I would like to be able to spend my whole time in admiring my beautiful heads."

"Then we will presently discuss this matter," said Ozma, "and try to find a way to liberate your aunt and cousins. But first you must liberate another prisoner—the little girl you have locked up in your tower."

"Of course," said Langwidere, readily. "I had forgotten all about her. That was yesterday, you know, and a Princess cannot be expected to remember today what she did yesterday. Come with me, and I will release the prisoner at once."

So Ozma followed her, and they passed up the stairs that led to the room in the tower.

While they were gone Ozma's followers remained in the drawing-room, and the Scarecrow was leaning against a form that he had mistaken for a copper statue when a harsh, metallic voice said suddenly in his ear:

"Get off my foot, please. You are scratch-ing my pol-ish."

"Oh, excuse me!" he replied, hastily drawing back. "Are you alive?"

"No," said Tiktok, "I am on-ly a ma-chine. But I can think and speak and act, when I am pro-per-ly wound up. Just now my ac-tion is run down, and Dor-o-thy has the key to it."

"That's all right," replied the Scarecrow. "Dorothy will soon be free, and then she'll attend to your works. But it must be a great misfortune not to be alive. I'm sorry for you."

"Why?" asked Tiktok.

"Because you have no brains, as I have," said the Scarecrow.

"Oh, yes, I have," returned Tiktok. "I am fit-ted with Smith & Tin-ker's Improved Com-bi-na-tion Steel Brains. They are what make me think. What sort of brains are you fit-ted with?"

"I don't know," admitted the Scarecrow. "They were given to me by the great Wizard of Oz, and I didn't get a chance to examine them before he put them in. But they work splendidly and my conscience is very active. Have you a conscience?"

"No," said Tiktok.

"And no heart, I suppose?" added the Tin Woodman, who had been listening with interest to this conversation.

"No," said Tiktok.

"Then," continued the Tin Woodman, "I regret to say that you are greatly inferior to my friend the Scarecrow, and to myself. For we are both alive, and he has brains which do not need to be wound up, while I have an excellent heart that is continually beating in my bosom."

"I con-grat-u-late you," replied Tiktok. "I can-not help be-ing your in-fer-i-or for I am a mere ma-chine. When I am wound up I do my du-ty by go-ing just as my ma-chin-er-y is made to go. You have no i-de-a how full of ma-chin-er-y I am."

"I can guess," said the Scarecrow, looking at the machine man curiously. "Some day I'd like to take you apart and see just how you are made."

"Do not do that, I beg of you," said Tiktok; "for you could not put me to-geth-er a-gain, and my use-ful-ness would be de-stroyed."

"Oh! are you useful?" asked the Scarecrow, surprised.

"Ve-ry," said Tiktok.

"In that case," the Scarecrow kindly promised, "I won't fool with your interior at all. For I am a poor mechanic, and might mix you up."

"Thank you," said Tiktok.

Just then Ozma re-entered the room, leading Dorothy by the hand and followed closely by the Princess Langwidere.

Chapter 8

THE HUNGRY TIGER

THE first thing Dorothy did was to rush into the embrace of the Scarecrow, whose painted face beamed with delight as he pressed her form to his straw-padded bosom. Then the Tin Woodman embraced her—very gently, for he knew his tin arms might hurt her if he squeezed too roughly.

These greetings having been exchanged, Dorothy took the key to Tiktok from her pocket and wound up the machine man's action, so that he could bow properly when introduced to the rest of the company. While doing this she told them now useful Tiktok had been to her, and both the Scarecrow and the Tin Woodman shook hands with the machine once more and thanked him for protecting their friend.

Then Dorothy asked: "Where is Billina?"

"I don't know," said the Scarecrow. "Who is Billina?"

"She's a yellow hen who is another friend of mine," answered the girl, anxiously. "I wonder what has become of her?"

"She is in the chicken house, in the back yard," said the Princess. "My drawing-room is no place for hens."

Without waiting to hear more Dorothy ran to get Billina, and just outside the door she came upon the Cowardly Lion, still hitched to the chariot beside the great Tiger. The Cowardly Lion had a big bow of blue ribbon fastened to the long hair between his ears, and the Tiger wore a bow of red ribbon on his tail, just in front of the bushy end.

In an instant Dorothy was hugging the huge Lion joyfully.

"I'm *so* glad to see you again!" she cried.

"I am also glad to see you, Dorothy," said the Lion. "We've had some fine adventures together, haven't we?"

"Yes, indeed," she replied. "How are you?"

"As cowardly as ever," the beast answered in a meek voice. "Every little thing scares me and makes my heart beat fast. But let me introduce to you a new friend of mine, the Hungry Tiger."

"Oh! Are you hungry?" she asked, turning to the other beast, who was just then yawning so widely that he displayed two rows of terrible teeth and a mouth big enough to startle anyone.

"Dreadfully hungry," answered the Tiger, snapping his jaws together with a fierce click.

"Then why don't you eat something?" she asked.

"It's no use," said the Tiger sadly. "I've tried that, but I always get hungry again."

"Why, it is the same with me," said Dorothy. "Yet I keep on eating."

"But you eat harmless things, so it doesn't matter," replied the Tiger. "For my part, I'm a savage beast, and have an appetite for all sorts of poor little living creatures, from a chipmonk to fat babies.

"How dreadful!" said Dorothy.

"Isn't it, though?" returned the Hungry Tiger, licking his lips with his long red tongue. "Fat babies! Don't they sound delicious? But I've never eaten any, because my conscience tells me it is wrong. If I had no conscience I would probably eat the babies and then get hungry again, which would mean that I had sacrificed the poor babies for nothing. No; hungry I was born, and hungry I shall die. But I'll not have any cruel deeds on my conscience to be sorry for."

"I think you are a very good tiger," said Dorothy, patting the huge head of the beast.

"In that you are mistaken," was the reply. "I am a good beast, perhaps, but a disgracefully bad tiger. For it is the nature of tigers to be cruel and ferocious, and in refusing to eat harmless living creatures I am acting as no good tiger has ever before acted. That is why I left the forest and joined my friend the Cowardly Lion."

"But the Lion is not really cowardly," said Dorothy. "I have seen him act as bravely as can be."

"All a mistake, my dear," protested the Lion gravely. "To others I may have seemed brave, at times, but I have never been in any danger that I was not afraid."

"Nor I," said Dorothy, truthfully. "But I must go and set free Billina, and then I will see you again."

She ran around to the back yard of the palace and soon found the chicken house, being guided to it by a loud cackling and crowing and a distracting hubbub of sounds such as chickens make when they are excited.

Something seemed to be wrong in the chicken house, and when Dorothy looked through the slats in the door she saw a group of hens and roosters huddled in one corner and watching what appeared to be a whirling ball of feathers. It bounded here and there about the chicken house, and at first Dorothy could not tell what it was, while the screeching of the chickens nearly deafened her.

But suddenly the bunch of feathers stopped whirling, and then, to her amazement, the girl saw Billina crouching upon the prostrate form of a speckled rooster. For an instant they both remained motionless, and then the yellow hen shook her wings to settle the feathers and walked toward the door with a strut of proud defiance and a cluck of victory, while the speckled rooster limped away to the group of other chickens, trailing his crumpled plumage in the dust as he went.

"Why, Billina!" cried Dorothy, in a shocked voice; "have you been fighting?"

"I really think I have," retorted Billina. "Do you think I'd let that speckled villain of a rooster lord it over *me*, and claim to run this chicken house, as long as I'm able to peck and scratch? Not if my name is Bill!"

"It isn't Bill, it's Billina; and you're talking slang, which is very undig'n'fied," said Dorothy, reprovingly. "Come here, Billina, and I'll let you out; for Ozma of Oz is here, and has set us free."

So the yellow hen came to the door, which Dorothy unlatched for her to pass through, and the other chickens silently watched them from their corner without offering to approach nearer.

The girl lifted her friend in her arms and exclaimed:

"Oh, Billina! how dreadful you look. You've lost a lot of feathers, and one of your eyes is nearly pecked out, and your comb is bleeding!"

"That's nothing," said Billina. "Just look at the speckled rooster! Didn't I do him up brown?"

Dorothy shook her head.

"I don't 'prove of this, at all," she said, carrying Billina away toward the palace. "It isn't a good thing for you to 'sociate with those common chickens. They would soon spoil your good manners, and you wouldn't be respec'able any more."

"I didn't ask to associate with them," replied Billina. "It is that cross old Princess who is to blame. But I was raised in the United States, and I won't allow any one-horse chicken of the

Land of Ev to run over me and put on airs, as long as I can lift a claw in self-defense."

"Very well, Billina," said Dorothy. "We won't talk about it any more."

Soon they came to the Cowardly Lion and the Hungry Tiger to whom the girl introduced the Yellow Hen.

"Glad to meet any friend of Dorothy's," said the Lion, politely. "To judge by your present appearance, you are not a coward, as I am."

"Your present appearance makes my mouth water," said the Tiger, looking at Billina greedily. "My, my! how good you would taste if I could only crunch you between my jaws. But don't worry. You would only appease my appetite for a moment; so it isn't worth while to eat you."

"Thank you," said the hen, nestling closer in Dorothy's arms.

"Besides, it wouldn't be right," continued the Tiger, looking steadily at Billina and clicking his jaws together.

"Of course not," cried Dorothy, hastily. "Billina is my friend, and you mustn't ever eat her under any circ'mstances."

"I'll try to remember that," said the Tiger; "but I'm a little absent-minded, at times."

Then Dorothy carried her pet into the drawing-room of the palace, where Tiktok, being invited to do so by Ozma, had seated himself between the Scarecrow and the Tin Woodman. Opposite to them sat Ozma herself and the Princess Langwidere, and beside them there was a vacant chair for Dorothy.

Around this important group was ranged the Army of Oz, and as Dorothy looked at the handsome uniforms of the Twenty-Seven she said:

"Why, they seem to be all officers."

"They are, all except one," answered the Tin Woodman. "I have in my Army eight Generals, six Colonels, seven Majors and five Captains, besides one private for them to command. I'd like to promote the private, for I believe no private should ever be in public life; and I've also noticed that officers usually fight better and are more reliable than common soldiers. Besides, the officers are more important looking, and lend dignity to our army."

"No doubt you are right," said Dorothy, seating herself beside Ozma.

"And now," announced the girlish Ruler of Oz, "we will hold a solemn conference to decide the best manner of liberating the royal family of this fair Land of Ev from their long imprisonment.

Chapter 9

THE ROYAL FAMILY OF EV

THE Tin Woodman was the first to address the meeting.

"To begin with," said he, "word came to our noble and illustrous Ruler, Ozma of Oz, that the wife and ten children—five boys and five girls—of the former King of Ev, by name Evoldo, have been enslaved by the Nome King and are held prisoners in his underground palace. Also that there was no one in Ev powerful enough to release them. Naturally our Ozma wished to undertake the adventure of liberating the poor prisoners; but for a long time she could find no way to cross the great desert between the two countries. Finally she went to a friendly sorceress of our land named Glinda the Good, who heard the story and at once presented Ozma a magic carpet, which would continually unroll beneath our feet and so make a comfortable path for us to cross the desert. As soon as she had received the carpet our gracious Ruler ordered me to assemble our army, which I did. You behold in these bold warriors the pick of all the finest soldiers of Oz; and, if we are obliged to fight the Nome King, every officer as well as the private, will battle fiercely unto death."

Then Tiktok spoke.

"Why should you fight the Nome King?" he asked. "He has done no wrong."

"No wrong!" cried Dorothy. "Isn't it wrong to imprison a queen mother and her ten children?"

"They were sold to the Nome King by King Ev-ol-do," replied Tiktok. "It was the King of Ev who did wrong, and when he re-al-ized what he had done he jumped in-to the sea and drowned him-self."

"This is news to me," said Ozma, thoughtfully. "I had supposed the Nome King was all to blame in the matter. But, in any case, he must be made to liberate the prisoners."

"My uncle Evoldo was a very wicked man," declared the Princess Langwidere. "If he had drowned himself before he sold his family, no one would have cared. But he sold them to the powerful Nome King in exchange for a long life, and afterward destroyed the life by jumping into the sea."

"Then," said Ozma, "he did not get the long life, and the Nome King must give up the prisoners. Where are they confined?"

"No one knows, exactly," replied the Princess. "For the king, whose name is Roquat of the Rocks, owns a splendid palace underneath the great mountain which is at the north end of this kingdom, and he has transformed the queen and her children into ornaments and bric-a-brac with which to decorate his rooms."

"I'd like to know," said Dorothy, "who this Nome King is?"

"I will tell you," replied Ozma. "He is said to be the Ruler of the Underground World, and commands the rocks and all that the rocks contain. Under his rule are many thousands of the Nomes, who are queerly shaped but powerful sprites that labor at the furnaces and forges of their king, making gold and silver and other metals which they conceal in the crevices of the rocks, so that those living upon the earth's surface can only find them with great difficulty. Also they make diamonds and rubies and emeralds, which they hide in the ground; so that the kingdom of the Nomes is wonderfully rich, and all we have of precious stones and silver and gold is what we take from the earth and rocks where the Nome King has hidden them."

"I understand," said Dorothy, nodding her little head wisely.

"For the reason that we often steal his treasures," continued Ozma, "the Ruler of the Underground World is not fond of those who live upon the earth's surface, and never appears among us. If we wish to see King Roquat of the Rocks, we must visit his own country, where he is all powerful, and therefore it will be a dangerous undertaking."

"But, for the sake of the poor prisoners," said Dorothy, "we ought to do it."

"We shall do it," replied the Scarecrow, "although it requires a lot of courage for me to go near to the furnaces of the Nome King. For I am only stuffed with straw, and a single spark of fire might destroy me entirely."

"The furnaces may also melt my tin," said the Tin Woodman; "but I am going."

"I can't bear heat," remarked the Princess Langwidere, yawning lazily, "so I shall stay at home. But I wish you may have success in your undertaking, for I am heartily tired of ruling this stupid kingdom, and I need more leisure in which to admire my beautiful heads."

"We do not need you," said Ozma. "For, if with the aid of my brave followers I cannot accomplish my purpose, then it would be useless for you to undertake the journey."

"Quite true," sighed the Princess. "So, if you'll excuse me, I will now retire to my cabinet. I've worn this head quite awhile, and I want to change it for another."

When she had left them (and you may be sure no one was sorry to see her go) Ozma said to Tiktok:

"Will you join our party?"

"I am the slave of the girl Dor-oth-y, who res-cued me from pris-on," replied the machine. "Where she goes I will go."

"Oh, I am going with my friends, of course," said Dorothy, quickly. "I wouldn't miss the fun for anything. Will you go, too, Billina?"

"To be sure," said Billina in a careless tone. She was smoothing down the feathers of her back and not paying much attention.

"Heat is just in her line," remarked the Scarecrow. "If she is nicely roasted, she will be better than ever."

"Then," said Ozma, "we will arrange to start for the Kingdom of the Nomes at daybreak tomorrow. And, in the meantime, we will rest and prepare ourselves for the journey."

Although Princess Langwidere did not again appear to her guests, the palace servants waited upon the strangers from Oz and did everything in their power to make the party comfortable. There were many vacant rooms at their disposal, and the brave Army of twenty-seven was easily provided for and liberally feasted.

The Cowardly Lion and the Hungry Tiger were unharnessed from the chariot and allowed to roam at will throughout the palace, where they nearly frightened the servants into fits, although they did no harm at all. At one time Dorothy found the little maid Nanda crouching in terror in a corner, with the Hungry Tiger standing before her.

"You certainly look delicious," the beast was saying. "Will you kindly give me permission to eat you?"

"No, no, no!" cried the maid in reply.

"Then," said the Tiger, yawning frightfully, "please to get me about thirty pounds of tenderloin steak, cooked rare, with a peck of boiled potatoes on the side, and five gallons of ice-cream for dessert."

"I—I'll do the best I can!" said Nanda, and she ran away as fast as she could go.

"Are you so very hungry?" asked Dorothy, in wonder.

"You can hardly imagine the size of my appetite," replied the Tiger, sadly. "It seems to fill my whole body, from the end of my throat to the tip of my tail. I am very sure the appetite doesn't fit me, and is too large for the size of my body. Some day, when I meet a dentist with a pair of forceps, I'm going to have it pulled."

"What, your tooth?" asked Dorothy.

"No, my appetite," said the Hungry Tiger.

The little girl spent most of the afternoon talking with the Scarecrow and the Tin Woodman, who related to her all that had taken place in the Land of Oz since Dorothy had left it. She was much interested in the story of Ozma, who had been, when a baby, stolen by a wicked old witch and transformed into a boy. She did not know that she had ever been a girl until she was restored to her natural form by a kind sorceress. Then it was found that she was the only child of the former Ruler of Oz, and was entitled to rule in his place. Ozma had many adventures, however, before she regained her father's throne, and in these she was accompanied by a pumpkin-headed man, a highly magnified and thoroughly educated Woggle-Bug, and a wonderful sawhorse that had been brought to life by means of a magic powder. The Scarecrow and the Tin Woodman had also assisted her; but the Cowardly Lion, who ruled the great forest as the King of Beasts, knew nothing of Ozma until after she became the reigning princess of Oz. Then he journeyed to the Emerald City to see her, and on hearing she was about to visit the Land of Ev to set free the royal family of that country, the Cowardly Lion begged to go with her, and brought along his friend, the Hungry Tiger, as well.

Having heard this story, Dorothy related to them her own adventures, and then went out with her friends to find the

Sawhorse, which Ozma had caused to be shod with plates of gold, so that its legs would not wear out.

They came upon the Sawhorse standing motionless beside the garden gate, but when Dorothy was introduced to him he bowed politely and blinked his eyes, which were knots of wood, and wagged his tail, which was only the branch of a tree.

"What a remarkable thing, to be alive!" exclaimed Dorothy.

"I quite agree with you," replied the Sawhorse, in a rough but not unpleasant voice. "A creature like me has no business to live, as we all know. But it was the magic powder that did it, so I cannot justly be blamed."

"Of course not," said Dorothy. "And you seem to be of some use, 'cause I noticed the Scarecrow riding upon your back."

"Oh, yes; I'm of use," returned the Sawhorse; "and I never tire, never have to be fed, or cared for in any way."

"Are you intel'gent?" asked the girl.

"Not very," said the creature. "It would be foolish to waste intelligence on a common Sawhorse, when so many professors need it. But I know enough to obey my masters, and to gid-dup, or whoa, when I'm told to. So I'm pretty well satisfied."

That night Dorothy slept in a pleasant little bedchamber next to that occupied by Ozma of Oz, and Billina perched upon the foot of the bed and tucked her head under her wing and slept as soundly in that position as did Dorothy upon her soft cushions.

But before daybreak every one was awake and stirring, and soon the adventurers were eating a hasty breakfast in the great dining-room of the palace. Ozma sat at the head of a long table, on a raised platform, with Dorothy on her right hand and the Scarecrow on her left. The Scarecrow did not eat, of course; but

Ozma placed him near her so that she might ask his advice about the journey while she ate.

Lower down the table were the twenty-seven warriors of Oz, and at the end of the room the Lion and the Tiger were eating out of a kettle that had been placed upon the floor, while Billina fluttered around to pick up any scraps that might be scattered.

It did not take long to finish the meal, and then the Lion and the Tiger were harnessed to the chariot and the party was ready to start for the Nome King's Palace.

First rode Ozma, with Dorothy beside her in the golden chariot and holding Billina fast in her arms. Then came the Scarecrow on the Sawhorse, with the Tin Woodman and Tiktok marching side by side just behind him. After these tramped the Army, looking brave and handsome in their splendid uniforms. The generals commanded the colonels and the colonels commanded the majors and the majors commanded the captains and the captains commanded the private, who marched with an air of proud importance because it required so many officers to give him his orders.

And so the magnificent procession left the palace and started along the road just as day was breaking, and by the time the sun came out they had made good progress toward the valley that led to the Nome King's domain.

Chapter 10

THE GIANT WITH THE HAMMER

THE road led for a time through a pretty farm country, and then past a picnic grove that was very inviting. But the procession continued to steadily advance until Billina cried in an abrupt and commanding manner:

"Wait—wait!"

Ozma stopped her chariot so suddenly that the Scarecrow's Sawhorse nearly ran into it, and the ranks of the army tumbled over one another before they could come to a halt. Immediately the yellow hen struggled from Dorothy's arms and flew into a clump of bushes by the roadside.

"What's the matter?" called the Tin Woodman, anxiously.

"Why, Billina wants to lay her egg, that's all," said Dorothy.

"Lay her egg!" repeated the Tin Woodman, in astonishment.

"Yes; she lays one every morning, about this time; and it's quite fresh," said the girl.

"But does your foolish old hen suppose that this entire cavalcade, which is bound on an important adventure, is going to stand still while she lays her egg?" enquired the Tin Woodman, earnestly.

"What else can we do?" asked the girl. "It's a habit of Billina's and she can't break herself of it."

"Then she must hurry up," said the Tin Woodman, impatiently.

"No, no!" exclaimed the Scarecrow. "If she hurries she may lay scrambled eggs."

"That's nonsense," said Dorothy. "But Billina won't be long, I'm sure."

So they stood and waited, although all were restless and anxious to proceed. And by and by the yellow hen came from the bushes saying:

"Kut-kut, kut, ka-daw-kutt!" Kut, kut, kut—ka-daw-kut!" "What is she doing—singing her lay?" asked the Scarecrow.

"For-ward—march!" shouted the Tin Woodman, waving his axe, and the procession started just as Dorothy had once more grabbed Billina in her arms.

"Isn't anyone going to get my egg?" cried the hen, in great excitement.

"I'll get it," said the Scarecrow; and at his command the Sawhorse pranced into the bushes. The straw man soon found the egg, which he placed in his jacket pocket. The cavalcade, having moved rapidly on, was even then far in advance; but it did not take the Sawhorse long to catch up with it, and presently the Scarecrow was riding in his accustomed place behind Ozma's chariot.

"What shall I do with the egg?" he asked Dorothy.

"I do not know," the girl answered. "Perhaps the Hungry Tiger would like it."

"It would not be enough to fill one of my back teeth," remarked the Tiger. "A bushel of them, hard boiled, might take a little of the edge off my appetite; but one egg isn't good for anything at all, that I know of."

"No; it wouldn't even make a sponge cake," said the Scarecrow, thoughtfully. "The Tin Woodman might carry it with his axe and hatch it; but after all I may as well keep it myself for a souvenir." So he left it in his pocket.

They had now reached that part of the valley that lay between the two high mountains which Dorothy had seen from her tower window. At the far end was the third great mountain, which blocked the valley and was the northern edge of the Land of Ev. It was underneath this mountain that the Nome King's palace was said to be; but it would be some time before they reached that place.

The path was becoming rocky and difficult for the wheels of the chariot to pass over, and presently a deep gulf appeared at their feet which was too wide for them to leap. So Ozma took a small square of green cloth from her pocket and threw it upon the ground. At once it became the magic carpet, and unrolled itself far enough for all the cavalcade to walk upon. The chariot now advanced, and the green carpet unrolled before it, crossing the gulf on a level with its banks, so that all passed over in safety.

"That's easy enough," said the Scarecrow. "I wonder what will happen next."

He was not long in making the discovery, for the sides of the mountain came closer together until finally there was but a narrow path between them, along which Ozma and her party were forced to pass in single file.

They now heard a low and deep "thump!—--thump!—--thump!" which echoed throughout the valley and seemed to grow louder as they advanced. Then, turning a corner of rock, they saw before them a huge form, which towered above the path for more than a hundred feet. The form was that of a gigantic man built out of plates of cast iron,and it stood with one foot on either side of the narrow road and swung over its right shoulder an immense iron mallet, with which it constantly pounded the earth. These resounding blows explained the thumping sounds they had heard, for the mallet was much bigger than a barrel, and where it struck the path between the rocky sides of the mountain it filled all the space through which our travelers would be obliged to pass.

Of course they at once halted, a safe distance away from the terrible iron mallet. The magic carpet would do them no good in this case, for it was only meant to protect them from any dangers upon the ground beneath their feet, and not from dangers that appeared in the air above them.

"Wow!" said the Cowardly Lion, with a shudder. "It makes me dreadfully nervous to see that big hammer pounding so near my head. One blow would crush me into a door-mat."

"The ir-on gi-ant is a fine fel-low," said Tiktok, "and works as stead-i-ly as a clock. He was made for the Nome King by Smith & Tin-ker, who made me, and his du-ty is to keep folks from find-ing the un-der-ground pal-ace. Is he not a great work of art?"

"Can he think, and speak, as you do?" asked Ozma, regarding the giant with wondering eyes.

"No," replied the machine; "he is on-ly made to pound the road, and has no think-ing or speak-ing at-tach-ment. But he pounds ve-ry well, I think."

"Too well," observed the Scarecrow. "He is keeping us from going farther. Is there no way to stop his machinery?"

"On-ly the Nome King, who has the key, can do that," answered Tiktok.

"Then," said Dorothy, anxiously, "what shall we do?"

"Excuse me for a few minutes," said the Scarecrow, "and I will think it over."

He retired, then, to a position in the rear, where he turned his painted face to the rocks and began to think.

Meantime the giant continued to raise his iron mallet high in the air and to strike the path terrific blows that echoed through the mountains like the roar of a cannon. Each time the mallet lifted, however, there was a moment when the path beneath the monster was free, and perhaps the Scarecrow had noticed this, for when he came back to the others he said:

"The matter is a very simple one, after all. We have but to run under the hammer, one at a time, when it is lifted, and pass to the other side before it falls again."

"It will require quick work, if we escape the blow," said the Tin Woodman, with a shake of his head. "But it really seems the only thing to be done. Who will make the first attempt?"

They looked at one another hesitatingly for a moment. Then the Cowardly Lion, who was trembling like a leaf in the wind, said to them:

"I suppose the head of the procession must go first—and that's me. But I'm terribly afraid of the big hammer!"

"What will become of me?" asked Ozma. "You might rush under the hammer yourself, but the chariot would surely be crushed."

"We must leave the chariot," said the Scarecrow. "But you two girls can ride upon the backs of the Lion and the Tiger."

So this was decided upon, and Ozma, as soon as the Lion was unfastened from the chariot, at once mounted the beast's back and said she was ready.

"Cling fast to his mane," advised Dorothy. "I used to ride him myself, and that's the way I held on."

So Ozma clung fast to the mane, and the lion crouched in the path and eyed the swinging mallet carefully until he knew just the instant it would begin to rise in the air.

Then, before anyone thought he was ready, he made a sudden leap straight between the iron giant's legs, and before the mallet struck the ground again the Lion and Ozma were safe on the other side.

The Tiger went next. Dorothy sat upon his back and locked her arms around his striped neck, for he had no mane to cling to. He made the leap straight and true as an arrow from a bow, and ere Dorothy realized it she was out of danger and standing by Ozma's side.

Now came the Scarecrow on the Sawhorse, and while they made the dash in safety they were within a hair's breadth of being caught by the descending hammer.

Tiktok walked up to the very edge of the spot the hammer struck, and as it was raised for the next blow he calmly stepped forward and escaped its descent. That was an idea for the Tin Woodman to follow, and he also crossed in safety while the great hammer was in the air. But when it came to the twenty-six officers and the private, their knees were so weak that they could not walk a step.

"In battle we are wonderfully courageous," said one of the generals, "and our foes find us very terrible to face. But war is one thing and this is another. When it comes to being pounded upon the head by an iron hammer, and smashed into pancakes, we naturally object."

"Make a run for it," urged the Scarecrow.

"Our knees shake so that we cannot run," answered a captain. "If we should try it we would all certainly be pounded to a jelly."

"Well, well!" sighed the Cowardly Lion, "I see, friend Tiger, that we must place ourselves in great danger to rescue this bold army. Come with me, and we will do the best we can."

So, Ozma and Dorothy having already dismounted from their backs, the Lion and the Tiger leaped back again under the awful hammer and returned with two generals clinging to their necks. They repeated this daring passage twelve times, when all the officers had been carried beneath the giant's legs and landed safely on the further side. By that time the beasts were very tired, and panted so hard that their tongues hung out of their great mouths.

"But what is to become of the private?" asked Ozma.

"Oh, leave him there to guard the chariot," said the Lion. "I'm tired out, and won't pass under that mallet again."

The officers at once protested that they must have the private with them, else there would be no one for them to command. But neither the Lion or the Tiger would go after him, and so the Scarecrow sent the Sawhorse.

Either the wooden horse was careless, or it failed to properly time the descent of the hammer, for the mighty weapon caught it squarely upon its head, and thumped it against the ground so powerfully that the private flew off its back high into the air, and landed upon one of the giant's cast-iron arms. Here he clung desperately while the arm rose and fell with each one of the rapid strokes.

The Scarecrow dashed in to rescue his Sawhorse, and had his left foot smashed by the hammer before he could pull the creature out of danger. They then found that the Sawhorse had been badly dazed by the blow; for while the hard wooden knot of which his head was formed could not be crushed by the hammer, both his ears were broken off and he would be unable to hear a sound until some new ones were made for him. Also his left knee was cracked, and had to be bound up with a string.

Billina having fluttered under the hammer, it now remained only to rescue the private who was riding upon the iron giant's arm, high in the air. The Scarecrow lay flat upon the ground and called to the man to jump down upon his body, which was soft because it was stuffed with straw. This the private managed to do, waiting until a time when he was nearest the ground and then letting himself drop upon the Scarecrow. He accomplished the feat without breaking any bones, and the Scarecrow declared he was not injured in the least.

Therefore, the Tin Woodman having by this time fitted new ears to the Sawhorse, the entire party proceeded upon its way, leaving the giant to pound the path behind them.

Chapter 11

THE NOME KING

By and by, when they drew near to the mountain that blocked their path and which was the furthermost edge of the Kingdom of Ev, the way grew dark and gloomy for the reason that the high peaks on either side shut out the sunshine. And it was very silent, too, as there were no birds to sing or squirrels to chatter, the trees being left far behind them and only the bare rocks remaining.

Ozma and Dorothy were a little awed by the silence, and all the others were quiet and grave except the Sawhorse, which, as it trotted along with the Scarecrow upon his back, hummed a queer song, of which this was the chorus:

> "Would a wooden horse in a woodland go?
> Aye, aye! I sigh, he would, although
> Had he not had a wooden head
> He'd mount the mountain top instead."

But no one paid any attention to this because they were now close to the Nome King's dominions, and his splendid underground palace could not be very far away.

Suddenly they heard a shout of jeering laughter, and stopped short. They would have to stop in a minute, anyway, for the huge mountain barred their further progress and the path ran close up to a wall of rock and ended.

"Who was that laughing?" asked Ozma.

There was no reply, but in the gloom they could see strange forms flit across the face of the rock. Whatever the creations might be they seemed very like the rock itself, for they were the color of rocks and their shapes were as rough and rugged as if they had been broken away from the side of the mountain. They kept close to the steep cliff facing our friends, and glided up and down, and this way and that, with a lack of regularity that was quite confusing. And they seemed not to need places to rest their feet, but clung to the surface of the rock as a fly does to a window-pane, and were never still for a moment.

"Do not mind them," said Tiktok, as Dorothy shrank back. "They are on-ly the Nomes."

"And what are Nomes?" asked the girl, half frightened.

"They are rock fair-ies, and serve the Nome King," replied the machine. "But they will do us no harm. You must call for the King, be-cause with-out him you can ne-ver find the en-trance to the pal-ace."

"*You* call," said Dorothy to Ozma.

Just then the Nomes laughed again, and the sound was so weird and disheartening that the twenty-six officers commanded the private to "right-about-face!" and they all started to run as fast as they could.

The Tin Woodman at once pursued his army and cried "halt!" and when they had stopped their flight he asked: "Where are you going?"

"I—I find I've forgotten the brush for my whiskers," said a general, trembling with fear. "S-s-so we are g-going back after it!"

"That is impossible," replied the Tin Woodman. "For the giant with the hammer would kill you all if you tried to pass him."

"Oh! I'd forgotten the giant," said the general, turning pale.

"You seem to forget a good many things," remarked the Tin Woodman. "I hope you won't forget that you are brave men."

"Never!" cried the general, slapping his gold-embroidered chest.

"Never!" cried all the other officers, indignantly slapping their chests.

"For my part," said the private, meekly, "I must obey my officers; so when I am told to run, I run; and when I am told to fight, I fight."

"That is right," agreed the Tin Woodman. "And now you must all come back to Ozma, and obey *her* orders. And if you try to run away again I will have her reduce all the twenty-six officers to privates, and make the private your general."

This terrible threat so frightened them that they at once returned to where Ozma was standing beside the Cowardly Lion.

Then Ozma cried out in a loud voice:

"I demand that the Nome King appear to us!"

There was no reply, except that the shifting Nomes upon the mountain laughed in derision.

"You must not command the Nome King," said Tiktok, "for you do not rule him, as you do your own peo-ple."

So Ozma called again, saying:

"I request the Nome King to appear to us."

Only the mocking laughter replied to her, and the shadowy Nomes continued to flit here and there upon the rocky cliff.

"Try en-treat-y," said Tiktok to Ozma. "If he will not come at your re-quest, then the Nome King may list-en to your plead-ing."

Ozma looked around her proudly.

"Do you wish your ruler to plead with this wicked Nome King?" she asked. "Shall Ozma of Oz humble herself to a creature who lives in an underground kingdom?"

"No!" they all shouted, with big voices; and the Scarecrow added:

"If he will not come, we will dig him out of his hole, like a fox, and conquer his stubbornness. But our sweet little ruler must always maintain her dignity, just as I maintain mine."

"I'm not afraid to plead with him," said Dorothy. "I'm only a little girl from Kansas, and we've got more dignity at home than we know what to do with. *I'll* call the Nome King."

"Do," said the Hungry Tiger; "and if he makes hash of you I'll willingly eat you for breakfast tomorrow morning."

So Dorothy stepped forward and said:

"*Please* Mr. Nome King, come here and see us."

The Nomes started to laugh again; but a low growl came from the mountain, and in a flash they had all vanished from sight and were silent.

Then a door in the rock opened, and a voice cried:

"Enter!"

"Isn't it a trick?" asked the Tin Woodman.

"Never mind," replied Ozma. "We came here to rescue the poor Queen of Ev and her ten children, and we must run some risks to do so."

"The Nome King is hon-est and good na-tured," said Tiktok. "You can trust him to do what is right."

So Ozma led the way, hand in hand with Dorothy, and they passed through the arched doorway of rock and entered a long passage which was lighted by jewels set in the walls and having lamps behind them. There was no one to escort them, or to show them the way, but all the party pressed through the passage until they came to a round, domed cavern that was grandly furnished.

In the center of this room was a throne carved out of a solid boulder of rock, rude and rugged in shape but glittering with great rubies and diamonds and emeralds on every part of its surface. And upon the throne sat the Nome King.

This important monarch of the Underground World was a little fat man clothed in gray-brown garments that were the exact color of the rock throne in which he was seated. His bushy hair and flowing beard were also colored like the rocks, and so was his face. He wore no crown of any sort, and his only ornament was a broad, jewel-studded belt that encircled his fat little body. As for his features, they seemed kindly and good humored, and his eyes were turned merrily upon his visitors as Ozma and Dorothy stood before him with their followers ranged in close order behind them.

"Why, he looks just like Santa Claus—only he isn't the same color!" whispered Dorothy to her friend; but the Nome King heard the speech, and it made him laugh aloud.

"'He had a red face and a round little belly
That shook when he laughed like a bowl full of jelly!'"

quoth the monarch, in a pleasant voice; and they could all see that he really did shake like jelly when he laughed.

Both Ozma and Dorothy were much relieved to find the Nome King so jolly, and a minute later he waved his right hand and the girls each found a cushioned stool at her side.

"Sit down, my dears," said the King, "and tell me why you have come all this way to see me, and what I can do to make you happy."

While they seated themselves the Nome King picked up a pipe, and taking a glowing red coal out of his pocket he placed it in the bowl of the pipe and began puffing out clouds of smoke that curled in rings above his head. Dorothy thought this made the little monarch look more like Santa Claus than ever; but Ozma now began speaking, and every one listened intently to her words.

"Your Majesty," said she, "I am the ruler of the Land of Oz, and I have come here to ask you to release the good Queen of Ev and her ten children, whom you have enchanted and hold as your prisoners."

"Oh, no; you are mistaken about that," replied the King. "They are not my prisoners, but my slaves, whom I purchased from the King of Ev."

"But that was wrong," said Ozma.

"According to the laws of Ev, the king can do no wrong," answered the monarch, eyeing a ring of smoke he had just blown from his mouth; "so that he had a perfect right to sell his family to me in exchange for a long life."

"You cheated him, though," declared Dorothy; "for the King of Ev did not have a long life. He jumped into the sea and was drowned."

"That was not my fault," said the Nome King, crossing his legs and smiling contentedly. "I gave him the long life, all right; but he destroyed it."

"Then how could it be a long life?" asked Dorothy.

"Easily enough," was the reply. "Now suppose, my dear, that I gave you a pretty doll in exchange for a lock of your hair, and that after you had received the doll you smashed it into pieces and destroyed it. Could you say that I had not given you a pretty doll?"

"No," answered Dorothy.

"And could you, in fairness, ask me to return to you the lock of hair, just because you had smashed the doll?"

"No," said Dorothy, again.

"Of course not," the Nome King returned. "Nor will I give up the Queen and her children because the King of Ev destroyed his long life by jumping into the sea. They belong to me and I shall keep them."

"But you are treating them cruelly," said Ozma, who was much distressed by the King's refusal.

"In what way?" he asked.

"By making them your slaves," said she.

"Cruelty," remarked the monarch, puffing out wreathes of smoke and watching them float into the air, "is a thing I can't abide. So, as slaves must work hard, and the Queen of Ev and her children were delicate and tender, I transformed them all into articles of ornament and bric-a-brac and scattered them around the various rooms of my palace. Instead of being obliged to labor, they merely decorate my apartments, and I really think I have treated them with great kindness."

"But what a dreadful fate is theirs!" exclaimed Ozma, earnestly. "And the Kingdom of Ev is in great need of its royal family to govern it. If you will liberate them, and restore them to their proper forms, I will give you ten ornaments to replace each one you lose."

The Nome King looked grave.

"Suppose I refuse?" he asked.

"Then," said Ozma, firmly, "I am here with my friends and my army to conquer your kingdom and oblige you to obey my wishes."

The Nome King laughed until he choked; and he choked until he coughed; and he coughed until his face turned from grayish-brown to bright red. And then he wiped his eyes with a rock-colored handkerchief and grew grave again.

"You are as brave as you are pretty, my dear," he said to Ozma. "But you have little idea of the extent of the task you have undertaken. Come with me for a moment."

He arose and took Ozma's hand, leading her to a little door at one side of the room. This he opened and they stepped out upon a balcony, from whence they obtained a wonderful view of the Underground World.

A vast cave extended for miles and miles under the mountain, and in every direction were furnaces and forges glowing brightly and Nomes hammering upon precious metals or polishing gleaming jewels. All around the walls of the cave were thousands of doors of silver and gold, built into the solid rock, and these extended in rows far away into the distance, as far as Ozma's eyes could follow them.

While the little maid from Oz gazed wonderingly upon this scene the Nome King uttered a shrill whistle, and at once all the silver and gold doors flew open and solid ranks of Nome soldiers marched out from every one. So great were their numbers that they quickly filled the immense underground cavern and forced the busy workmen to abandon their tasks.

Although this tremendous army consisted of rock-colored Nomes, all squat and fat, they were clothed in glittering armor of polished steel, inlaid with beautiful gems. Upon his brow each wore a brilliant electric light, and they bore sharp spears and swords and battle-axes of solid bronze. It was evident they were perfectly trained, for they stood in straight rows, rank after rank, with their weapons held erect and true, as if awaiting but the word of command to level them upon their foes.

"This," said the Nome King, "is but a small part of my army. No ruler upon Earth has ever dared to fight me, and no ruler ever will, for I am too powerful to oppose."

He whistled again, and at once the martial array filed through the silver and gold doorways and disappeared, after which the workmen again resumed their labors at the furnaces.

Then, sad and discouraged, Ozma of Oz turned to her friends, and the Nome King calmly reseated himself on his rock throne.

"It would be foolish for us to fight," the girl said to the Tin Woodman. "For our brave Twenty-Seven would be quickly destroyed. I'm sure I do not know how to act in this emergency."

"Ask the King where his kitchen is," suggested the Tiger. "I'm hungry as a bear."

"I might pounce upon the King and tear him in pieces," remarked the Cowardly Lion.

"Try it," said the monarch, lighting his pipe with another hot coal which he took from his pocket.

The Lion crouched low and tried to spring upon the Nome King; but he hopped only a little way into the air and came down again in the same place, not being able to approach the throne by even an inch.

"It seems to me," said the Scarecrow, thoughtfully, "that our best plan is to wheedle his Majesty into giving up his slaves, since he is too great a magician to oppose."

"This is the most sensible thing any of you have suggested," declared the Nome King. "It is folly to threaten me, but I'm so kind-hearted that I cannot stand coaxing or wheedling. If you

really wish to accomplish anything by your journey, my dear
Ozma, you must coax me."

"Very well," said Ozma, more cheerfully. "Let us be friends,
and talk this over in a friendly manner."

"To be sure," agreed the King, his eyes twinkling merrily.

"I am very anxious," she continued, "to liberate the Queen of
Ev and her children who are now ornaments and bric-a-brac in
your Majesty's palace, and to restore them to their people. Tell
me, sir, how this may be accomplished."

The king remained thoughtful for a moment, after
which he asked:

"Are you willing to take a few chances and risks yourself, in
order to set free the people of Ev?"

"Yes, indeed!" answered Ozma, eagerly.

"Then," said the Nome King, "I will make you this offer:
You shall go alone and unattended into my palace and examine
carefully all that the rooms contain. Then you shall have
permission to touch eleven different objects, pronouncing at the
time the word 'Ev,' and if any one of them, or more than one,
proves to be the transformation of the Queen of Ev or any of her
ten children, then they will instantly be restored to their true forms
and may leave my palace and my kingdom in your company,
without any objection whatever. It is possible for you, in this way,
to free the entire eleven; but if you do not guess all the objects
correctly, and some of the slaves remain transformed, then each
one of your friends and followers may, in turn, enter the palace
and have the same privileges I grant you."

"Oh, thank you! thank you for this kind offer!" said
Ozma, eagerly.

"I make but one condition," added the Nome King, his eyes twinkling.

"What is it?" she enquired.

"If none of the eleven objects you touch proves to be the transformation of any of the royal family of Ev, then, instead of freeing them, you will yourself become enchanted, and transformed into an article of bric-a-brac or an ornament. This is only fair and just, and is the risk you declared you were willing to take."

Chapter 12

THE ELEVEN GUESSES

HEARING this condition imposed by the Nome King, Ozma became silent and thoughtful, and all her friends looked at her uneasily.

"Don't you do it!" exclaimed Dorothy. "If you guess wrong, you will be enslaved yourself."

"But I shall have eleven guesses," answered Ozma. "Surely I ought to guess one object in eleven correctly; and, if I do, I shall rescue one of the royal family and be safe myself. Then the rest of you may attempt it, and soon we shall free all those who are enslaved."

"What if we fail?" enquired the Scarecrow. "I'd look nice as a piece of bric-a-brac, wouldn't I?"

"We must not fail!" cried Ozma, courageously. "Having come all this distance to free these poor people, it would be weak and cowardly in us to abandon the adventure. Therefore I will accept the Nome King's offer, and go at once into the royal palace."

"Come along, then, my dear," said the King, climbing down from his throne with some difficulty, because he was so fat; "I'll show you the way."

He approached a wall of the cave and waved his hand. Instantly an opening appeared, through which Ozma, after a smiling farewell to her friends, boldly passed.

She found herself in a splendid hall that was more beautiful and grand than anything she had ever beheld. The ceilings were composed of great arches that rose far above her head, and all the walls and floors were of polished marble exquisitely tinted in many colors. Thick velvet carpets were on the floor and heavy silken draperies covered the arches leading to the various rooms of the palace. The furniture was made of rare old woods richly carved and covered with delicate satins, and the entire palace was lighted by a mysterious rosy glow that seemed to come from no particular place but flooded each apartment with its soft and pleasing radiance.

Ozma passed from one room to another, greatly delighted by all she saw. The lovely palace had no other occupant, for the Nome King had left her at the entrance, which closed behind her, and in all the magnificent rooms there appeared to be no other person.

Upon the mantels, and on many shelves and brackets and tables, were clustered ornaments of every description, seemingly made out of all sorts of metals, glass, china, stones and marbles. There were vases, and figures of men and animals, and graven platters and bowls, and mosaics of precious gems, and many other things. Pictures, too, were on the walls, and the underground palace was quite a museum of rare and curious and costly objects.

After her first hasty examination of the rooms Ozma began to wonder which of all the numerous ornaments they contained were the transformations of the royal family of Ev. There was nothing to guide her, for everything seemed without a spark of life. So she must guess blindly; and for the first time the girl came to realize how dangerous was her task, and how likely she was to lose her own freedom in striving to free others from the bondage of the Nome King. No wonder the cunning monarch laughed good naturedly with his visitors, when he knew how easily they might be entrapped.

But Ozma, having undertaken the venture, would not abandon it. She looked at a silver candelabra that had ten branches, and thought: "This may be the Queen of Ev and her ten children." So she touched it and uttered aloud the word "Ev," as the Nome King had instructed her to do when she guessed. But the candelabra remained as it was before.

Then she wandered into another room and touched a china lamb, thinking it might be one of the children she sought. But again she was unsuccessful. Three guesses; four guesses; five, six, seven, eight, nine and ten she made, and still not one of them was right!

The girl shivered a little and grew pale even under the rosy light; for now but one guess remained, and her own fate depended upon the result.

She resolved not to be hasty, and strolled through all the rooms once more, gazing earnestly upon the various ornaments and trying to decide which she would touch. Finally, in despair, she decided to leave it entirely to chance. She faced the doorway of a room, shut her eyes tightly, and then, thrusting aside the heavy draperies, she advanced blindly with her right arm outstretched before her.

Slowly, softly she crept forward until her hand came in contact with an object upon a small round table. She did not know what it was, but in a low voice she pronounced the word "Ev."

The rooms were quite empty of life after that. The Nome King had gained a new ornament. For upon the edge of the table rested a pretty grasshopper, that seemed to have been formed from a single emerald. It was all that remained of Ozma of Oz.

In the throne room just beyond the palace the Nome King suddenly looked up and smiled.

"Next!" he said, in his pleasant voice.

Dorothy, the Scarecrow, and the Tin Woodman, who had been sitting in anxious silence, each gave a start of dismay and stared into one another's eyes.

"Has she failed?" asked Tiktok.

"So it seems," answered the little monarch, cheerfully. "But that is no reason one of you should not succeed. The next may have twelve guesses, instead of eleven, for there are now twelve persons transformed into ornaments. Well, well! Which of you goes next?"

"I'll go," said Dorothy.

"Not so," replied the Tin Woodman. "As commander of Ozma's army, it is my privilege to follow her and attempt her rescue."

"Away you go, then," said the Scarecrow. "But be careful, old friend."

"I will," promised the Tin Woodman; and then he followed the Nome King to the entrance to the palace and the rock closed behind him.

Chapter 13

THE NOME KING LAUGHS

In a moment the King returned to his throne and relighted his pipe, and the rest of the little band of adventurers settled themselves for another long wait. They were greatly disheartened by the failure of their girl Ruler, and the knowledge that she was now an ornament in the Nome King's palace—a dreadful, creepy place in spite of all its magnificence. Without their little leader they did not know what to do next, and each one, down to the trembling private of the army, began to fear he would soon be more ornamental than useful.

Suddenly the Nome King began laughing.

"Ha, ha, ha! He, he, he! Ho, ho, ho!"

"What's happened?" asked the Scarecrow.

"Why, your friend, the Tin Woodman, has become the funniest thing you can imagine," replied the King, wiping the tears of merriment from his eyes. "No one would ever believe he could make such an amusing ornament. Next!"

They gazed at each other with sinking hearts. One of the generals began to weep dolefully.

"What are you crying for?" asked the Scarecrow, indignant at such a display of weakness.

"He owed me six weeks back pay," said the general, "and I hate to lose him."

"Then you shall go and find him," declared the Scarecrow.

"Me!" cried the general, greatly alarmed.

"Certainly. It is your duty to follow your commander. March!"

"I won't," said the general. "I'd like to, of course; but I just simply *won't*."

The Scarecrow looked enquiringly at the Nome King.

"Never mind," said the jolly monarch. "If he doesn't care to enter the palace and make his guesses I'll throw him into one of my fiery furnaces."

"I'll go!—of course I'm going," yelled the general, as quick as scat. "Where is the entrance—where is it? Let me go at once!"

So the Nome King escorted him into the palace, and again returned to await the result. What the general did, no one can tell; but it was not long before the King called for the next victim, and a colonel was forced to try his fortune.

Thus, one after another, all of the twenty-six officers filed into the palace and made their guesses—and became ornaments.

Meantime the King ordered refreshments to be served to those waiting, and at his command a rudely shaped Nome entered, bearing a tray. This Nome was not unlike the others that Dorothy had seen, but he wore a heavy gold chain around his neck to show that he was the Chief Steward of the Nome King, and he assumed an air of much importance, and even told his majesty not to eat too much cake late at night, or he would be ill.

Dorothy, however, was hungry, and she was not afraid of being ill; so she ate several cakes and found them good, and also she drank a cup of excellent coffee made of a richly flavored clay, browned in the furnaces and then ground fine, and found it most refreshing and not at all muddy.

Of all the party which had started upon this adventure, the little Kansas girl was now left alone with the Scarecrow, Tiktok, and the private for counsellors and companions. Of course the Cowardly

Lion and the Hungry Tiger were still there, but they, having also eaten some of the cakes, had gone to sleep at one side of the cave, while upon the other side stood the Sawhorse, motionless and silent, as became a mere thing of wood. Billina had quietly walked around and picked up the crumbs of cake which had been scattered, and now, as it was long after bed-time, she tried to find some dark place in which to go to sleep.

Presently the hen espied a hollow underneath the King's rocky throne, and crept into it unnoticed. She could still hear the chattering of those around her, but it was almost dark underneath the throne, so that soon she had fallen fast asleep.

"Next!" called the King, and the private, whose turn it was to enter the fatal palace, shook hands with Dorothy and the Scarecrow and bade them a sorrowful good-bye, and passed through the rocky portal.

They waited a long time, for the private was in no hurry to become an ornament and made his guesses very slowly. The Nome King, who seemed to know, by some magical power, all that took place in his beautiful rooms of his palace, grew impatient finally and declared he would sit up no longer.

"I love ornaments," said he, "but I can wait until tomorrow to get more of them; so, as soon as that stupid private is transformed, we will all go to bed and leave the job to be finished in the morning."

"Is it so very late?" asked Dorothy.

"Why, it is after midnight," said the King, "and that strikes me as being late enough. There is neither night nor day in my kingdom, because it is under the earth's surface, where the sun does not shine. But we have to sleep, just the same as the up-stairs people do, and for my part I'm going to bed in a few minutes."

Indeed, it was not long after this that the private made his last guess. Of course he guessed wrongly, and of course he at once became an ornament. So the King was greatly pleased, and clapped his hands to summon his Chief Steward.

"Show these guests to some of the sleeping apartments," he commanded, "and be quick about it, too, for I'm dreadfully sleepy myself."

"You've no business to sit up so late," replied the Steward, gruffly. "You'll be as cross as a griffin tomorrow morning."

His Majesty made no answer to this remark, and the Chief Steward led Dorothy through another doorway into a long hall, from which several plain but comfortable sleeping rooms opened. The little girl was given the first room, and the Scarecrow and Tiktok the next—although they never slept—and the Lion and the Tiger the third. The Sawhorse hobbled after the Steward into a fourth room, to stand stiffly in the center of it until morning. Each night was rather a bore to the Scarecrow, Tiktok and the Sawhorse; but they had learned from experience to pass the time patiently and quietly, since all their friends who were made of flesh had to sleep and did not like to be disturbed.

When the Chief Steward had left them alone the Scarecrow remarked, sadly:

"I am in great sorrow over the loss of my old comrade, the Tin Woodman. We have had many dangerous adventures together, and escaped them all, and now it grieves me to know he has become an ornament, and is lost to me forever."

"He was al-ways an or-na-ment to so-ci-e-ty," said Tiktok.

"True; but now the Nome King laughs at him, and calls him the funniest ornament in all the palace. It will hurt my poor friend's pride to be laughed at," continued the Scarecrow, sadly.

"We will make rath-er ab-surd or-na-ments, our-selves, to-mor-row," observed the machine, in his monotonous voice.

Just then Dorothy ran into their room, in a state of great anxiety, crying:

"Where's Billina? Have you seen Billina? Is she here?"

"No," answered the Scarecrow.

"Then what has become of her?" asked the girl.

"Why, I thought she was with you," said the Scarecrow. "Yet I do not remember seeing the yellow hen since she picked up the crumbs of cake."

"We must have left her in the room where the King's throne is," decided Dorothy, and at once she turned and ran down the hall to the door through which they had entered. But it was fast closed and locked on the other side, and the heavy slab of rock proved to be so thick that no sound could pass through it. So Dorothy was forced to return to her chamber.

The Cowardly Lion stuck his head into her room to try to console the girl for the loss of her feathered friend.

"The yellow hen is well able to take care of herself," said he; "so don't worry about her, but try to get all the sleep you can. It has been a long and weary day, and you need rest."

"I'll prob'ly get lots of rest tomorrow, when I become an orn'ment," said Dorothy, sleepily. But she lay down upon her couch, nevertheless, and in spite of all her worries was soon in the land of dreams

Chapter 14

DOROTHY TRIES TO BE BRAVE

MEANTIME the Chief Steward had returned to the throne room, where he said to the King:

"You are a fool to waste so much time upon these people."

"What!" cried his Majesty, in so enraged a voice that it awoke Billina, who was asleep under his throne. "How dare you call me a fool?"

"Because I like to speak the truth," said the Steward. "Why didn't you enchant them all at once, instead of allowing them to go one by one into the palace and guess which ornaments are the Queen of Ev and her children?"

"Why, you stupid rascal, it is more fun this way," returned the King, "and it serves to keep me amused for a long time."

"But suppose some of them happen to guess aright," persisted the Steward; "then you would lose your old ornaments and these new ones, too."

"There is no chance of their guessing aright," replied the monarch, with a laugh. "How could they know that the Queen of Ev and her family are all ornaments of a royal purple color?"

"But there are no other purple ornaments in the palace," said the Steward.

"There are many other colors, however, and the purple ones are scattered throughout the rooms, and are of many different shapes and sizes. Take my word for it, Steward, they will never think of choosing the purple ornaments."

Billina, squatting under the throne, had listened carefully to all this talk, and now chuckled softly to herself as she heard the King disclose his secret.

"Still, you are acting foolishly by running the chance," continued the Steward, roughly; "and it is still more foolish of you to transform all those people from Oz into green ornaments.

"I did that because they came from the Emerald City," replied the King; "and I had no green ornaments in my collection until now. I think they will look quite pretty, mixed with the others. Don't you?"

The Steward gave an angry grunt.

"Have your own way, since you are the King," he growled. "But if you come to grief through your carelessness, remember that I told you so. If I wore the magic belt which enables you to work all your transformations, and gives you so much other power, I am sure I would make a much wiser and better King than you are."

"Oh, cease your tiresome chatter!" commanded the King, getting angry again. "Because you are my Chief Steward you have an idea you can scold me as much as you please. But the very next time you become impudent, I will send you to work in the furnaces, and get another Nome to fill your place. Now follow me to my chamber, for I am going to bed. And see that I am wakened early tomorrow morning. I want to enjoy the fun of transforming the rest of these people into ornaments."

"What color will you make the Kansas girl?" asked the Steward.

"Gray, I think," said his Majesty.

"And the Scarecrow and the machine man?"

"Oh, they shall be of solid gold, because they are so ugly in real life."

Then the voices died away, and Billina knew that the King and his Steward had left the room. She fixed up some of her tail feathers that were not straight, and then tucked her head under her wing again and went to sleep.

In the morning Dorothy and the Lion and Tiger were given their breakfast in their rooms, and afterward joined the King in his throne room. The Tiger complained bitterly that he was half starved, and begged to go into the palace and become an ornament, so that he would no longer suffer the pangs of hunger.

"Haven't you had your breakfast?" asked the Nome King.

"Oh, I had just a bite," replied the beast. "But what good is a bite, to a hungry tiger?"

"He ate seventeen bowls of porridge, a platter full of fried sausages, eleven loaves of bread and twenty-one mince pies," said the Steward.

"What more do you want?" demanded the King.

"A fat baby. I want a fat baby," said the Hungry Tiger. "A nice, plump, juicy, tender, fat baby. But, of course, if I had one, my conscience would not allow me to eat it. So I'll have to be an ornament and forget my hunger."

"Impossible!" exclaimed the King. "I'll have no clumsy beasts enter my palace, to overturn and break all my pretty nick-nacks. When the rest of your friends are transformed you can return to the upper world, and go about your business."

"As for that we have no business, when our friends are gone," said the Lion. "So we do not care much what becomes of us."

Dorothy begged to be allowed to go first into the palace, but Tiktok firmly maintained that the slave should face danger before the mistress. The Scarecrow agreed with him in that, so the Nome King opened the door for the machine man, who tramped into the palace to meet his fate. Then his Majesty returned to his throne and puffed his pipe so contentedly that a small cloud of smoke formed above his head.

Bye and bye he said:

"I'm sorry there are so few of you left. Very soon, now, my fun will be over, and then for amusement I shall have nothing to do but admire my new ornaments."

"It seems to me," said Dorothy, "that you are not so honest as you pretend to be.

"How's that?" asked the King.

"Why, you made us think it would be easy to guess what ornaments the people of Ev were changed into."

"It *is* easy," declared the monarch, "if one is a good guesser. But it appears that the members of your party are all poor guessers."

"What is Tiktok doing now?" asked the girl, uneasily.

"Nothing," replied the King, with a frown. "He is standing perfectly still, in the middle of a room."

"Oh, I expect he's run down," said Dorothy. "I forgot to wind him up this morning. How many guesses has he made?"

"All that he is allowed except one," answered the King. "Suppose you go in and wind him up, and then you can stay there and make your own guesses."

"All right," said Dorothy.

"It is my turn next," declared the Scarecrow.

"Why, you don't want to go away and leave me all alone, do you?" asked the girl. "Besides, if I go now I can wind up Tiktok, so that he can make his last guess."

"Very well, then," said the Scarecrow, with a sigh. "Run along, little Dorothy, and may good luck go with you!"

So Dorothy, trying to be brave in spite of her fears, passed through the doorway into the gorgeous rooms of the palace. The stillness of the place awed her, at first, and the child drew short breaths, and pressed her hand to her heart, and looked all around with wondering eyes.

Yes, it was a beautiful place; but enchantments lurked in every nook and corner, and she had not yet grown accustomed to the wizardries of these fairy countries, so different from the quiet and sensible common-places of her own native land.

Slowly she passed through several rooms until she came upon Tiktok, standing motionless. It really seemed, then, that she had found a friend in this mysterious palace, so she hastened to wind up the machine man's action and speech and thoughts.

"Thank you, Dor-oth-y," were his first words. "I have now one more guess to make."

"Oh, be very careful, Tiktok; won't you?" cried the girl.

"Yes. But the Nome King has us in his power, and he has set a trap for us. I fear we are all lost," he answered.

"I fear so, too," said Dorothy, sadly.

"If Smith & Tin-ker had giv-en me a guess-ing clock-work at-tach-ment," continued Tiktok, "I might have de-fied the Nome King. But my thoughts are plain and sim-ple, and are not of much use in this case."

"Do the best you can," said Dorothy, encouragingly, "and if you fail I will watch and see what shape you are changed into."

So Tiktok touched a yellow glass vase that had daisies painted on one side, and he spoke at the same time the word "Ev."

In a flash the machine man had disappeared, and although the girl looked quickly in every direction, she could not tell which of the many ornaments the room contained had a moment before been her faithful friend and servant.

So all she could do was to accept the hopeless task set her, and make her guesses and abide by the result.

"It can't hurt very much," she thought, "for I haven't heard any of them scream or cry out—not even the poor officers. Dear me! I wonder if Uncle Henry or Aunt Em will ever know I have become an orn'ment in the Nome King's palace, and must stand forever and ever in one place and look pretty—'cept when I'm moved to be dusted.It isn't the way I thought I'd turn out, at all; but I s'pose it can't be helped."

She walked through all the rooms once more, and examined with care all the objects they contained; but there were so many, they bewildered her, and she decided, after all, as Ozma had done, that it could be only guess work at the best, and that the chances were much against her guessing aright.

Timidly she touched an alabaster bowl and said: "Ev."

"That's one failure, anyhow," she thought. "But how am I to know which thing is enchanted, and which is not?"

Next she touched the image of a purple kitten that stood on the corner of a mantel, and as she pronounced the word "Ev" the kitten disappeared, and a pretty, fair-haired boy stood beside her. At the same time a bell rang somewhere in the distance, and as Dorothy started back, partly in surprise and partly in joy, the little one exclaimed:

"Where am I? And who are you? And what has happened to me?"

"Well, I declare!" said Dorothy. "I've really done it."

"Done what?" asked the boy.

"Saved myself from being an ornament," replied the girl, with a laugh, "and saved you from being forever a purple kitten."

"A purple kitten?" he repeated. "There *is* no such thing."

"I know," she answered. "But there was, a minute ago. Don't you remember standing on a corner of the mantel?"

"Of course not. I am a Prince of Ev, and my name is Evring," the little one announced, proudly. "But my father, the King, sold my mother and all her children to the cruel ruler of the Nomes, and after that I remember nothing at all."

"A purple kitten can't be 'spected to remember, Evring," said Dorothy. "But now you are yourself again, and I'm going to try to save some of your brothers and sisters, and perhaps your mother, as well. So come with me."

She seized the child's hand and eagerly hurried here and there, trying to decide which object to choose next. The third guess was another failure, and so was the fourth and the fifth.

Little Evring could not imagine what she was doing, but he trotted along beside her very willingly, for he liked the new companion he had found.

Dorothy's further quest proved unsuccessful; but after her first disappointment was over, the little girl was filled with joy and thankfulness to think that after all she had been able to save one member of the royal family of Ev, and could restore the little Prince to his sorrowing country. Now she might return to the terrible Nome King in safety, carrying with her the prize she had won in the person of the fair-haired boy.

So she retraced her steps until she found the entrance to the palace, and as she approached, the massive doors of rock opened of their own accord, allowing both Dorothy and Evring to pass the portals and enter the throne room.

Chapter 15

BILLINA FRIGHTENS THE NOME KING

Now when Dorothy had entered the palace to make her guesses and the Scarecrow was left with the Nome King, the two sat in moody silence for several minutes. Then the monarch exclaimed, in a tone of satisfaction:

"Very good!"

"Who is very good?" asked the Scarecrow.

"The machine man. He won't need to be wound up any more, for he has now become a very neat ornament. Very neat, indeed."

"How about Dorothy?" the Scarecrow enquired.

"Oh, she will begin to guess, pretty soon," said the King, cheerfully. "And then she will join my collection, and it will be your turn."

The good Scarecrow was much distressed by the thought that his little friend was about to suffer the fate of Ozma and the rest of their party; but while he sat in gloomy reverie a shrill voice suddenly cried:

"Kut, kut, kut—ka-daw-kutt! Kut, kut, kut—ka-daw-kutt!"

The Nome King nearly jumped off his seat, he was so startled.

"Good gracious! What's that?" he yelled.

"Why, it's Billina," said the Scarecrow.

"What do you mean by making a noise like that?" shouted the King, angrily, as the yellow hen came from under the throne and strutted proudly about the room.

"I've got a right to cackle, I guess," replied Billina. "I've just laid my egg.'

"What! Laid an egg! In my throne room! How dare you do such a thing?" asked the King, in a voice of fury.

"I lay eggs wherever I happen to be," said the hen, ruffling her feathers and then shaking them into place.

"But—thunder-ation! Don't you know that eggs are poison?" roared the King, while his rock-colored eyes stuck out in great terror.

"Poison! well, I declare," said Billina, indignantly. "I'll have you know all my eggs are warranted strictly fresh and up to date. Poison, indeed!"

"You don't understand," retorted the little monarch, nervously. "Eggs belong only to the outside world—to the world on the earth's surface, where you came from. Here, in my underground kingdom, they are rank poison, as I said, and we Nomes can't bear them around."

"Well, you'll have to bear this one around," declared Billina; "for I've laid it."

"Where?" asked the King.

"Under your throne," said the hen.

The King jumped three feet into the air, so anxious was he to get away from the throne.

"Take it away! Take it away at once!" he shouted.

"I can't," said Billina. "I havn't any hands."

"I'll take the egg," said the Scarecrow. "I'm making a collection of Billina's eggs. There's one in my pocket now, that she laid yesterday."

Hearing this, the monarch hastened to put a good distance between himself and the Scarecrow, who was about to reach under the throne for the egg when the hen suddenly cried:

"Stop!"

"What's wrong?" asked the Scarecrow.

"Don't take the egg unless the King will allow me to enter the palace and guess as the others have done," said Billina.

"Pshaw!" returned the King. "You're only a hen. How could you guess my enchantments?"

"I can try, I suppose," said Billina. "And, if I fail, you will have another ornament."

"A pretty ornament you'd make, wouldn't you?" growled the King. "But you shall have your way. It will properly punish you for daring to lay an egg in my presence. After the Scarecrow is enchanted you shall follow him into the palace. But how will you touch the objects?"

"With my claws," said the hen; "and I can speak the word 'Ev' as plainly as anyone. Also I must have the right to guess the enchantments of my friends, and to release them if I succeed."

"Very well," said the King. "You have my promise."

"Then," said Billina to the Scarecrow, "you may get the egg."

He knelt down and reached underneath the throne and found the egg, which he placed in another pocket of his jacket, fearing that if both eggs were in one pocket they would knock together and get broken.

Just then a bell above the throne rang briskly, and the King gave another nervous jump.

"Well, well!" said he, with a rueful face; "the girl has actually done it."

"Done what?" asked the Scarecrow.

"She has made one guess that is right, and broken one of my neatest enchantments. By ricketty, it's too bad! I never thought she would do it."

"Do I understand that she will now return to us in safety?" enquired the Scarecrow, joyfully wrinkling his painted face into a broad smile.

"Of course," said the King, fretfully pacing up and down the room. "I always keep my promises, no matter how foolish they are. But I shall make an ornament of the yellow hen to replace the one I have just lost."

"Perhaps you will, and perhaps you won't," murmured Billina, calmly. "I may surprise you by guessing right."

"Guessing right?" snapped the King. "How should you guess right, where your betters have failed, you stupid fowl?"

Billina did not care to answer this question, and a moment later the doors flew open and Dorothy entered, leading the little Prince Evring by the hand.

The Scarecrow welcomed the girl with a close embrace, and he would have embraced Evring, too, in his delight. But the little Prince was shy, and shrank away from the painted Scarecrow because he did not yet know his many excellent qualities.

But there was little time for the friends to talk, because the Scarecrow must now enter the palace. Dorothy's success had greatly encouraged him, and they both hoped he would manage to make at least one correct guess.

However, he proved as unfortunate as the others except Dorothy, and although he took a good deal of time to select his objects, not one did the poor Scarecrow guess aright.

So he became a solid gold card-receiver, and the beautiful but terrible palace awaited its next visitor.

"It's all over," remarked the King, with a sigh of satisfaction; "and it has been a very amusing performance, except for the one good guess the Kansas girl made. I am richer by a great many pretty ornaments.

"It is my turn, now," said Billina, briskly.

"Oh, I'd forgotten you," said the King. "But you needn't go if you don't wish to. I will be generous, and let you off."

"No you won't," replied the hen. "I insist upon having my guesses, as you promised."

"Then go ahead, you absurd feathered fool!" grumbled the King, and he caused the opening that led to the palace to appear once more.

"Don't go, Billina," said Dorothy, earnestly. "It isn't easy to guess those orn'ments, and only luck saved me from being one myself. Stay with me, and we'll go back to the Land of Ev together. I'm sure this little Prince will give us a home."

"Indeed I will," said Evring, with much dignity.

"Don't worry, my dear," cried Billina, with a cluck that was meant for a laugh. "I may not be human, but I'm no fool, if I *am* a chicken."

"Oh, Billina!" said Dorothy, "you haven't been a chicken in a long time. Not since you—you've been—grown up."

"Perhaps that's true," answered Billina, thoughtfully. "But if a Kansas farmer sold me to some one, what would he call me?—a hen or a chicken!"

"You are not a Kansas farmer, Billina," replied the girl, "and you said—"

"Never mind that, Dorothy. I'm going. I won't say good-bye, because I'm coming back. Keep up your courage, for I'll see you a little later."

Then Billina gave several loud "cluck-clucks" that seemed to make the fat little King *more* nervous than ever, and marched through the entrance into the enchanted palace.

"I hope I've seen the last of *that* bird," declared the monarch, seating himself again in his throne and mopping the perspiration from his forehead with his rock-colored handkerchief. "Hens are bothersome enough at their best, but when they can talk they're simply dreadful."

"Billina's my friend," said Dorothy quietly. "She may not always be 'zactly polite; but she *means* well, I'm sure."

Chapter 16

PURPLE, GREEN *AND* GOLD

THE yellow hen, stepping high and with an air of vast importance, walked slowly over the rich velvet carpets of the splendid palace, examining everything she met with her sharp little eyes.

Billina had a right to feel important; for she alone shared the Nome King's secret and knew how to tell the objects that were transformations from those that had never been alive. She was very sure that her guesses would be correct, but before she began to make them she was curious to behold all the magnificence of this underground palace, which was perhaps one of the most splendid and beautiful places in any fairyland.

As she went through the rooms she counted the purple ornaments; and although some were small and hidden in queer places, Billina spied them all, and found the entire ten scattered about the various rooms. The green ornaments she did not bother to count, for she thought she could find them all when the time came.

Finally, having made a survey of the entire palace and enjoyed its splendor, the yellow hen returned to one of the rooms where she had noticed a large purple footstool. She placed a claw upon this and said "Ev," and at once the footstool vanished and a lovely lady, tall and slender and most beautifully robed, stood before her.

The lady's eyes were round with astonishment for a moment, for she could not remember her transformation, nor imagine what had restored her to life.

"Good morning, ma'am," said Billina, in her sharp voice. "You're looking quite well, considering your age."

"Who speaks?" demanded the Queen of Ev, drawing herself up proudly.

"Why, my name's Bill, by rights," answered the hen, who was now perched upon the back of a chair; "although Dorothy has put scollops on it and made it Billina. But the name doesn't matter. I've saved you from the Nome King, and you are a slave no longer."

"Then I thank you for the gracious favor," said the Queen, with a graceful courtesy. "But, my children—tell me, I beg of you—where are my children?" and she clasped her hands in anxious entreaty.

"Don't worry," advised Billina, pecking at a tiny bug that was crawling over the chair back. "Just at present they are out of mischief and perfectly safe, for they can't even wiggle."

"What mean you, O kindly stranger?" asked the Queen, striving to repress her anxiety.

"They're enchanted," said Billina, "just as you have been—all, that is, except the little fellow Dorothy picked out. And the chances are that they have been good boys and girls for some time, because they couldn't help it."

"Oh, my poor darlings!" cried the Queen, with a sob of anguish.

"Not at all," returned the hen. "Don't let their condition make you unhappy, ma'am, because I'll soon have them crowding 'round to bother and worry you as naturally as ever. Come with me, if you please, and I'll show you how pretty they look."

She flew down from her perch and walked into the next room, the Queen following. As she passed a low table a small green grasshopper caught her eye, and instantly Billina pounced upon it and snapped it up in her sharp bill. For grasshoppers are a favorite food with hens, and they usually must be caught quickly, before they can hop away. It might easily have been the end of Ozma of Oz, had she been a real grasshopper instead of an emerald one. But Billina found the grasshopper hard and lifeless, and suspecting it was not good to eat she quickly dropped it instead of letting it slide down her throat.

"I might have known better," she muttered to herself, "for where there is no grass there can be no live grasshoppers. This is probably one of the King's transformations."

A moment later she approached one of the purple ornaments, and while the Queen watched her curiously the hen broke the Nome King's enchantment and a sweet-faced girl, whose golden hair fell in a cloud over her shoulders, stood beside them.

"Evanna!" cried the Queen, "my own Evanna!" and she clasped the girl to her bosom and covered her face with kisses.

"That's all right," said Billina, contentedly. "Am I a good guesser, Mr. Nome King? Well, I guess!"

Then she disenchanted another girl, whom the Queen addressed as Evrose, and afterwards a boy named Evardo, who was older than his brother Evring. Indeed, the yellow hen kept the good Queen exclaiming and embracing for some time, until five Princesses and four Princes, all looking very much alike except for the difference in size, stood in a row beside their happy mother.

The Princesses were named, Evanna, Evrose, Evella, Evirene and Evedna, while the Princes were Evrob, Evington, Evardo and Evroland. Of these Evardo was the eldest and would inherit his father's throne and be crowned King of Ev when he returned to his own country. He was a grave and quiet youth, and would doubtless rule his people wisely and with justice.

Billina, having restored all of the royal family of Ev to their proper forms, now began to select the green ornaments which were the transformations of the people of Oz. She had little trouble in finding these, and before long all the twenty-six officers, as well as the private, were gathered around the yellow hen, joyfully congratulating her upon their release. The thirty-seven people who were now alive in the rooms of the palace knew very well that they owed their freedom to the cleverness of the yellow hen, and they were earnest in thanking her for saving them from the magic of the Nome King.

"Now," said Billina, "I must find Ozma. She is sure to be here, somewhere, and of course she is green, being from Oz. So look around, you stupid soldiers, and help me in my search."

For a while, however, they could discover nothing more that was green. But the Queen, who had kissed all her nine children once more and could now find time to take an interest in what was going on, said to the hen:

"Mayhap, my gentle friend, it is the grasshopper whom you seek."

"Of course it's the grasshopper!" exclaimed Billina. "I declare, I'm nearly as stupid as these brave soldiers. Wait here for me, and I'll go back and get it."

So she went into the room where she had seen the grasshopper, and presently Ozma of Oz, as lovely and dainty as ever, entered and approached the Queen of Ev, greeting her as one high born princess greets another.

"But where are my friends, the Scarecrow and the Tin Woodman?" asked the girl Ruler, when these courtesies had been exchanged.

"I'll hunt them up," replied Billina. "The Scarecrow is solid gold, and so is Tiktok; but I don't exactly know what the Tin

Woodman is, because the Nome King said he had been transformed into something funny."

Ozma eagerly assisted the hen in her quest, and soon the Scarecrow and the machine man, being ornaments of shining gold, were discovered and restored to their accustomed forms. But, search as they might, in no place could they find a funny ornament that might be the transformation of the Tin Woodman.

"Only one thing can be done," said Ozma, at last, "and that is to return to the Nome King and oblige him to tell us what has become of our friend."

"Perhaps he won't," suggested Billina.

"He must," returned Ozma, firmly. "The King has not treated us honestly, for under the mask of fairness and good nature he entrapped us all, and we would have been forever enchanted had not our wise and clever friend, the yellow hen, found a way to save us."

"The King is a villain," declared the Scarecrow.

"His laugh is worse than another man's frown," said the private, with a shudder.

"I thought he was hon-est, but I was mis-tak-en," remarked Tiktok. "My thoughts are us-u-al-ly cor-rect, but it is Smith & Tin-ker's fault if they some-times go wrong or do not work prop-er-ly."

"Smith & Tinker made a very good job of you," said Ozma, kindly. "I do not think they should be blamed if you are not quite perfect."

"Thank you," replied Tiktok.

"Then," said Billina, in her brisk little voice, "let us all go back to the Nome King, and see what he has to say for himself."

So they started for the entrance, Ozma going first, with the Queen and her train of little Princes and Princesses following. Then came Tiktok, and the Scarecrow with Billina perched upon his straw-stuffed shoulder. The twenty-seven officers and the private brought up the rear.

As they reached the hall the doors flew open before them; but then they all stopped and stared into the domed cavern with faces of astonishment and dismay. For the room was filled with the mail-clad warriors of the Nome King, rank after rank standing in orderly array. The electric lights upon their brows gleamed brightly, their battle-axes were poised as if to strike down their foes; yet they remained motionless as statues, awaiting the word of command.

And in the center of this terrible army sat the little King upon his throne of rock. But he neither smiled nor laughed. Instead, his face was distorted with rage, and most dreadful to behold.

Chapter 17

THE SCARECROW WINS *THE* FIGHT

After Billina had entered the palace Dorothy and Evring sat down to await the success or failure of her mission, and the Nome King occupied his throne and smoked his long pipe for a while in a cheerful and contented mood.

Then the bell above the throne, which sounded whenever an enchantment was broken, began to ring, and the King gave a start of annoyance and exclaimed, "Rocketty-ricketts!"

When the bell rang a second time the King shouted angrily, "Smudge and blazes!" and at a third ring he screamed in a fury, "Hippikaloric!" which must be a dreadful word because we don't know what it means.

After that the bell went on ringing time after time; but the King was now so violently enraged that he could not utter a word, but hopped out of his throne and all around the room in a mad frenzy, so that he reminded Dorothy of a jumping-jack.

The girl was, for her part, filled with joy at every peal of the bell, for it announced the fact that Billina had transformed one more ornament into a living person. Dorothy was also amazed at Billina's success, for she could not imagine how the yellow hen was able to guess correctly from all the bewildering number of articles clustered in the rooms of the palace. But after she had counted ten, and the bell continued to ring, she knew that not only the royal family of Ev, but Ozma and her followers also, were being restored to their natural forms, and she was so delighted that the antics of the angry King only made her laugh merrily.

Perhaps the little monarch could not be more furious than he was before, but the girl's laughter nearly drove him frantic, and he roared at her like a savage beast. Then, as he found that all his enchantments were likely to be dispelled and his victims every one set free, he suddenly ran to the little door that opened upon the balcony and gave the shrill whistle that summoned his warriors.

At once the army filed out of the gold and silver doors in great numbers, and marched up a winding stairs and into the throne room, led by a stern featured Nome who was their captain. When they had nearly filled the throne room they formed ranks in the big underground cavern below, and then stood still until they were told what to do next.

Dorothy had pressed back to one side of the cavern when the warriors entered, and now she stood holding little Prince Evring's hand while the great Lion crouched upon one side and the enormous Tiger crouched an the other side.

"Seize that girl!" shouted the King to his captain, and a group of warriors sprang forward to obey. But both the Lion and Tiger snarled so fiercely and bared their strong, sharp teeth so threateningly, that the men drew back in alarm.

"Don't mind them!" cried the Nome King; "they cannot leap beyond the places where they now stand."

"But they can bite those who attempt to touch the girl," said the captain.

"I'll fix that," answered the King. "I'll enchant them again, so that they can't open their jaws."

He stepped out of the throne to do this, but just then the Sawhorse ran up behind him and gave the fat monarch a powerful kick with both his wooden hind legs.

"Ow! Murder! Treason!" yelled the King, who had been hurled against several of his warriors and was considerably bruised. "Who did that?"

"I did," growled the Sawhorse, viciously. "You let Dorothy alone, or I'll kick you again."

"We'll see about that," replied the King, and at once he waved his hand toward the Sawhorse and muttered a magical word. "Aha!" he continued; "*now* let us see you move, you wooden mule!"

But in spite of the magic the Sawhorse moved; and he moved so quickly toward the King, that the fat little man could not get out of his way. Thump—*bang!* came the wooden heels, right against his round body, and the King flew into the air and fell upon the head of his captain, who let him drop flat upon the ground.

"Well, well!" said the King, sitting up and looking surprised. "Why didn't my magic belt work, I wonder?"

"The creature is made of wood," replied the captain. "Your magic will not work on wood, you know."

"Ah, I'd forgotten that," said the King, getting up and limping to his throne. "Very well, let the girl alone. She can't escape us, anyway."

The warriors, who had been rather confused by these incidents, now formed their ranks again, and the Sawhorse pranced across the room to Dorothy and took a position beside the Hungry Tiger.

At that moment the doors that led to the palace flew open and the people of Ev and the people of Oz were disclosed to view. They paused, astonished, at sight of the warriors and the angry Nome King, seated in their midst.

"Surrender!" cried the King, in a loud voice. "You are my prisoners."

"Go 'long!" answered Billina, from the Scarecrow's shoulder. "You promised me that if I guessed correctly my friends and I might depart in safety. And you always keep your promises."

"I said you might leave the palace in safety," retorted the King; "and so you may, but you cannot leave my dominions. You are my prisoners, and I will hurl you all into my underground dungeons, where the volcanic fires glow and the molten lava flows in every direction, and the air is hotter than blue blazes."

"That will be the end of me, all right," said the Scarecrow, sorrowfully. "One small blaze, blue or green, is enough to reduce me to an ash-heap."

"Do you surrender?" demanded the King.

Billina whispered something in the Scarecrow's ear that made him smile and put his hands in his jacket pockets.

"No!" returned Ozma, boldly answering the King. Then she said to her army:

"Forward, my brave soldiers, and fight for your Ruler and yourselves, unto death!"

"Pardon me, Most Royal Ozma," replied one of her generals; "but I find that I and my brother officers all suffer from heart disease, and the slightest excitement might kill us. If we fight we may get excited. Would it not be well for us to avoid this grave danger?"

"Soldiers should not have heart disease," said Ozma.

"Private soldiers are not, I believe, afflicted that way," declared another general, twirling his moustache thoughtfully. "If your Royal Highness desires, we will order our private to attack yonder warriors."

"Do so," replied Ozma.

"For-ward—march!" cried all the generals, with one voice. "For-ward—march!" yelled the colonels. "For-ward—march!" shouted the majors. "For-ward—march!" commanded the captains.

And at that the private leveled his spear and dashed furiously upon the foe.

The captain of the Nomes was so surprised by this sudden onslaught that he forgot to command his warriors to fight, so that the ten men in the first row, who stood in front of the private's spear, fell over like so many toy soldiers. The spear could not go through their steel armor, however, so the warriors scrambled to their feet again, and by that time the private had knocked over another row of them.

Then the captain brought down his battle-axe with such a strong blow that the private's spear was shattered and knocked from his grasp, and he was helpless to fight any longer.

The Nome King had left his throne and pressed through his warriors to the front ranks, so he could see what was going on; but as he faced Ozma and her friends the Scarecrow, as if aroused to action by the valor of the private, drew one of Billina's eggs from his right jacket pocket and hurled it straight at the little monarch's head.

It struck him squarely in his left eye, where the egg smashed and scattered, as eggs will, and covered his face and hair and beard with its sticky contents.

"Help, help!" screamed the King, clawing with his fingers at the egg, in a struggle to remove it.

"An egg! an egg! Run for your lives!" shouted the captain of the Nomes, in a voice of horror.

And how they *did* run! The warriors fairly tumbled over one another in their efforts to escape the fatal poison of that awful egg, and those who could not rush down the winding stair fell off the balcony into the great cavern beneath, knocking over those who stood below them.

Even while the King was still yelling for help his throne room became emptied of every one of his warriors, and before the monarch had managed to clear the egg away from his left eye the Scarecrow threw the second egg against his right eye, where it smashed and blinded him entirely. The King was unable to flee because he could not see which way to run; so he stood still and howled and shouted and screamed in abject fear.

While this was going on, Billina flew over to Dorothy, and perching herself upon the Lion's back the hen whispered eagerly to the girl:

"Get his belt! Get the Nome King's jeweled belt! It unbuckles in the back. Quick, Dorothy—quick!"

Chapter 18

THE FATE OF THE TIN WOODMAN

DOROTHY obeyed. She ran at once behind the Nome King, who was still trying to free his eyes from the egg, and in a twinkling she had unbuckled his splendid jeweled belt and carried it away with her to her place beside the Tiger and Lion, where, because she did not know what else to do with it, she fastened it around her own slim waist.

Just then the Chief Steward rushed in with a sponge and a bowl of water, and began mopping away the broken eggs from his master's face. In a few minutes, and while all the party stood looking on, the King regained the use of his eyes, and the first thing he did was to glare wickedly upon the Scarecrow and exclaim:

"I'll make you suffer for this, you hay-stuffed dummy! Don't you know eggs are poison to Nomes?"

"Really," said the Scarecrow, "they *don't* seem to agree with you, although I wonder why."

"They were strictly fresh and above suspicion," said Billina. "You ought to be glad to get them."

"I'll transform you all into scorpions!" cried the King, angrily, and began waving his arms and muttering magic words.

But none of the people became scorpions, so the King stopped and looked at them in surprise.

"What's wrong?" he asked.

"Why, you are not wearing your magic belt," replied the Chief Steward, after looking the King over carefully. "Where is it? What have you done with it?"

The Nome King clapped his hand to his waist, and his rock colored face turned white as chalk.

"It's gone," he cried, helplessly. "It's gone, and I am ruined!"

Dorothy now stepped forward and said:

"Royal Ozma, and you, Queen of Ev, I welcome you and your people back to the land of the living. Billina has saved you from your troubles, and now we will leave this drea'ful place, and return to Ev as soon as poss'ble."

While the child spoke they could all see that she wore the magic belt, and a great cheer went up from all her friends, which was led by the voices of the Scarecrow and the private. But the Nome King did not join them. He crept back onto his throne like a whipped dog, and lay there bitterly bemoaning his defeat.

"But we have not yet found my faithful follower, the Tin Woodman," said Ozma to Dorothy, "and without him I do not wish to go away."

"Nor I," replied Dorothy, quickly. "Wasn't he in the palace?"

"He must be there," said Billina; "but I had no clew to guide me in guessing the Tin Woodman, so I must have missed him."

"We will go back into the rooms," said Dorothy. "This magic belt, I am sure, will help us to find our dear old friend."

So she re-entered the palace, the doors of which still stood open, and everyone followed her except the Nome King, the Queen of Ev and Prince Evring. The mother had taken the little Prince in her lap and was fondling and kissing him lovingly, for he was her youngest born.

But the others went with Dorothy, and when she came to the middle of the first room the girl waved her hand, as she had seen the King do, and commanded the Tin Woodman, whatever form he might then have, to resume his proper shape. No result followed this attempt, so Dorothy went into another room and repeated it, and so through all the rooms of the palace. Yet the Tin Woodman did not appear to them, nor could they imagine which among the thousands of ornaments was their transformed friend.

Sadly they returned to the throne room, where the King, seeing that they had met with failure, jeered at Dorothy, saying:

"You do not know how to use my belt, so it is of no use to you. Give it back to me and I will let you go free—you and all the people who came with you. As for the royal family of Ev, they are my slaves, and shall remain here."

"I shall keep the belt," said Dorothy.

"But how can you escape, without my consent?" asked the King.

"Easily enough," answered the girl. "All we need to do is to walk out the way that we came in."

"Oh, that's all, is it?" sneered the King. "Well, where is the passage through which you entered this room?"

They all looked around, but could not discover the place, for it had long since been closed. Dorothy, however, would not be dismayed. She waved her hand toward the seemingly solid wall of the cavern and said:

"I command the passage to open!"

Instantly the order was obeyed; the opening appeared and the passage lay plainly before them.

The King was amazed, and all the others overjoyed.

"Why, then, if the belt obeys you, were we unable to discover the Tin Woodman?" asked Ozma.

"I can't imagine," said Dorothy.

"See here, girl," proposed the King, eagerly; "give me the belt, and I will tell you what shape the Tin Woodman was changed into, and then you can easily find him."

Dorothy hesitated, but Billina cried out:

"Don't you do it! If the Nome King gets the belt again he will make every one of us prisoners, for we will be in his power. Only by keeping the belt, Dorothy, will you ever be able to leave this place in safety."

"I think that is true," said the Scarecrow. "But I have another idea, due to my excellent brains. Let Dorothy transform the King into a goose-egg unless he agrees to go into the palace and bring out to us the ornament which is our friend Nick Chopper, the Tin Woodman."

"A goose-egg!" echoed the horrified King. "How dreadful!"

"Well, a goose-egg you will be unless you go and fetch us the ornament we want," declared Billina, with a joyful chuckle.

"You can see for yourself that Dorothy is able to use the magic belt all right," added the Scarecrow.

The Nome King thought it over and finally consented, for he did not want to be a goose-egg. So he went into the palace to get the ornament which was the transformation of the Tin Woodman, and they all awaited his return with considerable impatience, for they were anxious to leave this underground cavern and see the sunshine once more. But when the Nome King came back he brought nothing with him except a puzzled and anxious expression upon his face.

"He's gone!" he said. "The Tin Woodman is nowhere in the palace."

"Are you sure?" asked Ozma, sternly.

"I'm very sure," answered the King, trembling, "for I know just what I transformed him into, and exactly where he stood. But he is not there, and please don't change me into a goose-egg, because I've done the best I could."

They were all silent for a time, and then Dorothy said:

"There is no use punishing the Nome King any more, and I'm 'fraid we'll have to go away without our friend."

"If he is not here, we cannot rescue him," agreed the Scarecrow, sadly. "Poor Nick! I wonder what has become of him."

"And he owed me six weeks back pay!" said one of the generals, wiping the tears from his eyes with his gold-laced coat sleeve.

Very sorrowfully they determined to return to the upper world without their former companion, and so Ozma gave the order to begin the march through the passage.

The army went first, and then the royal family of Ev, and afterward came Dorothy, Ozma, Billina, the Scarecrow and Tiktok.

They left the Nome King scowling at them from his throne, and had no thought of danger until Ozma chanced to look back and saw a large number of the warriors following them in full chase, with their swords and spears and axes raised to strike down the fugitives as soon as they drew near enough.

Evidently the Nome King had made this last attempt to prevent their escaping him; but it did him no good, for when Dorothy saw the danger they were in she stopped and waved her hand and whispered a command to the magic belt.

Instantly the foremost warriors became eggs, which rolled upon the floor of the cavern in such numbers that those behind could not advance without stepping upon them. But, when they saw the eggs, all desire to advance departed from the warriors, and they turned and fled madly into the cavern, and refused to go back again.

Our friends had no farther trouble in reaching the end of the passage, and soon were standing in the outer air upon the gloomy path between the two high mountains. But the way to Ev lay plainly before them, and they fervently hoped that they had seen the last of the Nome King and of his dreadful palace.

The cavalcade was led by Ozma, mounted on the Cowardly Lion, and the Queen of Ev, who rode upon the back of the Tiger. The children of the Queen walked behind her, hand in hand. Dorothy rode the Sawhorse, while the Scarecrow walked and commanded the army in the absence of the Tin Woodman.

Presently the way began to lighten and more of the sunshine to come in between the two mountains. And before long they heard the "thump! thump! thump!" of the giant's hammer upon the road.

"How may we pass the monstrous man of iron?" asked the Queen, anxious for the safety of her children. But Dorothy solved the problem by a word to the magic belt.

The giant paused, with his hammer held motionless in the air, thus allowing the entire party to pass between his cast-iron legs in safety.

Chapter 19

THE KING OF EV

IF there were any shifting, rock-colored Nomes on the mountain side now, they were silent and respectful, for our adventurers were not annoyed, as before, by their impudent laughter. Really the Nomes had nothing to laugh at, since the defeat of their King.

On the other side they found Ozma's golden chariot, standing as they had left it. Soon the Lion and the Tiger were harnessed to the beautiful chariot, in which was enough room for Ozma and the Queen and six of the royal children.

Little Evring preferred to ride with Dorothy upon the Sawhorse, which had a long back. The Prince had recovered from his shyness and had become very fond of the girl who had rescued him, so they were fast friends and chatted pleasantly together as they rode along. Billina was also perched upon the head of the wooden steed, which seemed not to mind the added weight in the least, and the boy was full of wonder that a hen could talk, and say such sensible things.

When they came to the gulf, Ozma's magic carpet carried them all over in safety; and now they began to pass the trees, in which birds were singing; and the breeze that was wafted to them from the farms of Ev was spicy with flowers and new-mown hay; and the sunshine fell full upon them, to warm them and drive away from their bodies the chill and dampness of the underground kingdom of the Nomes.

"I would be quite content," said the Scarecrow to Tiktok, "were only the Tin Woodman with us. But it breaks my heart to leave him behind."

"He was a fine fel-low," replied Tiktok, "al-though his ma-ter-i-al was not ve-ry du-ra-ble."

"Oh, tin is an excellent material," the Scarecrow hastened to say; "and if anything ever happened to poor Nick Chopper he was always easily soldered. Besides, he did not have to be wound up, and was not liable to get out of order."

"I some-times wish," said Tiktok, "that I was stuffed with straw, as you are. It is hard to be made of cop-per."

"I have no reason to complain of my lot," replied the Scarecrow. "A little fresh straw, now and then, makes me as good as new. But I can never be the polished gentleman that my poor departed friend, the Tin Woodman, was."

You may be sure the royal children of Ev and their Queen mother were delighted at seeing again their beloved country; and when the towers of the palace of Ev came into view they could not forbear cheering at the sight. Little Evring, riding in front of Dorothy, was so overjoyed that he took a curious tin whistle from his pocket and blew a shrill blast that made the Sawhorse leap and prance in sudden alarm.

"What is that?" asked Billina, who had been obliged to flutter her wings in order to keep her seat upon the head of the frightened Sawhorse.

"That's my whistle," said Prince Evring, holding it out upon his hand.

It was in the shape of a little fat pig, made of tin and painted green. The whistle was in the tail of the pig.

"Where did you get it?" asked the yellow hen, closely examining the toy with her bright eyes.

"Why, I picked it up in the Nome King's palace, while Dorothy was making her guesses, and I put it in my pocket," answered the little Prince.

Billina laughed; or at least she made the peculiar cackle that served her for a laugh.

"No wonder I couldn't find the Tin Woodman," she said; "and no wonder the magic belt didn't make him appear, or the King couldn't find him, either!"

"What do you mean?" questioned Dorothy.

"Why, the Prince had him in his pocket," cried Billina, cackling again.

"I did not!" protested little Evring. "I only took the whistle."

"Well, then, watch me," returned the hen, and reaching out a claw she touched the whistle and said "Ev."

Swish!

"Good afternoon," said the Tin Woodman, taking off his funnel cap and bowing to Dorothy and the Prince. "I think I must have been asleep for the first time since I was made of tin, for I do not remember our leaving the Nome King."

"You have been enchanted," answered the girl, throwing an arm around her old friend and hugging him tight in her joy. "But it's all right, now."

"I want my whistle!" said the little Prince, beginning to cry.

"Hush!" cautioned Billina. "The whistle is lost, but you may have another when you get home."

The Scarecrow had fairly thrown himself upon the bosom of his old comrade, so surprised and delighted was he to see him again, and Tiktok squeezed the Tin Woodman's hand so earnestly that he dented some of his fingers. Then they had to make way for Ozma to welcome the tin man, and the army caught sight of him and set up a cheer, and everybody was delighted and happy.

For the Tin Woodman was a great favorite with all who knew him, and his sudden recovery after they had thought he was lost to them forever was indeed a pleasant surprise.

Before long, the cavalcade arrived at the royal palace, where a great crowd of people had gathered to welcome their Queen and her ten children. There was much shouting and cheering, and the people threw flowers in their path, and every face wore a happy smile.

They found the Princess Langwidere in her mirrored chamber, where she was admiring one of her handsomest heads—one with rich chestnut hair, dreamy walnut eyes and a shapely hickorynut nose. She was very glad to be relieved of her duties to the people of Ev, and the Queen graciously permitted her to retain her rooms and her cabinet of heads as long as she lived.

Then the Queen took her eldest son out upon a balcony that overlooked the crowd of subjects gathered below, and said to them:

"Here is your future ruler, King Evardo Fifteenth. He is fifteen years of age, has fifteen silver buckles on his jacket and is the fifteenth Evardo to rule the land of Ev."

The people shouted their approval fifteen times, and even the Wheelers, some of whom were present, loudly promised to obey the new King.

So the Queen placed a big crown of gold, set with rubies, upon Evardo's head, and threw an ermine robe over his shoulders, and proclaimed him King; and he bowed gratefully to all his subjects and then went away to see if he could find any cake in the royal pantry.

Ozma of Oz and her people, as well as Dorothy, Tiktok and Billina, were splendidly entertained by the Queen mother, who owed all her happiness to their kind offices; and that evening the yellow hen was publicly presented with a beautiful necklace of pearls and sapphires, as a token of esteem from the new King.

Chapter 20

THE EMERALD CITY

DOROTHY decided to accept Ozma's invitation to return with her to the Land of Oz. There was no greater chance of her getting home from Ev than from Oz, and the little girl was anxious to see once more the country where she had encountered such wonderful adventures. By this time Uncle Henry would have reached Australia in his ship, and had probably given her up for lost; so he couldn't worry any more than he did if she stayed away from him a while longer. So she would go to Oz.

They bade good-bye to the people of Ev, and the King promised Ozma that he would ever be grateful to her and render the Land of Oz any service that might lie within his power.

And then they approached the edge of the dangerous desert, and Ozma threw down the magic carpet, which at once unrolled far enough for all of them to walk upon it without being crowded.

Tiktok, claiming to be Dorothy's faithful follower because he belonged to her, had been permitted to join the party, and before they started the girl wound up his machinery as far as possible, and the copper man stepped off as briskly as any one of them.

Ozma also invited Billina to visit the Land of Oz, and the yellow hen was glad enough to go where new sights and scenes awaited her.

They began the trip across the desert early in the morning, and as they stopped only long enough for Billina to lay her daily egg, before sunset they espied the green slopes and wooded hills of the beautiful Land of Oz. They entered it in the Munchkin territory, and the King of the Munchkins met them at the border and welcomed Ozma with great respect, being very pleased by her safe return. For Ozma of Oz ruled the King of the Munchkins, the King of the Winkies, the King of the Quadlings and the King of the Gillikins just as those kings ruled their own people; and this supreme ruler of the Land of Oz lived in a great town of her own, called the Emerald City, which was in the exact center of the four kingdoms of the Land of Oz.

The Munchkin king entertained them at his palace that night, and in the morning they set out for the Emerald City, travelling over a road of yellow brick that led straight to the jewel-studded gates. Everywhere the people turned out to greet their beloved Ozma and to hail joyfully the Scarecrow, the Tin Woodman and the Cowardly Lion, who were popular favorites. Dorothy, too, remembered some of the people, who had befriended her on the occasion of her first visit to Oz, and they were well pleased to see the little Kansas girl again, and showered her with compliments and good wishes.

At one place, where they stopped to refresh themselves, Ozma accepted a bowl of milk from the hands of a pretty dairy-maid. Then she looked at the girl more closely, and exclaimed:

"Why, it's Jinjur—isn't it!"

"Yes, your Highness," was the reply, as Jinjur dropped a low curtsy. And Dorothy looked wonderingly at this lively appearing person, who had once assembled an army of women and driven the Scarecrow from the throne of the Emerald City, and even fought a battle with the powerful army of Glinda the Sorceress.

"I've married a man who owns nine cows," said Jinjur to Ozma, "and now I am happy and contented and willing to lead a quiet life and mind my own business.

"Where is your husband?" asked Ozma.

"He is in the house, nursing a black eye," replied Jinjur, calmly. "The foolish man would insist upon milking the red cow when I wanted him to milk the white one; but he will know better next time, I am sure."

Then the party moved on again, and after crossing a broad river on a ferry and passing many fine farm houses that were dome shaped and painted a pretty green color, they came in sight of a large building that was covered with flags and bunting.

"I don't remember that building," said Dorothy. "What is it?"

"That is the College of Art and Athletic Perfection," replied Ozma. "I had it built quite recently, and the Woggle-Bug is its president. It keeps him busy, and the young men who attend the college are no worse off than they were before. You see, in this country are a number of youths who do not like to work, and the college is an excellent place for them."

And now they came in sight of the Emerald City, and the people flocked out to greet their lovely ruler. There were several bands and many officers and officials of the realm, and a crowd of citizens in their holiday attire.

Thus the beautiful Ozma was escorted by a brilliant procession to her royal city, and so great was the cheering that she was obliged to constantly bow to the right and left to acknowledge the greetings of her subjects.

That evening there was a grand reception in the royal palace, attended by the most important persons of Oz, and Jack Pumpkinhead, who was a little over-ripe but still active, read an address congratulating Ozma of Oz upon the success of her generous mission to rescue the royal family of a neighboring kingdom.

Then magnificent gold medals set with precious stones were presented to each of the twenty-six officers; and the Tin Woodman was given a new axe studded with diamonds; and the Scarecrow received a silver jar of complexion powder. Dorothy was presented with a pretty coronet and made a Princess of Oz, and Tiktok received two bracelets set with eight rows of very clear and sparkling emeralds.

Afterward they sat down to a splendid feast, and Ozma put Dorothy at her right and Billina at her left, where the hen sat upon a golden roost and ate from a jeweled platter. Then were placed the Scarecrow, the Tin Woodman and Tiktok, with baskets of lovely flowers before them, because they did not require food. The twenty-six officers were at the lower end of the table, and the Lion and the Tiger also had seats, and were served on golden platters, that held a half a bushel at one time.

The wealthiest and most important citizens of the Emerald City were proud to wait upon these famous adventurers, and they were assisted by a sprightly little maid named Jellia Jamb, whom the Scarecrow pinched upon her rosy cheeks and seemed to know very well.

During the feast Ozma grew thoughtful, and suddenly she asked:

"Where is the private?"

"Oh, he is sweeping out the barracks," replied one of the generals, who was busy eating a leg of a turkey. "But I have ordered him a dish of bread and molasses to eat when his work is done."

"Let him be sent for," said the girl ruler.

While they waited for this command to be obeyed, she enquired:

"Have we any other privates in the armies?"

"Oh, yes," replied the Tin Woodman, "I believe there are three, altogether."

The private now entered, saluting his officers and the royal Ozma very respectfully.

"What is your name, my man?" asked the girl.

"Omby Amby," answered the private.

"Then, Omby Amby," said she, "I promote you to be Captain General of all the armies of my kingdom, and especially to be Commander of my Body Guard at the royal palace."

"It is very expensive to hold so many offices," said the private, hesitating. "I have no money with which to buy uniforms."

"You shall be supplied from the royal treasury," said Ozma.

Then the private was given a seat at the table, where the other officers welcomed him cordially, and the feasting and merriment were resumed.

Suddenly Jellia Jamb exclaimed:

"There is nothing more to eat! The Hungry Tiger has consumed everything!"

"But that is not the worst of it," declared the Tiger, mournfully. "Somewhere or somehow, I've actually lost my appetite!"

Chapter 21

DOROTHY'S MAGIC BELT

DOROTHY passed several very happy weeks in the Land of Oz as the guest of the royal Ozma, who delighted to please and interest the little Kansas girl. Many new acquaintances were formed and many old ones renewed, and wherever she went Dorothy found herself among friends.

One day, however, as she sat in Ozma's private room, she noticed hanging upon the wall a picture which constantly changed in appearance, at one time showing a meadow and at another time a forest, a lake or a village.

"How curious!" she exclaimed, after watching the shifting scenes for a few moments.

"Yes," said Ozma, "that is really a wonderful invention in magic. If I wish to see any part of the world or any person living, I need only express the wish and it is shown in the picture."

"May I use it?" asked Dorothy, eagerly.

"Of course, my dear."

"Then I'd like to see the old Kansas farm, and Aunt Em," said the girl.

Instantly the well remembered farmhouse appeared in the picture, and Aunt Em could be seen quite plainly. She was engaged in washing dishes by the kitchen window and seemed quite well and contented. The hired men and the teams were in the harvest fields behind the house, and the corn and wheat seemed to the child to be in prime condition. On the side porch Dorothy's pet dog, Toto, was lying fast asleep in the sun, and to her surprise old Speckles was running around with a brood of twelve new chickens trailing after her.

"Everything seems all right at home," said Dorothy, with a sigh of relief. "Now I wonder what Uncle Henry is doing."

The scene in the picture at once shifted to Australia, where, in a pleasant room in Sydney, Uncle Henry was seated in an easy chair, solemnly smoking his briar pipe. He looked sad and lonely, and his hair was now quite white and his hands and face thin and wasted.

"Oh!" cried Dorothy, in an anxious voice, "I'm sure Uncle Henry isn't getting any better, and it's because he is worried about me. Ozma, dear, I must go to him at once!"

"How can you?" asked Ozma.

"I don't know," replied Dorothy; "but let us go to Glinda the Good. I'm sure she will help me, and advise me how to get to Uncle Henry."

Ozma readily agreed to this plan and caused the Sawhorse to be harnessed to a pretty green and pink phaeton, and the two girls rode away to visit the famous sorceress.

Glinda received them graciously, and listened to Dorothy's story with attention.

"I have the magic belt, you know," said the little girl. "If I buckled it around my waist and commanded it to take me to Uncle Henry, wouldn't it do it?"

"I think so," replied Glinda, with a smile.

"And then," continued Dorothy, "if I ever wanted to come back here again, the belt would bring me."

"In that you are wrong," said the sorceress. "The belt has magical powers only while it is in some fairy country, such as the Land of Oz, or the Land of Ev. Indeed, my little friend, were you to wear it and wish yourself in Australia, with your uncle, the wish would doubtless be fulfilled, because it was made in fairyland. But you would not find the magic belt around you when you arrived at your destination."

"What would become of it?" asked the girl.

"It would be lost, as were your silver shoes when you visited Oz before, and no one would ever see it again. It seems too bad to destroy the use of the magic belt in that way, doesn't it?"

"Then," said Dorothy, after a moment's thought, "I will give the magic belt to Ozma, for she can use it in her own country. And she can wish me transported to Uncle Henry without losing the belt."

"That is a wise plan," replied Glinda.

So they rode back to the Emerald City, and on the way it was arranged that every Saturday morning Ozma would look at Dorothy in her magic picture, wherever the little girl might chance to be. And, if she saw Dorothy make a certain signal, then Ozma would know that the little Kansas girl wanted to revisit the Land of Oz, and by means of the Nome King's magic belt would wish that she might instantly return.

This having been agreed upon, Dorothy bade good-bye to all her friends. Tiktok wanted to go to Australia, too; but Dorothy knew that the machine man would never do for a servant in a civilized country, and the chances were that his machinery wouldn't work at all. So she left him in Ozma's care.

Billina, on the contrary, preferred the Land of Oz to any other country, and refused to accompany Dorothy.

"The bugs and ants that I find here are the finest flavored in the world," declared the yellow hen, "and there are plenty of them. So here I shall end my days; and I must say, Dorothy, my dear, that you are very foolish to go back into that stupid, humdrum world again."

"Uncle Henry needs me," said Dorothy, simply; and every one except Billina thought it was right that she should go.

All Dorothy's friends of the Land of Oz—both old and new—gathered in a group in front of the palace to bid her a sorrowful good-bye and to wish her long life and happiness. After much hand shaking, Dorothy kissed Ozma once more, and then handed her the Nome King's magic belt, saying:

"Now, dear Princess, when I wave my handkerchief, please wish me with Uncle Henry. I'm aw'fly sorry to leave you—and the Scarecrow—and the Tin Woodman—and the Cowardly Lion—and Tiktok—and—and everybody—but I do want my Uncle Henry! So good-bye, all of you."

Then the little girl stood on one of the big emeralds which decorated the courtyard, and after looking once again at each of her friends, waved her handkerchief.

"No," said Dorothy, "I wasn't drowned at all. And I've come to nurse you and take care of you, Uncle Henry, and you must promise to get well as soon as poss'ble."

Uncle Henry smiled and cuddled his little niece close in his lap.

"I'm better already, my darling," said he.

THE END